The Weight of a Moment

For Myrna, once again and always.

Chapter One

It was my own personal theory that most lifetimes could be summed up by ten to twenty moments, meaningful snippets ranging from a handful of seconds to a few spins around the clock face that contained both the best and worst of one's character and experiences. Like a home movie on Super 8 film, twenty impactful moments that told the story of a life. Often those moments were first glances, tearful goodbyes, fortunate turns, unfortunate accidents, promises kept, promises broken, triumphs, failures, and regrets. In my case, it only took thirteen moments from my forty-three years to convey an insightful understanding of my life, twelve recollections that I told proudly and one that always stung a little bit in the telling. As a writer and someone who examines the human experience for a paycheck, I knew that the best stories were the ones that stung a little bit in the telling; the ones that most people didn't volunteer to friends or family; the ones they kept locked deep within themselves.

For almost four years, I kept my moment locked deep within me, never willing to discuss my tragic choice and public humiliation. In a cowardly manner, I retreated to the small town where I was born and raised and tried to hide from my moment. But, my moment burned inside me like a steady flame in constant contact with the soft tissue of my soul. It was pain like I'd never experienced before—my discomfort ever-present, my regret weighty and overwhelming. On two occasions, clouded and emboldened by pills and alcohol, I even attempted to put my moment behind me and end my life. In hindsight, it was obvious that I didn't really want to kill myself, or I would have purchased a gun and a box of thirty-eight-caliber certainty. From my past life, I knew thugs who could get a gun for me, but pills and alcohol were my weapons of choice so I'd wake up after my bouts of extreme self-loathing.

When I arrived in Shelbyville in central Pennsylvania in the spring of 2008, I desperately wanted to make a new start and move forward with my life, but I had no idea how to do it. After settling into an efficiency apartment over the pharmacy, I acquired *The Sentinel*, the town's newspaper from Bob Wheaton, who was retiring, with the hope that honest work, ample column space as therapy, and a small contribution to the community would be my salvation. But I was too broken at the time, struggling each day to remain sober long enough to write coherent sentences and managing only to publish a mediocre (at best) bi-weekly newspaper which fortunately was good enough for the audience that read it. The church-going, kind-hearted townsfolk of Shelbyville were the opposite of harsh big-city critics. It was the schlockiest work of my career in journalism, but they accepted it and me like I was the new century's reincarnation of William Randolph Hearst. I knew I'd come to the right place to heal —I just didn't know how to do it.

During my "one thousand days of incoherence" or what most people referred to as the years of 2008 and 2009 and 2010, I could often be found passed out on the army cot I kept in the backroom of *The Sentinel*, sleeping off my intoxicants and sleeping away another fine afternoon. This being a small town, I got very good at disguising my bad habits and hiding the wreckage within my being. Townsfolk knew I drank a lot and dabbled in other distractions, but they never knew the full extent of the problem. They never knew I walked around in a constant stupor. Most would have been surprised to learn that I could put the newspaper together with my mind half-obliterated.

One fall afternoon, I remembered waking up around 4 p.m. in a panicked state, drenched by sweat and confusion, because my bi-weekly deadline was fast approaching. I always provided the copy to the printer every other Tuesday by 6 p.m. so I could publish every other Thursday morning. Sitting on the edge of the pea green cot, shaking my head in an attempt to clear the fog, it was Monday afternoon, and I had twenty-four hours to put the whole newspaper together. In those days, I typically worked in an unstructured manner that included lengthy stints of procrastination and flurries of productivity fueled by stimulants, but I seriously doubted that I could rally this time and meet my deadline.

I can't put a whole newspaper together in twenty-four hours, I thought. *This is truly my worst fuck-up in a long string of fuck-ups.*

Standing beside the cot, swaying in place, I reached deep into my pockets to ascertain what magic potions I might have to aid me with my literary endeavor. My cocaine vial was almost empty but thick with white dust around the inside, so I figured it would facilitate a quick revival. Next, I decided I'd walk to the local diner, The Bashful Rooster, where I'd get a quick meatloaf and mashed potatoes dinner and consume a pot of coffee. Finally, I'd purchase a bottle of Glen (fiddich) at the liquor store so I'd have companionship on an extended night that wouldn't end until late afternoon of the next day. Strangely enough, I felt comforted by my plan.

It won't be the best edition I've ever published, I told myself, *but I'll get it done.*

Beneath the leaded glass transom with *The Sentinel* scripted above the front door, I paused, tucked my shirttail into my black jeans, spit on the fingers of my left hand, and made a feeble attempt to make my hair presentable. I turned the antique silver doorknob, opened the front door of the simple white building—formerly a residence and row house built in 1910, and stepped onto the sidewalk of

Main Street. Out of habit, I squinted to prepare myself for the late-day sun, as sunshine was never a friend to those who lived like the undead, constantly searching the night for anything that would provide relief from their torment. As I turned toward the diner, I heard a voice from across the narrow street.

"Great paper yesterday, Nick," a man called out to me. "I read it over breakfast at The Rooster this morning."

"I'm glad you liked it," I returned, smiling though befuddled.

"Why did you leave a page blank?" he followed up, his face puzzled. "Was it to provide a space for your readers to doodle?"

"Exactly."

Immediately, I lowered my head and walked purposely toward the corner where the newspaper stand was located in front of the hardware store. Quite fortunately, when I reached into my pocket and extracted a fistful of coins, I had the four quarters required by the slots to open it. With his words still reverberating in my bleary mind, I opened the compartment and removed the newspaper. Much to my surprise, I held in my hand *The Sentinel* issue dated the previous day, but its front page was unfamiliar to me. Though editor and publisher, I was reading its cover for the first time, like a patron at the diner with eggs, toast, and coffee in front of him. It was safe to say that I'd created it, but I had no memory of the process or final product. It wasn't Monday; it was Friday, and I'd been granted a reprieve of ten days.

Oh well, I thought, not even surprised by this ridiculous turn of events, *I'm still getting meatloaf for dinner.*

Chapter Two

L   ying on my bed at the impressionable age of thirteen, with only a small book light illuminating the page before me, I decided to be a writer while reading *In Cold Blood* by Truman Capote. But, it wasn't his recounting of one of the most horrific crimes ever committed in the heartland that convinced me; it was simply the first five paragraphs of the book. In that tiny snippet, that magnificent fragment of American literature, Capote described a small town, its people, and the surrounding terrain in such elegant prose that I was in awe of his eloquence. There was nothing beautiful about the location—the dust, the mud, the twang, the plains—the beauty was manifest in his selection of words and his masterful use of imagery.

"The village of Holcomb stands on the high wheat plains of western Kansas, a lonesome area that Kansans call 'out there.'...After rain, or when snowfalls thaw, the streets, unnamed, unshaded, unpaved, turn from the thickest dust into the direst mud."

· · ·

I grew up in a small community, but I never visited or even imagined a town as desolate as Capote described. While reading his words, I knew I never wanted to vacation in Holcomb, maybe not Kansas altogether, but I also felt like he transported me there. In my mind, I walked the unpaved streets of Holcomb, and its thick, brown mud got caked on my boots. I witnessed the hardscrabble life of its gritty residents and the dilapidated state of the tiny town. I watched the wind blow across the open prairie and understood their isolation. But most importantly, in five paragraphs, seven hundred words or so, Capote demonstrated how powerful words could be in the hands of a gifted wordsmith. His words engaged the mind, expanded the imagination, touched the heart, and rallied the spirit. His words were arranged so masterfully that they were lyrical. As I read his opening pages, Capote's words spoke to me—even sang to me. In less than two minutes of reading, he provided the backdrop for his book, as well as a new direction for my life.

"Until one morning in mid-November 1959, few Americans—in fact, few Kansans—had ever heard of Holcomb. Like the waters on the river, like the motorists on the highway, and like the yellow trains streaking down the Santa Fe tracks, drama in the shape of exceptional happenings, had never stopped there."

At Shelbyville High School, the newspaper staff consisted of five writers and two photographers, and, believe it or not, there were frequent openings. To most high school students, writing for the newspaper was simply one more tedious class, one more pesky assignment. In the fall of 1985, when I arrived at the school of 500 students, securing a position on the staff and seeing my name adorn a byline on the paper's front page was my main objective. Unfortunately for me, I could identify exceptional writing like Capote's *In Cold Blood*, but I had no idea how to create it. Fortunately for me, the newspaper's moderator, Mr. Austin Sinclair, who taught English and history to eleventh and twelfth graders when not editing *The Falcon*, the school's monthly newspaper, was a former writer for *The Philadelphia Post* who knew more than a little about great journalism.

Shorter than an average eighth grader, Mr. Sinclair was diminutive in stature with a frame as frail as someone battling cancer—though he wasn't—and wildly uninhibited brown hair that seemed like it belonged on either a crazed physicist or an elderly orangutan. At forty-three years old, he strode quickly through the crowded hallways between classes, often bumping into students and hastily apologizing but continuing like he was constantly late for an appointment and had someplace to be. His small band of fledgling writers followed closely behind him with muddled expressions on their faces and black composition notebooks in their hands as they tried to keep up.

"You should always be writing in your mind," Mr. Sinclair told his new staff members during his standard orientation, "and that's why you should carry a composition notebook with you everywhere you go. You don't want your best thoughts and ideas lost during inopportune moments."

For my first six months on the staff of *The Falcon*, my submissions were severely edited by Mr. Sinclair and never made it into the front half of the paper. My problem was that I covered football games, debate competitions, and chess matches and tried to write like Truman Capote. With each successive submission, Mr. Sinclair told me that I needed to get out of my own way and stop overthinking it—I needed to write with my heart as much as I wrote with my brain.

"You need to find your own voice," he said one day in his office as he handed me an article that looked bloodied from his edits in red, "and stop trying to write like the authors of books you've read."

One day, in the hallway in front of the cafeteria, Robbie Reynolds dropped his books on the floor in front of me. In the middle of the textbooks, concealed, I noticed a substantial book on astronomy. Since the school didn't offer classes on that subject, I concluded that it must be his personal interest. Even though he was two years older, a full foot taller, and the best high school basketball player in the nation, I mustered my courage and approached him in the student parking lot. As he opened the door to his Mustang, I timidly asked, "Can I write an article for *The Falcon* about your interest in astronomy?"

"Why would anyone want to read about my interest in astronomy?" Robbie shot back. "My basketball career has been on the pages of *The Falcon, The Sentinel, The Philadelphia Post,* and even national magazines for the last three years."

"That's exactly why they want to read about it—they are interested in you."

About to respond, Robbie stopped. His expression turned pensive. Unclear about his thought process, I waited quietly because my writer's instincts told me I had his attention, and that was a start. Finally, he responded.

"Let me think about it."

Two days later, while changing classes, I slammed my locker door closed and found Robbie standing behind it. The hallway was full of nosey teenagers and it seemed like everyone was watching us.

"I don't want to be in *The Falcon* any more than I already am," Robbie said, "but it would be awfully nice to hear someone say something to me about something other than basketball."

"So you'll do it?"

"I'll do it."

A week later, in early April, Robbie drove us to a cornfield on the outskirts of town around 9 p.m. on a Wednesday. Standing in the middle of the field, with no homes, businesses, or other sources of light for miles in any direction, we turned our flashlights off and were instantly surrounded by the vacantness of night and the twinkling of bright stars. Nothing else existed. In central Pennsylvania, more than one hundred miles from any metropolitan area, this was a perfect location for stargazing. My neck bent skyward, the billions of bright, twinkling stars amazed me with their simple brilliance and colossal count. For the first time in my life, I was more than aware that our small planet was in the midst of an endless universe. I felt small and insignificant but also part of something that greatly exceeded my own understanding. Dumbfounded by my ignorance, I recognized that the stars had always been there, shining as they did—it was me who never really noticed.

After ten minutes of silence, a shooting star streaked across the southern horizon, creating intensely bright movement through the otherwise tranquil night.

"Did you see that?" Robbie asked me, as the light seemed to burnout at the horizon.

"I did," I said, thrilled by the flash. "I guess it's difficult to maintain that brilliance for long. It seemed to exhaust itself."

"That may be true," Robbie said, "but we're fortunate to have witnessed its brilliant moment."

For the next hour, Robbie pointed his telescope at different stars and constellations and regaled me with facts and legends concerning each one. He told me that the starlight we saw left the star more than four years ago, that our fastest spacecraft would take seventy thousand years to reach the closest stars, and that shooting stars were really dust and rocks entering our atmosphere and more correctly known as meteors. He told me that the moon was almost five billion years old and rotating in perfect synchronization with the earth, which meant that we always viewed the same side. He told me that Orion, the Greek hunter, was the brightest of the eighty-eight constellations and that Hydra, the sea serpent, was the largest one.

After three hours with Robbie, I really liked him. He was kind to me and giving of himself. He shared his love of astronomy in an infectious manner, and I knew I would never look at the night sky in the same way again. From that night forward, I shared his amazement. Robbie was a guy with an almost exalted existence, and, yet, he didn't have an ounce of cockiness in him. He wasn't the egotistical, narrow-minded jock I expected. The truth was that the most recruited high school basketball player in the nation was just a kid, much like me.

* * *

Ten days later, seated in a hard, wooden chair in front of Mr. Sinclair's desk, I waited for him to arrive after his last class of the day. Two hours earlier, he stopped me in the hallway between third and fourth period and arranged the meeting. Behind his desk in mahogany frames were three articles from the front page of *The Philadelphia Post* during the 1970s. Sitting there, I didn't make any effort to read the actual articles; I was more impressed by the presence of his name, Austin Sinclair, on the byline. After ten minutes of staring at the beautiful simplicity of a black and white newspaper, Mr. Sinclair entered the office from behind me and placed the new issue of *The Falcon* on the desk in front of me. Curious, I lifted the issue to eye level and was quite surprised to see my latest article, entitled "The Wonder of Shooting Stars," about Robbie Reynolds' interest in astronomy as the headline story.

"I thought you might be interested in an advance copy," Mr. Sinclair said as he sat down in his chair. "Your article is not only the lead article, but also your first to run completely unedited. I didn't change a single word."

"Wow," I declared. "I didn't expect the front page."

"It's your first great effort, and I expect that level of work from you going forward. You have a lot of talent, and I think you're finally finding your voice."

"It seems like Robbie stepped out of his comfort zone and helped me find mine."

"That may be true," he said, "but I want to be clear about one thing: Your article's placement on the front page has nothing to do with the fact that it's about Robbie Reynolds. It's on the front page because it's damn good—it's as simple as that."

"I'm going to get a mahogany frame and hang it over my desk at home," I informed him.

"It will be the first of many," he added, smiling.

Chapter Three

Is it possible to dream a dream so vividly, wish for it so
hopefully, and want it so badly that your dream actually finds
you? Ten days out of State College that was exactly what
happened to me. Early one morning, I received a call from someone
in the newsroom of *The Philadelphia Post* and, several days later, I
found myself sitting in the chaotic office of Stewart Brady, a hardcore
newspaper editor who learned the business in the 1950s when huge
mechanical presses still rolled in the basement of the building.
Having just crossed his sixtieth birthday, Stewart was an anachro-
nism, a crusty, old newspaperman fighting the passage of time, the
advancement of technology, the breaking of long-standing traditions,
and the evolution of journalism with every indignant, nicotine-laced
breath he took. While I waited, he stormed into his office, collapsed
into the large leather chair behind his desk, and was obviously
surprised to see me sitting in front of him.

"Who the hell are you?" he demanded, his shoulders squared.

"Nick Sterling," I said. "I'm here for an interview."

"Sterling," he grumbled as he searched the loose papers on his
desk for a note, "the name does sound familiar. Oh yes, here it is."

He was silent for a minute, and I recognized that he was trying to read his handwriting. Squinting at the paper, his scribbled note was only partly decipherable to him. Finally, he'd decoded enough and asked me, "Do you know why you're here, Sterling?"

I didn't have a chance to respond before he continued.

"You're here because Austin Sinclair, one of the best writers ever to pound a typewriter at *The Post,* called my boss and told him that you're going to be a great writer. He even went so far as to say that you'd be better than he ever was, and, you can bet, that endorsement carries a lot of sway in this building."

"Mr. Sinclair was my mentor at Shelbyville High School."

"Well, to me, kid, you still look like you belong in the halls of a high school. Do you even shave yet?"

"I shave every day."

"Good for you," he barked before continuing. "Personally, I'm not a fan of prodigies. Don't think for one second that you'll get any special treatment in my newsroom because Austin recommended you. You're going to learn the newspaper business the same way every rookie writer who came before you did—by writing obituaries, watching the news services, covering City Hall, attending charity events, covering grand openings, and doing any other grunt work I ask you to do. Hell, you'll deliver newspapers in the snow if that's what I tell you to do. You won't get any consideration from me until you earn it."

"Are you saying I'm hired?"

"You start Monday at 8 a.m."

My first three years at *The Post* were full of everything Stewart promised on my first day in his office: tedious tasks, mind-numbing assignments, and humbling activities. For the first eight months, I sat in a dark, drafty back corner of the newsroom and researched and wrote obituaries from the moment I got my first cup of black coffee in the morning until they turned out the fluorescent lights at night. Often, news organizations like *The Philadelphia Post* did the preliminary research and drafts of obituaries for notable people and celebrities in advance so that the obituary was nearly ready for print when the person passed. Regardless of the actual date of death of any notable person or celebrity, if they were old, feeble, or sickly in the 1990s, there was a good chance I wrote the preliminary draft of *The Post* obituary. All in all, I wrote more than five hundred obituaries. I used the words widow, widower, bereaved, and beloved so often that I swore I would never again use them in another sentence as long as I lived. Then, on one cold and cloudy mid-winter day, feeling a little down and gloomy over my unyielding focus on the Grim Reaper (and thinking it might cheer me up), I even wrote my boss' obituary though I skipped all the pesky research and fact-checking.

Stewart Hogsbreath Brady

Stewart Hogsbreath Brady was born on March 15, 1932, on the floor of a restroom in a bus station in Ames, Iowa, as his mother, Agnes Skank Brady, fled her husband, Horatio "Hard Luck" Brady, a convicted whore chaser, bigamist, and petty swindler. Lacking a proper blanket or swaddling clothes, the young infant was wrapped in the morning edition of *The Ames Telegraph*, and that was believed to be the spark for his life-long obsession with newspapers. On the run and without income, his mother shared her whiskey and cigarettes with the small boy and their daily saloon hour became the only nutrition little Stewart received until he began school years later. On his first day of grammar school, the five-year-old was ink-stained, hacked like a coal miner, and stank of whiskey so none of the other children would play with him. Rejected, young Stewart vowed to himself that he would dedicate his life to making all young people pay for his cruel treatment. His wife, Matilda Coonhound Brady, gave birth to eleven children, but unbeknownst to Stewart, he wasn't their biological father. As Matilda walked the railroad tracks daily and dreamed of returning to her beloved hometown of Huntsville, Alabama, an assortment of hobos and circus workers fathered the Brady children. After seventy-two years in the position of editor of *The Post,* Stewart Brady died in a freak office accident when he drank a quart of newspaper ink instead of his usual cheap whiskey. Between the ink and the alcohol, the corpse was basically drenched in lighter fluid, so the family decided to cremate the body. Funeral services will be held at the Greyhound Bus Station.

After writing obituaries for a solid eight months, Stewart begrudgingly told me to start attending the daily staff meetings where the coverage assignments for potential articles were handed out. As the junior, trainee, low-level, apprentice, cub reporter (my official title), my role in the staff meetings was to sit quietly and accept any assignments that none of the senior writers wanted. For instance, if there was a grand opening of a new playground at a daycare center that was being hosted by the owner and no one was expected to attend it or care about it, then the other writers would pass and Carrie Stanton, the coordinator of the meeting, would declare, "Looks like one for you, Sterling." And, if there was a reunion of the Fighting Eighth Tank Battalion of the U.S. Army that served in southern France during World War II and only four veterans were expected to be present, then the other writers would pass again and Carrie would declare, "You're going to be busy this week, Sterling." In the meetings, I quickly realized that I was going to write an awful lot of fluff pieces before I ever got to cover a real news story. However, what Stewart didn't understand about me was that I was still absolutely ecstatic to be on the staff of *The Philadelphia Post.* Though sometimes I thought it was his actual objective, he hadn't broken my spirit yet. I knew I'd eventually get my chance, and I'd make the most of it.

On the third anniversary of my first day at *The Post,* I sat before Stewart in his office for my annual review, something that he obviously hated to do. He made no effort to hide his disdain for the task and the process. Stewart was a man who lived every moment of his life with a deadline in view—he didn't have time for reviews; he didn't care about personnel policies. In my three years at the paper, I could honestly state that I'd never seen him smile or laugh, but, at that moment, he seemed even grumpier and more sideways than usual. While working for him, I'd concluded that he truly disliked people and would rather not have to deal with them. Stewart had my review form on the desk before him and a tumbler of scotch beside his telephone.

"You are doing fine, kid," he told me, making it evident that he had no intention of participating in this corporate ritual. In truth, Stewart only wanted my signature on the bottom of the review form so he could inform personnel that the review was complete. In an unsubtle manner, he slid the form and a pen in front of me. Aware of his organizational need, I thought I sensed an opportunity to get some kind of advancement on my side of the ledger.

"Maybe we can discuss the type of assignments I'll be working on this year?" I said, hoping to secure a commitment that I could write some serious articles in my fourth year.

"What's the matter, Sterling?" he demanded, glaring in my direction as he reached for his tumbler of scotch. "Am I delaying your plans to win a Pulitzer?"

"No sir. I was just hoping..."

"You may have worked here for three years, but you still have a long way to go before you become a contributing journalist in my newsroom. Hell, you still look like you belong in high school."

"I don't think my appearance should..."

"Here, have a drink," Stewart told me in a tone that was far more order than offer. "It'll put some hair on your chest."

He placed a murky glass in front of me and poured three fingers of scotch from the bottle he kept in his bottom right drawer. I watched the gold liquid flow between bottle and glass, and I marveled at its hypnotic quality.

"When I was your age, Sterling, I worked in the press room from midnight to 8 a.m. By the end of every shift, my hands were so black with ink that I had to scrub them with soap and water for a full fifteen minutes just to get them to a light shade of gray. After two years at *The Post*, I thought I'd never see my actual skin tone again."

"Do you think I...?"

"Goddamn it, you're not listening to me! There are dues to be paid and lessons to be learned if you want to make it in the newspaper business. You're writing obituaries and covering grand openings for a reason. In the long run, you're going to be a better newspaperman because of it."

"I know I'm learning a lot, sir, but..."

During the next fifty minutes in his office, I never even completed a sentence. Whatever opportunity I thought I sensed at the beginning of the review turned very fuzzy by the end as Stewart continued refilling my glass with scotch. I remembered three generous pours of scotch, signing the review form before he hustled me out the door, and his instructions to see Carrie about drafting another fifty obituaries. When I woke up in my bed the following day, I realized I'd taken a few steps backward on my path toward serious assignments, not forward. Lying there with a steady pounding in my head, I couldn't believe I had more obituaries to write. I'd clearly learned the hard way that three fingers times three pours was an old newspaperman's ploy.

That crusty, old, scotch-soaked bastard, I thought, *he played me.*

Chapter Four

I s it possible to dream a dream so vividly, wish for it so hopefully, and want it so badly that your dream actually finds you? Three and a half years into my tenure at *The Post* that was exactly what happened to me—again. One November morning, a veteran business columnist passed me with his coffee cup and remarked, "Did you hear the big news this morning, Nick? Stewart Brady is retiring."

"Say what?" I said, flabbergasted.

"Stewart is retiring. He's in his mid-sixties and a relic from a bygone era, so the time has come. They're going to introduce his replacement later this morning."

"Retiring," I repeated, still processing the news.

"How about we grab some lunch today?"

"Sure. Anywhere but the Korean place—it took three full days for the burning in my throat to go away."

After the columnist disappeared from my view, I was left pondering this rather morning-rattling news.

On the one hand, I thought, *I really haven't made a lot of progress with Stewart, so this must be good news. But, on the other hand, I have to start over again with a new editor, so maybe this is bad news. When all is said and done, I am as befuddled by this news as I am unclear about its implications.*

For the next two hours, I got very little done. I doubt the word count from my morning's efforts even exceeded two hundred words. Stopping frequently, I glanced about the newsroom as I waited for Stewart's replacement to make an appearance and meet the staff. In mid-morning, I finally spotted a small contingent going desk to desk at the far side of the newsroom, and I wondered if the new editor was amongst the three men and one woman. I could see the woman and one man, but the others were mostly blocked from my view. Rather than stare incessantly, I put my head down and tried to look busy. Three minutes passed and then I heard the woman say to me, "Nick Sterling, I'd like you to meet the new editor of *The Post.*"

When I looked up from my papers, a small man was in front of me with his hand extended in my direction, a more than familiar face.

"Nick and I are old friends," Mr. Sinclair informed the woman. "We were both on the staff of *The Shelbyville High School Falcon* several years ago."

"Mr. Sinclair," I blurted. "Are you the new editor?"

"I am," he said, "and I want you to start calling me Austin. We're colleagues now."

"I'm so happy to be working for you again," I exclaimed, barely able to contain my elation. "I learned so much from you."

"Well, we're in the big leagues now. We're both going to have to improve our games."

"You'll get my best every day, Austin," I assured him.

With the New Year, Austin Sinclair took over as editor of *The Post,* and while the annual turn of the calendar is always symbolic of a new start, this one was particularly relevant to me. Immediately, I sensed a new dynamic in the newsroom and felt reinvigorated. Unlike Stewart Brady before him, Austin attended the staff meeting each morning and participated in the assignment of articles to the writing staff. He understood the importance of matching his writers

18

to the appropriate assignments so he could get the best work. He wanted his staff working on subject matter and issues best suited to their particular talents and skillset. Unlike Stewart, Austin understood that each writer brought a different perspective to each story and that the selection of the writer would influence the story itself. Major stories continued to be awarded to the most senior writers, but the quality of my assignments improved greatly. Each morning, while I still got my fair share of low-level grunt work and unglamorous events, my assignments were peppered with some real news stories. In May of 1997, my articles started making it as far forward as the third page of the main section, which was enormous progress for me.

The newspaper business was similar to real estate in as much as it was all about location. The chance of an article getting read had a lot to do with its placement in the paper, the black-and-white real estate it occupied. The front page of any section was basically the newspaper equivalent of oceanfront property, and the front page of the paper itself was a beautiful beachfront home on a perfect white sand beach. It was far and away the most desirable place for an article to land because it was ensured a large number of readers. Still a junior writer, I had little chance of acquiring beachfront property because it was reserved for veteran writers with loyal readerships. In my junior position, when my articles landed on the second or third page of any section, it was the newspaper equivalent of being a block off the beach in a great beach town. It was not the most premium real estate, but it was real estate that most would be happy to occupy. There wasn't an ocean view, but you could smell the salty air and hear the surf. With Austin as editor, my flip-flops, sunscreen, and beach towel were getting a lot of use.

A week before my fourth anniversary at *The Post,* I sat before Austin in his office for my annual review. He began by commenting, "You know, I think the worst offense any manager can commit is holding back real talent, limiting their growth and potential. In my mind, the duty of managers is to get the best out of their people."

"Okay," I said, not knowing where this was going.

"For example," Austin elaborated with an analogy, "let's say a baseball manager doesn't play one of his players until the last month of the season, and then, in that month, the player bats 405. Without a doubt, that player should've been in the heart of the lineup all season, and his manager sure let his team down."

"That makes sense," I said, though confused and still unsure of where this analogy was heading.

"I want to make sure that doesn't happen to you."

"How so?" I asked.

"Going forward, I want you to pursue some of your own ideas, your own stories. I will reduce your assignments and give you time to cultivate your own material. I've always believed that you're talented, and I don't want to make the mistake of holding you back. Generally, this privilege is reserved for veteran writers with devoted readers, but I'm confident this will pay off for the paper in the long run, so I'm going to do it."

"I have a lot of ideas," I informed him.

"That's what I figured. Bring them to me when you're ready."

Over the next three months, I took full advantage of my opportunity and rattled off eleven articles in succession that all landed on the fifth page or better of the main section. Those efforts also established an initial level of name recognition for me amongst loyal *Post* readers. One article in particular, about a homeless man named Gus who frequented a busy street that I walked each day, caused such an emotional response amongst readers that it resulted in a barrage of phone calls to the newsroom. Many of the callers requested follow-up articles. In his previous life, Ferguson was a pastor for a large congregation in Houston before he gave it all up to live and work among the homeless. Gus told me that a voice called him to this new life, but I had difficulty believing it was the Lord. Whether his motivation was a spiritual calling or mental illness was one question I never quite answered in my time with him. My article was intended as a simple profile, but it turned into a three-part series that examined his daily struggles on the gritty backstreets of Philadelphia. There was so much interest in Gus that I would have written even more follow-ups, but he simply disappeared one day, ending the series. Due to the favorable reception of my eleven articles, a black-and-white sketch of my likeness was added to my byline—a treatment reserved for regular columnists and featured writers because, in the newspaper game, the facial sketch was the methodology for building a brand. With my smiling mug beside my words, I felt like good things were starting to happen for me but, most important to me, Austin was thrilled by the success of his gamble on me.

"Well done, Truman," Austin razzed me as he finished reading my latest submission. "This is your best work yet."

Over the next three years, my name did, indeed, become a valuable brand for *The Philadelphia Post*. According to extensive market research conducted by the company, more Philadelphians read and trusted articles by Nick Sterling than any other columnist or feature writer in the marketplace. Furthermore, my Name Recognition Quotient (whatever the hell that was) registered at thirty-one percent, and I was told that was far better than any result in the history of the research. Along with frequent articles, I began writing a regular column entitled "A Sterling Viewpoint" that appeared three days a week on the fourth page of the paper. The black-and-white sketch of my likeness proved to be a very good likeness as strangers bought me drinks everywhere I went. It had taken me almost eight years to arrive at this very favorable point in my career, but—little did I know—my truly major moments still lay ahead.

Chapter Five

Another one of my hard-learned theories about life was that redemption wasn't a solo endeavor. After my collapse, the attributes needed for redemption—insight, determination, and grace—were no longer available to me. I was too broken. While redemption might seem like something one envisions, works at, and journeys towards, it didn't happen that way for me. I didn't make it happen; redemption happened to me. Like someone lost in a dark labyrinth of underground caves, I wandered through the corridors until I saw a shimmer of light ahead and stumbled upon the way out. It was either divine intervention or dumb luck, but it wasn't my doing. For me, it was an unlikely meeting with a like-minded stranger that started me on my road to redemption.

When I met Tom Corbett in the summer of 2011, I knew we shared a connection that few others could relate to or even understand. We were members of an unfortunate fellowship—people whose worst moment was viewed by millions and who were recognized and judged based on that moment from that day forward. Everyone has moments they would like to forget, moments they would never want as their calling card. And fortunately for them, their bad moment was witnessed by one or two or even ten but not viewed by the whole world. In moments of weakness, Tom and I made unfortunate choices, and those moments impacted us in ways we never anticipated. We were mocked and ridiculed by numbers of people only possible in the modern world, the world connected by the internet and social media. Many never recover from these types of moments.

After our meeting, I realized that Tom and I had unique stories with a common tragic element that bound us. In my mind, the only difference between us was that I deserved the full measure and severity of my punishment while Tom was treated unfairly. For me at least, our meeting was a matter of life and death; having Tom as a friend pulled me out of my downward spiral and saved my life. In fact, both our crash courses corrected and both our trajectories in life improved. But the thing about our downward spirals was that they were unique to each of us—Tom's started with a lapse in civility followed by gradual descent while mine started with a tragic mistake followed by a steep descent to rock bottom. I lost everything: my column, my self-respect, my job, my home, my sanity, and the woman I loved. In Tom's case, it took over four months for him to land on his rock bottom, but, just like me, he knew it when he arrived...

Chapter Six

In March 2011, Tom Corbett and his wife Shannon had reached a level of success Tom never imagined, as both their careers flourished during the last decade, their forties. They lived in a five thousand square foot, multi-million dollar condominium in a prestigious hi-rise tower in downtown Philadelphia, a short walk from Independence Hall and the Liberty Bell. Their home was decorated with the finest furniture from five continents and art and collectibles with five-figure appraisal values. They enjoyed all their cosmopolitan city's offerings, shopping at the finest boutiques, dining at the chicest restaurants, and attending theater productions on opening night. Each afternoon when sorted, their mail contained more invitations to dinner parties, charity benefits, and society balls than bills or junk mail. Part of the "New Rich," which meant their money was earned and not inherited, the Corbetts were often in the background at social functions while the paparazzi focused on celebrities and trust fund heirs.

Tom and Shannon lived in their expansive condo with their nineteen-year-old daughter, Nicole, their sixteen-year-old son, Alex, and their housekeeper, Marta Elias. On an unseasonably warm Tuesday morning in late March, there was already much scurrying about the residence by 7 a.m. as the Corbett family prepared to start the new day.

Arriving at the dining room table, Tom said, "Good morning, sweetheart," as he kissed his wife on her forehead.

"Good morning, sweetheart," he repeated as he duplicated the gesture with Nicole.

Nicole, wearing the elementary school uniform where she worked as a teacher's aid, consisting of a white shirt, bluish-green plaid skirt, and white athletic shoes, rolled her eyes as her father passed.

"You know," Tom remarked, "I don't think I've ever seen you smile while wearing that uniform in the two months you've worked at that school."

"I'm barely awake, Dad, and besides, I hate this uniform. They make all the teacher's aids wear these silly outfits so we don't cause trouble by wearing something revealing or controversial."

"It is a Catholic school."

"I know, but I still think it's ridiculous that I must bring a complete change of clothes for when the school day is over, and I'm done with the little monsters."

"Well, I'm glad they make you wear it," Tom said as he reached for a blueberry muffin. "I get to think that my little girl isn't all grown up."

"I am."

"I know," he said with a hint of exasperation.

Noticing the time on her diamond-studded Rolex watch, Shannon blurted, "I've got to go! I'm late!" and rose from the table.

At forty-nine years old, Shannon Corbett was a woman who answered to her demanding schedule but otherwise challenged the passage of time. In mid-life, she still turned as many heads each day as she did in her twenties and thirties. On this day, her attire was eye-catching and professional—a dark gray suit with blue pinstripes, a pale blue silk blouse, blue Ferragamo shoes, and pearls. But it wasn't her tailored clothing or accessories that would turn the heads; it was her cobalt eyes, chiseled cheekbones, and short, boyishly cropped, blonde hair. Shannon took one last sip from her coffee cup, returned it to the saucer, and grabbed an apple from a bowl.

"Will you be late tonight?" Tom asked, though actually wondering about the couple's plans for the evening. As part of their normal modus operandi, Shannon managed their social calendar and coordinated all their activities on evenings and weekends.

"We have a fundraiser at AJ's gallery tonight," she reminded her husband in a tone miffed by his forgetfulness.

"Which one?" Tom followed up, knowing their long-time friend AJ Gaines was the owner of two art galleries near the business district: The AJ Gaines Gallery and Waterwheel.

"Waterwheel," she said. "I'll meet you there."

At six-foot-three inches tall, with thick, wavy brown hair, and billboard-worthy good looks, Tom Corbett was a kind, generous, and reserved man who really enjoyed the examination of daily life. In fact, Tom appreciated life and the world around him more than he aspired to partake in them. True to his nature and chosen profession, he watched from the sidelines, observed from a distance, and marveled at the talents and creations of others. Comfortable in the shadow of his rapacious wife, he quietly savored his own version of contentment. Typical of the dynamics of their marriage, Tom would have been satisfied with a monthly, twenty-dollar haircut at a local barber shop—where he'd really enjoy the chat that came with it—but got a bi-weekly, two-hundred-dollar haircut instead because his wife selected his stylist and wanted him well-groomed for social functions.

True to form, Shannon was very quickly out the door, and Tom followed after her five minutes later.

* * *

Formerly a stockbroker, Shannon Corbett was a partner in Hastings Corbett, an elite money management firm. The firm only accepted new accounts seeded with at least five million dollars, listed ninety-three clients on their exclusive roster, and managed almost a billion dollars. In the "men with cigars" world of Wall Street, Shannon was an exception to just about every rule or norm, studied by her competitors for insights from her daily transactions, and both well-known and well-respected. When asked about the secret of her success, she was recently quoted in a financial magazine saying, "Nothing breaks down stereotypes, changes long-standing traditions, or makes alliances faster than making a hell of a lot of money."

When the firm moved to their current offices five years ago, remodeling costs exceeded seven million dollars with almost three million spent on the reception area alone. The reception area rivaled any five-star hotel lobby with its Italian marble, original artwork, Romanesque statues, and cascading waterfall. Shannon and her partner, Martin Hastings, thought the price tag of the remodel was absurd but also knew they had to do it nonetheless. To attract the big investors, you have to look like you don't need or worry about money, and, since that was the stated objective, one could say their reception area dripped nonchalance and oozed apathy.

Around 9 a.m., Shannon arrived at their offices and found her partner waiting in reception. She'd already talked with him on her cellular phone from the car and was aware of the unscheduled, but very welcome, visitor in their conference room. Wallace Bennett, a stout, cantankerous septuagenarian, was one of the wealthiest men in the city, thanks to an uncountable fortune made in local real estate, and he did not provide the reason for his visit. Around town, Mr. Bennett was known as a man of many, many dollars but few words.

"I'll wait in your conference room," he gruffly advised the receptionist. "You do have a conference room, don't you?"

Side by side, Shannon and Martin hastily strode down a long hall toward the firm's conference room to meet with someone they've tried to schedule appointments with but never had any success.

Wallace Bennett was a difficult man to access, a hard hand to shake. Recently, Mr. Bennett told a good friend that now that he was old enough to be considered for historical landmark status, he had no time left to waste on the incompetent or self-important, or basically everyone he knew.

"Thanks to you, missy," Mr. Bennett began sourly, scowling at Shannon, "I can't go to my beloved Carlton Club anymore without listening to other members boast about the fabulous success you're having with their investments. They drone on and on about you like you are some sort of Houdini in pinstripes. Since I am unwilling to give up my club, I figure that leaves only one other avenue available to me at present."

With that said, the feisty old man withdrew a ten million dollar check from his inner coat pocket and placed it on the cherry wood table. Unusual in this century, the check was handwritten on a small, household-style check with only the Bennett family crest atop it. Elated on the inside, Shannon and Martin were careful to hide their exuberance and accept the check with restraint, modestly telling the old gentleman that they appreciated his trust and confidence. A few minutes later, as he placed his hat on his head and prepared to depart, he remarked brashly, "You better get to work and give me something to brag about for a change."

"This is really good timing," Martin told his partner once their new client left. "We can use fresh funds right now."

* * *

After five tedious years in real estate appraisal and as a result of an introduction made by his wife, Tom Corbett teamed up with Paul Desjardins, the proprietor of an antiques company fittingly named Desjardins House, and together they built it into a money-spinning antiques, art, auctions, and appraisal company. Tom's team of thirty appraisers spent most of their energy and effort valuing the assets of the well-heeled in the throes of divorce. Once again, Shannon's connections were highly beneficial as the company's appraisal revenue grew to more than thirty million dollars, and total revenue topped one hundred million dollars annually. Around town and at social functions, the Corbetts often joked that they were a full-service money management couple—Shannon helped clients accumulate wealth, and Tom helped them spend it and later divide it up.

Paul Desjardins was of French ancestry, born in Lyon in the southeastern Alps region of the country, and raised in Paris, but he'd lived in Philadelphia for more than twenty years. Despite his long residency, the petite Frenchman, who stood just five feet five inches tall and weighed just one hundred fifty pounds, retained an unmistakable accent and a Parisian *joie de vivre*. For both business and personal reasons, Paul traveled to Paris for at least three months annually and, on his return to the States, always proudly proclaimed that Paris was the most beautiful city in the world.

"I believe the city of Paris is the most compelling proof that divine inspiration exists," Paul often told his companions. "There is no other explanation for that degree of magnificence and beauty."

In mid-morning, Paul lured Tom to the receiving area of their building to view items received from a new consignment from an estate in liquidation and some other pieces. In the warehouse, the two men stood beside an eighteenth-century gilt-wood side table and marveled at the masterfully carved standing woman that adorned the ornate base. Unmistakably, like two young kids arriving at a carnival, a similar glassy, wide-eyed stare was present on both their faces.

"Look at the detail in that carving, the delicate waves in her dress," Tom said gleefully, admiring the small woman more passionately than he would an actual flesh and blood one.

It is said that a person is never alone when in a room with a thing of beauty. Without a doubt, Tom and Paul subscribed to this school of thinking, and both spent much of their spare time inspecting and savoring the historic and artistic items in their inventory. And the higher the price tag or estimation that each piece warranted, the more excitement it generated between the partners. Both men had truly found their passion in the world of art and antiques.

"I have to research it," Tom said, "but I'd guess this piece is worth twenty thousand dollars. It's in great condition, and I only see signs of minor touch-ups."

"It's gorgeous," Paul exclaimed, running his palm across the surface of the rich, dark wood, "and it wouldn't surprise me if it brought much more."

Out of the corner of his eye, Tom noticed a magnificent grandfather clock—the real reason that Paul lured him to the warehouse—being carefully uncrated forty feet away. Built between 1770 and 1780, the clock stood eight feet tall with a dark walnut veneer and gold face. To a serious collector, it was unmistakably the work of Eardley Norton, one of the most famous clockmakers in the world and, at one time, the official clockmaker of the Royal Family in England. Unique and exquisite, this clock would turn the head of any respectable collector of antiques so fast that it might cause whiplash.

"Is that an Eardley Norton?" Tom asked, his eyes wide, disbelief in his voice.

"It is," Paul responded, "and it's in wonderful condition."

"How much did you pay for it?"

"Fifty thousand dollars!"

"It's easily worth four times that amount."

On a recent trip through New England, Paul responded to an advertisement that offered a houseful of antiques for immediate sale. A woman whose teenage daughter had fallen while rock climbing, spent three months in intensive care, and required more surgeries before returning home had placed the ad. Though the clock had been in their family since the 1800s and had been passed down through seven generations, the woman told Paul she'd sell it for fifty thousand dollars if he gave her a check right there and then. Paul didn't hesitate.

"I wrote that check so fast I think I misspelled my last name,"

Paul told his partner, his chest puffed out, looking quite proud of his exploits.

"Put that in the conference room," Tom instructed two of the young men who worked in shipping and receiving. "We're not going to be in any hurry to sell that amazing piece of art and history."

"I couldn't agree more," Paul added.

Chapter Seven

Coincidentally, Tom and Shannon's town cars arrived at the same moment outside Waterwheel at 7:20 p.m. On the sidewalk, they pecked one another on the lips, and Shannon wearily declared, "Good God, I need a stiff drink, maybe several."

Softly lit by lamps behind awning-like structures made of copper, the front of the gallery was primarily glass with large windows framed by rectangles of weathered slate. Providing continuity to the design, the same slate was used as flooring throughout the gallery, and similar sheets of copper concealed the interior lighting. Through the large windows, Tom noticed an early crowd of approximately thirty invitees quietly milling, conversing, sipping cocktails, and listening to a solo cellist in the corner of the gallery.

After a stop at the bar, Tom and Shannon strolled toward their friend and gallery owner, AJ Gaines, who was busy with regular clients, a middle-aged couple with a fortune courtesy of five boutique hotels. A fascinating character, AJ had an unusual composition, one that sounded like the recipe for an exotic cocktail: three parts artist, three parts entrepreneur, three parts stage actor, two parts politician, and one part con man. Many believed AJ *was* an exotic cocktail. His arms crossed in front of him, AJ's focus moved between the couple and the large painting on the wall as he talked about its famous artist.

"I first met Sylvester more than twenty years ago when I was a starving young artist. He had a studio just a block from mine in what was, at that time, a low-rent warehouse district just a few blocks from here. One afternoon, as I walked around his studio and viewed his paintings, I had an epiphany—the only sober and lucid moment of my twenties. Like God himself shouted it into my ears, I was immediately aware of my limitations. In my heart, I knew I'd never paint anything like the works before me; Sylvester's magical use of color and light was like nothing I'd seen before or even imagined. He was brilliant, and, in comparison, I was ordinary. But this isn't a sad tale. At the same moment, I also realized that I wanted a place in the art world, just not as an artist. Two years later, I opened my first gallery on Market Street, and I featured eleven of Sylvester's works."

"Have you ever sold any of your own paintings?" the fifty-ish man in a black, turtleneck sweater asked AJ.

"I wouldn't dare," AJ replied. "I could wipe out twenty years of goodwill with one unfortunate exhibition."

They all laughed. Inconspicuously, AJ smiled at the Corbetts and signaled that he wanted them to stay put until he closed the sale. Even as late arrivals and fifteen feet away, Tom and Shannon recognized that AJ had this couple on the verge of a major purchase.

"I feel a real connection with the subject matter of this beautiful painting," the woman observed after a short sip of red wine, "and I believe I've got the right place for it. Would you take four hundred thousand for it, AJ?"

"I can never say no to you, Bella."

* * *

Andrew Jeremiah Gaines was born and raised on the poor side of Charleston, South Carolina, a mere three miles—but still a world away—from the classic Georgian-style homes of proper Charleston with their gated courtyards, manicured gardens, marble fountains, and majestic white porches. In a town where money, real estate, and family heritage meant everything, AJ and his family were clearly on the outside looking in. His mother cleaned motel rooms to keep her three sons fed while they lived in a shabby, one-bedroom apartment in a building where residents relied on temporary work and state assistance to survive. His father worked as an auto mechanic but left the family when AJ was only three years old, so he had no memories of his father at all. In the apartment for many hours every day, AJ spent his time painting, mostly family portraits and street scenes. He couldn't afford proper art supplies, so he painted on brown paper bags from the supermarket. With brush in hand, he was a natural, even gifted artist. But, as a poor, overweight, homosexual boy from a dubious bloodline, AJ knew the iron gates and stately front doors of the homes in Charleston would never swing open for him. Three weeks before his seventeenth birthday, AJ dropped out of high school and set off for Philadelphia. He knew the road ahead of him would be difficult, but he also believed he could build a life as an artist there—a city of immigrants where what your family did one hundred years ago has little impact on your own prospects in life.

* * *

Five minutes later, AJ joined Tom and Shannon in front of another painting by Sylvester, one with a price tag of two hundred fifty thousand dollars, but an absolute bargain if you listened to AJ long enough.

"I've got fantastic news," AJ said, seeming a bit too giddy for a two hundred seventy-five pound, fifty-four-year-old man. Like a teenager after his first sexual conquest, he looked like he would burst if he didn't speak his news soon enough.

AJ shaved his tanned head, wore a shiny diamond stud in each earlobe, and had a perfectly groomed, grayish-black goatee that accentuated his ever-present smile. On this occasion, he wore a loose-fitting, black buttonless shirt that draped over the top of his black pants. For many reasons, AJ Gaines was a man who was never overlooked.

"What?" Tom asked, his curiosity roused.

With much anticipation, the Corbetts were looking upward at their large friend.

"I'm going to open a third gallery," AJ blurted, his excitement overwhelming him.

"You should consider Washington Square," Shannon advised him, unaware that he had already chosen the location.

"It's going to be in Miami," he shrieked as he slapped Tom on the back. "I was just there last weekend, and I've got a couple of amazing locations picked out. It's such a vibrant, electric place, and I just love Cuban men."

"Wow, that's really big news, alright!" Tom said.

"I thought you looked tanned," Shannon observed.

"There's more," AJ said, still bubbling over. "I want you to consider being my partners in this gallery. I can get the money elsewhere, but I think it would be a lot more fun with you involved. We would have such a blast in Miami."

"That sounds interesting," Shannon said thoughtfully. "We should consider getting in on this investment, Tom. You know how well AJ's galleries do."

"Whoa," Tom said, feeling assailed by the excitement on both sides of him. "This is a little sudden, AJ, isn't it? You've only been out of rehab for a couple of months."

"Rehab is like a second home to me, you know that. Other people go on vacation—I go to rehab and dry out. I am a man of many demons, weaknesses, and addictions, but I've never let them affect my galleries. Just think about it, okay?"

After ten minutes of catching up, AJ excused himself so he could schmooze with his affluent clientele, Shannon headed back to the bar for another martini, and Tom was left alone to occupy himself with one of his favorite pastimes—chuckling privately over the ridiculous price tags on the works of several of the newer artists. Tom knew art valuations; it was a big part of his job. He also knew AJ would get his price, and that made it all the more amusing.

* * *

Around 10 p.m., the Corbetts climbed into the back of a town car for the short fifteen-minute drive to their condominium. On account of five olives and the vodka that accompanied them in her martinis, Shannon's tone was immediately antagonistic.

"We should invest in the Miami gallery," she said as soon as the car started moving. "We both know AJ makes a sizable commission on everything he sells."

"I'm not sure I'm comfortable with it," Tom said. "Let's think about it for a few days, and we'll talk about it over the weekend."

"Oh for God's sake, I invest ten times this amount on a daily basis. I make my living picking good investments, and I think this is a damn good one. Anyway, it'll give us an excuse to go to Miami each winter and spend some time in the sun."

"We'll talk about it over the weekend," he replied, repeating his previous request.

"You're afraid to take any risks, aren't you?" Shannon ranted, unwilling to honor his waiting period.

Shannon pressed on, slurring her words. "What you don't realize is that risks are actually good things; they get your heart pounding and make you feel alive again?"

"I take plenty of risks," Tom half-heartedly defended himself, as this subject matter was hardly fresh ground in their relationship.

"If I hadn't introduced you to Paul, you'd still be appraising houses for real estate transactions to this day."

"I get it," Tom grumbled. "I owe all my success in life to you. If we hadn't met, I'd be penniless."

"Oh, save the sarcasm. For once, just go for it. Don't overthink it. Just say we're in."

"AJ's been one of my best friends for more than twenty years and I'm not sure I want to be business partners with him. Okay?"

"Bastard," she mumbled.

"You're drunk," he said.

More often than not, Shannon drank a lot at social functions, but never to the point of stumbling inebriation, and she usually apologized the next morning for all her harsh comments or moments, most often involving Tom. Once again, Tom hoped this conversation was over and quietly stared out the car window at the faces of the strangers walking along Quince Street. One moment, a stylishly attired couple strolled together, and the next moment, a homeless person in rags leaned against a wall. From his passing glance, he thought he saw a common loneliness in the faces of all three strangers and wondered if his weary mug made four. Exhausted, Tom closed his eyes. With her head resting against the window, Shannon had already done the same.

Chapter Eight

Almost as rare as a total eclipse but never as eagerly anticipated, dinner with the entire Corbett family present at the table happened on the third Sunday in April. Total eclipses lasted for a short while and were remarkable; Corbett family dinners lasted about thirty minutes and were much less noteworthy. This night was an exception. Usually, the family dined in shifts, with the two children having dinner around 6 p.m. and the parents having dinner closer to 8 p.m. when they arrived home from work. Usually, Marta provided meals whenever the family members came to the kitchen and requested them. On this rare occasion, Tom, Shannon, Nicole, and Alex gathered at the south end of the grand dining room table with seating for sixteen where Marta was about to serve one of her most requested menus: roast pork, scalloped potatoes, fresh green beans, and crescent rolls. A glass of French chardonnay wine awaited each family member, and all four sampled the vintage as soon as they sat at the table. Tom and Shannon sipped like wine enthusiasts searching for subtle flavors while Nicole and Alex guzzled like teens chasing a buzz. One by one, Marta brought serving plates and bowls to the table and then retreated to the kitchen.

"Have you played in any games yet?" Shannon asked her son, currently the backup third baseman on the varsity baseball team.

"I haven't played one inning or had a single at-bat yet," Alex replied, "but on a few occasions, when Assistant Coach Davis was late, I filled in as third base coach. That's as close as I've come to playing my position in a game. Hopefully, I'll actually get to step on the field soon."

Alex's tone was acerbic, as he was unhappy with his bench-warming status and eager to see action soon.

"As soon as you get some playing time," Tom said, "I'd like to come to one of your games, so keep me posted."

"Sure, Dad," Alex returned in an appeasing manner, unsure which was more unlikely—that he would get playing time or that his father would actually come to the game.

"This is really good wine," Shannon remarked as she finished her first glass and reached for the bottle to pour a second one. Marta always placed an extra bottle near Shannon's place setting, knowing that she would want additional pours.

"I got some unexpected news on Friday," Tom said as the serving plates were passed around the table.

"Good news?" Shannon asked.

"I'm not sure how to categorize it," Tom answered, but the non-answer aspect of his reply caused his wife to bristle.

"Well, what is it then exactly?"

"I received a registered letter from a Pittsburgh lawyer named L. William Hathaway. He informed me that my Uncle Carl has passed away and that I am the sole heir to his estate, which largely consists of the family farm in Shelbyville, PA."

"How cool is that, Dad—you're a farmer!" Alex said mockingly, unable to picture his father driving a tractor or working in the fields.

"What's the farm like?" he followed up.

"I don't know," Tom said, as his demeanor turned reflective. "I was only seven years old when my father died, and my mom and I left for good. I don't remember the farm very well because I really don't have many memories from that time."

"Is it a large farm with cows and pigs and other livestock?" Alex asked.

"I don't think so," Tom said. "The letter describes it as a main farmhouse, guesthouse, two storage barns, and forty acres of farmland. I don't think it has livestock. I would imagine the property has been neglected and is in a state of serious disrepair. My Uncle Carl was seventy-eight years old and probably as bad a farmer as his brother."

"Your dad?" Alex asked for clarification.

"Yeah, my dad was a miserable farmer!"

"Should we sell it or lease it out?" Shannon asked, always quick to recognize the potential value of any asset.

"I haven't given it much thought."

For the next fifteen minutes, the four family members quietly focused on their meals, and the only sounds in the room were the taps of fine silverware on imported Portuguese china. Tom, Shannon, and Alex consumed their meals, while Nicole ate very little and mostly moved her food around her plate. As Marta came out of the kitchen to check on the meal's progress, Shannon noticed the uneaten pork and potatoes on her daughter's plate and inquired.

"You've been quiet this evening, Nicole, and have barely touched your meal. Are you feeling all right?"

"I have a lot on my mind," Nicole responded without glancing towards her mother.

"What could be weighing on your mind?" Shannon asked in a condescending tone. "You work with third graders."

"It's nothing, Mother. Just leave me alone."

Shannon, working on her third glass of chardonnay, was never good at leaving things alone when intoxicated. Normally outspoken, she was even more so after a few drinks. Further, she had been particularly hard on Nicole since she graduated high school last year and opted not to attend college. For most of the fall and winter, Nicole was purposeless because she had neither school nor work to occupy her time. She stayed out late at night regularly and slept in past noon often. Finally, in early January, Shannon reached out to contacts on the school board and arranged for Nicole's teaching aid position at the elementary school. Shannon had always hoped her only daughter would follow her trailblazing footsteps into the world of finance, but Nicole never demonstrated the temperament necessary for the profession. Unlike her mother, Nicole was sweet, sensitive, and nurturing.

"What's the worst thing that can happen in your workday?" Shannon chided her daughter. "Some kid forgets her milk money, and you have to spot her fifty cents? Honey, I simply don't understand how you can say you have a lot on your mind."

"I'm pregnant, Mother. Are you happy now?"

"You slut!" Alex blurted.

"Alex!" Tom shouted.

"What do you mean—you're pregnant?" Shannon demanded.

Marta, who was busily retrieving plates from the table, immediately placed the two plates in her hands back onto the tabletop when the word "pregnant" was spoken and scurried to the kitchen.

"*Diocito dame fuerza,*" she whispered in her native language as she made the sign of the cross with her right hand and opened the kitchen door with her left.

Marta was fluent in English but figured her "God, give me strength" plea was better kept between herself and the Lord. In her almost twenty years with the Corbetts, she'd fled to the sanctuary of her kitchen many times when family discussions intensified.

"Everyone calm down," Tom called out, trying to create a quieter moment so he could process his daughter's announcement.

"Tom," Shannon said through gritted teeth, "our nineteen-year-old daughter has just told us she is pregnant. I will not calm down. In fact, I have every right to do the opposite."

"It doesn't seem like you've known this boy very long," Tom observed, trying to mediate the situation.

"Scratch and I just celebrated our six-month anniversary," Nicole advised her father, seeming proud of the milestone.

"Oh, isn't that sweet?" Shannon said, her eyes narrowed, glaring at her daughter. "Is the six-month anniversary cardboard or plastic?"

"We're going to get an apartment and live together," Nicole added defiantly as if she wanted to inflict greater emotional pain on her mother.

At that moment, mother and daughter squared off against one another. They glared intensely across the table at one another. Their ongoing disagreements about Nicole's lack of plans and direction had finally reached a flashpoint.

"Oh God," Tom remarked quietly to himself, his head lowered momentarily, "I'm going to have a son-in-law named Scratch."

His mental state had turned toward bewilderment.

"Don't think for one second that I'm going to burp this kid or change any poopy diapers," Alex asserted as he departed the table for his bedroom.

"I'm leaving, too," Nicole said as she rose from the table. "You think you know everything," she added, irked, directed at her mother, before she followed her brother out of the room.

"Not so fast," her mother shouted.

"Let her go," Tom advised. "We need to talk."

"You can't drink alcohol when you're pregnant, Nicole," Shannon screamed in frustration.

"We need to talk," Tom repeated.

"What about, Tom? I think it's a little late for us to develop a parenting plan."

Chapter Nine

S omehow, more than twenty years ago, when Paul Desjardins founded his antiques and auction company, he managed to find the one building in Philadelphia that looked like it belonged on the *Avenue des Champs-Elysees* in Paris. Known as Desjardins House, the building was built in the early 1800s of limestone and brick and featured seven tall arched windows with concrete dormers on its top floor and stone steps in front that led to an ornate wrought iron entryway. The magnificent wood front door, salvaged from a church in the Bordeaux wine region of France, had meticulously carved grapevines along its edges and dated back to the reign of Napoleon. Appropriately, in a building that exuded European sensibilities, Paul and Tom had built a business dedicated to the appreciation and preservation of art, history, and beauty.

It was clearly "one of those days" inside Desjardins House, unusual for a Friday when the enthusiastic anticipation of the weekend normally softened any snags or difficulties. Earlier that morning, one of the workers in the shipping area, which was running four days behind schedule, dropped a large porcelain palace vase from the late 1800s, and it shattered into one hundred little pieces.

The vase was royal blue with gold handles and a lid and was quite unique in detail and condition. At auction, it had sold for eleven thousand dollars, almost twice its appraised value. The loss would be covered by insurance, but the piece was irreplaceable, and Tom was always turned a little sideways whenever a historic item was nicked or damaged, much less destroyed. On top of the mishap, irate customers had been calling because shipments that hadn't even left the warehouse yet were already expected at their destinations. And, adding one final pressure point to an already difficult morning, appraised asset values for a settlement meeting that afternoon at Clyde, Delaney, and Peat were not complete, and Tom was pushing his appraisers to finish the work. This law firm was one of Desjardins' largest and most lucrative clients and the reports simply couldn't be late.

It can't get any worse, Tom comforted himself after he hung up the phone. On the call, he'd just talked with and appeased his fifth disgruntled customer of the morning.

Exhausted already at only 10:15 a.m., Tom shut his office door and collapsed behind his desk in an effort to regain his composure during a few quiet minutes. His office was a hodgepodge of items from different eras and locales. An early American desk and an ornate Italian Baroque walnut chest on a stand that served as a credenza were a striking combination. Though few styles matched or naturally complemented one another, they created an exotic setting that spoke volumes about the tastes and interests of the man who occupied the office. Entering Tom's office was the equivalent of going on a whirlwind world tour during exciting, historically relevant periods.

During his quiet moment, Tom's cell phone vibrated against his desk, and he noticed the name AJ Gaines on its screen. Three weeks had passed since the conversation at Waterwheel about opening a Miami art gallery, and Tom knew he owed AJ a response, but he hadn't talked with his wife about the investment since that evening. He touched the screen and put AJ on speaker.

"We owe you an answer regarding your invitation to invest in the Miami gallery," Tom told the gallery owner after they exchanged pleasantries.

"That's not why I am calling," AJ corrected him. "Shannon gave me a check two weeks ago. We've already selected a location and signed a five-year lease with the owner. I assumed you knew."

"No, we haven't discussed it since that night."

"Well, that's not right, but we can fix it. I can find another partner and refund your investment."

"No AJ, we both know how stubborn Shannon can be once she has made up her mind. She won't be willing to reverse course. Besides, I know it's a solid investment—I just don't want it to impact our friendship. We've been friends for too long to let that happen."

"Tom, I would burn the gallery to the ground before letting it impact our friendship."

"Well, partner," Tom said enthusiastically, "we'll have to grab a drink one evening to celebrate, and I look forward to traveling to Miami for the grand opening."

* * *

Fifteen blocks south at Hastings Corbett, the morning had developed a similarly tense tone. Martin Hastings was on a phone call with a contact in the merger and acquisitions department at the Bauer Group, a prestigious investment banking company, and the news wasn't good. Beneath two seventy-year-old oil paintings—one that depicted the stock exchange floor during the crash of 1929 and the other a portrait of financier J.P. Morgan—Martin paced back and forth in the area behind his desk. In the portrait above him, J.P.'s facial expression looked almost as annoyed as Martin's.

"What do you mean, 'it ain't gonna happen?'" Martin shouted angrily into the telephone receiver. "Three weeks ago, it was a sure thing. We've got almost twenty million dollars of our client's money invested in Carbide Technologies. This is a real problem, Bob."

"It's not exactly something I have control over," the voice on the other end of the call responded defensively. "We are caught in a very unfavorable position also."

Five minutes later, Martin slammed his phone down and shouted, "Shannon, we've got a big problem."

Immediately, she appeared in his doorway with a concerned look on her face because she knew her partner didn't anger easily.

"Close the door," he instructed her, seething as he did. As soon as it was closed, Martin continued.

"Bob Wilson at Bauer just told me that Agilleon is no longer interested in buying Carbide Technologies. Suddenly, they think the price is excessive and they're questioning how well the two cultures will merge."

"That's a problem alright," she said. "Once the news gets out, Carbide Technologies could take a thirty percent hit, maybe more."

"No shit."

"Well, goddamn it, Martin," Shannon squawked. "You said this acquisition was a sure thing."

"I thought it was."

"We'll dump the Carbide shares as quickly as possible."

"Keep the lots as small as you can."

* * *

Tom and Shannon made it home later than usual that evening. Both had stopped for a couple drinks along the way, and both poured another at their bar as soon as they entered the living room. In their hands, the bottles lingered while the alcohol flowed, giving ample time for the level to rise in the glass. They knew they didn't have the energy to return to the bar later. Husband and wife were physically and mentally drained from what had been a tumultuous day for each of them, and it was readily apparent in their eyelids and shoulders, all hanging low, feeling heavy.

"I'm exhausted," Tom said.

"Me too," Shannon replied.

Four words were all they could muster and neither made any effort to explain their weary condition or inquire about their spouse's weary condition. Only routine carried them to the dining room table, not appetite or interest, and it was just the two of them because their kids had already eaten and retreated to their bedrooms. For thirty minutes, they barely looked up from their plates, eating their meals like they were using their last ounces of energy to maneuver the knives and forks and chew. Beneath a chandelier salvaged from a theater in Rome, they were in trance-like states; the dining room was silent until Tom finally broke the silence.

"I understand we are partners in the Miami gallery."

"Yes we are," Shannon said with no further explanation.

Around 10:30 p.m., Marta cleared their plates, and Tom and Shannon gradually and independently relocated to the burgundy sofas in the living room, each positioning themselves at opposite corners of the L shape when they arrived. Tom had a manila folder that contained the report compiled for the 3 p.m. settlement meeting that afternoon, appraisal values that went to the client without Tom's normal review. Shannon had a blue binder that contained all account transactions for that day so she could review the progress made on selling the more than one million shares of Carbide Technologies that the firm owned. Neither had the energy or focus needed to be productive.

Chapter Ten

On the following Monday at 11 a.m., Alex and his best friend, Jacob Stein, were alone in the Corbett condominium. Even under the most innocent of circumstances, two teenage boys, with a total of eleven shaves and not a single driver's license between them, at home alone and unsupervised was a precarious situation in any household. In Alex's bedroom, the posters on his walls illustrated his confused mid-puberty status with equal parts sports heroes, rock stars, rappers, social causes, and supermodels. A raucous energy existed in the room as the teens played a video game named Armed Assault, where they worked as a unit to overtake an enemy stronghold on a battlefield. Together, they hooted and hollered as they killed enemy combatants and made their way toward their opponent's weapons stockpile. In the video game, both boys had commander status—the highest ranking that usually required more than one hundred hours of game experience.

"Cover me!" Alex shouted.

"No," Jacob blared as a warning. "It's a death trap."

But, Jacob's warning was too late. In an instant, Alex's avatar was surrounded by the enemy, taking fire from all sides. It collapsed, withered, and died a convulsing death.

"Crap," Jacob said, now alone and outnumbered.

Less than a minute later, his avatar suffered the same fate as Alex's did, horrible convulsions and death.

"How about a couple of beers and some chips?" Alex suggested as Jacob's avatar writhed and convulsed on the screen before them.

"I'm down for that," Jacob said.

By early afternoon, both boys had two beers, shared a joint, and were feeling very good. On the large screen in the bedroom, Will Farrell was naked and trotting down a street in the middle of the night as the boys watched the movie "Old School" for the umpteenth time. As Will Farrell's wife in the film pulled alongside him in their SUV with her friends in the vehicle and asked, "Frank, what the hell are you doing?" the boys broke into gut-busting laughter. They only stopped when they noticed a text on Alex's phone in front of them.

Wat up, read the text from a girl named Emily, one that Alex knew from history class and was interested in.

Home watchn Old School w Jacob, Alex returned.

Home w Anna, come over

In 30

Immediately, Jacob grabbed the brown paper bag with the empty beer cans in it, the two boys retrieved their coats from atop the bed, and both rushed out without even turning off the television. They scampered through the living room towards the front door where Alex stopped at a small writing desk in the entryway and opened its middle drawer. He retrieved a set of car keys like he was grabbing a prize.

"We'll take the Jag," he said, referring to his parent's Jaguar automobile.

"Are you sure?" Jacob asked. "We've had several beers and a joint."

"I'm fine, dude," Alex responded.

"What about your parents?"

"They won't be home until after 8. And anyway, they never drive the car. I've put as many miles on it as either of them."

Emily's home was only eight miles from the condominium, and Alex and Jacob made the drive in less than twenty minutes. A precarious situation in the Corbett residence had now escalated into a dangerous situation in the Lancaster residence, as there were now two teenage boys and two teenage girls home alone and unsupervised. More beers and another joint served as the icebreakers. After a short while, the four teenagers split into two couples and adjourned to separate bedrooms on the second floor. For more than an hour, they engaged in pleasurable stroking and thrusting activities that would've caused their parents great displeasure if they knew what was going on while they were at work. For two of the teens, this afternoon marked the end of their virginity, their first experience with sexual intercourse, the first time they officially "hooked up." It was almost 5 p.m. when Jacob and Alex exited the residence in the direction of the Jaguar, walking the light-heeled walk of two teenage boys who just had sex.

"Did you use a condom?" Alex asked Jacob in the car.

"Of course I did!" he replied.

"Good," Alex returned. "I'm already living with one foolish, pregnant teenager."

"Nicole is pregnant?" Jacob asked with astonishment.

"Yeah. Isn't that ridiculous?"

"With that Snatch guy?" he followed up.

"His name is Scratch."

"Equally ridiculous," Jacob observed, shaking his head.

Miss u already, Alex texted to Emily before he pulled away from the curb.

Alex drove the same twenty-minute route home. With only four blocks to go until the garage entrance at his family's condo, Alex suddenly saw flashing red lights in his rear view mirror. Also sensing the lights, Jacob spun around and saw the cruiser following so closely that he found himself staring into the face of the officer. He freaked out.

"Holy shit!" he cried out. "It's a cop car, alright."

"Grab some mints from the glove box," Alex instructed him.

"Mints? You don't even have a driver's license!"

"One thing at a time," Alex said, remaining unusually cool for a sixteen-year-old about to suffer the biggest setback of his life.

"License and registration," the officer said as he stood outside the driver's window, appearing ten feet tall to the boys inside the car.

* * *

Two hours later, Tom received a call at his desk at Desjardins. On the screen of his phone, the caller was identified as PPD Precinct 11— PPD designating the Philadelphia Police Department—and though Tom recognized the caller, he assumed it was a fundraising call. In a calm manner, Tom touched his phone to activate the speaker.

"This is Tom Corbett."

"Mr. Corbett, this is Officer Randolph Hudson of the Philadelphia Police Department and I am calling to advise you that we have arrested your son, one Alexander Michael Corbett, on the charges of driving under the influence, operating a motor vehicle without a proper license, and failure to stop at a traffic signal."

"What?"

"Mr. Corbett, this is..."

"I'm sorry," Tom said, interrupting the officer as he began repeating his initial statement. "I heard you the first time."

After ten minutes on the phone with Officer Hudson, listening to the details of his son's infractions, Tom called AJ.

"Alex was arrested," Tom blurted as soon as AJ answered.

"Oh my gosh, what has my godson done?"

"DUI, driving without a license, and running a red light."

"I'd have to call that the trifecta of adolescent stupidity," AJ said with a touch of lightheartedness in his voice.

51

"This isn't funny. Alex is about to start applying to Ivy League schools. He'll never get into one now."

"I'm sorry. I know it's serious. If it's any consolation, I'd been charged with all those infractions before I was twenty."

"That's not consolation."

"Well, what can I do? How can I help?"

"I need the best lawyer for these types of charges. Who do you recommend?"

"You need a lawyer so you immediately think of me?"

"Well, yeah."

"Call Abigail Stone at Clyde, Delaney, and Peat. She is the best when it comes to DUI defenses."

"Really, I know Abby. I'll give her a call. Thanks."

Chapter Eleven

As two crises involving teenagers unfolded within the Corbett household, Marta darted from room to room like someone evading a fire, doing her best to avoid the many heated conversations. She loved the Corbett children like her own, so her mind was troubled. Raised voices and even name-calling became regular occurrences as frustration on the part of the parents and sniping between the children reached epic levels. Frequently, as she fled the room, Marta mumbled, "Dios, ayuda a estos ninos," (God help these children) to herself.

At 7:15 a.m., two days after his arrest, Alex and Nicole were the first to arrive at the dining room table. The two siblings sat opposite one another at the table and exchanged terse glares; then, they barely looked at one another. And, all the while, Marta scurried about the room with plates of crepes, fresh muffins, and glasses of juice.

"What are you doing up so early?" Nicole finally asked her brother. "You're never up this early."

"I have an appointment at my lawyer's office."

"How will you get there? Are you planning on stealing a car or hijacking a cabbie at knifepoint?"

"Very funny," Alex said. "Mom is driving me."

"If I were you, I wouldn't get in a car with Mom alone."

"You're not one to talk, Nicole," Alex objected, a blatant attempt at deflection. "At least my screw-up won't require me to change poopy diapers five times a day for two years."

"Are you kidding me?" Nicole said, quite miffed. "You are going to carry that DUI with you like a poopy diaper for a long time. It's a colossal screw-up."

"I'll be just fine," Alex responded dismissively. "Don't you worry your pretty little head about me; you need to focus on your Lamaze classes."

"That's exactly right," Nicole shot back. "I'll be in Lamaze class, and you'll be in jail."

"Oh, give me a break, sis. I'm a juvenile and a first-time offender. I'm not going to jail."

"I will give you credit, though," Nicole declared in a biting tone, "you're the first person I know to get a DUI before you even have a driver's license. Who does that?"

Hearing only that last remark, Tom and Shannon entered the dining room and assumed the sniping between the siblings had restarted with the new day, which it had.

"Can we change the topic?" Shannon said with impatience in her voice, unaware of the current topic.

"Scratch and I have decided to move in together in August," Nicole advised her parents. "He has some business opportunities he wants to execute before we do."

Tom and Shannon exchanged subtle glances, each wondering if a follow-up question was warranted about the business opportunities portion of her statement. Both knew Scratch had no means to support himself, much less Nicole and a child. He was a twenty-three-year-old with a GED who still lived in the basement of his parent's home. Independently, they decided it was too early in the morning to solicit such information and instead took their usual seats at the table. Once seated, Shannon turned her attention to her son.

"Marta will be keeping track of your comings and goings, so you'd better comply with the terms of your grounding."

"I will, Mom," he said. "I promise."

"You're going to have to earn back my trust again," she added coldly.

"And by the way, Alex," Tom said as he reached for his orange juice, "AJ asked me to give you a good, hard swat across the back of your head for him."

"Is AJ mad at me?"

"No one is mad at you," Tom told Alex though he was quite distressed by the incident. "We're disappointed. We know you are much smarter than that."

"Speak for yourself," Shannon said. "I'm mad as hell at him!"

Chapter Twelve

As a columnist at *The Post*, I received more than five hundred emails each day, and on some days, the count could be as high as one thousand. Though I tried to read, or at least scan, all the messages, on some days I had to delete large blocks because I simply couldn't get to them all. On those days, I always wondered what I might be missing and what was the opportunity cost of that action. Was the potential for an important article or a significant moment in my life amongst those deleted emails?

One day, amongst more than eight hundred fifty emails, I received an email from the wife of an Iraq War veteran who returned from his tour of duty on the battlefield four months earlier, only he didn't. In her email, she told me that my readers needed to understand that the war's casualties weren't limited to the dead and those with bodily injuries. Every soldier was traumatized by the war. The war spared no one. And, the casualties were not always obvious; not all were missing arms or legs or blinded or rolling about in wheelchairs. Many simply couldn't find their way home and couldn't return to the families and the lives they left behind. They wandered our streets like the walking wounded, unable to reclaim their spirit and identity from before the battlefield. Like so many, her husband was fighting a second war on our soil, his own private battle to return to everyday life as a productive husband, father and citizen.

I arranged to meet Tracy and Mark Miller (not their real names) at their home on separate occasions so we could talk without their spouse or children present. Even with spouses who theoretically share everything, I had found it better to talk with each separately as they'd often share things with me that they hadn't told their spouse. Their home was a beautiful colonial in a neighborhood two or three notches above middle class, with fine furnishings and family portraits adorning the walls and mantle of the living room. In the pictures, each more than three years old, I saw a family with glowing faces and smiles, not yet touched by war. Providing their upscale lifestyle, Tracy was well compensated as a software engineer at a communications company on the nearby I-270 corridor as well as her husband's income from the Army.

When I first met him and shook his hand, Lieutenant Mark Miller was a man both with and without presence. He was six feet three inches tall and as solidly built as any man I knew, but his eyes were vacant, and his handshake was lifeless. He was standing in front of me and simultaneously not present with me. Mark was a shell of a man, and, while I'd heard the expression before, I'd never encountered someone who so fit the bill. His physique was imposing, but he seemed hollow and empty inside. One thing I knew for certain, he wasn't the same guy I saw in the family portraits in the living room. Mark looked like him and could've been his brother, but he wasn't the same guy.

After fifteen minutes of small talk, I asked Mark to tell me what it was like for him to be stationed in Iraq. Listening to him, I felt fortunate that I'd never been sent to a battlefield.

"In a war zone, the stress level is simply indescribable," he told me, his eyes welling at the remembrance. "I can't compare it to anything I've experienced in civilian life. My seemingly inevitable death was a constant thought in my mind, and it weighed on my shoulders like an intolerable gravity. Every waking moment, and even at night while I tried to sleep, I waited for an IED (Improvised Explosive Devise) to explode, a shoulder-launched rocket to land, a sniper's bullet to strike me, or a truck bomb to crash through our perimeter fence. I was always aware that death might be a moment away, as close to me as the dry air that made my nose bleed. I often wondered: Would I know it happened, or would it happen so quickly that I would just cease being—alive one instant and gone the next. After my tour of duty, I concluded that the constant stress of the battlefield is mentally and emotionally more than soldiers can handle. No one comes home intact. Human beings are not built to live in constant fear of death. It's just too much."

"How many deaths did you witness in Iraq?"

"I witnessed the deaths of seven of my fellow soldiers and countless Iraqis."

"Were you close to any of the soldiers?"

"My best friend."

"Was that your worst day in Iraq?"

"Far and away."

Back off, I told myself, wary of continuing. *It's too soon to broach the subject of the death of his best friend.*

It was only our first interview. From my first question, Mark's eyes pooled with tears, and I knew that if I wanted to learn his whole story, I didn't want to push him so far as actual tears. It was too early. Before we went there, I needed to create a bond and build trust.

"Did your view of death change while in Iraq?"

"I don't know how to answer that one," Mark said. "I know I was much sadder the first time it happened than later. It certainly became less tragic and unexpected."

Born and raised in Maryland, Mark graduated from Duke in 1997 with an engineering degree that he completed in three years. Ten days after his twenty-second birthday, he married his childhood sweetheart on a hillside surrounded by cherry blossoms, and they welcomed a son before his next birthday. Two years into their marriage, Mark and his wife had prestigious jobs and a first home in Arlington, Virginia; they were the American dream personified. Prior to his service in Iraq, he was a guy with the necessary skill set to succeed in life, and he was confident he would. In a detached voice, he told me he wasn't that guy anymore.

"I didn't die in Iraq, but I think part of me did."

"What's so different now?"

"I can't focus on anything for any extended period," he declared in a clearly frustrated tone.

Ironically, Mark paused like he'd lost his train of thought, but then he continued.

"Before Iraq, I was a capable and productive person who had much to contribute to my family and society. Now after serving, I'm struggling every day, barely making it through my days, and a burden to my family and society."

* * *

During my first hour with Tracy Miller, I wondered if the human gestation period included a strengthening of the mother's will, the development of a mindset that she would do whatever it takes for as long as it takes to nurture and protect her children. Whether physiological, chemical or simply part of the loving bond that forms between mother and fetus, I detected a level of commitment in Tracy's tired eyes that made it quite clear she would never allow anything to harm her children or family. Without so much as a complaint or whimper, she would shoulder the burden, whatever the burden. It was as simple as that. Over more than two years, during their most trying times, Tracy put her family on her back and carried the load. In my mind at least, she should've worn a long red cape and chest emblem to our interview, as her actions over the last couple years were clearly that of a superhero. Tracy worked full-time at her employer, managed the home front, and cared for their two children, taking on the roles of mother and father while Mark was absent. And, now that Mark had returned, she was taking care of one more. Casualties of war were not always readily apparent and, from my research, that was also true of those who served.

"One day," Tracy said, "my daughter, Gail, asked me why Daddy gets so grumpy. She was only six years old and far too young for me to discuss the hardships of war, so I kept it simple. I told her that when people we love confuse us, the best thing we can do is hug them, simply give them a long, tight hug. A couple of days later, Mark was having a bad day, and he snapped at Gail. Without any hesitation, she walked right over and hugged him. At the time, I was standing beside the sink drying the dinner dishes, and I could not stop my tears from streaming down my face. I know my Mark, I thought, and he won't let that little girl down."

Chapter Thirteen

Entitled "The Stride," my five-part series about the Millers was published in October 2004 and was extraordinarily well received. By the time the third installment landed on the newsstands, I had received invitations to appear on several television shows to discuss the challenges faced by soldiers returning home. My article made one fact clear: The transition from a war zone to civilian life was far more perilous than most thought. When invited, I always wished I could bring Mark and Tracy along, but our arrangement called for anonymity, and their intent never wavered. I had to honor that. But I also knew that Mark and Tracy were what made my series special; individually and as a couple, they were remarkable people. Thousands of couples were working through the challenges of a loved one returning home from serving their country, but I was fortunate enough to find a couple doing it with such love and compassion and grace. Their story, as it turned out, would be the high watermark of my fourteen-year career with *The Philadelphia Post*.

On a bitterly cold January afternoon, Austin strolled into my office with a bottle of Cristal Champagne in his hand and a big smile on his face. This was unusual for two reasons: Austin never came to my office; he always called me on the phone and told me to come to his office, and Cristal cost over three hundred dollars per bottle so it was a luxury that humble wordsmiths like Austin and me couldn't afford. As he placed two plastic tumblers on the edge of my desk and began to remove the gold foil from the neck of the bottle, I questioned both his presence and the celebratory bottle.

"Are you getting married?" I asked with a perplexed look on my face. "Are you getting knighted?" I continued after I noticed that the bottle was Cristal.

In no hurry to share his news, Austin carefully poured two glasses of the fine bubbly, handed one across the desk to me, and sat in the chair before my desk, still smiling the ear-to-ear smile of a lottery winner, a first-time father, or someone who just pulled off a big heist. He didn't make a toasting motion; instead, he rested his hand on his knee and began reminiscing.

"Can you believe it has been almost twenty years since we first sat together in my office at Shelbyville High School?"

"At that time," I said, joining the reminiscing, "I could barely write my own name, much less a good article."

"Oh, don't be so hard yourself," he replied. "You were rough around the edges, but you had more talent and desire than any young writer I'd ever met."

"Maybe so, but that never stopped you from mercilessly editing my work. I swear you must've gone through ten red pens in our time together."

"You were a quick study."

"You taught me well."

"I guess I did," he acknowledged as he finally raised his glass to a toasting position about eye level. With a left-handed motion, he encouraged me to do the same. I hoisted my glass though I still had no idea what this celebration was all about. I awaited his announcement. In a serious tone, he continued.

"A little more than an hour ago, I received a call from the Director of the Fenwick Foundation at Stanton University and she informed me that Nicholas Gordon Sterling will be awarded the Fenwick Prize for Excellence in Journalism for the newspaper series, "The Stride," that appeared in *The Philadelphia Post*. The awards ceremony is scheduled for the third Saturday in February in New York City. Congratulations, Nick; this award is the highest honor attainable in our profession, and you truly deserve it. That determined kid in my office is now the best damn journalist I've ever known."

Chapter Fourteen

One of the wonders of a great city like New York is the daily juxtaposition of lives. At their birth, the odds of a boy born in Boulder, Colorado, meeting and marrying a girl born in Sao Paulo, Brazil, are astronomical. In the courses of their lifetimes, they must travel a million miles and turn a million times to find one another. So when it happens amid eight million other people, beneath the bright lights of a vibrant city, the boy and girl have surely won a lottery of sorts. They have claimed the big prize. And though marriage is an extreme example, lives intersect in New York City every day that would never cross otherwise, and each person is, for better or for worse, altered by the experience.

Though I lived in a big city, New York was different and unique; the buildings were so tall and dense that I felt like I was walking through the Grand Urban Canyon as I strolled toward the Winston Hotel for the awards ceremony. It was a cold, clear Saturday night in the Big Apple, and the sidewalks were bustling with people in winter coats who seemed to be scurrying about in search of warm places, each puffing cold air like locomotives as they rolled along. When I arrived at the hotel around 6 p.m., I paused in the lobby to view the splendor, but what caught my eye was a petite woman in a red beret whose natural beauty seemed like a beacon, as she was not wearing makeup but simply radiant on her own. She stood out like green space in a gray city block. While other women in the lobby were painted and prepped for an evening on the town, her long blonde hair, blue eyes, and perfect complexion required no enhancement or alteration.

Chelsea Yarborough, a celebrity chef with a small following on cable television, was a thirty-three-year-old native of Queensland, Australia, whose liquid blue eyes would remind any Aussie of the aquamarine waters of the Great Barrier Reef. She grew up in Brisbane on the Gold Coast of Australia in an A-frame house just four blocks from the beach. At nineteen, Chelsea married her childhood sweetheart and gave birth sixteen months later to a daughter named Miranda. In true Aussie form, she had a good bloke, no worries, and an ankle-biter with the bluest eyes on the continent. But, at the age of five, their daughter drowned, and Chelsea faced such grief and guilt daily that she didn't think she could go on living. Her marriage slowly collapsed, and, convinced that only a drastic reinvention and new scenery could save her, she moved to the United States. When she arrived in New York five years ago, she joined a support group that proved to be her salvation. Since her cooking show first aired almost three years ago, its distribution had grown to include several major U.S. markets, and she'd achieved a minor degree of celebrity status.

Though confident I could find the Grand Ballroom on my own, as it was larger than a football field, I noticed her hotel name tag, so I approached and asked for directions.

"Hi Chelsea," I said, "I'm attending an event in the Grand Ballroom this evening. Do you know where it's located?"

Startled by my inquiry, Chelsea quickly regained her composure and casually replied, "Follow me—I'll take you there."

From her very first word, her Aussie accent was apparent, and, when I asked about her homeland, Chelsea told me about growing up in eastern Australia. As soon as she could walk, her father, who owned a charter fishing business, taught her to swim and fish and, together, they spent many hours in or on the blue waters of the Pacific. She told me about the white sand beaches and warm water near her home and, in turn, I told her about the tall trees and wide-open fields surrounding mine. I told her I also swam and fished a lot as a young boy, but the settings were usually muddy lakes and rivers. Through a warm and comfortable smile, she remarked that we both had fortunate childhoods.

"We certainly have that in common," she added.

Chelsea and I walked down several long hallways only to reach an impassable point where we reversed course and retraced our steps backward. En route to the Grand Ballroom, we took three escalators and two elevators and passed the same coffee stand three times. At the coffee stand, I noticed the small stack of *The Philadelphia Post* newspapers amongst the other periodicals beside the counter. As our walk surpassed the thirty-minute mark, she told me that Aussies were sincere people who placed great emphasis on family and community, and I told her that Shelbyville was the kind of small town where everyone looked out for their neighbors. Even though we grew up half a world apart in different hemispheres, there was a lot of commonality in our childhood stories.

"Shelbyville sounds like a great place," she observed as we walked. "Even the name sounds idyllic."

After we roamed the hotel hallways for nearly forty-five minutes, I finally asked her, "Do you have any idea where the Grand Ballroom is located?"

"I must confess, Nick, I don't."

"Well, why did you tell me you did?" I asked, amused by her apparent lie.

"You looked so good in your tuxedo that I wanted to meet you. I figured we'd stumble on the Grand Ballroom eventually. With a name like Grand Ballroom, it seemed hard to miss."

"I am surprised we didn't find it," I returned with a laugh. "I think we've covered most of the hotel."

"I guess we weren't paying attention."

"Do you work here or did you steal that nametag?"

"I'm hosting a cooking seminar in the hotel. I don't work for the hotel, but the hotel manager gave it to me to wear."

"Is your name even Chelsea?"

"Yes, it is," she said, laughing as she did.

"Are you actually Russian?"

We decided to meet after our events at the same spot where we first met, where I first saw her standing in the crowded lobby. I had a feeling that moment would be significant to me as my life moved forward. We planned to have a drink together and continue our conversation.

Chapter Fifteen

Beneath one hundred chandeliers, one thousand journalists gathered in formal wear on the Upper Eastside to celebrate the written word. The program for the evening was three hours long and included cocktails, dinner, eleven awards, and several musical interludes. My award was the final award of the evening, and, when the emcee finally beckoned me, I tried to make my way to the podium without revealing my nervousness. Accepting the award, a tall, bronze quill in an inkwell base, I was impressed by its heft and elegant design.

Don't drop it, I thought. *A loud thud is never a good beginning to an acceptance speech.*

Standing before the most proficient in my profession, I removed a single index card from my inner coat pocket and placed it on the podium. Like Lincoln at Gettysburg, I was much more concerned about the content of my speech than its length. In this ballroom, most appreciated a smooth sentence, a smartly coined phrase, and a well-constructed paragraph, so I knew my speech must be a sample of my best work. After all, the very award I was receiving that evening was for excellence with the written word, so there was no winging it. Quite unexpectedly, when I looked out into the glare of the bright lights that shielded the audience from my view, an assuring sensation quieted my kinetic nerves—a sense that this was my moment and nothing would go wrong. Until now, like many others, I'd never been comfortable with public speaking, yet, I wasn't nervous.

What a night! I told myself calmly. *I was just handed the Fenwick Prize for Journalism, and I think I've met the love of my life. I know I'll never forget a single detail about this night.*

I addressed the crowd.

"Anyone who has ever stared at a blank sheet of paper for an extended period of time understands the writing sentiment, 'I hate to write, but I love having written,' because writing is hard. A blank page can cause a writer to question his ability and self-worth, as well as his career choice and aspirations. It can mock him like a bully on a playground and belittle him in ways that tear his heart open. Depending on the moment and the writer's state of mind, a blank page can be either an opponent or a blank canvas. But, when words begin to fill the page and thoughts and ideas emerge, there is nothing more beautiful than the black-and-white simplicity of the printed page. While artists have a palette of colors, writers have only the twenty-six black letters of our alphabet and the unwavering belief that, if arranged perfectly, the resulting work will be as beautiful as any Renaissance masterpiece. In fact, words can move us as much as any work of art; words can evoke emotions, change minds, teach lessons, convey ideas, lift spirits, or simply make us smile. I am here to tell you that as a young boy when I read the great authors, the words sang and danced for me; the words caused me to dream; the words caused me to laugh and smile; the words gave me hope; the words brought me to tears. Young and unaware, I wondered how this was possible—how could words on a page in a book have such a profound effect on me? So many years later, I believe I finally know the answer to that question: Words are the foundation of our humanity. We exist in our words. We are the words that we choose. Words matter. It's as simple as that. Thank you for saying that my words have mattered and that my words have made a difference. I'm grateful for your acknowledgment."

Chapter Sixteen

Chelsea and I shared the miles and turns that brought us to each other in a quiet corner of the hotel lobby. For more than two hours, we expressed beliefs and confidences like we had known one another for our entire lifetimes, like our journeys forward would be combined and our futures interwoven. Though we had just met, we were instantly connected. We were soul mates. Between us, we had enough life experience to recognize that this was a once-in-a-lifetime occurrence. Unlike typical first meetings where the going forward was on a "to be determined basis," we understood that courtship and a deeper connection were inevitable. Our newfound relationship was not a casual one, and we intuitively knew that we'd be lovers and partners for the rest of our days.

In my suite at 2 a.m., Chelsea and I made love for the first time, and the act was physical confirmation of the spiritual and emotional connection we sensed when our eyes first met in the lobby. Wrapped in a passionate embrace, we writhed in ecstasy like angels had blessed our union and christened our new love. At one moment, our love-making was as delicate as a wispy cloud and later as energetic as a thunderstorm. Well past the age of backseat fumbling, I thought I understood the act of making love. Still, this encounter produced a union that exceeded anything I'd experienced before, one that far exceeded the introduction of a penis to a vagina. Unlike my previous lovers, a spiritual bond transcended our physical bodies, one that seemed to unite our souls. More intense than my physical pleasure, I felt overwhelmed by this newly discovered, nonphysical aspect of sexual intercourse. For the first time in my life, sex had more meaning and purpose than I ever realized; in the quiet afterglow, I experienced a deeper level of human connection than ever before. Both bare and depleted, I pulled our warm bodies together beneath the sheets.

"Wow," Chelsea said, stroking the side of my face as she did. "That was amazing."

"Wow is right," I returned, wondering if she experienced the same mystical union I did.

I had never believed in love at first sight or that there was one soul mate for every person, but I knew, with every fiber of my being, that this woman in my arms was the love of my life.

Chapter Seventeen

At his office, during a quiet moment, Tom noticed yesterday's mail resting untouched in the middle of his desk, and one letter, in particular, caught his eye. It was a square, white linen envelope, four inches by four inches, stamped with twice the required postage, addressed to Tom Corbett, not Desjardins, with no return address, and boldly marked "Personal and Confidential" in the bottom left corner. His curiosity aroused, Tom retrieved the letter from the scattered pile, examined its tightly printed markings, and finally pierced its top with an antique letter opener. Enclosed, Tom found a single piece of heavy stock paper that contained twenty-four words that would make all his other concerns of the day seem trivial.

"Your wife is having an affair with David Nathan," it read. "They meet every Thursday at 1 p.m. in room 715 at the Saint Marcus Hotel. Sorry."

Instantly, Tom was devastated. Nicole's pregnancy and Alex's arrest had previously unsettled his world and left him feeling shaky, but this news struck him even harder. Whatever remaining tidbits of security Tom had in his being were instantly obliterated by this betrayal, and he felt like he had been transported back in time—so insecure and unsure of everything in his life that he felt seven years old again.

Earlier in the marriage, Tom sometimes wondered if Shannon was too attractive and whether her allure might lead to affairs. Everywhere she went, Shannon attracted the attention of men. After twenty-five years and two children, he hoped they'd outlasted that threat, but in his heart, Tom also knew that their marriage started to dissipate as much as ten years ago. With each passing year, there was always a little less reason to look into one another's eyes, always less pulling them toward one another, and always less connecting them on their journey through life. In his heart, he knew their marriage was not likely to go the distance, but like so many parents, he also assumed it would outlast their children's childhood. When Nicole and Alex were firmly planted in their mid-twenties with solid foundations of their own, Tom and Shannon would, more than likely, end their marriage. But, despite this reality, the thought of Shannon cheating on him was still very painful. It still cut very deep.

Would Shannon cheat on me? Tom wondered. *Has she cheated on me in the past? Would she leave me?* he asked himself, taking his concern one step further. *I'll confront her tonight. I've got to know the truth.*

Tom lowered his head as his anguish rose.

I can't confront her, he quickly corrected himself. *If I confront her, she'll only deny it, and I won't know. I've got to know the truth. I've got to go to the Saint Marcus, wait in the lobby, and see for myself. It's the only way. I've got to wait until next Thursday.*

Seeking comfort and assurance, Tom looked toward a framed photograph of Shannon on his credenza taken at a New Year's Eve party about twenty Auld Lange Synes ago. Wearing a sequined, royal blue evening gown, she had been caught turning in mid-laugh, like something surprised her from behind, and it has always been his favorite picture of her. That photo captured a softness that Tom knew was inside her, a quality he saw more frequently in their early days, that Shannon seldom displayed anymore. He loved that photo because she was the woman he fell in love with so many years ago.

Interrupting his reminiscing, an appraiser opened the door and peeked his head into Tom's office.

"We've got a problem out here," he said.

"Just handle it," Tom snapped back, stunning the young man and causing him to backpedal out of the doorway. "Handle it, damn it," he yelled again, much louder this time.

The response was very un-Tom like.

* * *

In life, some moments defy preparation. Waiting for the day, Tom had no inclination about what he would say or do if his worst fears were confirmed, and Shannon had, indeed, forsaken their vows and taken up with a lover. He knew there wasn't any point in trying to prepare for such a moment, and all he could do was deal with his emotions as they occurred. More often than not, life must be lived in the moment.

On Thursday at noon, Tom was seated on a sofa in an area of the Saint Marcus Hotel lobby shielded by large, leafy plants while still offering a slightly obstructed view of the front desk. His second gin and tonic was on a coaster on the table before him, and he was nervously checking the time on his watch every three or four minutes. In his anxious, disheveled condition, Tom looked like someone about to commit adultery and not someone planning to catch adulterers in the act.

Don't let me down, Shannon, Tom wished in his mind; *please don't let me down.*

At 12:49 p.m., David Nathan entered the hotel lobby and strode purposefully toward the front desk, where the hotel manager handed him a passkey across the counter. The transaction seemed routine and prearranged, as David didn't register or even sign his name. A minute later, he stepped into the elevator, the doors closed, the light indicated his arrival at the seventh floor, and Tom was left to wonder if his wife was, indeed, the woman that he was meeting. In David Nathan, there was much for Tom to dislike as Shannon's paramour: He was only thirty-five years old, tall, blonde, and handsome, never married, father of two by different mothers, and heir to a cosmetics fortune.

In truth, David's presence crushed Tom's desperate hope that the handwritten note was merely a cruel hoax. With half of the duo present, that seemed less probable now. Also, Tom was aware of David's reputation as a ladies' man and knew he wasn't at the hotel for a business meeting. Previously, Tom had allowed himself the comfort of blind optimism, but even he realized that the truth was slowly finding the light.

"I'll have another," Tom barked at the cocktail waitress as she passed. In light of his predicament, numbing his mind with alcohol seemed both prudent and appropriate.

At 1:13 p.m., Shannon entered the lobby and proceeded directly to the elevators. Despite her brisk stride, she checked her makeup in a small compact mirror and didn't notice her husband watching from behind a fig plant. Once she boarded an elevator, Tom abandoned his cocktail, quickly crossed the lobby, pressed the up arrow, and boarded a second elevator bound for the same floor. He arrived at the seventh floor just in time to peer out the open doors and witness Shannon enter room 715, halfway down the corridor from the elevators on the left. Immediately, his eyes welled up, his heart broke, his stomach ached, and he was sure of only one thing: There was no way he could have prepared himself for this moment.

Ten steps away, a red velvet chair with gold trim and a small marble table served as a wait station beside the elevators. Tom walked to the chair, slowly sat down, and despondently placed his head in his hands.

It is true was his only thought and he repeated it a hundred times in his mind.

Time lost all meaning and measure, and Tom was still in that chair almost two hours later when Shannon departed the room. Outside the door, she froze when she recognized the figure near the elevator, but there was no other way down to the lobby, no way to avoid this reckoning. Gathering her thoughts, she slowly walked the corridor toward Tom. He was unaware of her approach.

"Tom," she said as she placed her right hand on his shoulder. "What are you doing here?"

Tom looked up but didn't speak. After several minutes of heartbreaking silence, he finally mumbled, "How could you?"

"I'm sorry. I never meant to hurt you."

Shannon got down on her knees before him, so they were closer to eye to eye. She placed her hands on his knees.

"Doesn't twenty-five years and two children mean anything?" he asked. When she didn't respond, he asked a more basic question, "Why?"

"I guess I needed more," she said like it was a suitable rationale for her behavior, an understandable excuse.

"More," he muttered to himself.

Though Tom's mind was hazy and confused, he believed he had found the single most important question.

"Do you love him?" he asked, unknowingly holding his breath once the words left his mouth.

"I don't know."

The door opened at room 715, and David stepped out into the hallway. As it closed behind him, he noticed the scene by the elevator and froze in place, the same way Shannon had. Staring at the floor, Tom was unaware of the presence of her lover fifty feet away. As dread scaled the back of her neck, Shannon waved her hand inconspicuously, signaling for him to return to the room, so David waved the passkey in front of the lock and quietly reentered their suite. Safely out of view, she breathed a silent sigh of relief, knowing that an already painful moment had almost gotten much worse.

Neither Tom nor Shannon spoke for almost five minutes as she searched her mind for words of consolation. It would've been good to lessen his anguish, but she realized no words would do that. Though this crisis was only fifteen minutes old, Shannon had already measured the damage, examined the consequences, and come to terms with it. In her world, there was always a calculation and a cost.

I didn't want this to happen, she thought, *but maybe it's for the best.*

"I don't want you to come home," Tom instructed her, having difficulty even looking at his wife. "I think you should check into a hotel somewhere or stay with him for all I care."

"I understand. I'll just go by and get some things. You're not going to do anything reckless, are you?"

"Oh, don't be absurd!"

"What will you tell Nicole and Alex?"

"I'll tell them that we need some time apart."

Tom stood, pressed the down arrow, and looked at his wife in a parting manner like he was boarding a plane and wouldn't see her for a long while. All at once, his look was studious and grievous, but most significantly, his look conveyed goodbye. Subconsciously, Tom had reached two conclusions that he was too shaken and dazed to even be aware of: Shannon didn't need him anymore, and he needed to focus on his children and himself. As soon as the doors opened, Tom boarded the elevator, pressed the lobby button, and didn't glance at Shannon again. She watched him as the doors closed.

Slowly, Shannon moved to the chair her husband had previously occupied and sat in much the same position, head in her hands, staring at the floor. Finishing her calculations, she remained in that position for fifteen minutes before returning to room 715.

"Are you okay, darling?" David asked when she entered the suite. Accustomed to encounters with angry husbands, David was hardly affected by the encounter.

"How did he find out?" Shannon asked. "I can't believe he followed us here."

"I don't know."

"I was so careful," Shannon said in a slightly uneven tone. "Were you careful, David?"

"I was. I promise."

"We should've switched hotels. We were too predictable."

"It'll be alright," David consoled her. "I'll tell the hotel manager that I need the suite indefinitely. I'll take care of everything. You can stay here as long as you need."

"I'm going to need some time. I've got to sort things out. I'll call you later," she told him, signaling that she wanted to be alone.

He leaned forward and kissed her, then departed.

Ten minutes later, her cell phone was in her hands, and she touched the screen to initiate a call to her office.

Chapter Eighteen

Outside a downtown nightclub just before midnight, Nicole waited beside an imposing bouncer nicknamed "Mountain" because the young man physically resembled one. He had a black metal flashlight in one hand that doubled as a Billy club and a silver energy drink can in his other, filled with Patron tequila, making it a tequila shot that would stagger most men. On the other side of the mountain, a line of about twenty club-goers, wearing mostly second-hand clothes that revealed fragments of colorful tattoos, stretched in the opposite direction up the alleyway. Nicole was wearing a simple yellow sweater and faded blue jeans, appearing subdued compared to the line where partying was the obvious objective. Eventually, Scratch, a lanky, unshaven Romeo with shoulder-length black hair from the suburbs north of the city, emerged through the doorway and embraced Nicole, but she moved quickly backward. Instead, she took him by the hand and led him thirty paces up the alley for privacy.

"Come inside," Scratch urged. "Blade and Ian saved a table for us."

"I'm not in the mood for a club," she told him, stroking his shoulder as she did. "Let's go someplace quiet."

"These will get you in the mood real fast," Scratch countered, removing a handful of little orange pills from his pocket.

"I am pregnant," she objected. "Did you forget?"

"Of course, I know you're pregnant—I was there when it happened, baby," he said with a sly, boyish grin.

"We've got to get our lives together, Scratch; the baby will be here in December."

"Don't be such a buzz-kill," he said, his patience tested. "I told you we'd have our own place in August. Blade says the record company is very close to offering us a deal. It could be as early as next month. He says they loved our demo tracks—called us a mix of U2 and Coldplay infused with a big dose of hip-hop. Just be patient, baby."

"It's only six months until parenthood."

"Don't you have faith in me, baby?"

"I do. I'm just concerned."

"Don't be," he said while he stroked her face. "I'm going to take good care of you and little Scratch."

With those words hanging in the air, Scratch paused, looked skyward, and seemed to have an epiphany of sorts, like he was receiving a communiqué from above. His mention of little Scratch started him thinking.

"We should name the baby Nick," Scratch continued. "After all, a nick is a little scratch."

"Oh dear God, I'm going," Nicole told him in an exasperated tone. "Are you coming with me or not?"

"I can't just bail on Blade and Ian. They are my bandmates. I'll see you soon."

Scratch fist-bumped Mountain as he passed, proceeded through the doorway back into the club, and an instant of loud music and flashing lights rushed into the alley. After watching him disappear into the club, Nicole stared at the large bouncer and the line of waiting club-goers, wondering if Scratch meant the things he said.

He is not going to be there for you, Nicole thought to herself, expressing the doubts she didn't want to acknowledge for the very first time. *Scratch will never be a good husband or father.*

After a minute of soul-searching, Nicole turned away from the club entrance and walked up the dirty, dimly lit alley, one that no young woman should walk alone at night, much less a pregnant one.

Chapter Nineteen

With the dawn of the new millennium, the coffee store emerged and established its place in everyday life. Once satisfied with home-brewed coffee from a tin can, coffee drinkers flocked to stores for gourmet, five-dollar cups of coffee. Gone were the days of pouring a black cup of Joe from the pot in the back of a convenience store; getting coffee required a barista, sophisticated equipment, special terminology, and basic Italian. Typical orders heard while waiting in line included "I'd like a triple, venti, soy, no foam latte" and "Give me a double, grande, half sweet, nonfat, caramel macchiato." At most urban intersections, coffee stores were a significant part of the cityscape, often occupying two or three corner locations. On the streets, the green Starbucks logo was as common as yellow cabs, and the only sight more prevalent on the busy sidewalks than coffee cups was the ever-present cell phone in the hands of passersby. It seemed we, as a people, had finally realized our Maker's intent—humans have two hands, one for coffee and one for a cell phone.

Four doors down from Desjardins House was a small coffee store named Interlude that had five small, two-seat tables and two areas with overstuffed sofas for those who preferred a communal experience with their aromatic cups. Paul and Tom usually ventured to Interlude around 3 p.m. to get a cup and savor the quiet break because the store was seldom busy at that time of day. On this occasion, Paul was occupied with several regular customers who dropped in to view new arrivals, so Tom walked up the street alone.

Seated in Interlude with his cup of Brazilian roast before him, Tom heard scenes from the last six weeks echo in his mind. He heard Nicole saying, "I'm pregnant;" he heard AJ saying, "Shannon gave me a check two weeks ago;" he heard Officer Hudson saying, "We have arrested your son;" and he heard Shannon saying, "I never meant to hurt you." The voices were as clear and distinct, and the pain was as real as the first time he heard the words. Feeling insecure and shattered, he wondered what his life would be like if this troubling streak continued for another six weeks, if he suffered more unsettling events. He knew he couldn't withstand it. The voices continued to echo over and over in his mind, and he felt as if his head would explode.

This has been the worst period of my adult life, Tom thought as he gazed out the window at the traffic.

Five feet from Tom, seated on two sofas near the window, were four Temple University students, two men and two women, who were discussing their economics assignment. Just two hours earlier, their professor tasked them with one question: As the latest generation in line to make their mark, what changes would you like to make to our nation? On the window ledge beside them were four backpacks, one with the Temple crest facing into the store, and on the tabletop in front of them were four coffee drinks topped with whipped cream. It seemed the coffee store infiltration of American culture had reached all the way to college campuses. The four students were talking loudly in voices more suited to a classroom than a coffee store like they'd already had several cups of coffee.

In the coffee store, soft background music played at a low setting of three on the volume dial, but it sounded abnormally loud to Tom, almost blasting. The echoing that continued in his mind—"I'm pregnant, a check two weeks ago, arrested your son, never meant to hurt you"—combined with the sound of the college students talking loudly near the window made Tom feel like he was being bombarded by noise.

I come here for a quiet, peaceful break each afternoon, he wondered to himself, *so why is it so noisy in here today?*

Tom and the college students were the only customers in the store. The store manager, a twenty-something technology geek in a red flannel shirt, was twiddling with his phone behind the counter.

"We should ban fossil fuel vehicles by the start of the next decade," one of the female students suggested as their debate raged on. "With alternative energy vehicles becoming more efficient and practical, we could lower greenhouse gases and impact the overall condition of the planet. As a nation, all we need is the resolve."

"That's a good idea, Monica," one of the male students said. "My idea is that all education should be free to anyone who wants it. Education is critical to the advancement of our people, so we should make sure that it's available to all. No one should ever pay a penny for their schooling regardless of how far they want to go—high school, college, graduate school, medical school, law school, whatever; it should all be free."

"Man, I sure wish that was true today," the other male student said. "I already have more debt than I wanted to accumulate in the full four years."

All his life, Tom had been a calm person and one who passed through this world in a measured and considerate manner. Usually, he was kind, humble, and reserved. But seated in the coffee store, listening to the students, Tom was not himself. His thoughts were frazzled; his emotions frayed. Rage was swelling within his troubled mind, and he knew he couldn't restrain himself much longer. Some kind of breakdown or blow-up was looming and both emotional states were foreign and frightening to him. In his forty-nine years, he had never felt this way—the turmoil of the last six weeks had greatly affected him.

These kids are both naive and obnoxious, he observed to himself. *Why don't they take their raucous discussion somewhere more appropriate? They are annoying the hell out of me!*

"Wouldn't the world be a better place if corporations were more altruistic and less profit minded?" one of the female students asked. "I saw a shoe company on the evening news the other night that donates a pair of shoes to the poor for every pair they sell. What if every corporation did something like that?"

"These are really good ideas," the other female said. "Can you hand me my backpack, Ethan? I need my notepad so I can start typing some notes."

"Speaking of the news," Ethan said as he reached for the backpack, "I saw a segment where a charity group was building tiny, ten thousand-dollar homes for the homeless. What do you think of that idea?"

"Sounds like a good idea to me. I hate to see the homeless beneath underpasses and alongside the road. It makes me sad!"

As Tom's unraveling continued, the echoing in his mind narrowed to just one chorus, "I never meant to hurt you," over and over, while the volume on the background music seemed to increase another four digits. Hearing Shannon's voice repeating that empty sentiment while simultaneously annoyed by the music and the college students, Tom couldn't restrain his anger any longer.

"Are you kidding me?" he cried out as he rose from his seat. "Are these the young minds that will shape the future of our country? Is this the kind of thinking we can look forward to in the coming years? I can't even begin to tell you how silly you sound, spouting your naive, utopian bullshit."

Tom took a step toward their sofas and looked down upon the young students as they cowered beneath him, each unsure what to make of the crazy old man towering over them.

"Have you ever even worked at a corporation?" he asked the young woman who talked about more altruistic corporations.

"Well, no," she said, scooting to the far end of the sofa.

"By definition," Tom returned, pointing his finger like a man with six weeks of angst inside him, "the very purpose of a corporation is to make profits for its shareholders. No one would invest their hard-earned money without the promise of large profits. In your ridiculous world, our capitalist system would grind to a halt. Your suggestion would mean the end of the entrepreneurial age, the end of life-saving drugs and devices, the end of world-altering technologies, and the end of our high standard of living. Our nation would enter a steep and perilous decline."

"I'm sorry," the young woman stammered.

"And you," Tom exclaimed, looking toward the young man who passionately advocated for free education. "Nothing is ever free. Someone has to pay for everything. If students don't pay for their educations, then the taxpayers will pay through higher taxes. It's as simple as that. To fund your free educations, politicians will raise our sales taxes, and the next time I come to Interlude for my afternoon cup of coffee, it will cost eleven dollars because the cost of free educations has been rolled into it. Nothing is ever free. Someone always has to pay for everything. Don't forget that."

"Geez, mister, lighten up!" the student said. "What happened to you that made you this cynical about life?"

"Nothing happened to me, kid. I live in the real world, not that fairy tale world that you and your fellow students live in. Wait until you join me in the real world; you'll feel exactly the same."

"God, I hope not."

"But, the truth is that your entire generation is just a coddled band of losers who, inevitably, move back into their parent's basement after their first encounter with real life. Your generation has no idea how to function without someone holding your hand and telling you everything will be okay."

"Well, at least we don't go around calling ourselves "The Greatest Generation.""

"Oh, no one will ever mistake you for that!" Tom insisted.

"Okay, okay," the student conceded, raising his hand to eye level, trying to request a cease-fire.

"In the meantime," Tom continued his rant, "let me suggest that each of you pour the contents of your coffee cups into the gutter out front of the store, return to your dormitories, and allow your minds a full twenty-four hours to refresh their cells. I can only hope that your foolhardiness is a byproduct of too much caffeine and not just plain stupidity. Once you have come down from your caffeine highs, maybe you will be able to come up with some practical ideas that have some small measure of value in the real world. Those ridiculous ideas that I overheard would surely get you kicked out of your university, so the truth is I've saved each of you from great humiliation today. Have a good day."

As Tom returned to his table, the four college students quickly gathered their backpacks and coffee drinks and made their way out the front door, just a few feet from the sofa. Through the front window, the group could be seen laughing as they turned toward Temple University.

"What the hell just happened?" one student remarked after he sipped from his cup.

"If that guy lives in the real world," a second student said, "then I live on Pluto."

Chapter Twenty

L ater that evening, in an efficiency apartment near Franklin
Plaza, the manager of Interlude, Steven Sweeney, a twenty-
four-year-old in a red flannel shirt and gray sweat pants, was
working on his laptop computer with two digital files on the screen
before him: security video from the coffee store and cell phone video
that he shot from behind the counter. Both files contained the activities in the coffee store between 3:10 p.m. and 3:18 p.m. that afternoon, the time period that included Tom's tirade involving the college
students. From behind the counter, Steven had found the whole incident hilarious and wanted to edit the two videos together so he could
post an amusing video of the incident on the internet. Aiding his
cause was the security system feature that zoomed in on customers'
faces as they moved about the store. The feature was designed to
facilitate the identification and capture of criminals, but Steven knew
that close-ups of Tom during his tirade would add to the entertain-
ment value of his video.

At 10 p.m., a pizza deliveryman who Steven knew well arrived at
his darkened apartment with a large pepperoni pizza in hand. As
Steven stumbled about in the darkness trying to locate his wallet, the

deliveryman wandered toward the light from the laptop and asked, "What are you working on this evening?" On previous deliveries, the two men had talked at length about Steven's constant and popular social media postings. Steven hit the play button on the screen as he walked past the laptop so the deliveryman could watch the three-minute video of Tom's tirade. By the time Steven counted out twenty-five dollars for payment and tip, the deliveryman was laughing hysterically at the video.

"That's off the hook!" the deliveryman said as he wiped a tear from his cheek.

"It happened in my store today."

"That's the funniest thing I've seen in a long while. It is hilarious! The dude is a total jackass!"

"Do you have time for a beer, Brandon?" Steven asked as he handed him the cash.

"Sure. You're my last delivery of the night."

Chapter Twenty-One

Tom was alone for almost an hour at breakfast the next morning with his newspaper. While unfortunate, his outburst at the coffee shop had the side benefit of releasing a lot of tension and frustration that had built up inside him. As a result, he had slept well and felt much better. His schedule for the day was light so he planned a short walk from Desjardins House to Independence Hall at lunch to distance his thoughts from his recent troubles. He recognized that the incident at Interlude was a sign that he needed to relax, take some time, and work through the events that caused him such upheaval in the first place.

Those poor college students, he thought, amused by his recollection, *they sure crossed my path at the wrong time.*

Around 8:30 a.m., Nicole finally arrived at the table with a very concerned expression on her face. Earlier that morning, she received several texts from friends who also forwarded a video she watched in her bedroom.

"Are you okay?" she asked when she first saw her father.

"I'm fine. I slept well last night. Why do you ask?"

When Nicole reached her father, she pressed play on her cell phone and handed it to him. For the next three minutes, Tom watched the video of himself berating the college students at Interlude the prior afternoon. As it progressed, his expression grew more and more tortured because his behavior was ruder and more condescending than he remembered. At that moment, that incident was two minutes and fifty-five seconds of his life that he regretted and wished he could get back. When the video ended, he placed the cell phone on the table, lowered his head, and covered his mouth in shame. He was silent for a full minute.

"Where did you get that video?" he finally asked Nicole.

"It's on the internet. Some friends forwarded it to me."

"That's not good!" Tom replied, his unsettled demeanor from yesterday returning just that quickly. "How do we take it down?"

"We can't. Once something is posted on the internet, it's out there forever. Unfortunately, you've just joined the millions of people who have stuff on the internet they'd like to take down—like the foolish young girls who sent topless pictures to their boyfriends before they broke up."

That unsolicited information caused Tom to pause.

"Have you sent Scratch any topless photos of you?" Tom asked, temporarily distracted from his predicament.

"No, I haven't," Nicole answered him, "but your fatherly concern during your own moment of crisis is very sweet."

Tom returned to the topic of the video.

"I was having a really bad day!" he said.

"Well, obviously," Nicole responded. "It doesn't seem like you at all. You seem a little possessed while you're talking."

"We can't take it down?"

"Don't worry about it. It only has thirty-five views. It will fade off into the obscurity of the Internet."

"Let's hope so, but I have a really bad feeling about this!"

Tom arrived at Desjardins an hour later and proceeded directly to his office. He knew he had a meeting in ten minutes with a large law firm that was a significant appraisal client, one that generated almost a million dollars of work annually, but he noticed three messages on his voice mail. He glanced at his watch and figured he had enough time to handle any important inquiries, so he pressed the flashing white button.

"Hey Tom, it's AJ. I just watched a video that was forwarded to me by Jack Carter. It's a video of you in Interlude railing at some college students. What's going on? Are you okay? Give me a call."

"This is Robert Samuelson of Reid & McClaren. We are running a little late and will be at your office around 10:30 a.m. I hope this doesn't create any problems for you. See you then."

"What an asshole!" the final voicemail began. "Are you out of your mind? Who beats up on college students? You're just a fucking bully! You've obviously got serious mental health issues. Get some help!"

Tom sighed. He looked around his office for comfort at several treasured antiques that always struck him as particularly beautiful. On his credenza, a French bust of Louis XIV carved in the year of his death, 1715, by a renowned artist of the era, softened Tom's furrowed brow. He sighed a second time. With some unanticipated free time on his hands, courtesy of the second voicemail, he decided to grab a cup of coffee. Rising from his desk, he opted to walk up the hallway to their company coffee machine rather than up the street to Interlude because he was unwilling to return to the site of his great humiliation. Truth be told, it might be a very long time before he returned to that coffee store.

Fortunately, Tom offered himself as consolation, *seven coffee stores are within a five-block radius of Desjardins.*

After the meeting with a trio of lawyers from Reid and McClaren, Tom set off from Desjardins for his much-anticipated walk to Independence Hall. His well-rested feeling from earlier in the day had been replaced by an anxious feeling about the internet video. When he arrived at the hall, he didn't notice the tourists milling about or the beautiful yellow flowers in bloom in the shadow of the brick tower that once housed the Liberty Bell. Surrounded by distractions that he had so desperately sought, Tom was lost in thought. Nothing was distracting him from his problems; nothing was unburdening his mind. Instead of distancing himself from his old problems, his walk seemed to draw him closer to his new one.

Socrates wrote, "An unexamined life is not worth living." Much like the ancient philosopher, Tom always needed to find rhyme and reason in his daily affairs, to live an examined life. Determined to examine his current situation, he located a quiet spot on a park bench beneath a sprawling oak tree where he could reflect on the last few days. In the shade of the tree, he examined his predicament, analyzed it from every angle, determined what the worst repercussions might be, and then decided that it wasn't nearly as bad as he was making it. Relieved, he set off to get some lunch.

Just as Nicole said this morning, Tom told himself as he walked, *this incident will fade away into the obscurity of the internet.*

At a café just up the street from the hall, Tom purchased a turkey and Swiss sandwich and then wandered back to the same bench as before, more determined than ever to enjoy his sandwich and the pleasant afternoon. Finally, Tom noticed the architecture of the stately Georgian building and the beautiful yellow flowers in front of it. While chewing, Tom thought he heard someone behind him utter the word "jerk," but when he turned around and saw only a crowd of tourists milling and taking photographs, he dismissed it.

Just shy of 3 p.m., Tom felt much better when he arrived at his desk until he noticed the voicemail count on his phone. Twenty-five voicemails were far more than he would've expected under normal circumstances so he was concerned that many of the voicemails related to the video. Slumped forward, staring at the flashing light, he dreaded the touch of his finger on the white button. In his mind, Tom knew he either had a lot of urgent work to accomplish, or he was about to be mercilessly harassed, and neither scenario made him want to hear his messages. Finally, with much trepidation, Tom pressed his finger against the white button.

"Hello Tom. This is Robert Samuelson. I just wanted to thank you for all your support today during our meeting. You guys are doing a great job for us."

"Man, you're something else. Are you really that little of a person that you have to make yourself bigger by belittling college students? What the hell is wrong with you?"

"I just watched your video on the internet. I thought it was hysterical! It's about time someone told those coddled, good-for-nothing college kids how the world really works. I'm a big fan. You should start posting weekly videos with your viewpoint."

"Hey fucker. I'm also a student at a local college, and I don't appreciate you trashing my fellow students. Knock it off, asshole."

Seventeen of the twenty-one remaining messages were related to the video and "agitated" best described their tone. As Tom listened to the callers assail his character, one after another, he got the sinking feeling that the impact of this incident was not ending but rather just beginning. With his head in his hands as the last message played, Tom's cell phone vibrated on the desk, indicating an incoming text, and he received all the confirmation he needed.

Hi Dad, the text from Nicole began, *the views of your video have now crossed 1,000. I'm getting a little concerned.*

Chapter Twenty-Two

The next morning, no one made it to the breakfast table before the residence erupted in shouting a little after 7 a.m. With her cell phone in her hand and an upset look on her face, Nicole rushed into her father's bedroom. She found Tom seated on the edge of the bed lacing his shoes.

"Oh my God," she shrieked at her father. "Your video has fifteen thousand views. This isn't good! It's going to go viral."

"Why would anyone watch that video?" Tom asked.

"You don't get it. You're becoming a joke. In the comments section of the posting, they're starting to refer to you as "The Dream Squasher." This is really bad. How could you do this?"

With his cell phone in his hand and a bothered look on his face, Alex stormed into the room, almost mimicking his sister's entrance from five minutes earlier. He pushed his way past her to a position in front of his father.

"What the hell is going on?" he blasted. "Over forty kids have texted me a video of you shouting at some college kids in a coffee store. I can't go to school today! What will I tell my friends?"

"I wish I could stay home today," Tom mumbled under his breath.

"You can stay home from school today," he told his son.

"I'll tell you one thing," Alex continued, still angry despite his excused absence from school, "by this time next week, my DUI is going to look like a parking ticket compared to this mess. How could you do this?"

After both children exited his room in a manner similar in tone to their heated entrances, Tom was left contemplating the most glaring and obvious observation from their encounter. His children had asked him the same question, both using the same five words, "How could you do this?" Alone, he realized he'd let his children down and disappointed them. Even worse, he'd embarrassed his son so much that he didn't want to go to school and face his friends. And, of all the things he valued in the world, Tom knew the love and respect of his children topped the list. Three months ago, he felt like a decent father; not perfect, no one was, but overall he thought he was doing a good job. Now, however, he had no idea how to reverse this humiliation and redeem himself in their eyes. What could he do?

On his way to the office, Tom wondered whether he was becoming paranoid or whether strangers on the sidewalk were actually glancing his way more often and staring a little longer. He felt their glances included recognition of his notoriety; they'd watched him on the internet and knew his shame. Often, he thought he noticed a slight upturn in the corner of their mouths, a tiny hint of amusement on their faces. Because of his moment in the coffee store, Tom wondered if he would ever walk anywhere again without leaving the stench of embarrassment in every footprint.

Four times that day, Tom received texts from Nicole that required no elaboration. The texts didn't contain words—only numbers—but Tom understood the digits. Stressed by what was happening online, Nicole followed the web page closely. She refreshed often, sometimes sighing as she did. Periodically, she advised her father of the view count for the video. Tom grew more stressed also as the numbers climbed.

17,513, Nicole texted at 9:21 a.m.
  19,555, she texted at 12:15 p.m.
  23,975, she texted at 4:21 p.m.
  29,110, she texted at 7:05 p.m.

Chapter Twenty-Three

The following afternoon, in room 715 at the Saint Marcus Hotel, Shannon and David Nathan had just finished two hours of sex acts that would make a seasoned prostitute blush. At this point in their exploits, the two lovers were well versed on one another's sexual penchants as well as the appropriate arousal and teasing techniques to heighten their sexual gratification. Finished her shower, Shannon toweled off in the center of the suite while David tied his necktie and prepared to resume his day. In the mirror, David admired her shimmying motion as she moved the towel back and forth across her back, causing her breasts to dance ever so sweetly.

"You are so beautiful," he told her, and she smiled.

"I'm going to have to purchase that writing desk from the hotel," Shannon remarked coyly, "as, in good conscience, I can't allow anyone to work at it knowing the things we've done on top of it."

"In that case," David responded with boyish glee, "we'll have to purchase all the furniture in the suite."

"I think this was our best session yet!"

"And unfortunately," David said, "our best and last session."

"What are you talking about?" Shannon followed up, a wisp of concern in her voice.

"Have you seen your husband's video? It's creating quite a sensation on the internet."

"Of course, I've seen it. It has been forwarded to me about one hundred times!"

"I can't be associated with it. My family's name has been highly respected in this city for seven generations. Our businesses and investments could be affected by it."

When she was introduced to David, one of her friends warned Shannon that he had a relationship rule that he never dated any one woman for more than fifty days. At the time, Shannon figured it was the type of slanderous talk started by jilted lovers that made its way around the rumor mill and became legend.

That's not true, she told herself at the time. *He seems like such a nice guy.*

Though she acknowledged that the video was embarrassing, she also consulted the calendar in her mind to determine whether or not it was just an excuse.

It has been about seven weeks, she thought, *which makes the tally just shy of fifty days. That son of a bitch!*

"Maybe we can resume in the future," David told her, "but we have to cool it for now."

"You are the louse everyone warned me about," she shouted back. "Just get the hell out of here, and don't come back!"

David exited the suite. No more than five minutes passed before Shannon was on her cell phone with Tom.

"I'm coming home today," she informed him. "I've ended my affair with David Nathan. I told him I can't do this any longer."

"Alright," Tom said, and they both simultaneously ended the call without saying any more.

Chapter Twenty-Four

Coincidentally, almost seven days to the minute after the incident happened, the video surpassed two hundred thousand views. More stressed and embarrassed with each tick of the view count, Tom hoped that interest in the video would wane soon, but truthfully, at this point, he wasn't even sure it had peaked yet. As a coping mechanism, Tom stopped listening to voicemails altogether, came and went using the garage entrance at his condo, and wore a red Phillies baseball cap and dark sunglasses as a disguise. Several times a day, he told himself that it couldn't get any worse, but it always did.

Leaving his downtown office with the red baseball cap and sunglasses in place, a television news crew ambushed Tom before he reached the sidewalk. Cynthia Meade, an attractive, blonde field reporter, waited on the front steps of Desjardins House with a microphone in her hand as her cameraman, a heavyset man with scraggly brown hair and an unkept beard, waited beside the news van at the curb. Not fooled by his disguise, both moved in Tom's direction as he exited the building.

"I'm a reporter from KPLD, and I'm doing a human interest

piece for the evening news about the video of you at the coffee store," Cynthia explained as if Tom didn't know why she was there.

"There is nothing interesting about it," Tom shot back in a snippy tone as he tried to pass right by her.

"I want to get your side of the story, Mr. Corbett. I've already talked with the four students."

"Please, just leave me alone."

"This is your chance to correct the public's image of you. I've talked with several of your friends and co-workers, and they all speak kindly of you, saying you must have been having a bad day or something to that effect. They say the video doesn't depict the Tom Corbett they know."

"You've talked to my friends and co-workers?"

"I did say I was a reporter, didn't I?"

Suddenly, Tom stopped in his tracks, realizing that this was indeed an opportunity for him. If he was going to be viewed and judged by thousands of strangers, which was exactly what was happening, then he wanted to provide input regarding the content and message. At present, all people knew about him was his worst moment; they had no idea who he was or what kind of man he was. Tom decided to use this interview to set the record straight and add balance to the situation.

He smiled. He nodded his head.

"Okay," Tom instructed her. "Get your cameraman."

After a minute of sound checks, both Cynthia and Tom were ready to go to work. A crowd had gathered on the sidewalk beside them to watch the interview.

"I am standing a block from Interlude with Tom Corbett, a local man with newfound fame courtesy of a video making the rounds of his recent encounter with four Temple students in the coffee store. Tom, what is your view of what happened that day?"

"What happened, Cynthia, was that I was disrespectful to those four students, and I want to use this opportunity to apologize for my behavior. I hope they will accept it."

"Were you having a bad day, Tom?"

"I was having a horrible day, actually, a horrible week, but I don't want to use that as an excuse for my actions. We all move about this city daily, and we encounter fellow Philadelphians everywhere we go —on the sidewalk, in coffee stores, restaurants, at the ballpark, or wherever. We all need to be courteous and good to one another. I wasn't that day, and I'm ashamed of my conduct."

"Well, you heard it here first, Philadelphia, the man that the internet has nicknamed The Dream Squasher isn't such a bad guy after all. This is Cynthia Meade reporting for KPLD News on the streets of downtown."

"Well done, Tom," she said as she removed her earpiece.

Until now, Tom had felt powerless in the situation. By doing the interview and telling his side of the story, he finally felt like he'd done something, like he'd struck back against the forces that were assaulting him. Maybe now he'd get some rest that night; maybe now things would be better in the morning. He strode away from the interview feeling like some of his confidence had been restored, though he was still relying on his red hat and sunglasses to travel home inconspicuously.

*   *   *

After the segment aired on KPLD News, views of the video skyrocketed, accelerating to a pace that far exceeded any of the previous days. The video started clicking off more than two hundred views per minute, more than ten thousand views per hour. As it turned out, Tom's apology for his bad behavior only made people want to see his bad behavior that much more. The truth was that people found consolation for their own bad behavior by watching other people during their worst behavior. Overnight, the view count for the video surpassed five hundred thousand as more and more people forwarded it to family, friends, and co-workers. By midnight, it was official—the video of Tom, now known as "The Dream Squasher," and the four students from Temple University had "gone viral." In the vernacular of the internet, a video went viral when people forwarded it to their friends who forwarded it to their friends and so on. The exponential effect of the forwarding to more and more people was known as "going viral." Viral videos were often viewed by millions of people in a short period of time, often just a matter of hours or days.

Worse still, on the following evening, the parent network in New York City picked up this human-interest story from their affiliate, KPLD in Philadelphia, and broadcasted it nationally. The video of Tom's most regrettable moment, previously viewed mostly in the Philadelphia area, became a national and even international phenomenon. Within three days of the segment airing on the national news program, the view count for the video surpassed five million. Within a week, the view count surpassed fifteen million. While the view count continued to skyrocket, Tom's life and emotional state spiraled downward.

Even worse still, Tom's family was collateral damage. Nicole, who didn't handle difficult times and stress well, wouldn't leave the condominium. Since the news segment aired, she had barely eaten, slept very little, and even stopped showering. With the covers pulled over her head and the television blaring, she spent most of her time in bed. During rare moments when she got out of bed, she wandered the condo like a zombie with only short bouts of awareness, which she usually used to yell at her father.

"Your big mouth created this mess," she shouted one evening. "What could make you believe that your big mouth could fix it?"

Alex skipped several school days but eventually returned to the classroom. He was the target of merciless ribbing and ridicule in the hallways between classes. He often heard, "Hey, it's Dream Squasher Junior" or "How's it feel to have a video star for a father?" shouted his way. Alex was stronger and more stress-tolerant than his sister so he was holding up much better, though his mental state could best be described as pissed off. He, too, had some choice comments for the source of his aggravation, his father.

"Thanks to your damn video, the kids at school make fun of me all day long," Alex blared. "Do you have any idea what assholes teenagers can be?"

The video was humiliating for Shannon personally, but what angered her most was its impact on her reputation and business. Her partner, Martin Hastings, often complained that half of his company's good name, Hastings Corbett, was being assailed on a daily basis. Hoping to minimize the damage, Shannon and Martin spent a large portion of their time on the phone with clients trying to assure them that there was no reason for concern. Many clients threatened to pull their accounts and a few actually did. Both partners knew there would be a very real cost for this public relations nightmare, and it could amount to hundreds of thousands of dollars.

"We'll see how this disaster plays out," Martin said in his office one afternoon, "but one thing is certain—your partnership distribution will pick up the cost, not mine."

Chapter Twenty-Five

Tom spent much of his time at Desjardins in his office with the door closed. The room had always been his sanctuary and refuge, but now it felt like his hideout. He could accomplish little in the way of productive work, as he couldn't even retrieve his messages from his phone. Mostly, he stared at the art and history surrounding him and tried to find comfort in the fact that there was still beauty in the world, no matter how harsh the world had become. On his desktop beside a letter opener was a hefty 1886 silver dollar that his grandfather gave him when he and his mother moved to Philadelphia after his father's death. The coin had always held special meaning for him and had always been a source of reassurance. Early in his life, while dislocated from his childhood home and intimidated by the big city, that shiny coin comforted him; he carried it in his pocket everywhere he went. Now, during his hard times, Tom gripped the coin in his hand as reminder that there was, indeed, goodness in people, even though he hadn't felt that goodness in recent days.

Early one evening, when most of the staff had gone home, Paul decided it was time to discuss the "embetement," a French word that basically meant problem. As he walked up the hallway toward Tom's office, he shook his head in a mournful manner, as he was very distressed about the situation. Paul couldn't bear the fact that his friend was being tormented. When he arrived, he took a seat on a red leather chair in front of Tom's desk, and his face revealed his deep sadness. Like many French men, Paul was not able to conceal his emotions. On the emotional scale, he was one notch away from tears.

"I know these have been hard days for you, my friend," Paul said as a prelude to their conversation.

"Hard days indeed," Tom echoed his sentiment.

Paul knew the significance of the silver dollar and noticed that Tom was holding it in his hand. His heart sank even lower.

"We've been friends and business partners for almost twenty years, and you know you're part of my family," Paul told him, his words spoken softly.

"It has been a great association and friendship."

"In all the years I've known you, I've never told you the real reason I left Paris and came to Philadelphia."

"I didn't know we had any secrets."

"We do."

With that said, Paul leaned forward in his chair to draw his audience in, like any great storyteller would at the start of a tale. He took a long, deep breath to bolster himself while sharing a story from a painful time in his life. It was a story that stung a little in the telling.

"When I was a young man of twenty-two and just starting to make my way in the business world, my father was arrested for collusion. His company made large payments to government officials to ensure that they would get the work when contracts were awarded. It was a horrible time in my life. Once held in high esteem, my family name became a scarlet letter on my chest. To this day, my soul has never been completely cleansed of that disgrace. I left Paris and came to Philadelphia to find a new path for my life, to find a new road to journey along. Needless to say, I met you, and the road we have journeyed together has been one of blessings and good cheer.

107

Without my father's scandal, none of this would have happened in my life."

"Why have you never told me about this?" Tom asked.

"I was too ashamed."

"I'm sorry you had to endure that at such a young age."

"Tom, you are about to have that kind of journey in your own life. You are going to have to put this embarrassment behind you and find a new road to travel along. I can only hope that your road will be as beautiful and productive as our shared road."

"Are you firing me?"

The thought clearly angered Tom.

"I have to let you go. Our business has always been reliant on relationships and trust. We can never allow anything to damage our business by corroding the trust of our clients."

"Et tu, Paul—the most unkindest cut of all," Tom recited, directing his words at his partner, mixing his tragic quotes.

"You own thirty-five percent of this business. I was hoping you would see that your departure is in your own best interests."

"This is all I have left," Tom declared, in a tone that clearly reflected the amount of damage that had been done to his life in recent weeks. "My family barely speaks to me anymore; they mostly shout disparaging remarks at me."

"You have to step away and find that new road. We'll see what happens a year or so from now. Maybe there will be a time when you can return. I honestly don't know."

Tom said nothing more. He looked around the office like he was confused, like he didn't know what to do next. He stared blankly.

"Come on," Paul said as he moved around the desk to help his long-time friend rise from the chair. "I'll drive you home."

All the while, the silver dollar was tightly clenched in Tom's right hand.

Chapter Twenty-Six

I t was mid-June in Philadelphia, a typically beautiful time of year with colorful flowers in bloom and temperatures not yet scorching, but Tom had spent the last three weeks sequestered in his residence. He wore t-shirts and pajama bottoms, played daily bouts of gin rummy with Marta, and walked nightly around midnight once the streets cleared. His razor had not met his skin since his last day at his office, and the result was a full beard that provided a natural mask for his embarrassed mug. His relationship with his family was still quite volatile, and even he participated in the daily disparagement, having retreated backward to the anger stage of the healing process when he grew weary of apologizing. Aside from Shannon's several sniping comments about his unshaven face and still being in pajama bottoms at 7 p.m., Tom and Shannon had said little to one another since she returned home. Theirs was truly a marriage in crisis. A few days earlier, on June 10th, the video of Tom and the Temple University students surpassed twenty-five million views, though the rate of increase had decreased significantly since it peaked after the national news program aired its segment. None of the Corbetts were aware of the recent milestone because they stopped following the view count weeks ago.

Everyday at 11:30 a.m., Tom relaxed on an Italian Renaissance settee in the living room and watched as the late morning sun created kaleidoscope rainbows in the liquor bottles on top of the bar. He first noticed this phenomenon on his first day home after his termination and has not missed the dancing colors in the bottles since. Only drunks and hobos drank before noon, so Tom maintained a daily ritual of watching the rainbows form while watching the minute hand on his watch creep toward noon. As soon as the minute hand arrived at the twelve, Tom poured a stiff drink, usually bourbon or gin, depending on the sun's position and the planet's tilt, and then he called Marta to the dining room table for their daily games of gin rummy.

"I'm feeling confident today," he informed Marta as she emerged from the kitchen with a deck of cards in her hand. "I need to win back some points from yesterday's trouncing."

"Why don't you take a walk this afternoon and enjoy some fresh air and sunshine?" Marta asked Tom daily.

"Soon, Marta," he always responded.

Tom spent much of his day in his study with his cherished items from his old office at Desjardins. The day after Tom's departure, Paul tasked his shipping personnel with packing and transporting the items to Tom's residence, not because Paul wanted the office cleared or needed the space, but because he knew the items would comfort Tom. Scattered throughout the room were three busts from the French and Roman Empires, two urns that once resided in a court-yard in Florence, Italy at the beginning of the twentieth century, and a weathervane handcrafted in Boston around the start of the American Revolution. Even Tom understood that he was lost in those days and appreciated the vestiges from his previous life that provided comfort.

According to her doctor, Nicole was fourteen weeks pregnant, just beginning to show, hopefully near the conclusion of what had been horrific morning sickness, and due around December 1st. With all this newfound time on his hands, Tom had spent some quality time with his soon-to-be son-in-law Scratch on afternoons when he dropped by to visit Nicole, but she was too sick for company. Tom listened to his endless blather about an imminent record contract as well as the band's newest music that would surely be their breakthrough effort. While he would never use the term "lost cause" when talking with Nicole, the term regularly popped into his mind whenever Scratch was around or mentioned in conversation.

Two weeks ago, during the final game of the season, Alex made his first appearance in a varsity baseball game and played three innings at third base. He had one at-bat and singled to left field; he had two ground balls hit in his direction that he fielded cleanly and threw the runners out. Because father and son hadn't talked in three weeks, Tom didn't know Alex might get some playing time and was not present at the game. Whether Alex wanted his father to attend or Tom would have attended had he known was unclear.

One afternoon, shortly after their gin rummy game had ended, Tom heard a knock on the front door. Peering through the peephole, he saw a deliveryman with an overnight envelope, so he opened the door and signed where requested. Immediately, he recognized the sender, L William Hathaway, the Pittsburgh lawyer for his Uncle Carl's estate, and he retreated to his study to review the contents. Sitting at his desk, slicing open the business letter, a momentary sense of position and purpose flashed across his mind, a stark and stinging reminder of his life before the incident. Tom knew he was a man who valued productivity and contribution, and he knew those qualities were missing from his life.

After many paragraphs of indecipherable formalities that had Tom remarking to himself about the ridiculously inefficient nature of the practice of law, he finally arrived at the purpose of the letter.

"I am writing to inform you that the process of settling your uncle's estate is almost complete, so we should schedule a time and place for the execution of all documents related to the transfer of the

Shelbyville real estate and other personal property. The meeting can take place in Philadelphia, Shelbyville, or Pittsburgh, at your choosing. Since your father, Samuel Corbett, passed away in 1968, the property title has listed Marie Margret Corbett, Carl David Corbett, and Thomas Alexander Corbett as owners, with rights of survivorship held by all. With two of the owners now deceased, you are the sole owner of the Shelbyville property. A condition of your uncle's will specifically requires that the transfer of keys, a box of personal property, and a handwritten letter from your uncle must happen in person between you and representatives of our law firm. Please contact us at your earliest convenience to arrange the meeting."

Immediately, Tom was taken aback by the fact that his uncle had left a box of personal property and a letter that he must receive in person and formerly accept. He hadn't seen or even talked with the man in forty-two years. Tom knew there were no brooches or precious heirlooms to pass down, no photo albums or scrapbooks of cherished family memories, and no porcelain china, silverware, or serving trays. For generations, the Corbett side of the family had been poor, even dirt poor—the kind of poor that barely meets its daily food and clothing needs, much less sets aside any savings for hard times. Their family farm went back six generations, and all six generations had struggled to keep it viable, never producing surpluses in any form, money, crops, or otherwise. It was just not enough land to make it a profitable farm.

I'm going to Shelbyville, Tom thought, a little tingly at the prospect of taking a road trip. He knew that getting out of the residence would do him good. *Paul told me I needed to find a new road in life—maybe that road is Interstate 76, the Pennsylvania Turnpike, which crosses the state near the southern border and takes me directly there.*

Chapter Twenty-Seven

I first met Tom Corbett on a sticky July afternoon in The Bashful Rooster around 3 p.m. when there were no other customers in the diner. Finished with my BLT and fries, I noticed Tom sitting alone in a booth near the tall glass case with fresh cakes and pies on display on the far side of the restaurant. I recognized him immediately from the internet video as The Dream Squasher, but I knew not to mention his notoriety as I strolled toward his booth. Better than most, I knew what it meant to run from yourself, and I figured that was the reason he'd come to our little town.

"I'm Nick Sterling," I said when I reached his table. "I am the owner of the local newspaper, *The Sentinel*."

Immediately, I wanted my words back. The last thing Tom wanted was another encounter with a person from a newspaper. His life had already been turned upside down by several segments of our modern media, and he wanted nothing more to do with any of it. He recoiled immediately, just as I'd expect someone in his position to do. I knew I had to put him at ease and make him believe I didn't recognize him.

"What brings you to our little slice of paradise, stranger? We don't see a lot of unfamiliar faces around here."

Bring it back a notch or two, I thought, *you're clearly overcompensating for your introduction.*

"Tom Corbett," he said, extending his hand. "I inherited my uncle's farm, and I came to Shelbyville to have a look at it."

"Carl Corbett?" I asked, making the obvious connection.

"Yes, he was my uncle."

"He was one ornery son of a bitch, you know."

"I would assume so. I haven't talked with him in many years. I know that his brother, my father, was an ornery son of a bitch."

"You're going to like it here, Tom."

"Oh, I'm not staying. I'm just here to see the farm."

"That's exactly what I thought when I came here almost four years ago, but Shelbyville is a difficult place to leave. It's a quaint and beautiful little farming community, almost poetic in its placement in the center of the state between the City of Brotherly Love and Steel City, the birthplace of our nation and a key location in our Industrial Revolution. Shelbyville is a place of balance and harmony."

"You're a writer, alright!"

"Yes, I am. And if you want to read more drivel like that, pick up a copy of my newly minted edition at the newsstand out front. I'd be lying if I told you it's a real page-turner, but you will keep a washed up wordsmith off the streets."

Tom didn't say much during our first encounter—I did most of the talking—but I knew I liked him right away. He was a kind and gentle person you felt you could trust after sharing a diner booth for just fifteen minutes. Sitting before me, he had a sad, tormented look in his eyes, like someone who'd endured a trying ordeal, a look I saw in the mirror every morning. I knew that if I'd met him a year ago, his eyes would've shined more brightly; he would've been more forthcoming and less reserved. I knew that because I changed a lot during my ordeal—I shut myself off from the world. Almost instantly, I realized Tom Corbett and I were kindred spirits, and we would play a key role in one another's life.

"Do you know your way to the farm?" I asked him.

"Not exactly."

"How about I ride along and show you where it is? I have nothing but free time and serendipitous wandering on my schedule this afternoon. I am a man without purpose or commitment, a totally free and adventurous spirit."

"You're doing that writer thing again."

"Sorry."

"Anyway, it'd be great if you rode along with me," Tom told me. "I have a meeting at the farm in twenty minutes with the estate lawyers to execute some paperwork. They tell me it will only take ten or fifteen minutes."

* * *

The house at the end of Misty Hollow Road was a simple two-story farmhouse with four bedrooms and a bathroom upstairs, and small rooms downstairs for the living room, dining room, kitchen, guest bathroom, and mudroom. When the home was built in 1891, space was a luxury that few could afford. On the exterior, the white paint was dirty and faded to off-white, and the extensive chipping and peeling seemed to hint that the condition of the interior wouldn't be much better. In front of the house, a shiny, black Cadillac was parked alongside the porch that stretched the length of the domicile, and the front door was wide open.

As Tom and I entered the house and were greeted by L. William Hathaway, our eyes were immediately drawn to the dining room table, about twenty feet from where we stood. On the small table, four stacks of papers were in front of a single chair and a metal box with a white envelope propped up against it. The box was the size of a small footlocker, and, judging from the faded black paint and manufacturing techniques, probably used in World War II to carry munitions into battle. It was scuffed and dented and showed its age, but a shiny, new lock dangled on the front of it. Looking at it, I couldn't decide if it was Pandora's box or one full of precious family items, and, from Tom's expression, he wasn't sure either. He looked anxious, though the fact that he was standing in his childhood home was probably part of that. Standing beside him, I sensed this was not a fully joyous homecoming. The letter, resting against the front of the metal box, was in a standard white business envelope with a square of melted red wax to ensure its unopened status, something Uncle Carl must have applied, not the law firm.

I stood in the corner near the entrance to the kitchen while the lawyer explained each document and pointed to the places where Tom must sign. The first three documents pertained to the real estate transfer and the filing requirements for the estate papers with the court. The final document was included so Tom could acknowledge his receipt of both the metal box and the letter as was specified in his uncle's will. For reasons unknown, Carl sure wanted to make sure the box and letter were given to Tom.

"No one but your Uncle Carl knows the contents of that box and letter," L. William informed Tom as he signed the document. "Your uncle specified that it was a handwritten letter when he turned it over to us, but he told us nothing about the subject matter of the letter. I hope it is a heartfelt note and a box of treasured items."

You obviously didn't know Carl Corbett very well, I thought to myself as Tom handed the pen back to the lawyer.

With the execution of documents complete, the lawyer handed Tom a key ring with thirteen keys on it, some antique, some modern, and told him that the keys covered everything from the front door to the machinery in the barn to the padlock on the box. He picked up his briefcase, shook our hands, and remarked to Tom, "I am very sorry for your loss, Mr. Corbett." Less than two minutes later, we watched as the black Cadillac left the property on the long, unpaved driveway that wound through an open field, kicking up a large wake of brown dust behind it.

For the next hour, Tom and I walked the rooms of the house first, and then the outbuildings and grounds of the property next. Everything we saw—from bedding to furniture to appliances to windows to flooring to machinery to tools—was old and dilapidated. Everything was in need of restoration, maintenance, or discarding. The house itself was old and rundown; the barn was ramshackle and might not withstand the next wind gust; the guesthouse was filthy because it was long ago converted into a garden and tool shed. Basically, the entire property was in a state of total neglect and disrepair.

"What are your plans, Tom?" I asked as we completed our walk and settled down on the front porch steps.

"Well, it's really a day to day thing for me, but I think I'll stay for the summer and see if I can improve the condition of the property."

"Have you ever done this kind of work before?" I followed up.

"Not at all," he said, "and that's why I want to do it. I think a new challenge will be good for me."

Tom saw a project in the Shelbyville property, or more correctly, he saw about one hundred projects. Since he left Desjardins, he'd felt adrift—rudderless—and the property represented a chance to direct his energies toward productive work again. He could remain safely out of the public eye, free from the scrutiny and ridicule commonplace in Philadelphia, while doing work that would help him feel better about himself. While refurbishing the property, Tom hoped to rebuild his life also.

"You could make real progress by simply getting rid of all the junk and trash," I observed. "That's surely the place to start."

"Yeah, you're right about that."

"It's going to take a lot of trips to the dump in your Jaguar," I remarked with a hint of amusement in my voice. "How about I drop by in my pickup truck around 2 p.m. each afternoon for the next couple of days, and I'll help you haul the stuff away."

"You would do that?" Tom asked in an astounded tone.

"You're not in the big city anymore. In Shelbyville, we help our neighbors when they need a hand."

"Well, thank you, Nick, but I will insist on buying dinner at The Bashful Rooster each night when we're done."

"That's a deal."

Later that evening at my apartment in town, I thought about the metal box and white envelope and wondered if Tom had opened them. Their contents were none of my business, but, as a journalist, I couldn't help but be curious—it was my nature and hard-wired into the circuitry of my brain. I knew I couldn't ask him about them; I'd have to wait until he brought them up again. Until then, I knew it would eat away at my psyche like a missed opportunity.

Over the next five days, while Tom and I disposed of his uncle's large piles of trash and junk, I noticed that Tom had moved the metal box and white envelope to a shelf in the mudroom. The items were tucked away in the back behind a pile of work gloves, but I couldn't help but notice them. The red wax on the envelope hadn't been intruded upon, so I assumed that was also the case with the contents of the box. Perplexed, I wondered what it was about his family's history that caused him such hesitation. After all, who puts off opening a surprise package? In my apartment each evening, I was one frustrated newspaperman.

Chapter Twenty-Eight

I'd witnessed transitions before, but never as quick, dramatic, and thorough as Tom's transition during his first week in Shelbyville. On the first afternoon, when we met in the diner, Tom was dressed in expensive clothing, wearing Italian shoes, and driving a light blue Jaguar. One week later, when I saw him on Main Street, Tom was dressed in Carhartt overalls, wearing Timberland work boots, and driving a used Ford pickup truck that he'd purchased in nearby State College. All traces of the urban dweller had been wiped away, and Tom looked like he'd been walking the streets of a small town all his life.

Chapter Twenty-Nine

The Bashful Rooster was the main gathering spot for the townsfolk of Shelbyville and the heart and soul of the town. The tight bonds and deep connections between this small community's neighbors were on display every day within the walls of the simple, forty-seat diner. Each day around noon, locals filed into the diner and took their usual seats at their usual tables to enjoy their lunch break and interact with their neighbors. Whether the conversation or the food was better depended on the day and menu item. On a beautiful mid-July afternoon, after a morning spent applying a coat of paint to the walls of two bedrooms at the farm, Tom and I sat at the counter as the diner was quickly filling up.

At 11:53 a.m., Chet Riley, a tall man with black-rimmed glasses who owned the local hardware store, entered the diner and proceeded to a table near the window. Owning the hardware store in a small farming community made Chet as well known and essential as the mayor or the police chief, his usual lunch companions. Sitting at the table, Chet heard a familiar voice call out from across the restaurant.

"Hey Chet," Martha Gladstone, the owner of a large apple

orchard near the edge of town and a direct descendent of the town's founder, inquired of the store owner as she frequently did. "How can a shovel cost thirty-nine dollars? I believe the gosh darn thing should be gold-plated for that much money."

"I tell you all the time," Chet said with annoyance in his voice, "things cost what they cost. I don't have any control over what it costs to manufacture a shovel. We buy stuff, attach a reasonable markup, and then sell the stuff to the good people of Shelbyville."

"That's the same damn answer you give me every time."

"So why do you keep asking?"

At 11:58 a.m., coincidentally, the mayor and the police chief entered the diner and joined Chet at their usual table by the window.

At 12:05 p.m., Robbie Reynolds, who won the state basketball championship for the town twenty-four years ago with a jump shot at the buzzer, entered the restaurant and proceeded to the other end of the counter, seven stools away from Tom and me. Before he sat, Davy Preston popped up from a booth and called out to him.

"Hey Train," his nickname during his high school days due to his size, speed, and initials, "I watched the tape of the game last night. What a great day that was for this town!"

Robbie only smiled and nodded as he sat down.

But Davy wasn't finished yet. Loudly and enthusiastically, as if the moment was happening all over again, Davy began reciting the announcer's call of the game at the point where fifteen seconds remained on the clock.

"The pass is inbounded to Davy Preston near the half-court line. He dribbles the ball toward the top of the key, allowing the clock to tick down to nine seconds, now eight, now seven. He looks to his right and passes the ball to Robbie Reynolds as he comes off a high pick set by Marvin Kennedy. Reynolds turns as he catches the pass, plants his feet, and rises for a fifteen-foot jump shot. The shot arches toward the basket—it swishes through the net as the buzzer sounds. Shelbyville has won the state title! The Falcons have done it!"

"Go Falcons," someone called out.

"Hey, everyone," Davy reminded the townsfolk, laughing as he did. "I threw that pass to Robbie. Let's not forget the pass. Without the pass, there is no game winning shot."

"Oh, sit down, Davy," the same voice called out from the back. "We know you made the pass. You remind us of that fact regularly."

At 12:15 p.m., Milt Wallace, a grumpy sixty-year-old with a white beard and uncombed hair who owned the liquor store, entered the diner, grabbed a napkin off one of the tables, and began vigorously wiping his shoulder.

"What's the problem, Milt?" Chet asked his friend from two tables away.

"That goddamn bird!" Milt said, his face turning bright red as he spoke. "I know it's the same bird that crapped on me two times last week."

"They are creatures of habit," Chet responded. "You walk the same route at the same time each day, and that bird flies over and craps on you. Take a different route or leave a little earlier. That will solve the problem."

"I'm not changing my routine to accommodate a goddamn bird. I am the superior creature; I am much further up the food chain than that little winged bastard. Let him change his damn routine!"

"Milt," Chet said with a big smile on his face, "if the bird is crapping on you every day, I'd have to say that makes him the superior creature."

With that observation, the entire diner broke out in boisterous laughter.

At 12:55 p.m., while exiting, the mayor paused momentarily at the door and called out to his fellow townsfolk.

"I want to take this opportunity to thank Nick Sterling," the mayor announced like he was standing on a soapbox in a town square, "for that excellent article in this week's newspaper about the founding of our town by Digby Morton in 1853. Great job, Nick, *The Sentinel* is a wonderful asset for our community."

"Thank you, Mayor," I called to him as I rose to my feet at the counter. "And I want to warn everyone that copies are selling out quickly so make sure you get your copy early."

"I see old copies in the bin every other Wednesday before the new edition comes out," Martha said to me, puzzled.

"Help me out, Martha," I replied, urging her silence by placing my index finger in front of my mouth, the librarian's salute, "I am trying to sell newspapers."

Once again, laughter filled the diner.

"Our mayor is quite the politician," I remarked to Tom quietly as I retook my seat at the counter.

Chapter Thirty

Early one evening, I diverted from an errand to check on Tom's progress on his many projects. A few days earlier, I saw him in town at the hardware store, and I watched him load a rented sanding machine into the back of the old pickup, one generally used to refinish flooring. On my visit to the farm, I hoped to see beautifully restored pine floors. As I drove up to the farmhouse, I noticed Tom standing in the middle of an overgrown field amongst tall grasses and weeds. About one hundred yards from the house, knee-high in unkempt vegetation, he was staring in the direction of a stunning orange sunset and didn't see or hear me approach him from behind.

"What are you doing out here—surveying your land?" I asked in a lighthearted tone.

"My father died on this spot," Tom answered with reflection in his voice, instantly taking the mood of our interaction one hundred eighty degrees in the opposite direction.

He looked down at the earth beneath his feet, kicked the dry dirt, and caused dust to rise. In his eyes, there was a faraway look, one relating to time, not distance. His mind was revisiting 1968, a time as different from this time as the paved roads that led to his house.

"I'm sorry," I said, not knowing what else to say.

"My father had purchased a used tractor from a large farm in another county. It arrived that day."

He paused as if he was remembering the details as he spoke.

"Before dinner, he started drinking as he always did, but he drank a lot more than usual that night. I guess he was celebrating or something. He was nowhere to be found when my mother and I woke up the next morning, so we went outside to look for him. I remember walking into this field, feeling the mist on my face, and seeing the fog settled on the ground. We could only see about fifteen feet in front of us. It took us a couple of minutes to even spot the tractor."

Once again, Tom paused. I resisted my urge to ask any questions and remained silent so he would continue with his recollection. He had a pained expression on his face, almost as if he was locating his father's body all over again.

"He was lying on this spot," Tom confided. "He had fallen off the tractor, which was only about a dozen paces ahead of his body, and been crushed by the large back wheel. We figured he'd gone out for a late night, drunken joyride on his new tractor and killed himself. As soon as my mother saw the mangled body, she rushed me away from the ghastly scene. Fortunately, I don't think I got much of a look at him. I only remember seeing his body in a heap on the ground."

"You were seven at the time?"

"Yeah, we left for Philadelphia just a few days later, and I had never been back until I inherited the farm."

Chapter Thirty-One

While emptying the attic of boxes of old clothing that moths and time had rendered unsalvageable, Tom stumbled upon wooden easels, canvases, paintbrushes, and small baby food jars of hard, caked paint. Concealed from view, the art stash was hidden behind several large boxes in a corner of the attic. His mother, Marie Corbett, was a well-known artist in Philadelphia with works on display in many of the East Coast's finest galleries, including The AJ Gaines Gallery, which was how Tom and AJ met. Raised by a college professor and an elementary school teacher, Marie started painting at seven years old and put brush to canvas all her life, except for five years in her mid-twenties while she lived in Shelbyville.

Sitting in the dusty attic, leaning against a support beam, Tom recalled a conversation with his mother on a weekend home from college almost thirty years ago. He was in his early twenties at the time, a young man in his mother's eyes, and she spoke the harshest words he had ever heard her speak. The subject matter and memory clearly angered Marie, and her facial expression and tone were consistent with the victim of an injustice, someone with deep-seated pain that was otherwise uncharacteristic of her. Tom remembered the conversation well because he'd never seen his mother that way. In the sunroom of their home in Philadelphia, where his mother had an art studio, she told Tom why she didn't paint while they lived in Shelbyville. For Tom, it also explained why she seldom spoke of his father or Shelbyville.

As part of that conversation, Marie told Tom that his father, Sam Corbett, objected to her painting and often told her that art supplies were a luxury their family couldn't afford. Sam constantly complained about the cost of brushes and canvases and even converted their costs into seed and fuel and asked, "Which is more important, Marie?" When Marie suggested that she get the money from her parents, Sam's disposition instantly went from mad to incensed. He told her that no wife of his would ask her parents for money for anything, especially a foolish hobby. True to his backward upbringing, Sam shouted words he often shouted, "Marie, you'd better learn your place."

Growing more emotional with each word, Marie also told her son that she normally cowered and backed away from Sam because he had a fierce temper, but she was absolutely unwilling to give up her beloved painting. On that day, in her studio in Shelbyville, quite uncharacteristically, she stood her ground and defended her need to express herself in paint, something she viewed as fundamental to her well-being as the air she breathed. In firm rebuttal, Marie told Sam she would rather die than stop painting. Mustering her strength, she insisted she would never give it up. Livid, Sam stormed out of her studio and slammed the door behind him, something he frequently did.

When Marie returned from the grocery store the next afternoon, her art studio, previously located in a room in the guesthouse, had been completely emptied. Her baby food jars full of paint were gone; her collection of brushes was gone; her finished and unfinished canvases were gone; the two wooden easels that her father had given her as a gift were gone; even her rags and cleaning supplies were gone. When Sam saw his wife standing in the guesthouse door, he walked from the field to the door where she stood with tears streaming down her face.

Marie said Sam flatly informed her that he threw everything out and then turned and walked back towards the field. He never even blinked.

"Sam and I never spoke of my painting again," Marie told her son, tears streaming down her face, just as they had on that miserable day in Shelbyville.

He put the paintings in the attic and never told her, Tom thought to himself. *He was a cruel man.*

Tom sighed deeply. He was troubled by the recollection.

* * *

With the attic project complete, Tom settled down on an old rocking chair on the front porch with a cold beer and his cell phone in his hands. He touched the screen to dial AJ. In front of him, only a sliver of the orange sun remained above the horizon.

"I was in the attic today and found thirteen canvases tucked away in a dark corner. Four are blank, but nine are oil paintings by my mother of landscapes around the farm."

"That's incredible!" AJ said. "What's the condition?"

"Surprisingly good."

"Oh dear God, I just want to jump in my car and come see them. I know they're early works and might not even be salable, but I still want to see them."

"They're early, alright, probably around 1962 or 1963. They're not the quality of the her work later in life, but I'm just thrilled to rescue them. I'm going to hang them in every room of this house."

"I miss her," AJ remarked. "Has it been a decade yet?"

"Almost, she died eight years ago. I know I look a lot like my father," Tom said, seated on the porch of the only home his parents ever shared, "but my heart and everything else came from my mother. She made me the man I am. She was special."

Chapter Thirty-Two

On a Tuesday in mid-August, Tom took his seat beside me at the counter in The Rooster. In a little more than a month, Tom had suitably integrated into the slow and steady rhythms of the town, and he was known and well-liked by many of the townsfolk. As it was Tuesday, I faced my usual 6 p.m. deadline to turn the next issue over to the printer, but I was actually ahead of schedule for the first time in a long while. After lunch, I'd make some final tweaks to the copy and then casually stroll up Main Street to the print shop with the file on a flash drive. Strangely enough, I'd been so busy helping Tom at the farm that I didn't have as much time for my usual routine, my usual bad habits. I still drank more than I should and still dabbled in my pharmaceutical adventures but not as zealously. I guess it's true what they say—idle hands are the devil's workshop.

"I've got a proposition for you," Tom told me while Connie placed his usual iced tea in front of him.

"Are you talking to Nick or me, honey?" the comely waitress asked, "because it has been a long while since I've heard a good proposition."

"Are you any good at sanding and painting?"

"I sure hope that is slang for something other than hard work," she said as she grabbed plates from the window and set off for a table.

"I'm going to start painting the exterior of the house next week," Tom continued, directed at me, "so I can finish before summer is gone."

"That's going to be a lot of hard work," I observed, "scraping all that peeling paint from the sides of the house."

"I know," he said, wincing at the acknowledgment. "Do you have any interest in helping me with the project? I would pay you the same amount that I'd pay a painter."

"Well, I sure could use the extra money. Believe it or not, *The Sentinel* doesn't provide me with as many extravagances as you might think."

"I'll hire a painter to help me if you're not interested. I just think it would be more enjoyable working with you."

"Let's do it, Tom. You know, I think a fresh coat of paint will make a huge difference. That house could look very nice by the time we're done."

"My thinking exactly."

"Are we going to paint it white?"

"Of course!"

Chapter Thirty-Three

For the first three days of the project, Tom and I scraped paint chips off exterior walls until our wrists felt limp and mushy. With temperatures in the eighties and a scorching sun beating down upon us, we worked long days into early evening, breaking often for cold water to keep hydrated, and then, at day's end, we relaxed with cold beers on the porch as the sapped sun fell from the sky. On the third day, each of us atop two twenty-foot ladders on the south side of the house, Tom, with sweat streaming down his sunburnt face, called out to me.

"I'm going to double the amount we agreed to, Nick. This work is much harder than I thought, and it's going to take much longer than I thought."

Going in and out the back door frequently for water and restroom breaks, I walked through the mudroom, and I couldn't stop my eyes from locking on the metal box and white envelope on the shelf beside the new washing machine—two nondescript items on crowded shelves that stood out, in my mind at least, like a hooker in a room full of nuns. Each time I passed, I didn't know how much longer I could keep myself from asking Tom about them. Even worse, I worried I might snap one afternoon and, without his consent or knowledge, break their seals to view the contents, an action that would be a huge betrayal of our new friendship.

One evening at sunset, my newspaperman's curiosity finally overwhelmed my restraint, and I asked Tom the question that had been burning in my mind since the first day we met.

"Are you ever going to open the metal box and white envelope that your uncle left for you?"

"I will," Tom said coolly, "when the time is right."

"What is holding you back?"

"I feel like I have unfinished business here, like I came back to Shelbyville for a bigger reason than the farm. My mom and I left this town to go live with my aunt in Philadelphia just four days after my father died, almost as if we were fleeing. When you leave someplace in that manner, you risk leaving a part of you behind. The next time I leave Shelbyville, I want to leave on my own terms, healthy and whole.

"Are you afraid to open the box? It might be some family photographs or a stamp collection."

"A little," Tom replied after a long swig of beer. "I don't trust that side of the family, and I don't want to be run out of here until I'm ready to leave. Like you told me the first day we met, my uncle wasn't a nice man."

"You know, Tom, the first time I met Carl Corbett, he told me *The Sentinel* was a waste of paper and ink, and I should find a more productive purpose for my life. Your uncle was just plain mean."

Chapter Thirty-Four

W hen Tom typed my name, Nick Sterling, into Google, the first three items returned by the search engine were: "Writer and Columnist at The Philadelphia Post, 1993-2007," "Nick Sterling Wins Prestigious Fenwick Prize for Journalism," and "Excerpt from 'The Stride,' Nick Sterling's award winning five-part series about a vet returning from Iraq with a long journey still ahead." Curious, he selected the final item.

The Stride
By Nick Sterling, Columnist

While her husband, Mark, served two tours of duty in Iraq, Tracy Miller held down the home front, working days at her tech job near Arlington, Virginia, while also taking care of the couple's two young children, both under the age of seven. Alone in their bed each night, she counted the days until he'd complete his military commitment and return to civilian life. Lying there, Tracy worried about him. She couldn't wait to hold him again. According to Tracy, Mark returned from Iraq and crossed the threshold of their home on Belmont Street on January 29, 2004, but it was a full eight months more before he actually came home. Mark struggled with his difficult readjustment to civilian life for all that time.

"I could see it in his eyes," Tracy recalled, "the very moment he returned, he just wasn't there. Mark hadn't come home yet. His eyes were empty—no longer the bright, beautiful eyes that left two years earlier to serve his country."

It was difficult for Tracy and her children to see her husband and their father struggling with daily life as he suffered from frequent bouts of depression and anxiety. Though Mark tried to hide it from his family, he exuded sadness and unease. Often, he snapped at his wife and kids, something he never did before his time in Iraq. Mark tried to contribute by driving the kids to and from school and making an occasional dinner, but he couldn't get Iraq out of his mind. The battlefield haunted him in ways he never anticipated. Every day in Iraq, he told himself he just needed to survive another day and make it home to his family. Everything would be better then. But it wasn't.

War is soul-altering. It requires soldiers to face off against one another on a battlefield in a life or death struggle. It is kill or be killed in the name of national interests far exceeding most soldiers' comprehension. No amount of training can prepare them for the battlefield, or the sights and sounds they will witness—painful injuries, bloody wounds, horrific disfigurements, and tragic deaths—that hold a mind hostage long after the smoke clears. Few return from the battlefield without bringing the battlefield home with them.

The most difficult memory for Mark to put behind him was the death of his best friend while on patrol in Baghdad. They were standing only four feet apart when a sniper's bullet struck him. His friend was standing beside him one moment, dead on the ground the next. It was that quick, and his only memory of the incident was the sound of the bullet whistling through the air. During his first six months back in the States, Mark often heard that bullet whistling by him in a taunting manner.

"On the night of our first date," Tracy told me in a sweet, nostalgic tone, "I watched from my bedroom window as Mark walked the sidewalk to our front door. At six foot three, Mark's walk was brisk and purposeful, with long strides that covered ground at an impressive rate. He strode toward my front door with such confidence and purpose that I thought to myself, 'that man is going places.'"

In the months that followed Mark's return from Iraq, her husband's stride became a source of comfort for Tracy. Though times were hard and confusing, she'd watch him walk up their front walkway or stride across the parking lot at the grocery store, and she'd tell herself, "He's still in there. I just need to give him time. Mark has always walked with such direction and purpose that he'll find his way back."

The thing about a stride is that it's such a simple thing, the act of placing one foot in front of the other while moving forward. It doesn't involve any looking back or doubtful hesitation, to stride is to move forward, one step at a time. It might just be the secret to life that so many have searched for unsuccessfully. It was indeed the answer to Mark's problems.

Mark went to the VA for individual and group counseling and began coaching his son's little league baseball team. He just put one foot in front of the other and moved forward. He went to an employment center for resume and job placement assistance until he found a good job. He just put one foot in front of the other and moved forward. He began going to church with his family every Sunday morning, and together they established pizza night every Thursday. He put one foot in front of the other and moved forward.

The amazing thing about the stride is that after you put one foot in front of the other over and over, it's often quite surprising how far you've gone and how much progress you've made. If you have any doubts, just ask Mark and Tracy Miller.

Chapter Thirty-Five

In need of a break after a morning of white-knuckle scraping, Tom and I drove away from the farmhouse, now reduced to mostly bare wood—and sweat and blood—and set off to The Rooster for lunch. Both extremely hungry, we made quick work of the scenic, five-mile cruise along Stony Creek Road, past open fields and apple orchards, until we arrived in town about ten minutes later.

"I might have to ask Connie to spoon-feed me today," Tom said. "I'm not sure my hands can manage a knife and fork."

As we entered the diner, we were greeted by a commotion as Martha Gladstone was quibbling with Connie over the price of a slice of pie. At her table near the door, Martha looked upward at her waitress with a scowl on her face.

"How can a slice of pie cost four dollars?" Martha asked. "I should get the whole damn pie for that much money."

"I don't set the prices," Connie replied. "I take the food orders and deliver the plates."

"I'm not going to pay four dollars for a slice of berry pie."

"If I slice an extra-large piece, will that make you happy?"

"I just told you I'm not going to pay four dollars for a slice of pie. Weren't you listening to me?"

"Have it your way," Connie said and then placed her check on the corner of the table.

Tom and I made our way to our usual seats at the counter.

"Did you notice the special today is chicken pot pie?" I remarked as we sat on our stools. "They make good chicken pot pies."

"What is the word of the day?" Tom asked.

Years ago, I signed up on a website to receive the "Word of the Day" in my email each morning. As a writer, I already had a prodigious vocabulary and seldom discovered a new word, but I looked forward to its arrival each morning and thought about the word during the course of the day. As part of this ritual, I focused on the simple beauty of the words and their obscure or lesser-known meanings, and I tried to develop a greater appreciation for them. Lately, Tom seemed to derive some kind of vicarious pleasure from my daily words.

"Wherewithal," I answered.

"That is a really good word," he observed smugly, "a word with real gravitas."

His observation complete, Tom grinned like the Cheshire Cat because he was proud of his obvious reference to the word of the day from three days earlier: gravitas—a noun meaning seriousness or solemnity.

"It's good to know you're paying attention," I said.

"You are a noteworthy individual."

"The means for the purpose or need," I continued, quoting the definition I'd read earlier that morning. "It's a word that brings to mind an all-important question in life: Do I have the wherewithal?"

"That seems like a question we should ask ourselves more than we do, one that will bring about some serious soul-searching."

"Exactly," I declared. "It should be a mantra."

At 11:59 a.m., Robbie Reynolds entered the diner and strolled toward the counter, but he was thwarted and kept from his usual stool when a hand from within a booth grabbed his right elbow. In the booth were the Baxter brothers, Alan and Brian, owners of The Baxter Hotel.

"Hey Robbie, Brian told me the umbrella insurance policy we bought last month only applies if it's raining while the loss occurs. That's not true, is it?"

"Well, of course not, Alan," Robbie replied, holding back his laughter as he readied his explanation. "The weather has nothing to do with your insurance policy or coverage. Brian is just pulling your leg!"

"So, just to clarify, if our hotel burns to the ground on a perfectly sunny day, we are covered, right?"

"That's correct!"

"You're so gullible!" the other man remarked as Robbie continued toward the counter.

When Robbie reached his usual stool at the counter, I asked him a question that only he and I understood.

"Have you seen the northern lights yet, Robbie?"

"Not yet," he said, "but someday."

"We're not getting any younger, you know," I advised him.

"Yeah, I know."

At 12:15 p.m., Milt Wallace entered the diner, grabbed a napkin off a nearby four-top, and began vigorously wiping off his shoulder.

"Oh no, not again," Chet said.

"That goddamn little bird," Milt shouted, his face turning red as he did. "I swear to God he is waiting for me above the bank when I leave my store every day for lunch."

"Well, Milt," Chet counseled his friend as a follow-up on this long-running saga with the bird, "I guess that inferior creature is fully determined to show you that he's not so inferior."

"I'm going to get a damn shotgun and kill that little winged bastard," Milt said as his face reached a deep shade of crimson.

"Hey Milt," the police chief called from his table, "I don't want to hear that kind of talk. You can't discharge a shotgun in town. It's against the law."

"Maybe you can challenge the little bird to a duel and have him meet you outside town limits?" Chet suggested.

With that suggestion, the diner erupted with laughter.

Chapter Thirty-Six

By the seventh day of our painting project, we'd finished the paint removal and preparatory taping of doors and windows and were finally ready to start spraying paint on the house. Seated on the front porch in the cool of the morning, enjoying a cup of coffee before getting at our task, Tom and me spotted a black Porsche about three hundred yards down the road approaching the house at a very fast clip. With a big smile on his face, Tom informed me that I was about to make the acquaintance of someone I'd never forget. Less than a minute from our first spotting the car, it came to a screeching halt in front of the porch, and a large man emerged from the sports car dressed in peach and blue.

"Thomas, my friend," the man called out in a booming voice that woke any neighbors who'd slept through the roosters.

"What a great surprise," Tom answered back. "It's so good to see you, AJ."

When he reached the porch, AJ grabbed Tom and hugged him so vigorously that he lifted his feet off the ground.

"This is my friend, Nick. He owns the local paper."

"How about a handshake?" I suggested as I extended my hand. "I prefer introductions that don't involve broken ribs."

"Any friend of Tom's is a friend of mine," AJ said as he shook my hand. He said it like he really meant it.

"What brings you to Shelbyville?" Tom asked though he knew why his friend was standing on his front porch.

"Don't play coy with me," AJ responded. "You know damn well that I drove all this distance to see Marie's paintings."

"The paintings are hung throughout the house."

With that information, AJ practically pushed Tom and I off the porch and made a beeline for the living room. Inside, we found him standing in front of a canvas depicting the property's barn on what appeared to be a beautiful spring afternoon. The entire scene was in place, but small details were missing, as Marie didn't finish it. However, its unfinished state did not detract from AJ's interest.

"Those were better days for that barn," Tom remarked as we joined AJ. "It's pretty ramshackle now."

"This work is less mature than her later works but still as beautiful," AJ said.

Standing before an early work by one of his favorite clients, AJ told me how he met Marie and became her agent. Tom had heard the story many times.

* * *

In the fall of 1983, just months after AJ opened his first gallery, the most frequent visitor was a forty-four-year-old woman who came in around noon and wandered the gallery admiring the art on its walls. Almost as if she was committing each work to memory, she spent long periods in front of each painting. Gradually, AJ learned the woman was Marie Corbett, and she was employed as a paralegal at a prestigious law firm a few doors down from the gallery. Allied by their love and appreciation of art, AJ and Marie became friends and, one afternoon, while standing before an oil painting by an artist named Sylvester, Marie confided in the young gallery owner.

"By now, I'm sure you've figured out that I can't afford any of the paintings in your gallery."

"And even so, Marie, you're still my favorite customer," AJ told her as he reached for her hand. "I so enjoy your company when you come by."

On occasion, AJ and Marie enjoyed lunch together at one of the local eateries, and eventually, Marie invited AJ to their home for dinner, and that was when Tom and AJ met. In the sunroom of their modest suburban home, which spanned the length of the back of their house, Marie had a comfortable, well-lit studio where she loved to read and paint, most often on Sunday afternoons. As soon as AJ viewed her work, he asked Marie if she'd allow him to sell some of her landscapes in his gallery. He told her that her talent was surely part of the reason that they met.

"Your paintings are beautiful," AJ gushed, as astonished as when he first saw the work of Sylvester, his most successful client. "Your delicate treatment of light and shade is simply remarkable."

Though flattered by the request, Marie politely rebuffed him, saying she'd never compromise their friendship by allowing him to represent her. And anyway, she could never imagine her paintings on a wall beside the brilliant works of Sylvester. In her mind, he was a modern-day artist with talent comparable to the greats like Rembrandt, Whistler, or Waterhouse. For the next six months, on a very regular basis, AJ pleaded with Marie to allow him to display just three works in his gallery.

Finally, one Saturday evening, AJ showed up at the Corbett's front door without notice, but with two of his best customers standing beside him, Howard and Eva Mayfield. They had purchased many items of fine art from AJ in the past. Their attire and extravagant jewelry made it clear that they were a couple with more money than they knew what to do with. A few days earlier, AJ told the wealthy couple that they simply must view the works of this new artist before the rest of the art world discovered her. Though reluctant, Marie was absolutely on the spot and allowed the Mayfields to view her works in the sunroom. In less than an hour, Howard and Eva purchased seven paintings for the tidy sum of twenty-nine thousand dollars, and Marie Corbett became a featured artist in The AJ Gaines Gallery from that day forward.

* * *

"I don't believe it," AJ said as he moved to a painting hung on the dining room wall, tears welling in his eyes. "It's the silo."

"It's just west of the property," Tom advised AJ. "You can see it from the front porch."

"I remember Marie telling me about that silo years ago," AJ elaborated. "She said that for a few days every July, the sun would set directly behind the silo, and she thought it was magical when it paused above it and seemed to rest upon it. She told me you were born on one of those days, which confirmed its magical nature for her. Marie called it Shelbyville's small-town version of Stonehenge."

"As a child," Tom remarked wistfully, "I remember her telling me that story often. She always said my birthday was a magical day."

"You know," AJ added, "I believe that was the one and only time Marie ever mentioned Shelbyville to me."

"Even with me," Tom said, "it was a time and subject matter that she seldom brought up."

"You realize she probably painted this canvas on your first or second birthday?"

"I know."

"I loved your mother so much," AJ said as tears overflowed from his eyes. "If I wasn't a gay man, I believe I would have asked her to marry me."

From that point forward, the tour of the home and its artwork was an emotional endeavor for AJ. He wept a little before each painting, stared at each like a long-lost friend, glanced skyward as a tribute to

Marie, and solemnly bowed his head in quiet reflection. His love for Marie was apparent, and his lingering grief for her loss was still palpable. An hour later, AJ was absolutely drained and asked to sit alone on the sofa in the living room so he could regain his composure. While he did, Tom and I waited outside on the porch. At that point, I'd only known AJ for a couple of hours, but I could tell he was a man who lived his life in a raw, uncensored manner.

"The house looks better than I expected," AJ remarked once he'd recuperated. "Originally, you described it as unlivable, but it's better than that now. I wouldn't live in it, mind you, but it's livable."

"I've still got a long way to go with the refurbishments," Tom said, "but I'm actually enjoying both the work and the process. It'll be a major milestone once we finish painting it."

Sitting on the front porch at a little after 3 p.m., Tom and I once again watched as the Porsche maneuvered along the road like it was racing on the winding roads near Nurburgring. About a quarter mile down the road, just as it was about to leave our sight, the car once again came to a screeching halt. After a lot of engine revving, wheel spinning, and dust raising, the Porsche turned around and retraced its tracks back to the farmhouse.

"I almost forgot," AJ called out the driver's side window, a cloud of dust floating between his car and the porch, "the grand opening for the Miami gallery is scheduled for the second Saturday in November. You have to come to Miami for it."

"I'll let you know."

"Oh, don't be a fuddy-duddy. You have to be there. I simply won't take no for an answer."

Rather than wait for an answer and risk a second less than enthusiastic response, AJ unleashed the engine of the Porsche and took off down the road again.

Chapter Thirty-Seven

Tom and I lost a full day of painting due to AJ's unscheduled appearance at the farm, and I turned my focus to the next edition of *The Sentinel,* so finishing the painting project seemed more likely in early September than end of August. But, neither of us was concerned because, other than my bi-weekly publishing deadline, we were two men who paid little attention to clocks or schedules. For our own reasons, we both traveled apart from the mainstream. Case in point, three hours after I delivered my next edition to the printer, Tom wandered into *The Sentinel* office and joined my friend Glen (fiddich) and me in our usual celebration of my latest issue. From his first swig, Tom knew our little party would further delay the project, but he didn't care. We'd finish when we finished.

With my fifth pour, my inquisitive nature and the booze started to get the better of me, and I asked Tom if he had any good memories of his father during his years at the farm. Since meeting Tom, I'd heard so many bad things about Sam Corbett that I wondered if the man had any redeeming qualities at all. As a writer, individuals' character and their interactions with other people had always fascinated me.

"Did he ever play catch with you in the yard or teach you to ride a bicycle?" I asked.

"That's not how I remember him," Tom said. "My memories of my father have to do with the times he yelled at me about money."

"You were just a little kid in elementary school," I followed up. "Why would he yell at you about money?"

"One evening after dark, I remember my father came in from the field, and my winter coat was lying on the floor next to the sofa. Immediately, he went off on me, shouting, 'Do you know how much a coat like that costs? Well, I'll tell you. That coat costs around twenty dollars. Don't you think something that costs twenty dollars deserves better care than being left on the dirty floor? I sure as hell do! Get that damn coat off the floor and then get out of my sight.'"

"Holy shit!" I exclaimed, shaking my head. "I asked because I figured he couldn't have been nearly as bad as I thought, but he was worse. Don't you have any positive memories of him?"

"I'm sure there were good moments, even some when we all laughed," he responded, "they're just not what I remember."

"What about Marie?" I asked. "Tell me about her."

"Oh, I could talk for hours about my great memories of my mother —she was kind and sweet, and she always made me feel special. The thing you have to know about my mother was that she had a lot of exuberance in her, an absolute joy about living and life. My mother cooked, played piano, painted, sculpted, spun pottery, ice-skated, ran 10ks, practiced yoga, volunteered, and loved old movies and animals. And those are just a few things that come to mind. Most of us go through our days in a trance and barely participate in our own lives, but my mother lived each day like it was a contest, like she was not going to let a single minute get by without enjoying it, without savoring it. The French call it '*joie de vivre*' and my mother just oozed it."

"She sure left her mark on AJ."

"Oh, she left her mark on a lot of people."

"Here's to Marie," I said, knocking back a swig of Glen.

"I think my father was a lot like his brother, Carl. If Sam Corbett left his mark on someone, whether verbally or physically, it left an enduring scar."

Unable to let the mention of Carl pass without addressing the metal box and white envelope, I asked Tom again.

"Have you thought any more about when you'd open the box and envelope?

"Actually, I have thought about it. I think I'll open the box and envelope when we finish painting the house. I feel like I'm almost ready."

"Are you just saying that to get me to work harder?"

"Absolutely not, but I know you will."

"Are we painting tomorrow?" I asked, knowing we wouldn't be effective as it was almost 1 a.m.

"Oh God no," Tom answered as he started towards the door. "I'll see you Thursday."

Chapter Thirty-Eight

I could not remember the last time that I practically counted the minutes until something happened, the last time I so eagerly anticipated a moment or event. It might have been in eighth grade when I invited Debbie Jo Corcoran to the movies on a Saturday night and thought I might get to touch a boob for the first time. I could only hope that the opening of the metal box and white envelope was more satisfying than my evening with Debbie Jo. Oh, she was willing all right—I couldn't get her bra unhooked. And, the theater was sold out for the first weekend of Ghostbusters, so I couldn't exactly walk behind her seat and unfasten it.

On the second Saturday in September, Tom and I sat at the dining room table at the farm with the metal box and white envelope in front of us. For more than a couple of minutes, we just stared at them. Though I was bursting at the seams with anticipation, I knew I had to respect whatever process Tom had in mind for the conduct of this event. After all, it was his family history we were about to delve into. Finally, he broke the silence.

"I think we need a couple of beers, don't you?"

I almost knocked my chair over as I rushed to the refrigerator, grabbed two beers, and hustled back to the table.

"Here you go," I said, placing the bottles in front of us.

"Which should I open first?" he asked me.

"Well, I think the letter probably addresses what's in the box, so I think you should open the box first. That way, we'll better understand the letter when you read it."

"You've given this a lot of thought, haven't you?"

"Maybe a little."

Tom picked up the key ring the estate lawyer gave him on his first day at the property and, one by one, he began attempting to insert each key into the lock. It was the seventh key that finally sprung the padlock open. In an apprehensive motion, like the box might be full of snakes or scorpions, Tom slowly raised the lid of the metal box until it remained in place at the ninety-degree mark. We leaned in and peered into the box from opposite sides of the table.

"Is that blood?" I asked, breaking a long, tense silence.

"I believe it is," he replied. "Let me get some gloves."

Tom retrieved a pair of disposable latex gloves from a kitchen drawer and pulled them onto his hands once he returned to the dining room table. Standing over the box, he slowly reached into it and raised a pair of blue overalls, large enough to fit a sizable man and caked with dried, brown blood. From their styling and wear, the work clothes appeared very old—possibly even decades old. The bloodstain started at the chest and continued to the knees, causing me to surmise that whoever wore these overalls probably didn't survive the incident. It was an awful lot of blood. I had no medical training, but it seemed to me that a stain like that one would require at least a couple of pints of blood, and the term "bled out" came to my mind.

"Dear God," I blurted.

"I think these are the work clothes my father was wearing on the night he died," Tom uttered.

"That Carl wasn't just mean—he was sick also!"

Tom sat back down in his chair, so I did the same. There were more items in the box, but we both felt like we needed a minute or two, a pause to regain some sense of equilibrium. We were both knocked off balance by the presence of the bloody overalls in the box and felt like we were victims of a horrible prank. What family passes bloody clothing down to their heirs? Gazing at Tom across the table, overwhelmed by the work clothes and the blood, I wished it had been a coin or stamp collection in the box.

"What else is in there?" I finally asked.

"I see a bloody, flannel shirt, a pair of work boots, and a John Deere hat."

"Unbelievable," I stammered.

Eventually, Tom reached for the white envelope. I saw intense anger in his eyes, and he practically seethed as he ripped it open. The note was indeed handwritten, the writing style was simple printed letters as opposed to cursive, and the level of education appeared to be about tenth or eleventh grade. Holding the single sheet in his right hand, he read it to me.

"Tom, your mother killed my brother. I knew it all these years, but no one would listen to me. For all her remaining days, Marie lived with blood on her hands. And now, that blood is passed to you. I hope your mother burns in hell. Carl."

Tom was right, I thought to myself. *He knew not to open the box. He knew it contained nothing but heartache.*

We were both thunderstruck and silent. The anger in his eyes seemed to slowly dissipate and a meditative veneer replaced it. I'd pushed Tom to open the box, and I felt horrible. I couldn't look him in the eyes at that moment. With my head hung, I told him, "I'm sorry," across the table, but he didn't respond. He was thinking. There was stillness and silence for what seemed like an eternity and then frenzied activity.

"Grab your keys," Tom said, quickly rising from the table, knocking his chair over as he did.

Whack! The chair landed on the wooden floor.

"Where are we going?" I asked.

In a hurried manner, Tom grabbed the white envelope and the letter and placed them in the metal box. He slammed the lid closed and reattached the padlock to the front of it. Still, without answering my question, he raced into the kitchen, retrieved two flashlights from a drawer beside the refrigerator, and returned to the dining room. All of a sudden, Tom was a man on a mission.

"Bring the box," he said as he started toward the front door.

"Where are we going?" I asked for a second time.

"Drive away from town on Stony Creek Road."

Around Shelbyville, the two-lane roads were very dark at night—even pitch black—as there were no streetlights and only the lights from farmhouses set back from the roads to provide any illumination. Pitch is the black residue that results from distilling wood tar, and, on this moonless night, it felt like we were driving through it. The blackness seemed to create its own type of resistance, almost stickiness, so we made our way at a cautious thirty miles per hour. All I could see ahead of me was the blacktop within the narrow strip of light created by my truck's hi-beams. We drove for about fifteen minutes until Tom finally instructed me to pull over along the side of the road. Gravel crunched beneath the tires as I turned off the paved road. While he handed me a flashlight, I realized for the first time that we were parked alongside the town's cemetery. Hastily, Tom grabbed a flashlight and the metal box from the bed of the pickup and started off into the trees.

"Wait for me," I called as he was walking briskly. His strides were long and purposeful, like a man with dirty money in his pockets. I had to hustle to catch up with him.

After climbing a small hill, we flashed our lights on the grave markers around us, and I noticed that Corbett was common on many. I saw John William Corbett on one headstone, and I saw Patricia Jean Corbett on another. Apparently, we had entered his family's section of the cemetery. Even in the dark of night, Tom knew exactly where he was going; he'd obviously been here since he returned to town. Finally, after briskly walking more than one hundred yards into the cemetery, Tom stopped in front of two side-by-side headstones, chiseled to read Samuel Gerard Corbett and Carl David Corbett.

"Take your damn box of lies back, Carl," Tom shouted as he hurled the metal box at his uncle's headstone, striking it near the top and taking a sizable gray chip out of it.

"You burn in hell," he continued angrily. "You were nothing but a mean, spiteful son of a bitch. How dare you talk about my mother like that! She was full of kindness and love—two things you never showed anyone in your whole pathetic life."

His tirade over, we stood in front of the two headstones for several minutes, but there was no respect being paid on either of our parts for either of these men. Instead, it felt like we were squared off against adversaries, staring into eyes that could not stare back, searching for acknowledgment in the vastness of eternity. But ours was a futile search. My flashlight illuminated the stone that read Samuel Gerard Corbett, 1931 – 1968; his flashlight illuminated the stone that read Carl David Corbett 1933 – 2011. In my mind, a writer's mind, the dash between the years signified the negativity within their years as well as the slashing effect both men had on the people in their lives. They definitely earned their dashes. I'd never met Tom's father, but I knew Carl Corbett, and standing there, I felt like I knew both men. In my heart, I knew I wouldn't have liked either of them. Few people did.

"Feeling any better?" I asked.

"Maybe a little."

Chapter Thirty-Nine

The Pennsylvania Avenue Apartments were constructed during the Kennedy administration and hadn't been renovated since Reagan left office. All twenty-four units were tan or cream-colored, with mismatched appliances and carpets darkened by years of dirt. If the complex had a rental brochure—which it didn't—the main selling point was cheap monthly rates, with one and two-bedroom apartments costing only five and seven hundred dollars respectively. Residents were rarely professionals and turned over regularly, with the longest tenures generally capping out near the two-year mark. In apartment nineteen, Nicole and Scratch were its newest residents, occupying a two-bedroom apartment with an unobstructed view of the gas station and car wash. Scratch selected this apartment complex because his bandmate Blade, his girlfriend, and their seven-month-old daughter lived four doors down in apartment twenty-three.

Nicole was thirty weeks pregnant, and her belly protruded so far in front that it was visible to Scratch on the sofa before she turned the corner and exited the kitchen. Every time it appeared, he broke out in juvenile laughter and sometimes mimicked the "Jaws" theme for added effect. After many renditions, Nicole had yet to think it was funny. A blue and yellow nursery occupied the second bedroom because they'd long ago learned they were having a boy. Though living on Scratch's modest income from his part-time job in a warehouse, the nursery was nicely furnished and well stocked with diapers and wipes because Nicole arranged for subsidies from both her parents. One advantage of uninvolved, affluent parents was that they were easy marks, particularly when it came to their first grandchild.

Supposedly, the band's contract had lingered for over nine months in the legal department of the record company like groupies at a stage door in an alley. Whether they still believed it or not, the bandmates regularly bragged that the deal was imminent, and, two or three nights a week, Scratch and Blade celebrated their imminent signing. They'd even gone so far as to boast that their new material would surely result in Grammy wins and flip the music world upside down. Their working title for their release was "Silicon Dream," but it was unclear whether the title was intended as technology or boobs-related. All things considered, it was probably boobs-related.

While Nicole napped in the bedroom, Scratch and Blade talked in the living room.

"We need to get out on the road and do a dive bar tour up and down the east coast," Scratch told his bandmate. "We'll build a loyal fan base so online sales go ballistic when we drop our tunes."

"Say what?" Blade followed up. "We've got the girls and the kids depending on us."

"That's why we're crashing four doors apart. They'll have one another's back while we're touring the clubs. Our music needs to be heard!"

"The new riffs are really badass, man. That's the righteous truth. But, shouldn't you focus on Nicole right now? She looks like she is about to pop. You're going to have a little dude very soon."

"Hey man, I'm a guitarist, not a doctor! What the hell am I going to do for her?"

"You've got a point! Maybe we should talk with Bruno about a tour—we'll see if he can hook us up."

"Are you out of your mind, Scratch?" Nicole asked as she waddled down the hallway with a side-to-side stride that resembled a mother duck. "Did I hear you say something about a tour?"

"We need to create our fan base for when we drop our songs on the internet, babe."

"Our son will be here in seven weeks. I'm going to need you here with us."

"Come on, Blade," Scratch said as he rose from the sofa, "let's go chill at your place. Nicole has been a real bitch lately."

Chapter Forty

Back at The Rooster, during the third week of October, the usual crowd was arriving for lunch on a Wednesday afternoon. Already seated on my usual stool at the counter, Tom approached with a perplexed look on his face. As soon as he sat beside me, he addressed me in a hushed tone.

"I just passed Martha Gladstone, and she's eating a sandwich and potato chips out of a brown bag at her table."

"Yeah," I replied, "she brings her lunch once or twice a week because she says she can't afford to eat at The Rooster every day."

"She's the richest person in Shelbyville, she owns a seven-thousand-acre orchard at the edge of town, and her face is on the labels of apple sauce jars in grocery stores all across the U.S. How is it that she can't afford to buy lunch in a diner?"

"Go figure."

"Well, why does she bring her brown bag into The Rooster?" Tom followed up, looking more perplexed than when he sat down.

"I guess she likes to come here. She enjoys the company."

"I've never heard her say a kind word to anyone in all the times I've been here."

"Yeah, I know," I said, "but she doesn't want to miss a day of it."

At 12:15 p.m., Milt entered the diner and addressed his friend Chet who was seated at a table to the right of him.

"I'm very happy to report that I'm back to walking my usual route to the diner. The little winged bastard is nowhere in sight."

"Well," Chet responded, "that's because the little winged bastard has flown south for the winter."

"I don't give a damn where he is as long as he stays the hell out of my little town," Milt returned defiantly.

"He is in Daytona Beach right now, relaxing in a palm tree while enjoying the sunshine and warm breezes," Chet said. "Where will you be spending winter, Milt?"

"What kind of a stupid question is that—you know damn well that I always spend winter in Shelbyville. I am not a Rockefeller with a second home in Palm Beach."

"Once again, Milt, I think you have to ask yourself who the superior creature really is? The little winged bastard is working on his tan right now and waiting for his turn at shuffleboard."

"The little winged bastard is not the superior creature," Milt said, recognizing the trap he'd stumbled into. "I am!"

"Speaking of Florida," Tom observed as we waited for Connie to take our lunch orders, "I've decided to go to Miami for the gallery's grand opening after all. Why don't you come along?"

"A weekend in Miami," I replied thoughtfully as I began to contemplate the invitation.

I continued. "Miami is a beautiful city that combines the vibrant colors and pulsing rhythms of its Spanish heritage with the Art Deco styling and uproarious chic of the Roaring Twenties. The city is known for its white sand beaches, palm trees, and gorgeous women. I have always wanted to holiday in Miami, so I could relax in an outdoor cafe while enjoying the tropical breezes, drinking Puerto Rican rum, smoking a fine Cuban cigar, and seducing a beautiful woman."

"You're doing that writer thing again," Tom said. "Do you want to go with me or not?"

"Sure, I'll go with you."

Chapter Forty-One

As night descended on Miami, the tinny, bouncy, rhythmic sounds of a Jamaican steel drum band, located in the loft of a new art gallery named simply "AJ," reverberated through the thick Florida air, alerting invited guests, passersby, and tourists alike that it wasn't an ordinary night on the avenue. Along with the musicians, seven youthful dancers in white linen pants and floral tops bounced and bounded with the music, providing a zesty Caribbean floorshow that usually required a fan boat ride to observe. Watching the festivities, AJ Gaines, in yellow culottes, a loose-fitting indigo shirt, and a Panama hat, stood beside the entrance greeting guests and reporters as they arrived. Between the outfit and the wily smile on his face, he had a certain P.T. Barnum quality about him. Irrefutably, AJ was a man who knew he was about to make a lot of money.

"The gallery looks amazing," Shannon said on arrival.

Aglow, AJ returned, "You look amazing, my dear."

Flanked by art deco buildings trimmed in neon—a real estate company and a boutique hotel—AJ was unique in the South Beach landscape. While coral, lavender, and watermelon were the colors of the other two buildings, AJ was metallic in appearance with varying tones of silver, brass, and copper, and its design suggested an architectural melding of the Guggenheim Museum and an old aircraft hangar. In the newspapers, its presence on the strip had been both lauded and denigrated, which was the exact response AJ Gaines wanted. He'd knocked around the art world long enough to know that there was no such thing as bad publicity; art sells best when cutting-edge and controversial.

"It's not art unless it's loved or hated," AJ once told an interviewer early in his career. "Art moves people to the extreme reaches of their emotions."

A half-hour later, while the band took its first break, Tom and I moved from one painting to another, viewing the first collection of fine art offered for sale at the gallery. Many were bright and colorful and depicted Mexican and Cuban subject matter, like the one we were viewing, a sunset scene over a Mexican mission and young women.

"The brush strokes in that sky are remarkable," I said, noticing the dramatic blending of orange, yellow, and red, like the sun was melting into the horizon.

"Alejandro Ruiz," Tom stated as he read the artist's name aloud. "He did several of these next paintings," he added, pointing to the framed works just ahead of us.

"You look great, Tom," Shannon said as she strolled over to join us. She had a martini glass in her hand and a smirk on her face. "Farm life suits you."

"You always look great, Shannon," Tom returned as he gave his wife a hug and a quick kiss.

This was the first time that husband and wife had been in the same room since Tom left for Shelbyville a little more than three months ago. And, their total amount of time spent conversing on the phone had not yet topped sixty minutes. The past three months had basically been an undeclared trial separation. Tom was no longer bitter or angry about her affair and felt instead like he had left those unpleasant circumstances far behind.

161

"I don't know why you came," she remarked. "I have every intention of taking our ownership in the gallery as part of the divorce settlement, so you really have no involvement here."

"You've filed for divorce?"

"I haven't seen you in three months, so that seems like the next step. I've retained a lawyer at Garfunkel, Barton, and Mason to work on divorce papers."

"So, we're going the traditional route, huh?" Tom remarked. "We'll both hire high-priced, cutthroat lawyers and fight like dogs in the street?"

"Well, that's my plan, sweetheart," Shannon replied, grinning. "I can't speak for you."

"Let me just tell you this going in—if you and your lawyer put a reasonable division of assets forward, we can do this quick and easy. I really don't care about the particulars."

"You have always been so naive," Shannon observed. "What could make you think I have any intention of being reasonable?"

"Fine, Shannon, let's fight like dogs until we are both bloody and exhausted. I'll let you know the name of my attorney next week."

"Cheers," Shannon declared, hoisting her martini glass into the air while turning and walking away.

"Holy cow," I remarked once she was out of earshot.

"I didn't introduce you because her demeanor seemed toxic from the start. I wanted to spare you the aggravation."

"You did me a favor. If you had introduced me as your friend, I would've been looking over my shoulder for the rest of the night."

As soon as Shannon turned the corner and left our sight, AJ approached from the other side. He had a tall, fruity concoction in his hand and a big smile on his face.

"Alejandro is my latest discovery," AJ said as he stepped in between us, "and, frankly, one of my best. He is definitely top tier—right up there with Sylvester and Marie."

"That sunset is mesmerizing," I told him, pointing to the painting

Tom and I had just viewed. "I don't know a lot about art, but that is beautiful."

"Obviously, you have a good eye for art, Nick, and for a mere seventy-five thousand dollars you can hang that masterpiece on your office wall in Shelbyville."

"I would have to sell a kidney to afford it."

"Fortunately, Nick," Tom said, chuckling as he did, "AJ can broker that deal for you, too."

AJ had a loud, echoing laugh. When he laughed at Tom's remark, he drew the attention of two tattooed men in their late twenties who were off to our right in front of another Alejandro. One, wearing a stocking cap and lightly tinted sunglasses, looked over at Tom several times, apparently trying to figure out why Tom looked familiar. It took him about five minutes before he finally made the connection and addressed Tom.

"Hey, I know you—you are The Dream Squasher! Nice try with the beard, man, but I'd know you anywhere. I've watched your video about fifty times. What an asshole! How could you rip into those college kids like that? Don't you have anything better to do with your time?"

Immediately, AJ grabbed the man by the back of his shirt collar, pulled him up the aisle toward the front door, and hurled him out of the gallery and onto the sidewalk.

"I am AJ Gaines," he told the young man as he stumbled onto the sidewalk and then looked back like he didn't understand what just happened. "You're not welcome in my gallery any longer. That man you called an asshole is my friend."

"AJ," Tom advised him when he returned from his sideline as a bouncer, "you're going to lose a lot of business if you kick everyone out of here that has seen my coffee store video."

"I really don't care," AJ shot back, miffed. "You are one of the best men I know, and I'm never going to stand idly by while someone disparages you. That is never going to happen!"

"You're a good man, too," Tom returned, touched by his friend's comments.

"No, I am not but maybe someday."

I learned that night at AJ that the grand opening of a Miami art gallery was not the best place for someone like me, someone with a penchant for cocaine. Whenever I went into the restroom, someone was doing lines in the corner, and they always offered me one. Like Blanche DuBois in *A Streetcar Named Desire,* I had always been a person who appreciated the kindness of strangers. All night long, I never said no; I always accepted. In fact, I found myself returning to the restroom with far more frequency than my need to pee. Between 9 p.m. and midnight, I was in and out of the restroom more than a dozen times.

Around 1 a.m., with the steel drums silenced and the guests in the gallery whittled to a baker's dozen, AJ noticed my condition and wandered over to Tom near the bar.

"I'm concerned about Nick," AJ said in a hushed manner, knowing that discretion in these matters was always appreciated.

"What do you mean?"

"We were talking near the restroom and he was speaking really fast. His eyes were dilated, his arms were twitching, and I'm sure his heart rate was going through the ceiling. I'm an addict, Tom, and I know all the warning signs."

"Are you telling me that Nick is overdosing?"

"I'm telling you that you better take him to a hospital."

"Hey AJ," one of his clients said as he joined them at the bar. "That guy you were talking to a while ago is doubled over in the bathroom, holding his gut, and puking something fierce. Is he a friend of yours?"

"He is a friend of mine," Tom declared as he and AJ took off in the direction of the restrooms.

Tom and I arrived at the gallery that evening in a town car, but I left in the back of an ambulance with lights and sirens blaring. Until my dying day, I will always be able to close my eyes and hear the screeching whine of the siren as we sped through the streets of Miami in the middle of the night. I was only semiconscious and felt like I was in a dream. In the emergency room, the doctor told me that I had suffered a heart attack. Basically, my heart was pumping so fast that it damaged its tissue, so hard it could have burst inside my chest. Several times during his explanation, the doctor used the term "self-induced" to attach a degree of stupidity to my heart attack and distinguish it from natural ones. Though I'd had several confrontations with my own mortality in the past, this incident was entirely different, one hundred percent accident, with absolutely no harm intended. I almost died, but I didn't mean to, I wasn't attempting suicide—maybe there was some growth in that.

"I'm sorry I ruined the grand opening," I told Tom when I saw him in the hospital the next morning. He'd been there all night.

"I don't care about the grand opening," he replied, his eyes narrowed. "I hope you're sorry that you almost killed yourself."

"I am."

"Why do you do that to yourself?"

"A man is dead because of me, Tom—a good woman lost her husband, and two little girls lost their father."

Chapter Forty-Two

F ive days into May, our aircraft rumbled down the runway at JFK and lifted smoothly upward as Chelsea and I departed for two weeks in Paris, where she would be a featured lecturer at the renowned Lafayette Institute for the Culinary Arts. From her window seat, Chelsea watched as the aircraft gained altitude, and the highways, interchanges, and vehicles beneath the wings shrank and faded from view. Within minutes, our viewpoint was high above puffy white clouds that stippled an otherwise clear blue sky, with the green waters of the Atlantic Ocean visible on the horizon. Holding hands and smiling at thirty-three thousand feet, we were thrilled to be traveling to the City of Lights together, as Paris was truly one of the most beautiful and romantic cities in the world and one that neither of us had ever visited.

Our first nine weeks as a couple had been a continuation of our first night at the Winston Hotel, and our bond had only grown as we learned more about one another. We spent most of our time together either laughing or making love, and sometimes both at once. It was one hundred nineteen miles from the door of my apartment in Philadelphia to the door of her apartment in New York City, but that distance had yet to prove difficult. Chelsea's cooking show was taped in marathon sessions, meaning three or four episodes in one long day, so she was usually at the studio two days per week. Thanks to the condensed nature of her work schedule, she stayed with me in Philadelphia for three and four-day increments, and I traveled to New York for long weekends with her. In actuality, we felt fortunate about our arrangement in as much as we spent our time together in two great cities. Furthermore, it was clear to both of us that our mutual instincts on that first evening had only been confirmed by the passage of time.

"Two weeks in Paris with the man I love," Chelsea whispered beneath the sound of the jet engines. "I've never been happier in my whole life."

Our reservation was for thirteen nights at the Hotel Bisset, a narrow, six-story, white stone inn with leafy green boxes adorning the black railing of the four tall windows that spanned each level, just south of the River Seine near the center of Paris in an area known as *St. Germain Des Prix*. Just a block or two west of the hotel was an area of stores and boutiques near the Museum D'Orsay that included many art galleries and antique shops. From May to August, the dark of night did not arrive in Paris until almost 11 p.m., creating a magical three hours of twilight when pedestrians filled the narrow streets, and the neon signs of restaurants, outdoor cafes, bars, sandwich shops, and crepe stands illuminated. In that magical twilight, the tone and tenor of the evening felt like a deep satisfied sigh. At 9:30 p.m., two hours after registering, we first stepped out onto the crowded streets to wander the neighborhood near the hotel and find a romantic restaurant for dinner.

As we strolled, I noticed the soft light and its effect on the buildings around us. Like an aging screen actress shot in soft light to conceal her age lines, this magical twilight softened the avenues of Paris and produced an elegant scene not unlike a movie. Lining the street ahead of us, the buildings were constructed of solid white stone and more than one hundred years old, but all traces of age or dirt were diffused by the twilight, while their classic French architecture was center stage and highlighted. Fifty Parisians, the bluish cobblestones of the sidewalk, glowing neon, and a colorful outdoor flower stand on the corner completed the scene in front of us. Overwhelmed and in awe of the setting, I stopped and stared silently ahead.

"Do you want to eat here?" Chelsea asked, wondering if that was the reason I suddenly stopped.

"No," I said. "I'm noticing all the beauty that surrounds us. This street is unlike any street I've ever walked in my life. I'm quite content to keep walking. You tell me when you see a restaurant that interests you."

* * *

At breakfast the following day, Chelsea had a large map of Paris that showed the locations of about a hundred tourist attractions wide open on the white tablecloth beside her eggs, croissants, and hot chocolate. In bold, black marker, she had placed a large X near the center of the map that indicated our hotel's location and circled about thirty sites she wanted to visit. Beside the map, a manila folder with "Paris Trip" written neatly on its tab contained about fifty pages that she printed off the internet in advance of our flight. In our short time together, I had discovered what a great traveling companion Chelsea was—she loved to research and plan when that was appropriate, but she was also flexible and spontaneous when it wasn't. She would make a fantastic tour guide.

"How far is the Eiffel Tower?" I asked between sips of coffee.

"Two miles," she responded, after consulting the legend and calculating the distance using her bent knuckle.

"It's such a nice day that I think we should walk," I said. "What do you think?"

"Absolutely."

At 9:20 a.m., we departed the hotel and began walking west toward the tower. Chelsea had a small, red backpack with a map, cell phone, sunglasses, bottled water, sunscreen, a bottle of red wine, two cups, and a box of crackers stowed in it. We were hand in hand, walking slowly down the avenue, pausing at many windows to peruse the offerings. The traffic was light, and the sky was clear, but the temperature was expected to approach ninety degrees that day.

When we arrived at the Eiffel Tower, we sat on the grassy lawn and marveled at the majesty of the landmark. It had a simple and solid industrial splendor, the same type of splendor that the Brooklyn Bridge, Golden Gate Bridge, or the Gateway Arch possessed. Rising in a brilliant design, merging steel elements bent toward the sky and culminated at a tip that seemed to point the way to heaven. From her backpack, Chelsea removed a printed page she brought along that told the history of the structure. She read it aloud as we sat.

"Completed in 1889, the Eiffel Tower was constructed as an attraction for an international exposition. The invention of Gustave Eiffel, a French engineer who specialized in steel construction, the tower was the tallest structure on earth until 1929 when the Chrysler Building in New York surpassed it. It is still the tallest structure in Paris. At nine hundred eighty-four feet, its conspicuous height almost resulted in its dismantling after the exposition, as it has not always been popular with Parisians. Many petitioned for its removal, calling the tower a monstrosity and blight on the city's skyline. Even though it weighs over seven thousand tons, the tower is considered a brilliant feat of engineering because the pressure on the earth beneath it is less than three hundred pounds."

"Let's go to the top," Chelsea beckoned me after we'd spent more than an hour sitting on the grass, sipping red wine and munching on crackers.

There was a scary roller coaster sensation to the elevator ride as visitors ascended the tower—not because of speed or trajectory—but because of the aged nature of the wheels and wires that pulled the compartment ever higher. It was a slower version of a death-defying thrill ride, but the breathtaking views made any nail-biting or silent screaming worthwhile. From the top platform, one could assess the enormity of the city, as it seemed to go on endlessly in all directions, and identify many familiar landmarks. The Arc de Triomphe stood regally above the buildings surrounding it in the north, and the gold dome of the Hotel de Invalides and the gray dome of the Pantheon lined up in the east. In an unhurried manner, we moved from one vantage point to another while Chelsea took more than twenty photographs along the way. As city dwellers, we'd both seen views from tall buildings, but this was different and special.

"Almost four hundred people have fallen or committed suicide from the tower since it was constructed," Chelsea said as we walked about the platform.

"How many celebrity chefs have been tossed off the tower?" I asked, grabbing her in a menacing grip that quickly turned into a warm embrace.

From the Tour Eiffel, we took a green taxicab to the Arc de Triomphe, walked through the underground tunnel to the monument, and then broke for lunch at an outdoor café on the Avenue des Champs Elysees. From there, it was a short walk from the restaurant through the Jardin des Tuileries, a beautiful park with a tree-lined walkway and a large fountain at each end, to the Musee du Louvre, where Chelsea posed in front of the Mona Lisa. As she did, I stood four feet from her, framing the shot on my cell phone.

"Those are wonderful smiles," I said as I pressed the button.

Every day was as full and engaging as the first one as Chelsea and I were unrelenting in our quest to see as much of Paris in the time allotted. Making good on her commitment, Chelsea spent most afternoons teaching young chefs the culinary arts, but we made the most of her free time. Each morning, we journeyed to several sites around the city, and each night, we wandered the city streets until we happened upon a small café that suited our appetites. On our final day in Paris, we stood on the grand steps of Sacre Coeur or Sacred Heart, a magnificent basilica that sat high atop Montmartre Hill and overlooked the city. Looking out at Paris, we reflected on our time in this amazing place.

"I'm a different person than when I arrived two weeks ago," Chelsea remarked. "This city has a wonderful effect on one's spirit."

"I know what you mean," I said. "I'm leaving Paris with a much deeper appreciation of life. I feel changed also."

In every lifetime, sometimes more than once, a circumstance opens the heart to its fullest measure, where meaningful change is possible, failures and shortcomings are absolved, and a person is reborn. Some are healed or renewed by the experience, while others fail to recognize the opportunity, and it simply passes by. When it happened in my life, I had the unbelievably good fortune to be with Chelsea in Paris.

* * *

Once again, the aircraft climbed skyward, and Chelsea sat in the seat by the window. She watched as the highways, interchanges, and vehicles beneath us shrank and faded from view. Twenty minutes into the flight, when the aircraft reached its cruising altitude, she moved away from the window and sat back in her seat. We were both sad to be leaving Paris.

"What was your favorite part of our trip?" I asked.

"The hot chocolate at breakfast," she answered jokingly with a pursed smile, referring to the French custom she enjoyed each morning.

I grinned and nodded.

"What was your favorite part?" Chelsea asked in return.

"My tour guide," I answered. "She was amazing."

Her smile widened.

Chapter Forty-Three

I understood relativity. Every other theory by Albert Einstein eluded me, but I understood relativity. Einstein said that the passage of time is relative to circumstance, meaning that an hour spent with a beautiful woman passes much quicker than an hour spent waiting on a reprimand. Though always constant, time seems to accelerate when the mind is light and slow when the mind is weighted. After meeting Chelsea, the best and worst periods of my life followed in succession, so I got it—I lived his theory. My next five years illustrated Einstein's theory perfectly as they included the thirty best months of my life, as well as the thirty worst months of my life. And believe me, just as Einstein postulated, the best months passed quickly, and the worst months passed in a slow, torturous manner. The passage of time is truly relative to circumstance.

Chapter Forty-Four

When we returned from Paris, Chelsea and I purchased a small row house near Rittenhouse Square using the fifty thousand dollars I received as part of the Fenwick Prize to bolster our down payment. In July 2005, Chelsea relocated the filming of her show from New York City to downtown Philadelphia, so we could live together on a full-time basis like regular couples, eliminating the frequent one-hundred-mile journeys along Interstate 95. While we truly enjoyed living in both cities simultaneously, the feeling of having a home together was much better. I quickly learned that Chelsea was as good at homemaking as she was at cooking when she took the modest two-bedroom fixer-upper and transformed it into a warm, comfortable home with nightly meals that rivaled any four-star restaurant. Now a Fenwick Prize winner, I was able to supplement my income by making appearances on television programs as a guest commentator. Though I tried not to let the award and the recognition go to my head, I have to admit that every time the host of a news program said, "Now joining us from Philadelphia, Fenwick Prize winning journalist and columnist for *The Philadelphia Post*, Nick Sterling," I got goose bumps. For two years, Chelsea and I lived in a perpetual state of domestic bliss, one that I never imagined as a younger man, a cozy by the fire, nowhere I'd rather be, nothing I'd rather be doing type of bliss. We were simply happy and content whenever we were together; we wanted for nothing else. But, just as Einstein warned us, the two years passed too quickly.

Early in the summer of 2007, I decided to write a column about an infamous shooting in Philadelphia a decade earlier, a gang-related incident that the local papers branded "The Death of Innocence." Often in cities, as crime spirals out of control, a single incident causes such shock and outrage that citizens collectively declare, "Enough is enough!" On the night of April 19, 1989, in Central Park in New York City, a gang of about thirty hooligans—in the midst of an hour-long rampage and spree of violence—attacked and raped a jogger. Due to the pack-like nature of their actions, their malicious activities that night became known as "wilding." In the media, the idea was advanced that wild animals were taking over the streets of the city, and that imagery was the impetus for a drastic shift in the city's polit-ical and budgetary priorities, resulting in the hiring of hundreds of police officers, a steep reduction in crime, and much safer streets by the end of the century. The wilding incident changed New York City in much the same way "The Death of Innocence" changed Phil-adelphia.

On July 15, 1997, two rival Latino gangs squared off against one another near a park in South Philadelphia, and the resulting gunfire killed two young brothers who were playing soccer in the park. Only eight and nine years old, Ivan and Luka Divac were the children of Yugoslavian immigrants who fled their war-torn country in 1991 to seek safety and asylum in the United States. Their parents, Stefan and Mina, owned a successful market and delicatessen in South Phil-adelphia, and the transplanted family was, by all measures and accounts, thriving in their new homeland. Both thirty-eight years old, attractive, and fluent in English, the Divac's appearances on the evening news were heartbreaking, as they explained that their two sons were the reason they risked everything to make the dangerous journey out of Yugoslavia and come to America. The couple were kind, hard-working people who contributed a lot to their community, and this incident caused the citizens and politicians of Philadelphia to collectively declare, "Enough is enough!" Making matters worse, as the days, months, and years clicked off, no one was ever arrested for the murders.

* * *

Sadly, Stefan Divac aged twenty years in the decade since the horrendous murders of his young boys. In my mind, I remembered him as a young man in the prime of his life, but he looked old and weary, his black hair had thinned and spoilt to a scraggily, peppered gray, and his face was sad and creased. Even his hands had the veiny, withered look of a sixty-year-old though he was in his late forties. As he sat in front of me, his reluctance was apparent, and he voiced it.

"I would not do this interview," he said, "but I know you are respected reporter. I have seen you on the evening news and in the newspapers. I can only hope that something good will come from your article. Maybe, we will finally get justice for our boys."

"That is my hope also, Stefan."

My first question was a formality, as I knew the answer. I had sat with many heartbroken parents who'd lost young children, and I knew it never got better. There was no closure; there was no healing. Contrary to popular belief, time does not heal all wounds.

"How are you and Mina doing?"

"Not good," he answered, just as I expected. "These are hard days for us because our boys would be at university now. When we came to United States, Mina and I promised one another that our boys would go to university. They would be the first in our family. We were determined to make that happen."

"Do you still own your store?"

"We do, but it is hard for me to work there. When the punks from the neighborhood come into our store, I stare in their eyes and I

175

wonder if they killed our boys, if they killed Ivan and Luka. I wish I did not have this anger in me, but I do. I can't stop it."

"Tell me about Ivan."

"The Saturday before he was killed," his father began, tears welling in his eyes, "he scored his first goal in the soccer league. He was so proud. He was so happy. I always try to remember his face with his big smile on that day."

"Tell me about Luka."

"He loved his mother so much. He was always doing things for her. He would help her with groceries and clean his room. He followed her everywhere. He was good boy."

As part of this interview, I should've asked Stefan about the social and political ramifications these murders had on his neighborhood and the city of Philadelphia as a whole, but I couldn't bring myself to make this horrific crime about more than his two little boys, about more than his and Mina's loss. I knew that was all that mattered to them. His opinion was relevant to my story, but as we spoke, I could see that this man was holding on by a thread; he was mustering every ounce of strength in his being to maintain his composure and keep from breaking down in front of me. His boys were his sole focus, and I accepted that.

"Can I speak with Mina one day this week?"

"No."

I can't remember a time when one word has said so much, I thought. *It's not a scheduling issue—she can't bear it.*

* * *

On the seventh floor of our building was an archive room where photographs were stored, some of the photos were featured in the newspaper but many others had not been used. I found more than three hundred photographs taken as part of the coverage of this story in 1997, about one hundred that had to do with the crime scene and the remaining from all the follow-up stories, including those related to the funerals, family, neighborhood, gang activity, and police investigation. For more than an hour, I flipped through dusty images until I finally found a black-and-white photograph of the crime scene that captured the stark brutality of the day. In the image, in the middle of the park, two small bodies lay with bloodstains on their white jerseys while crime scene investigators gathered evidence and uniformed police officers kept onlookers behind crime scene tape. Near the feet of the victims, as a touch of tragic irony, a soccer ball punctured by a bullet lay still and deflated. This photograph filled half of the front page of *The Post* the day after the murders. I remembered it because it was an image that was hard to forget; it communicated the harsh reality of the tragedy in an uncensored manner. Immediately, I knew it was the photograph that should accompany my follow-up story, which I titled, "The Aftermath of 'The Death of Innocence.'"

* * *

On July 15, 2007, ten years to the day after the tragic deaths of Ivan and Luka Divac, my article and the crime scene photograph were the front-page of *The Post*. About 8:15 a.m. that morning, I departed our home with a folded copy of the newspaper tucked under my arm, without any notion that my newly printed article about the aftermath would produce more aftermath, a third murder as tragic and shocking as a decade ago and a second family added to the list of victims. I had no awareness of the despicable actions and horrible turn of events that I'd set in motion or the drastic turn that my life was about to take. If the Fenwick Prize was the high watermark of my career, this beautiful summer day was surely my low point.

"You know, Nick," Austin told me when I arrived at his office around 9 a.m., "I'd only been editor of *The Post* for six months when this crime occurred, and I hate to admit it, but it scared me. I feared for our city. It was a horrible day."

"I think a lot of people felt that way," I said. "They wondered how a crime this horrific could happen in our city?"

177

"And then, it only got worse," Austin observed, shaking his head as he remembered. "When there were no arrests, we realized how powerful and organized the gangs were."

"The death of Ivan and Luka was the reason the police chief created the special task force to reduce gangs and gang violence. It didn't rid the city of the gangs, but it reduced their street presence and the amount of violence."

"It's made a difference," Austin added. "The gangs that exist today are drug trafficking organizations and not the territorial street gangs from that era. I guess that's some improvement."

"It was a tough article to research. No one wanted to revisit that time in their memories."

"I think we'll get a lot of calls and emails about your article today. I warned the call center last week."

"Probably. Anniversaries have a way of opening old wounds."

"How are you and Chelsea doing?" Austin asked, changing the subject matter from work to personal as he did.

"Really great. I've never been happier."

"I see that," Austin said. "You have a lightness these days that you didn't have before you met her. You were a very serious young man."

"I know. She has a good effect on me."

"When are you going to bend your knee before her?"

"Oh, I don't know. We'll marry whenever the inspiration strikes us. We both know it's inevitable."

"Well, I think you should do it soon. Don't let that woman get away from you. She's a keeper."

"And I intend to keep her, Austin, for all of my days."

Chapter Forty-Five

In the foreground of the photograph that accompanied my article on the front page of *The Post* was a young police officer named Louis Maxwell, who'd just graduated from the police academy a mere forty-two days earlier. A rookie at such a significant crime, he was one of three uniformed police officers managing the crowd while crime scene investigators collected samples and evidence near the bodies behind them. Officer Maxwell, with his young face and big, wide eyes, appeared too young to be wearing a police uniform and, at the same time, overwhelmed by his first truly horrific crime scene. In the photograph, he looked like someone who was both uncomfortable in his circumstance and unsure of his role. Flanking him, the other two uniformed officers wore more business-as-usual facial expressions customary for seasoned officers at a crime scene.

Despite his baby face, Louis Maxwell became a dedicated cop who loved his career choice and sincerely wanted to protect and serve the citizens of Philadelphia. He was a person who truly wanted to make a difference in the world. Near the end of his first year on the police force, Louis received a commendation for thwarting a convenience store robbery and apprehending the suspects. As he handed the certificate to the young patrolman, the mayor declared that Louis Maxwell was a hero, and his actions that afternoon saved the lives of the people in the store at the time.

"We are fortunate to have Louis Maxwell serving on our police force," the mayor added in a clip that aired on the evening news.

Off-duty, Louis was a family man who really enjoyed his role as a husband and a father. During his first three years on the force, he and his wife, Sandra, welcomed two beautiful baby girls to their family and purchased a simple home in South Philadelphia. Without any doubt, his wife and daughters were his purpose in his life, the reasons he dragged his weary butt out of bed every morning and trudged off to work. In his mind, his job as a police officer was all part and parcel with his role as father, as he wanted his city and their neighborhood in particular, to be healthy and safe places for his family to live and his children to grow up. Louis Maxwell was a man who lived for a larger purpose than most ordinary men.

Deeply affected by "The Death of Innocence" and the fact that their new home was only five blocks from the park where the shooting occurred, Louis transferred to the special task force created to target gang activity. Two years after the transfer, Louis volunteered to work undercover and infiltrate a gang so the department could learn their methods for acquiring, moving, and distributing drugs. The gang that he infiltrated, the Saints of Tenth Street, were a notoriously violent gang that was believed to be responsible for as much as twenty percent of all illegal drug activity in Philadelphia, Baltimore, and New York City. At the time of the shooting, it was also believed that the Saints of Tenth Street and Deseo de la Muerte, or Death Wish, were the two gangs that created the crossfire that killed Ivan and Luka Divac. His undercover assignment was particularly dangerous work for a father with two young daughters, but his precious little girls were exactly why he felt the need to do it.

Unbeknownst to me, when I selected the ten-year-old photo to accompany my story, I was unknowingly outing an undercover police officer that had infiltrated the Saints of Tenth Street. His photograph from a decade earlier wearing the uniform of the Philadelphia Police Department alerted the gang of his true mission and resulted in his tragic death. Within seven hours of *The Post* landing on the news-stands, the body of Officer Louis Maxwell was found in a littered alleyway in the warehouse district with his hands tied behind his back, two bullet wounds in the back of his head, and his tongue cut out. Making the crime all the more horrific, the coroner later deter-mined that his tongue was cut out before the bullet wounds, prior to his cold-blooded execution, and that sequence was clearly meant as a gangland warning that "the Saints of Tenth Street don't tolerate snitches."

While eating lunch, I saw the news story posted as a breaking news item on *The Post* website, and I was absolutely devastated when I read the details. I couldn't decide whether I died in that alley with Officer Maxwell or I killed him, but either way, it was clearly my fault. And it only got worse from there. The more I learn about the officer and his young family, the worse I felt about my article and its aftermath. Five days later, from my car across the street, I watched as his family and what seemed like the entirety of the Philadelphia Police Department laid his body to rest at the cemetery. Even from a distance, it was a heartbreaking ceremony. With a very heavy heart, I read his obituary as well as several other articles my paper published about the decorated officer, and one thing was abundantly clear to me —he was a really good man. Louis Maxwell was a man who was making a difference, and, while we hear that expression often, it was rare that people actually did make a difference. He did. Louis died making a difference.

In the days that followed the funeral, I didn't write a single word. I couldn't think. On most days, I never even turned my laptop on. In the restroom one morning, a sportswriter offered me cocaine, and I sniffed the thick white line hoping that its powdery dust would cloud my mind. His intent was to help me escape my grief, but I would say that its effect was more like a trip where my grief came along. No matter how much powder I sniffed or how many whiskey shots I threw back, my grief was always nearby, always lurking like a shadow, reminding me of my tragic mistake and my tongue-less victim. I never forgot any of it, not for a second. When I nodded off from exhaustion, whether at night or during the day, Louis often appeared with blood oozing from the corners of his mouth. He seemed to want to say something to me, but he could not speak. On several afternoons, I followed his wife and daughters to a park near their home and, once again, I sat in my car across the street and observed. More often than not, I bawled like a little baby knowing those little girls were fatherless because of me; their lives were forever damaged because of me. In no small measure, my mind was tormenting me.

At home, I couldn't look Chelsea in her eyes, and I couldn't look at myself in a mirror—either reflection was just too painful. Making matters worse, I wasn't sure what it was exactly that I could not face: my mistake or what it was doing to me. I knew I was coming apart at the seams and fraying around the edges. Simply put, I was falling apart. Seeking escape from my guilt, I was destroying my mental capacities, physical health, and journalistic abilities. I drank alcohol and snorted cocaine all day long and never arrived home until well after midnight. Previously capable of insightful articles, my mind was stilted and unable to produce coherent thoughts. Recent articles by competing newspapers as well as conversations on local television talk shows had even posed the question: Is Nick Sterling a cop killer? In my pained confusion, I asked myself that same question every day.

Within three weeks of the incident, I was essentially run off of the internet, chased away in a manner that combined the worst elements of schoolyard bullying and road rage into a technological and psychological assault. My followers on Twitter morphed into an angry mob, and my friends on Facebook became downright unfriendly. Eventually, I closed my social media accounts because the dialogue was appalling, the posts were cruel and vindictive, and the taunts were mean-spirited and threatening. My email accounts were so packed with ugly messages that I couldn't even find the ones from associates, friends, or relatives, so I closed those accounts too. The irony of our connected world was that the same technologies that connected and empowered us could also be used to isolate and belittle us. I was isolated, just my guilty conscience and me.

As the days shortened and the temperatures fell, I had not published a column or article in *The Post* since Officer Maxwell was killed. I was conspicuously absent from the Philadelphia journalism scene. Hell, I was conspicuously absent from my own life.

After a five-day absence from our home, I returned one evening to find Chelsea had moved out. Her clothes were gone, her large binders of recipes were absent, and her perfume was missing from the air. In the cold house, I felt both relief and anguish, but mostly I felt emptiness. In truth, Chelsea watched my personal disintegration longer than any etiquette handbook would require, and her leaving was understandable. She left a simple, two-sentence note on the dining room table beside a photo of us beaming and obviously very much in love in front of Sacre-Coeur in Paris.

"Nick, I could help you with the sorrow and pain, but I won't enable your drug use and self-destruction. When you forgive yourself and heal, I look forward to seeing the man I love so much again."

Staring at the note, the writer in me loved her conciseness and eloquence—the rest of me just plain loved her.

Chapter Forty-Six

On December 3, 2011, at 11:49 p.m., screaming as loudly as the lead singer of a heavy metal band, Bartholomew Matthew Ackerman made his entrance into the world as his grandparents, Tom and Shannon Corbett, nervously paced the white tile floor in a nearby waiting room. The newborn weighed in at a healthy seven pounds, eleven ounces, and the mother, Nicole, was exhausted but feeling joyful and well after a five-hour delivery. Matthew Arnold Ackerman, the name of the father on the birth certificate, also known as Scratch to his contemporaries, was as excited and energetic as he'd be playing before a sell-out crowd in Madison Square Garden. In a loose-fitting hospital gown and paper slippers, he rushed into the waiting room to deliver the good news to the Corbetts.

"He's the bomb," Scratch informed Tom and Shannon as he arrived, sliding across the tile floor as he tried to stop.

"What the hell does that mean?" Shannon blurted. "Is the baby okay? Is Nicole okay?"

"They're dope," Scratch followed up.

"What the hell does that mean?" she blurted again. "You better say something in English real soon, or I'm going to smack you upside your head."

"Everyone is fine," Tom said, though he didn't understand Scratch either. His assessment was based on the smile on Scratch's face, but he was also aware that Shannon seldom bluffed, so he was trying to avoid a scene.

"Nicole and Bart are doing great," Scratch continued, finally adjusting his message to his audience and stepping backward out of Shannon's reach as he did. He may have been new to the family, but he also knew that Shannon seldom bluffed.

"Let's meet our grandson," Tom said as he took Shannon by the arm.

"I sure hope Bart is smarter than that one," Shannon remarked, glancing over her shoulder at Scratch.

Chapter Forty-Seven

Around midnight in mid-December, in the dimly lit dining room of the farm, Tom sat by his lonesome with a glass of beer in front of him. His mind was growing weary due to the late hour, and he traveled back to a time when he was barely fifty-five pounds and four feet tall. He returned to the final night of his father's life, a night that had weighed heavily on his mind since opening the metal box and white envelope Carl left him. In his memory, he was sitting at the table in the very position he was sitting while his mother was fifteen feet away preparing dinner in the kitchen. Startling both of them, his father burst through the kitchen door—sweaty, soiled, and excited about the tractor delivered less than an hour earlier. He made his way directly to the refrigerator, opened its scuffed white door, removed a six-pack of bottled beer, placed it in the middle of the table, and sat across from his son.

"That tractor will do the work of ten men," Sam said, directed at his son.

"Can I drive it?" Tom asked. He had driven other equipment on the property, so it wasn't an outlandish request.

"We'll see about that," his father replied. "It might be too much tractor for you."

His father continued on a familiar theme.

"Do you know how much that tractor costs?"

"How much?"

"I paid two thousand dollars for that tractor. It would cost close to seven thousand dollars if it were brand new. You might have to wait until you get a little older before you drive this one."

"That's a lot of money alright."

"Go wash your hands for dinner, boys," Marie called from the kitchen.

An hour later, with leftovers of baked chicken, white rice, and green beans before them, Sam got up from the table and retrieved a second six-pack of beer from the refrigerator. He took one and placed the other five bottles in the middle of the table as he always did. His mood was starting to turn disagreeable as he continued to drink beer after beer, and he broadened the focus of his words to include both the tractor and his wife.

"I should be able to plow our whole farm in five days now," he declared. "That's more work than you do in a month around here," he added, directed at Marie.

"Then maybe you can fix that kitchen door for me, Sam. It still gets stuck every time it rains. It's so much harder to bring the groceries in the front door."

"Goddamn it, Marie! Would you just let me enjoy one thing without your constant complaining?"

"I'm not complaining. It would just be a big help to have the door fixed."

"Well, how about you just clean the dishes and shut your damn mouth for once?"

Timidly, Marie rose and reached for the dinner plates, but, as she did, her husband grabbed her right wrist to keep her from taking his plate away. He twisted it firmly and pulled her face downward and toward him so they were eye to eye.

"I'm not done yet! I'm going to have more chicken and rice. Is that okay with you?"

"Can I watch television?" Tom asked his mother, knowing it was time to move away from his father. Tom and Marie stayed away from Sam when he was drunk.

"Keep the sound down so you don't disturb your father."

Tom moved to the sofa in the living room just fifteen feet away, and Marie retreated into the kitchen to begin cleaning up after the meal. Around 8 p.m., Sam came into the kitchen to the refrigerator for the third six-pack of beer, and Marie held her breath as he did, knowing that these nights usually turned violent. One six-pack of beer made her husband ornery, two six-packs of beer made him pissed off, but three six-packs of beer made him violent. Rarely did three six-pack nights come and go without Marie winding up bruised and bloodied. As he slammed his third six-pack onto the table in the dining room, Marie felt dread wash over her. She hastened her cleaning effort so she could put Tom to bed.

"I'm going to go drive my new tractor around the fields," Sam said thirty minutes after finishing the third six-pack.

"Can I drive it, too?" Tom asked as he scurried into the dining room and followed his father to the kitchen.

As his father moved closer to the kitchen door, Tom pleaded again.

"Can I drive it, too, Dad?"

"Goddamn it, Tom," Sam returned angrily.

Sam turned around quickly and faced his son, slapping him hard across his freckled face as he did—the slap lifted Tom from the floor, and he flew into the wall.

"Didn't I tell you earlier that you're too young to drive this tractor? Why can't anyone listen to me when I speak?"

"How dare you?" Marie cried as she leapt between her son and her husband. "You will not strike our son. Do you hear me? You will not hurt him."

"I will do whatever I damn well please within the walls of this house. This is my home! Don't you ever forget who puts this roof over our heads."

"I won't have it!" she shouted.

In a motion similar to his previous slap, Sam hauled off and slapped Marie across her face, lifting her off the floor and sending her stumbling into the stove. Her face caught the sharp edge of the oven handle and sliced her forehead open. Immediately, her face was bloodied.

"Mom," Tom shrieked when he saw the blood.

Sam walked out the kitchen door without any concern or interest and slammed it behind him, leaving the entirety of his family shaken, bloodied, and cowering on the kitchen floor.

* * *

A few days into the New Year, Tom recounted his memory of his father's final night to me. The image of young Tom and his bloodied mother cowering on the floor after being struck by Sam stayed with me.

"That was the one and only time my father struck me," Tom said. "I know he struck my mother often because I heard her screams at night, and I saw the bruises in the morning. He was a mean and violent man."

His memory of that night started both of us wondering about three questions: Would Marie kill Sam to keep him from hurting Tom, could Marie commit the murder though Sam was significantly larger than her, and finally, and most simply, did she do it?

* * *

Knowing that *The Sentinel* was first published in 1959 as a monthly, I wondered if the issue containing Sam's death was in my archives. In my crowded office, the archives consisted of three file cabinets in a dusty back corner beneath a staircase that contained a sampling of previous issues. It was by no means a complete historical reference library, and, making matters worse, the archives were not even in chronological order. They might have been in order sometime long ago, but at this point, the issues were randomly stuffed in the drawers. I knew it would be dumb luck if a copy of the November 1968 issue was on file, but I rifled through the drawers anyway.

After almost an hour of fending off spiders and dust mites, I found the issue in the drawer marked 1980 – 1985. A few years older than myself, the issue was yellow and crisp but readable just the same. In the middle of the third page, I found the article I had searched for:

Corbett Killed in Tractor Mishap

On Tuesday, October 15, 1968, Samuel Gerard Corbett, the owner of a farm on Misty Hollow Road, took delivery of a used tractor that he purchased from the Jake Thompson Farm in Bucks County. Overcome by excitement, Sam operated his tractor without the proper familiarity to ensure his safety. On the evening of the delivery, Sam fell off his tractor and was crushed by the rear wheel. Alcohol was a factor in his death. His blood alcohol measure was 0.21. Sam died at the scene. The death certificate identified massive internal injuries as the cause of death. Sam leaves behind his grieving widow, Marie, and his seven-year-old son, Thomas. According to Maddie Stover, the widow's best friend, Marie is devastated by the loss. Funeral services will be held on Saturday...

Chapter Forty-Eight

W hile hectic was never an apt description for life in Shelbyville, the holiday season added activities and distractions that altered the town's normal pace and natural rhythms. Throughout the holiday season, annual events like the holiday pie contest, the tree lighting ceremony, and the parade on Main Street produced diversions. Add holiday shopping and out-of-town visitors to the mix and normal routines bent and flexed like garland draped on tree branches.

On the second Monday in January, the crowd at The Bashful Rooster filed into the diner around noon in their usual workweek manner for the first time since the start of the holiday season about twenty days ago. On the whole, the mood seemed light and upbeat amongst the townsfolk because their routines were being restored. Routines were appreciated and honored in Shelbyville.

At 11:51 a.m., Hal Donaldson entered the diner and addressed the police chief, Walt Garrison, already seated at his usual table.

"Damn it, Walt," Hal called out in an agitated manner, "when are we ever going to replace the four-way stop with a traffic light? The line was eleven cars long when I arrived at it last Friday."

"That's horrible," the police chief returned. "You must've felt like you were in Los Angeles? Was there road rage to accompany such a ridiculous wait?"

"That's not funny!" Hal said. "It's time we acknowledge that a traffic light would be more efficient than stop signs and make the change."

"I don't know what to tell you; some people actually prefer the stop signs. They think it's quaint."

"Oh, for God's sake, we're up to our eyeballs in quaint in this little town, and a damn traffic light isn't going to change that!"

"Well," the police chief offered as a conciliatory comment, "maybe it'll finally happen this year. We'll see what the mayor and the city council think when they meet at the end of the month. In the meantime, Happy New Year, Hal."

"Yeah, yeah," Hal mumbled as he headed for his seat.

"Speaking of the New Year," Davy Preston announced to the diner as he rose from his seat. "I want to remind everyone that this year will mark the twenty-fifth anniversary of 'The Pass.' On March 13th, it will be exactly twenty-five years since I threw that perfect pass to Robbie Reynolds so that he could hit the jump shot that won Shelbyville its only state championship."

"Oh, sit down, Davy," someone called from the back of the diner. "You and that damn pass."

"Now, I often hear some of you refer to it as 'The Shot,'" Davy continued in a lighthearted tone, "but I want to remind everyone that without the pass, there is no shot; without the pass, there is no state championship. From now on, I'd appreciate it if you would all refer to it as 'The Pass.'"

"Someone please stick a wad of napkins in his mouth," the same voice in the back called out again.

"Would everyone like to hear me do my beloved reenactment of the announcer's call of 'The Pass' from that game again? I'd be happy to do it for you all right now."

"Sit down, Davy," several diners called out.

"Alright then," Davy said, smiling as he did, "we'll save my beloved reenactment for our anniversary lunch."

Tom and I sat at our usual seats at the counter. Connie poured Tom his usual glass of iced tea.

"I've got a proposition for you," Tom said as Connie placed a lemon wedge on the side of his glass.

"I sure hope you are talking to Nick," Connie responded to Tom, "because the last time you propositioned me, I wound up feeling very unsatisfied."

"Sorry, Connie, I was talking to Nick."

"What's on your mind?" I asked.

"I've decided to build a guesthouse on the northwest corner of the property, and I was hoping you might want to help again. We've done some good work on our previous projects, but this will be a much larger undertaking. We'll start in spring and hopefully finish at the end of summer or early fall."

"Have you ever done anything like this before?"

"Absolutely not!"

"Well then, count me in. What could go wrong?"

"Great. I'm thinking it'll be a small, one-story structure that's about seven or eight hundred square feet. I've already been looking on the Internet for plans to purchase."

"That's encouraging. It'll be the first thing we've done that involves a plan, so that seems like progress right there."

Chapter Forty-Nine

Earl Reynolds and Julia Sanders were the king and queen of the prom at Shelbyville High School in the spring of 1959. Earl was a six foot six inch, two hundred twenty pound basketball, football, and baseball star, and Jules, as her classmates called her, was the captain of the cheerleaders and the star of the senior class production of "Cat on a Hot Tin Roof." Earl was voted "Most Likely to Succeed," and Jules was voted "Most Destined for Stardom." In truth, there was a couple just like them in every high school graduating class in the U.S., but that didn't make them any less of a big deal in little Shelbyville; they were the couple everyone admired. True to script, Earl and Jules married in the spring of 1961 in a beautiful ceremony beside a drawbridge on the Susquehanna River. Shortly thereafter, Earl was appointed the local representative of the Keystone Insurance Company, and Jules sold cosmetics from behind the counter of the local drugstore. It might not have been a fairy tale ending, but the two were happy together.

But, most of the 1960s proved to be a difficult time for the couple as Jules suffered four miscarriages in succession, and husband and wife wondered if they might not be able to have children.

"Maybe it isn't meant to be," they confided in one another.

Before the miscarriages, everyone assumed that Earl and Julia Reynolds's children would be beautiful and talented and gifted and destined to live extraordinary lives. In this part of the country, where farmers meticulously bred livestock to ensure the best possible outcomes, Earl and Jules were the best of the breeding stock; the best this small community had ever produced, so their children would surely be prizewinners. Every time word of another miscarriage circulated, the townsfolk breathed a collective sigh.

Then, on December 25, 1969, Robert Earl Reynolds was born at Shelbyville Hospital, and the whole town celebrated the event like it was the birth of a savior. Two by two, the good people of Shelbyville made their way to the viewing area of the paternity ward to gaze upon the newborn infant, all carrying gifts for the baby, as they'd wanted to do for such a long time. Staring through the viewing window, Robbie lay before them, wrapped snuggly in a white cotton blanket with royal blue stars, oblivious of all the adoration. Late into the night, proud father Earl greeted his neighbors with chocolates, flowers, and cigars and told anyone that would listen that he was the luckiest man on earth. On Christmas day, before the close of the decade, the golden couple regained their luster.

"Jules and I never gave up," Earl boasted as he stood before the viewing window, "and now we have a beautiful son."

* * *

Robbie Reynolds was a sensation from his very first game at Shelbyville High School. He was a natural basketball player, six feet five inches tall, strong, far quicker than most players his size, and able to out-jump much larger opponents. His jump shot was smooth and precise, and his dribbling and passing skills were remarkable. As a freshman, he was in the top ten in the state in scoring and rebounding and was named first team All-State. With just one high school season in the record books, Robbie was one of the most recruited high school players in the nation by top-ranked colleges.

In his second season, Robbie led the Shelbyville Falcons to a 24-5 record and a fourth-place finish in the state championship. He finished in the top five in the state for scoring and rebounding and was again named first team All-State. In Shelbyville, where the basketball team had never previously played in the state tournament, some townsfolk speculated about the possibility of actually winning one. At The Bashful Rooster, few afternoons passed without lengthy conversations about Robbie Reynolds, the Falcon squad, and the team's chances next year.

"Robbie will be the best high school basketball player in the nation next year," his father Earl was quoted as saying in *The Sentinel*, "and he'll only be a junior."

Despite hopes for a state championship, Shelbyville delivered another outstanding season in Robbie's junior year and posted a 26-3 record but settled for a second consecutive fourth place finish in the state tournament. Many newspapers and sporting concerns named Robbie Reynolds the National High School Player of the Year and predicted that Shelbyville would win the state championship in the next season. For the entire off-season at The Bashful Rooster, all conversations about anything other than Robbie Reynolds and Falcon basketball seemed banned as barely a word was spoken on any other subject.

In his much-anticipated senior year, the Falcons got off to a wobbly 3-3 start because two starters were injured, and townsfolk questioned whether this was Shelbyville's year or not. Determined to pick up the slack for his injured teammates, Robbie played the best basketball of his high school career and led the team to twenty-two straight wins while averaging thirty-seven points per game. In the town, the excitement level reached a pitch not experienced since Patrick Collier won the blue ribbon in the Aberdeen Angus category at the state fair a decade earlier. Though many thought it impossible, Robbie had become more legendary than blue ribbon winner Abigail.

During the first ten days of March of 1987, the Shelbyville Falcons easily defeated their first three opponents in the state tournament and made their way to the title game. Robbie scored one hundred thirty-five points in those games and established a new tournament record with a full game still to play. As fate would have it, their opponent in the championship game was Sunnydale High School of Pittsburgh, the same team that eliminated Shelbyville from the last two state tournaments and forced them to settle for fourth place both times. Another twist of fate, the tournament was being played in Pittsburgh, so the game was essentially a home game for Sunnydale. Neither school had ever won a state championship, and both wanted the victory badly.

With almost every resident of Shelbyville in attendance, on March 13, 1987, the two teams met at half court for the tip-off of the championship game. Typical of Robbie, he outjumped the Sunnydale center who was a full four inches taller than him, and tapped the ball to his teammate, Davy Preston, to start the game. Many familiar with the Pennsylvania State Basketball Tournament regarded the next forty-eight minutes as the best state championship game ever played because neither team ever led by more than four points. It was the horseracing equivalent of two great thoroughbreds running the entire length of the race neck and neck, staring one another in the eye with every stride. As fate would have it, it all came down to the final possession.

Barely audible over the frenzied crowd, the announcer called the action on the court during the final fifteen seconds of the game.

"The pass is inbounded to Davy Preston near the half-court line. He dribbles the ball toward the top of the key, allowing the clock to tick down to nine seconds, now eight, now seven. He looks to his right and passes the ball to Robbie Reynolds as he comes off a high pick set by Marvin Kennedy. Reynolds turns as he catches the pass, plants his feet, and rises for a fifteen-foot jump shot. The shot arches toward the basket—it swishes through the net as the buzzer sounds. Shelbyville has won the state title! The Falcons have done it!"

As the ball dropped through the nylon net, securing the state championship for his hometown, Robbie Reynolds had every reason to believe his life would be extraordinary, one of great accomplishments and success. Everyone else believed it.

* * *

There were two hotels in Shelbyville, The Silo Inn, located on the outskirts of town with twenty-three rooms and a bed and breakfast style of accommodation, and The Baxter Hotel, located on Main Street near The Bashful Rooster, with thirty-one rooms and a quaint, small-town style of accommodation. During Robbie Reynolds' senior year at Shelbyville High School, both hotels were booked more than three weeks in advance as college coaches flocked to the little hamlet to watch the small-town sensation. Never before had so many middle-aged men walked the streets of Shelbyville in loud sport coats of their school's colors: bright oranges for Syracuse, Clemson, and Texas, deep purples for Northwestern, Washington, and LSU, reds for USC, Stanford, Alabama, and Louisville, and blues for UCLA, North Carolina, Michigan, and Kentucky. For nine months, the town looked as if it was hosting a convention for either used car salesmen or real estate agents.

A week after the state championship game, Robbie Reynolds announced he'd attend the University of Notre Dame in South Bend, Indiana, in the fall of 1987 and, almost immediately, the two hotels returned to their normal occupancy rates, and the streets of Shelbyville became ordinary and less colorful again. True to *The Sentinel's* small-town roots, the paper's front page proclaimed, "Robbie Selects Notre Dame." And during the first three weeks of April 1987, much to the dismay of the manager of the Notre Dame bookstore, baseball caps with the "ND" logo suddenly sold out, with the majority being shipped to Shelbyville, PA. The small town's love and admiration for their hardwood hero weren't going to end because he was going to college in another state.

By the time the Notre Dame Fighting Irish opened their season against their cross state rival, Butler University, Robbie had secured a position as a starter, and the Irish faithful were elated that the most sought-after high school prospect in the nation was playing for their school. In the first game of the season, Robbie demonstrated his remarkable prowess as he led the team to a win over their rival, scoring twenty-five points and grabbing eleven rebounds as he did. He made the transition from high school to college with relative ease and still stood out as exceptional when compared to any of the other players on the court. When the buzzer sounded ending his college debut, the speculation over whether he would be named a first team All-American as a freshman began in earnest. In familiar territory, Robbie was, once again, a freshman sensation.

When mid-season rolled around, the Fighting Irish had posted a record of 13-1, and Robbie Reynolds was fifth in the nation in scoring with an average of twenty-seven points per game. His nickname from high school, "Train," had been co-opted by Fighting Irish fans, and they howled, "Choo-Choo" periodically throughout games, especially after his baskets. Around campus, Robbie was recognized and treated as a celebrity everywhere he went, particularly at fraternity events and campus parties. Robbie never purchased any pints for himself in the campus pub and always left a couple of full pints on the table when he departed; he simply couldn't drink all the beers that students sent his way. He was doing well in his schoolwork, carrying a double major in economics and marketing while earning a 3.7 grade point average. His girlfriend from high school, Christie Logan, a petite, blue-eyed blonde who was majoring in chemistry, also attended the university, and the two high school sweethearts had continued their relationship at college. True to form, Robbie's life was progressing exactly as expected.

In early March, with the NCAA tournament fast approaching, a television newswoman from a South Bend station interviewed Robbie after practice one afternoon. Standing beneath the scoreboard on the practice court, wearing a light gray practice jersey darkened by sweat in the chest area, Robbie towered over the much shorter woman by so much that she held the mic above her head whenever he spoke.

"You've had an incredible freshman season," the newswoman said at the start of the interview. "How excited are you to play in your first NCAA tournament?"

"I can't wait," Robbie replied, smiling like a kid who got everything he wanted for Christmas. "As a young kid shooting hoops in our backyard in Shelbyville, playing in the NCAA tournament was always the ultimate dream."

"Are you dreaming about a national title?"

"No, not at all. What we do as a team is go out onto the court every night and try to win every game. It is one game at a time. We'll see how far that takes us."

"What do you think of this new tradition where the fans chant "Choo Choo" as support after you score? It sure has caught on."

"It's great. I'm so thrilled to walk onto the court every night and play in front of such a large and enthusiastic crowd—they make it a lot of fun for me."

Favored by eleven points in the first round of the tournament, the Notre Dame Fighting Irish met the Dayton Flyers on a Thursday night in Tucson, AZ. With seven minutes remaining in the first half, the Irish led their opponent by a score of 27-23 when Robbie leapt high above the rim in pursuit of a defensive rebound. Surrounded by three Flyers, Robbie secured the ball but landed with his foot awkwardly atop the foot of one of his opponents, and his right knee bent in a way that the human knee was never intended to bend. It violently jutted to the right and severely tore the cartilage within. In agony, Robbie slumped onto the hardwood floor.

Immediately, the medical staff rushed to his aid. As the trainer examined his right knee, the grimace on Robbie's face told the whole story because he knew his injury was serious; he knew it would be a long time before he played again. His face showed both the pain and the heartbreak of the injury. It was so quiet in the large arena that a cough echoed through the building. A few minutes later, the stunned crowd was silent as he left the court on a motorized cart. Several surgeries followed as well as months of rehabilitation, but Robbie never played in another college basketball game. Like shooting stars in the night sky above, Robbie flashed brilliantly for a while but burned out in an instant.

Chapter Fifty

"I've got some interesting news," I called out to Tom as he walked into *The Sentinel* office one afternoon.

"Good news, I hope," Tom said as he sat in the wooden chair beside my desk.

In the 1960s, the large farm west of the Corbett property was referred to as The Stover Farm because it was owned and operated by Fred and Madelyn Stover, who grew mostly potatoes on more than seven hundred acres. It was a beautiful expanse of land and the location of the silo that Marie once painted where the sun set behind it in July like Stonehenge. In subsequent years, the farm was passed down through their family to their grandchild, Heather White, who now operated it as both dairy and farmland with her husband, Peter, under the moniker of The White Bridge Farm. Until a few days ago while talking with a group of men at The Rooster, I hadn't made a significant family connection. Having returned to Shelbyville just four years ago, I didn't know the lineage.

"Do you remember that article from *The Sentinel* about your father's death that I showed you a while back?"

"Of course, I remember it. I may be older than you, but I'm not senile."

"The article referred to a woman named Maddie Stover as your mother's best friend at the time. It even quoted her."

"I remember that."

"Well, Maddie is seventy-seven years old and lives with her granddaughter on The White Bridge Farm. She still lives here in Shelbyville. From your front porch to her front door is about two miles at most."

"I've got to speak with her."

"You do."

"Do you want to come with me?"

"I'd like to, but I think she'll be more forthcoming in a conversation that's just between the two of you."

"Yeah, you're probably right. I'll talk to her alone."

* * *

Madelyn Grace Stover was a relic from another time and place. Maddie was born in Oklahoma in 1935—in the midst of the Dust Bowl and the Great Depression—at a time when struggle or perish was the norm. Though too young to remember the hardships, she heard stories about her family's struggles every day as a child, and those admonitions influenced her character and values. In her entire life, she never purchased an indulgence or wasted an ounce of anything. Even as a young woman, she never wore makeup or perfume, never applied lotions or body oils, and never wore lacy undergarments or frilly dresses. At this late stage in life, the things that Maddie held dear to her heart were unchanged: family, community, hard work, clean living, and belief in God and country. In retrospect, the framework of her entire life was fixed on that bleak day when she was born in a three-room shack on the desolate plains of the Sooner State. Sitting before Tom, with her warm smile, weary eyes, and loose skin on her forearms that resembled tanned leather, she was happy to learn that he was the son of her dear friend, Marie Corbett, with whom she conversed at the kitchen table on many afternoons so many years ago.

"Your mother was so warm and welcoming," Maddie remarked as they began their chat. "We talked over coffee on the coldest Pennsylvania afternoons, and I forgot all about the bone chilling temperatures outside."

On another cold Pennsylvania afternoon in early March, Tom and Maddie sat beside a roaring fireplace in the great room of what was now her grandchild's house. Despite her advanced age, there was nothing frail or feeble about Maddie, and she was still active on the family farm. At 6 a.m. that morning, Maddie braved subfreezing temperatures and snowflakes to feed the chickens and collect a dozen eggs for breakfast. Though life on a farm had always been strenuous and not always recompensing, she'd never considered any other life. Farm life was all she knew.

"How would you describe my father?" Tom asked.

"Not so warm and welcoming!" she said, grimacing at the recollection. "Your father was not a nice man."

"I remember that he hit my mother often."

"Your father had a real meanness inside of him. I don't know what put it there, but he had it. More often than not, when I visited Marie, she was bruised."

"Do you know how my parents met?"

"I do, but it's not a pleasant story."

"I want to hear it anyway, Maddie."

"Some couples have sweet stories about how they met—this isn't one of those stories," the old woman warned him. "This is a story of mistreatment and abuse."

"Please don't hold anything back. I need to know the truth."

"While your mother attended college," she began, reluctance slowing the tempo of her initial words, "she had a handful of students that she taught piano on weekends. After she graduated, the parents of one of those students asked Marie to find an inexpensive upright piano for their family. Coincidentally, Sam did some work for a farmer who couldn't pay him, and he took their piano as settlement of the debt. Sam placed an ad in the newspaper to sell the piano and Marie responded. It was hardly love at first sight, but Sam asked Marie to dinner, and she accepted. After dinner, Sam and Marie had sex in his pickup truck. Marie told me she didn't believe in sex before marriage, but Sam insisted. She said he forced himself on her."

"You mean he raped her?" Tom asked indignantly.

"Your mother never used that word, but that is what I saw in her eyes. I saw a lot of anguish."

"That son of a bitch!"

"It was a case of a lamb wandering into the path of a wolf. He showed her no mercy or decency."

"Why did she marry him?" Tom asked, bewilderment in his voice.

"You must understand that in 1960, women were basically second-class citizens. It was not like today. Marie couldn't report the rape, she couldn't go forward as an unwed mother, she couldn't be a single parent, and so she had to marry Sam. It was as simple as that."

"All those years, she must've hated him."

"She described their marriage as tolerable for the first two years but very difficult after that. His drinking and violent temper got worse with each year that passed."

"How could such a good person suffer such a fate?"

"This world is not a fair place. A lot of bad happens to very good people. But, your mother sure loved you—that was never in question, and I'm sure you know that."

"I know."

For several minutes, Maddie and Tom sat in silence, and she reached over to grasp Tom's right hand. He smiled as she held it because he knew she was a good friend to his mother during a difficult time. He was comforted by the fact that his mother had such a friend. Maddie smiled also, as she remembered the young boy who scurried about the home as she and Marie conversed and how much her friend loved that small child. She found comfort in sitting with the small boy who had grown to be such a good man so many years later. Maddie saw a lot of her friend in Tom.

"I have to ask one more question before I leave," Tom asked, breaking a long but very comfortable silence.

"What is it, dear?"

"Do you think my mother could have killed my father?"

Startled, Maddie's head rocked backward.

"Honestly, in all these years," she answered after a moment, "I never considered that possibility. At the time, the reports said Sam was drunk and fell off his tractor, so I never questioned it. I had no reason to—it seemed reasonable. I don't think anyone questioned it. I guess all I can say about that now is that if Marie killed Sam, he made her do it. Your mother was a smart woman, and if she felt that the situation was a matter of life or death, she would've protected herself and you. She would never let him hurt you."

"My Uncle Carl questioned it."

Her face grimaced. Her brow V'ed.

"Oh dear God," Maddie replied, "please don't get me started on that horrible man."

Chapter Fifty-One

Honk! Honk!

Alerted by two sharp blasts of a horn one evening long after dark, Tom opened his front door and saw a man standing between the headlights of a 1936 Ford pickup truck with the engine off and a shotgun in his hands. In the glare of the headlights, the man was a shadowy silhouette and unrecognizable, but the shotgun was unmistakable; the shadow of the barrel was exaggerated by the headlights and spanned the front of the house. Concerned, Tom remained in the doorframe and called out to the stranger.

"What are you doing in front of my house with a shotgun, mister?"

"I carry it for protection," the stranger said. "I didn't come to harm you."

As he spoke, the stranger's voice quivered and unwittingly conveyed to Tom the fact that he was much older than him. The apparent frailty in his words lessened his menacing presence. Tom wasn't emboldened but less threatened.

"If you want to talk to me," Tom told him, "you're going to have to put that shotgun down."

Reluctantly, the stranger placed the butt of the gun on the dirt beside him and rested the barrel alongside one of the large headlights. In the doorway, Tom breathed a silent sigh of relief.

"Who are you?" Tom demanded.

"My name is Calvin Purdy, and I was a friend of Carl Corbett."

Calvin was a mechanic by trade who worked at the local filling station for almost thirty years until he retired five years ago at the age of seventy-two. A wanderer and loner in 1967, he drifted into Shelbyville with a tin of Tiger (chewing tobacco), a switchblade knife, and nineteen singles in his pocket. When asked where he hailed from, Calvin always answered, "Here, there, and everywhere, but never long enough to be known." He lived in a small residence near the railroad tracks that housed the station agent while the Penn Express stopped there. A large man during his prime, Calvin withered considerably with the graying and walked slumped slightly forward.

"Carl was my uncle," Tom said.

"I know who you are," Calvin returned.

"What can I do for you, Calvin?" Tom asked, trying to ease the tension by personalizing his words.

"I came here to speak for Carl because he cannot speak for his self anymore."

"I'd like to hear what you have to say. Would you like to come inside my house for a while? You'll have to leave the shotgun there."

"I'm fine right here."

"I understand Carl did not like my mother."

"Carl hated Marie. He always said she thought she was better than the rest of the family. She was all educated and such. He didn't like her fancy talk."

"Marie was an intelligent woman."

"Marie was an uppity bitch who wouldn't mind her man."

The remark offended Tom, but he wanted to hear what the stranger had to say. He bit his tongue and responded.

"Well, we are obviously not going to be friends, Mr. Purdy, so why don't you speak your mind and then leave."

"Carl told me more than a hundred times that Sam did not fall off the tractor. It was no accident. It was murder. He said it wasn't possible to fall under the back wheel that way."

"The police chief and the coroner said it was possible. They said he was too drunk to operate the tractor safely."

"They didn't like Sam, that's all. Sam could drink twenty shots of whiskey at Finley's Tavern and still drive home just fine. He could handle his booze."

"I'd say it was the other way around—booze sure handled Sam Corbett. It made him mean and ornery."

"Now, there you go. Folks said you have been badmouthing Carl and Sam around town. You may be their relation, but you need to stop saying those lies right now. I won't have none of it. Carl Corbett was my only friend."

"Sounds like you came here to threaten me after all."

"You just remember, Tom Corbett, a life sentence don't mean diddly to a man almost eighty years old."

"You'd better leave and don't come back."

Resembling slow motion, Calvin picked up his shotgun, walked to the door of his pickup truck, climbed behind the wheel, and turned the key to start the engine. It cranked a bit and finally turned over, and Calvin drove sluggishly away, so slowly that barely any dust rose in its tracks. The old truck glided across the driveway like a memory across a mind. Still standing in the doorframe, Tom realized that he didn't even know what Calvin Purdy looked like; on this moonless night, he never saw the face of his late-night visitor. In many ways, Calvin was just a disquieted ghost from the past.

Chapter Fifty-Two

Spring is the season of renewal, when flowers and leaves burst upon plants and trees that wilted only months ago. The monochrome days of winter are in the past as resplendent colors emerge and transform the landscape from bleak and barren to vibrant and alive. Reds, yellows, greens, and purples return in abundance as millions of flowers speckle the fields and roadsides, bringing with them the promise of warmer days and bluer skies. The time has come for all who endured winter captivity to embrace their newfound freedom by frolicking outdoors.

Unfortunately for Tom and me, complications from the past in the form of unanswered questions and unfortunate choices followed us like gray clouds into the bright new season. From my own experience, the past resided in memory in two forms: warm and pleasurable memories that felt like summer and cold and troublesome memories that felt like winter. At that time, my mind felt much more like December than May. In the spring of 2012, the winter thaw was prolonged.

Chapter Fifty-Three

"Goddamn it," Milt said as he entered The Bashful Rooster, grabbed a fistful of napkins off a nearby table, and vigorously wiped his left shoulder. "The little bastard is back!"

"How can you possibly know it is the same bird, Milt?" Chet called out from his table near the window.

"It's him alright," Milt continued angrily, his face reddening as he did. "I recognize his beady black eyes, the smirk of his beak, and the arrogant way he sits atop the bank building. It's the little winged bastard alright."

"Well, Milt," Chet replied, laughing as he did, "I guess the little guy missed you so much that he returned to Shelbyville from his winter home in Florida."

"As soon as I stepped out of the front door of my store, he swooped down at me like a Kamikaze pilot on a mission."

"Looks like you'll have to resort to your alternative route again and avoid him altogether."

"I know," Milt replied glumly, his tone mellowed, resigned to the detour and defeat at the talons of his little opponent.

"Hey, Milt," the police chief called from his table with the mayor, "don't forget what I told you about retaliation last year. You can't discharge a shotgun in town."

"Don't worry," Milt returned. "At this point, I wouldn't dare fire a shotgun at that crazy little bird. I am afraid of what he might do in retaliation."

"He might eat some really spicy food before he poops on you next time," Chet warned his friend.

"Or," the police chief added, "he could round up a flock of his little friends and run you out of town."

"It's not funny," Milt shot back, "that little bird is making my life miserable. You better hope one of those birds doesn't set his sights on you."

Weary of the counter, Tom and I relocated our usual spot in The Rooster to a table beside the dessert case, which meant we stared at fresh-baked pies and tall layer cakes as we waited, making us all the more susceptible to the lure of the baked goods. A local widow named Kathy Gabriel made the desserts for the diner, and each one was quite tempting in its own gooey or flakey or creamy decadence. We'd each added an inch or so to our normally trim waistlines and three or four dollars to our meal tabs in this location. As he lifted his fork of chocolate crème pie to his mouth, Tom insisted we'd burn off these calories once we started building the guesthouse.

"We've got five months of hard labor ahead of us once we start," he said as he licked the excess chocolate from his fork. "Get yourself a slice of something."

Barely prodded, I asked Connie for a slice of berry pie. After all, I didn't want to be weak and depleted on the work site.

That afternoon, Tom and I spent an hour discussing the tools, building materials, and supplies we would need because we hoped to break ground in the next few days. Over the course of the meal and dessert, we compiled a lengthy shopping list to fill at the hardware store up the street, one that would require both our trucks to transport it all. Around 2 p.m., Tom and I were the only customers remaining in our section of the diner, and I redirected our conversation to a matter that had been on my mind lately, one that was more than forty years old.

"I've been thinking about the night your father died."

"How so?"

"I've been putting the pieces together and trying to develop a theory of what might have happened. My biggest dilemma is whether Marie would have been physically up to the task of killing Sam? If she did it, I think she outwitted him in some way."

"So, what have you come up with?"

"Well, we know Sam was very drunk that night, and he struck both you and Marie."

"He struck me when I asked if I could drive the tractor, and then he struck my mother when she came to my defense."

"And then Sam stormed out the kitchen door to go out into the field to drive his new tractor."

"That's correct."

"When you and your mom were still in the kitchen, was she upset that Sam struck you?"

"She was livid. She said it would never happen again."

"That's interesting. You never told me that before."

"She said it in a very determined way."

"Now, Marie was half the size of Sam, so we know she didn't overpower him in any way."

"That's a given. My father was six feet two inches tall and weighed about two hundred twenty pounds, while my mother was five feet four inches tall and weighed about one hundred twenty-five pounds. He had the sturdy build of a farmhand, and she had the diminutive build of a piano teacher. Physically, she was no match for him."

"But she knew how to drive the tractor, right?"

"Yes, she did."

"Here's what I think happened," I began, leaning forward in my chair. "If Marie killed Sam, I think she took a large metal flashlight and followed him out to the field where he was driving the tractor. She shined the light at him so he'd stop the tractor, and then she told him it was late and he should come inside. When Sam got down off the tractor, Marie shined the light under the tractor and told him that something looked broken or dented or something to that effect. She created some reason for him to look under the tractor. Naturally, Sam got down on his knees to inspect his new tractor, and, when he did, she struck him on the back of his head with the metal flashlight. With Sam unconscious beneath the large wheels of the tractor, Marie climbed up into the operator's position and drove the tractor forward over his body. She may have even backed over him a second time to make sure he was dead."

"He was so drunk that a good wallop to his head would have knocked him unconscious and allowed her to drive over him."

"The more I think about it, Tom, the more I think that Marie outsmarted Sam and killed him."

"My mother was very smart."

"I know."

"And, I think she was adamant that she would never let him harm me again, or her for that matter. I think she'd reached her limit. When my father hit me, he crossed the line."

"I think so, too."

"I've thought a lot about that night also," Tom confided, "and do you know what I find particularly interesting?"

"What?"

"Your theory about that night matches my theory exactly, right down to the details about my mother shining the flashlight under the tractor, telling him she sees a problem and then striking him on the back of the head."

"The scenario fits the facts that we know."

"It does."

"In your mind, have you taken our theories any further?"

"What do you mean?"

"If we are right," I said, "Sam has blunt force trauma on the back of his skull. He will, most likely, have a small fracture on his skull."

"That's not necessarily true," Tom objected. "She could've knocked him unconscious without fracturing his skull."

"But Sam was her drunken, violent abuser," I offered in firm rebuttal. "Marie knew that if she was going to hit him over the head, she'd better knock him out, or else he'd beat her severely, or even kill her. If we're right and she hit him over the head, she hit him with all her might. She slammed his head with that flashlight. His skull will be fractured."

"So, where are you going with this?" Tom asked.

"If you exhume his body and the medical examiner finds blunt-force trauma on his skull, we'll know Marie killed him."

"But, to do that, I must accuse my mother of murder and dig my father up from his grave."

"Oh, I recognize the difficulty of this course of action."

"And, to what end? They are both dead. My father has been dead for forty years."

"The truth," I said. "As a journalist, I believe in the truth. And you, my friend, need to know the truth."

We both sat quietly for a few minutes while Tom absorbed the serious implications of our conversation. His expression revealed shock and confusion like he'd just seen a ghost or expected to be visited by one. My suggestion actually required him to disturb two ghosts—his deceased mother and his deceased father—one with an accusation of murder and the other with a backhoe. In an attempt to ease his overwrought mind, I stated the obvious.

"The good news is that Sam isn't going anywhere. He has been in that same spot for four decades, and we know where to find him. You don't have to decide this right now."

"I know. I've got to give this a lot of thought."

Chapter Fifty-Four

Probably the most scenic swath of the forty acres, the northwest corner of the farm was a small piece of rural paradise. On an acre or so of land, an unhurried stream flowed beside a spattering of fifteen birch trees with peeling, paper-like white bark shards and translucent yellow leaves, and the view to the west in the summer was of sunsets over the silo that Marie loved so much. The land was mostly flat with one modest rise where Tom had sited the guesthouse. With a wood deck planned for the west side of the structure, Tom knew his mother would have loved the location. He could envision Marie on the deck with her palette and easel in mid-July, contentedly painting the evening away as the orange sun slipped slowly downward in the sky towards her beloved silo. He intended to create a peaceful idyllic place the likes of which the farm had never known.

When I arrived at the farm in early morning, Tom had already positioned the excavator at the work site. An excavator was a tractor with tank-like treads for mobility and a large arched arm and claw for digging and trenching; in profile, its silhouette was reminiscent of some prehistoric creature that roamed the fields millions of years ago and died out because it was too dumb and clumsy to survive all this time. The attached claw had steel fingers to rip into the earth and a bucket shape for removing the loose soil. As I walked across the open field, I glimpsed the excavator for the first time.

"That beast looks up to the task," I said as I approached Tom and the yellow earthmover he rented for the day.

"Did you think we'd do this job with a couple of shovels?"

"Well, no," I responded, marveling at the brutish nature of the machine, "but I also didn't expect something that looks like it dredged the Erie Canal either."

"It's the right tool for the job," Tom advised me, grinning from ear to ear like a kid with a brand-new toy.

"We could dig a swimming pool while we're at it."

"Let's just focus on the guesthouse for now."

With kite string and wood stakes, Tom and I mapped out the areas that would be dug up, consisting of a forty by twenty-foot area for the guesthouse foundation, a three by fifteen-foot area for the septic tank, and a one hundred twenty foot trench for water pipes from the well to the build site. A popping sound and a small black cloud of smoke came from the engine compartment as Tom started the excavator and steered the mammoth machine toward the guest-house stakes. Maneuvering the levers in front of him, Tom raised the steel arm upward to the yoga position equivalent of upward facing elephant trunk and then guided it downward into the soil to officially break ground on our project. With a few jerky movements of the arm's bucket, Tom removed the first load of rich, brown dirt from the foundation. Remaining a safe distance from Tom's erratic piloting of the big yellow machine, I moved in and out of the expanding hole with a shovel and cleaned up the loose soil. Just in time for a late lunch, we finished the excavation of the guesthouse around 2 p.m. and walked to the farmhouse before we moved on to the well and septic tank.

"You know," Tom said as we put together a couple of turkey sand-wiches in the kitchen, "maybe you should bring some clothes and set yourself up in one of the extra bedrooms while we work on this project. It'll save you a lot of trips to town."

"That's a good idea," I replied, "particularly during the off-weeks when I don't publish *The Sentinel*. We'll be able to start early and put in productive days."

"There are three extra bedrooms—take your pick."

By the time we started the final task of the day, the large hole for the septic tank, Tom and I were quite proficient with the excavator and shovels; frankly, we were trained and ready for backup careers as gravediggers. In less than an hour, we carved out a perfect five-foot-deep rectangle that looked like a cemetery plot for either a very tall man or a giraffe. The walls of the hole were straight and smooth, and the corners were as tight as a well-made army bunk. After I turned off the excavator, Tom called out to me from within the grave.

"Hey, climb down in here and take a look at this."

Standing beside Tom in the hole, he pointed to an irregularity in the south wall of our hole that looked like the jawline of a large animal with five jagged teeth and a nostril. The jaw extended about two feet before it reached the corner of the rectangle, so the remainder of the skull was still buried beneath four feet of dirt. Together, we tried to imagine what the rest of the skull would look like and decided that it must be about four feet long. We also concluded that it was at least three or four times larger than the skull of any bear or large cat that roamed central Pennsylvania.

"What the hell is it?" Tom asked me, his fascination with his discovery on clear display.

I shrugged.

"I've no idea," I said. "You're the expert on old stuff."

"That may be true, but only the last few centuries. This thing could be millions of years old."

"It's too large to be anything in the modern era. I think we're looking at something that dates back to the dinosaurs."

Tom ran his fingers along its jagged teeth. "Whatever it was, it definitely killed its dinners."

"I think our project just got bigger."

"You're right about that. We've got to unearth this thing."

"Don't you think this is a job for paleontologists?"

"Have we ever let the fact that we know nothing about the work keep us from taking it on?"

"Not yet."

"And we're not going to start now. When you go to town to get your clothes, go to the hardware store and get us some small picks, chisels, paintbrushes, and anything else you think might be useful in unearthing this creature. Try to think like Indiana Jones."

"You know, Tom, once we get the skull unearthed and visible, I know a guy at the museum in Philadelphia that would surely come out and tell us what we've got here. He's an expert in the field, and I know he'd come all this way just to see it."

"Give him a call. Tell him we'll need about two weeks to have it ready for him."

* * *

In actuality, it took twenty-nine days. In that time, we built the molds, poured the foundation for the guesthouse, constructed the framing of the exterior walls and roof, and selected contractors to install the plumbing and electrical wiring. Three weeks into the work, the shape of the guesthouse emerged onto the landscape, and it was a good fit in its surroundings. In our free time, we ran extension cords from the farmhouse to the work site and set up large spotlights that lit our paleontological dig after dark. Each night, we both worked to unearth the skull by clearing away the four feet of dirt above it and then delicately chipping the attached sediment away and gently dusting with paintbrushes. As the massive skull emerged in what was previously the wall of the septic trench, we named our dinosaur Digby after the founder of Shelbyville, Digby Morton. During our many hours in the grave-like setting with the large reptile, we both found ourselves talking to him whenever we were alone. As it turned out, Digby was a wise old soul and a very good listener.

As I chiseled away at the hardened sediment each night, I told Digby about Chelsea. I told him about her adorable accent, brilliant smile, bright blue eyes, and how she often played music and danced about the kitchen while she prepared dinner. I told him that it always made me happy to see her so happy. In his eye sockets, I saw skepticism because he doubted that anyone could be as wonderful as I described her. I told him about how I first met Chelsea at the Fenwick Prize awards ceremony; again, he was skeptical about my story. From his empty look, it was obvious that Digby didn't believe in love at first sight or subjective awards. I also told him about Officer Maxwell and how my publication of a ten-year-old photograph cost the young family man his life. I told him about the officer's widow and his two young girls. Though it made us both a little sad, I told him all about that time in my life.

For twenty-nine days, I confided in Digby in the same way that most people confided in therapists, and, for some inexplicable reason, it was cathartic for me. Digby had been dead for millions of years, but I still enjoyed talking to him. Every night when I climbed out of that hole, I felt a little better, a little lighter. Sometimes, I guess it helps just to say things out loud.

Chapter Fifty-Five

A former professor at Cambridge University as well as an advisor to several distinguished museums, August Reese was widely regarded as the most knowledgeable and respected archeologist and paleontologist in the world. At sixty-three years of age, he regularly traveled to elite universities to lecture and host symposia about our world during prehistoric times. Augie, as friends and colleagues knew him, was the driving force behind the founding of the Woodbury Museum of Natural History in Philadelphia in the 1980s, where he still played an active role in the curating of exhibitions. In its most popular attraction, the museum housed one of the largest and most complete collections of dinosaurs on the planet with more than seventy on exhibit.

"The irony of my current stage of life," Augie was quoted as saying in a recently published feature article, "is that I have become a modern version of the dinosaurs that I spent my whole life studying; done with all the adapting that I am capable of, I'm at the mercy of the harsh world and my own mortality. The truth is I am much more interested in the world that existed two hundred million years ago than the one I live in today."

More than a decade ago, I met Augie while writing an article about a new dinosaur exhibit at the Woodbury. Grateful for a decent assignment, I did my research and read all the available literature about this legendary guru of the prehistoric community. While I expected a snooty university professor, I was quite surprised when he turned out to be one of the most fascinating characters I'd ever met. Augie was engaging and animated, and, by the time we finished the interview, he had me wishing that I'd majored in paleontology and worked alongside him in the fossil fields of Wyoming. Augie made the paleontological sites seem like the most glamorous place for a young, industrious man to make a name for himself—just as he did. He made it both cool and relevant when he spoke of stuff millions of years old.

With great anticipation, Tom and I sat on the front porch in the late afternoon, waiting for this world-renowned expert on dinosaurs and all things prehistoric to arrive.

True to my memory of him, Augie made a grand entrance, motoring up to the front porch of the farmhouse in a battered Land Rover that looked like it had logged a million miles on the plains of Africa with its rooftop luggage rack full of trunks and equipment. When he lowered himself from the passenger seat onto the familiar terrain of the dirt driveway, the esteemed paleontologist was wearing a tan, long sleeve shirt, khaki shorts, hiking boots, and pith helmet, attire more suitable for an elephant hunt in Zimbabwe than a farm in Shelbyville. Like an entourage for a rock star, a curator from the museum and three eager young students accompanied him.

"Nicholas, my good man," Augie called out in his staunch Massachusetts accent. "It's good to see you again. I have to tell you that I knew there was a Fenwick in your future when we did that interview a decade ago. I wasn't surprised when I heard the news."

"That's so nice of you to say," I said as I greeted him with a handshake. He had a royal heir quality that made even the most formal hug seem wildly inappropriate.

I introduced Tom, and we led the small contingent across the grassy field to the guesthouse.

"Oh, my gracious!" Augie exclaimed as he looked down at the skull, now about three-quarters exposed as it protruded from the south wall of the hole. "That is one fine looking allosaurus, and it roamed the earth about one hundred fifty million years ago."

"One hundred fifty million years ago," Tom said, echoing the professor's words with much more wonder in his voice. "That is almost incomprehensible."

"He lived during the Jurassic period," one of the students added, "and was one of the most feared hunters of his day."

"Go on, Patricia," the professor urged his disciple, "tell our friends a little bit about their find."

"Well," the twenty-two year old in black onyx-rimmed glasses and white cotton blouse continued, "judging by the length of its head, which appears to be approximately fifty inches, this specimen was a mature allosaurus, so its body was thirty to forty feet in length from the tip of its snout to the tip of its tail. That large head would have had small horns above the eyes and would have been mounted on a short neck. It had large, powerful hind legs and was bipedal, meaning it moved about on its two back legs. Its forelimbs were small with three fingers, and its tail was long, muscular, and heavy to balance itself while it walked or ran. It was a fierce predator with razor-sharp teeth, and it hunted other dinosaurs, everything from large herbivorous dinosaurs to other predators to another allosaurus. It was at the top of the food chain, and some believe that the allosaurus even, on occasion, hunted in packs with other allosaurus. Few dinosaurs stood a chance against a hungry allosaurus so a hunt by a group would have been indefensible. Your dinosaur was the badass of its day."

"Forty feet long," I said. "That means the tail could extend all the way to those birch trees."

"It sure could," the student confirmed.

"Well done, Patricia," Augie said. "Your description of the specimen was perfect."

"We've named him Digby," Tom advised them.

"I did the same thing at our sites," Augie informed us. "The alphanumeric identifiers were simply too impersonal for me, so I named them. My first excavation was a brontosaurus that I named Bessie. She's the first dinosaur you see when you enter the Woodbury."

Two of the students climbed into the hole for a better look at the skull, and, shortly thereafter, Professor Reese dropped to his knees and climbed into the hole beside them. They ran their hands along the snout and jawline and remarked to one another about the pristine condition of the remains. They were all familiar with dinosaur bones, and still, they seemed gleeful to be standing before another specimen; even Professor Reese, who'd worked with dinosaur fossils for forty years, had a child-like joy in his face. In their field, a new discovery is a very good day.

Augie climbed out of the hole.

"Gentlemen," he said, "this specimen is a remarkable find, and our museum is interested in acquiring the rights to these fossils."

"Wait a minute," Tom protested, "we didn't invite you here to sell the bones. We only wanted your help identifying it. Nick said you would want to see it."

"I am thrilled to view it, but the entire specimen belongs in a museum. It is a historical artifact."

"I won't let you dig it up and put it on display so people can gawk at it," Tom stated. "These bones have been here for millions of years, and I won't allow you to disturb them. Digby is staying right here."

"Are you going to leave the fossils in the ground?" Augie asked, confused by Tom's reaction.

"That's exactly right," Tom said. "We're going to respect the sanctity of a grave. Graves are hallowed ground."

"But Thomas, I can arrange for a significant payment from the museum for the rights to this specimen," the professor shot back as an inducement, "something around the one million dollar mark."

"I'm not interested."

"Please be reasonable," Augie pleaded. "At least let me send out a team with ground penetrating radar equipment so we can see what we've got here."

"Absolutely not."

"Nicholas, help me out here. Can you talk some sense into your friend?"

"It's his land and his dinosaur," I told Augie flatly.

Tom's curt response to Angie alerted me that the prospect of exhuming his father's remains weighed more heavily on his mind than I realized. Since our conversation in the diner a month ago, Tom and I had not revisited the issue. Listening to him, it seemed this dinosaur had become a proxy for his deceased father. He was resisting this exhumation as validation of his reluctance to exhume his father. In his mind, Tom had created an unequivocal opposition to any sort of digging up the past, regardless of whether it affected human beings or dinosaurs.

"Please stay for as long as you like," Tom told the professor and his entourage, "but I have work to do in the house."

With that said, Tom turned and walked off in the direction of the farmhouse and left us all behind. As he did, his shoulders were hunched like he was carrying a lot of weight.

"Is there anything you can do to persuade your friend?" Augie asked me minutes later when Tom reached the front door.

"Tom is going through a difficult period right now," I said as an intentionally vague response to his question. "He is dealing with a lot of complicated history pertaining to this farm—it's been in his family for nearly a century. Without revealing anything of a personal nature, I'll only tell you that the past is weighing heavily on his mind, and it seems like he has integrated this dinosaur into an existing family tragedy. He needs some time to sort it all out."

"Is there anything we can do to help him?" Augie asked.

"You need to back off and let him deal with his family issues. We can talk again later in the summer, and I'll let you know if he has changed his mind."

"Will you help him understand the significance of this find?"

"I will."

"You've been to our museum, Nicholas. You know we will provide an excellent home for Digby."

Chapter Fifty-Six

In the San Antonio Airport terminal of Equatorial Airlines, two federal agents in dark suits waited amongst passengers bound for Caracas, Venezuela. Two hours earlier, when Shannon Corbett and Martin Hastings boarded a plane in Philadelphia, their impromptu air travel caught the feds off guard, resulting in a scramble to obtain arrest warrants. Two days earlier, the partners were tipped off that their names were making their way onto the subject line of warrants, and, unnerved, they hastily made plans to flee the country. When Shannon and Martin reached the gate, looking like they had eaten an awful lot of airline food during their flight, the two agents approached them.

"Shannon Corbett and Martin Hastings," the senior agent announced with his credentials displayed. "I am placing you under arrest for violations of the Securities Exchange Act of 1934, and I have court orders in my possession to facilitate your extradition back to the state of Pennsylvania."

As the two suspects were patted down, the same agent recited the Miranda rights statement and asked if they understood their rights. In agitated tones, both declared, "Yes," with Shannon adding, "goddamn it," to her affirmation. During this time, all boarding activities ceased as even the airline employees watched the federal agents at work.

Inside the airport security office, Shannon was perspiring profusely and couldn't bear her overheated condition any longer—heat generated and retained by a thick layer of one hundred dollar bills taped to her body. Knowing the agents were aware of the stash, discovered during their pat-down at the gate, she asked if the hand-cuffs could be temporarily removed so she could remove the one hundred thousand dollars of currency causing her discomfort. In a similarly bloated and overheated condition, Martin had almost two hundred thousand dollars strapped around his torso and thighs.

"Sorry, lady," the agent said, directing her into the cell. "You're going to have to wait until we can get a female security officer to unload it for you. I can't take the chance that you've got a weapon in there."

"I'm not a criminal," Shannon shot back, miffed, "so you can stop acting like you've arrested a notorious outlaw. I'm a prominent member of this country's financial community, and, most impor-tantly, I haven't committed any crime."

"In my experience," the agent told her smugly, "innocent people don't transport cash by strapping it to their bodies. I suggest you exer-cise your right to remain silent, and we'll get that evidence removed as quickly as possible."

"Will you just shut up, Shannon," Martin barked in a pissed-off tone. "We need to talk to counsel before we say anything more."

In the weeks that followed, the investigation resulted in insider trading indictments for five persons from two well-respected financial services companies and four independent investors. Insider trading is the act of trading stocks based on information that hasn't been released to the public, giving those with advanced knowledge an advantage in the stock market. Typical of these transactions, Hastings Corbett purchased one million shares of DigiWare, a maker of data-base technologies, in August of 2010 at an average price of eight dollars per share. On October 18th, when Delta Technologies announced the purchase of DigiWare at twenty dollars per share, Hastings Corbett and their clients pocketed twelve million dollars, a one hundred fifty percent profit in little more than a month.

Summarily, the government charged that Shannon Corbett and Martin Hastings developed a sophisticated network of mergers and acquisitions specialists and private portfolio managers who, for more than a decade, traded the securities of public corporations based on illegally obtained insider information related to financial performance and planned acquisitions. Worse still for Shannon and Martin, several co-conspirators, including Robert Wilson of the Bauer Group and Julie Graham of Sullivan, Flannery & Haywood Investment Bankers, negotiated deals and had been cooperating with prosecutors. When all was said and done, the evidence against the partners was substantial and convincing, and Shannon and Martin were likely to serve lengthy sentences in a federal penitentiary.

"Hey, J Edgar," Shannon called out, "can I at least make a phone call while I'm waiting for the female agent?"

"Just sit tight, Ms. Corbett," the agent replied, "we'll take care of everything in good time."

"I'm entitled to make a phone call."

"And you will, ma'am. Are you going to be this difficult during our entire trip back to Philadelphia?"

"She is always this difficult," Martin advised the agent.

Chapter Fifty-Seven

Though Tom flatly refused the museum's request to unearth Digby, I found him deep in the hole on several subsequent evenings removing buckets of dirt from beneath the skull. He told me that he viewed online pictures of an allosaurus that piqued his curiosity and made him want to see more of Digby, most particularly his small front legs and long fingers. Without further explanation, Tom was suddenly more flexible than his original position when he vehemently rejected any intrusion upon the sanctity of Digby's grave, and his change of heart caused me to wonder if it applied to his father's grave also. But I didn't press Tom or even inquire about his thought process because I was trying to heed the same advice I gave Augie by backing off and allowing him to work through his family tragedy on his own. Instead, I climbed down into hole, and helped Tom with the excavation.

Fresh from his high school graduation, Tom and I looked up one evening to see Alex standing over us at the edge of the hole with a well-worn backpack over his left shoulder and a perplexed look on his face. From his perspective, Tom and I were quite a sight—beneath two large spotlights, we were delicately chiseling away at centuries of sediment like two Renaissance artists at work on a marble statue in a piazza in Venice. Driving from Philadelphia to Shelbyville in the five-year-old Jeep Cherokee that his parents gave him as a graduation gift, he never expected to see this scene upon arrival. He lowered his backpack onto the dirt beside him and addressed us.

"What the heck are you doing?" he asked, not having noticed Digby's skull yet.

"We're digging up a dinosaur," Tom said, smiling as he did, amused by the sheer ridiculousness of his statement.

"What the fuck!" Alex exclaimed, finally noticing the large white skull protruding from the dirt wall.

"It's an allosaurus," I said.

As quickly as I spoke the genus of our dinosaur, Alex typed it into his phone, and a picture of an allosaurus appeared.

"Awesome!" he declared. "That creature looks wicked!"

"He was the badass of his day," I said, repeating the words of the young paleontologist a week ago.

"Mom got arrested," Alex told Tom, his innocent enthusiasm for the dinosaur changed to seriousness.

"I know," Tom said. "AJ called."

"I had to get out of there," Alex said. "She is under house arrest, really pissed-off at the world, and taking it mostly out on me. Can I stay for a couple of days?"

"Why don't you stay for the summer?"

"What would I do here in Mayberry?"

"You can help Nick and me with our guesthouse project. I'll pay you for your efforts."

"How much?"

"Once I see how hard you're willing to work, I'll tell you how much I'm willing to pay you."

Like many teenagers, Alex asserted his independence during high school by detaching from his parents, a normal part of the maturation process, though the extent of the detachment is unique to each child. In his case, Alex's detachment was severe and culminated with his arrest for driving without a license and under the influence. While Tom and Shannon never doted over either of their children, Tom, in particular, was close to Alex during the first ten years of his life, taking on such paternal tasks as teaching him to ride his first bicycle and coaching his little league baseball team. When Alex started high school, their bond loosened, and the mentoring lessened. Typical of high school students, Alex's relationships with his peers became more central to his daily life than his relationship with his father, and the two gradually drifted apart. Exacerbating the change, Tom's Dream Squasher incident was hard on Alex because his classmates were brutal with their ridicule. The truth was that Tom's bad moment in the coffee store caused Alex many bad moments in the hallways and resulted in ongoing resentment by his son. Tom would love to heal their relationship, and the thought of Alex spending the summer at the farm delighted him.

"I've got calls to make," Alex said as he walked away.

"Are you going to work with us tomorrow?" Tom called out, uncertainty in his voice, like a father who had no idea how to connect with his teenage son.

"I don't know," Alex returned without pausing his stride.

* * *

Reluctantly, Alex emerged through the screen door and walked across the field around 10 a.m., two hours after Tom and I started work. The sun was at seventy degrees in the eastern sky, and the morning dew had long since evaporated. Our focus for that week was finishing the framing and exterior walls and doing the preparatory work required to put the metal roof in place. It was work that consisted of repeated measurements and then cutting the wood to match the requirement. During the last three weeks, we had both become quite proficient with band saws and nail guns while, very fortunately, managing to not spill any of our own blood. Without expressing my concern, I hoped we could add a teenager to our crew without incurring our first injury.

For his first half hour onsite, Tom provided Alex with an orientation concerning the task at hand and the power tools involved while I continued nailing beams and boards into place. Watching from the roof, I was acutely aware of Alex's obvious lack of enthusiasm and Tom's sincere desire to generate some. It wasn't until our lunch break at The Rooster that I finally detected the first glimmer of enthusiasm in Alex's eyes when Tom told him he'd pay him seventeen dollars per hour for his efforts.

"I'll make it twenty dollars per hour in a month when your skillset improves," Tom added as an incentive to keep him around. "At that rate, you should be able to put aside some spending money for when you go off to Brown in the fall."

Alex had been accepted for the fall semester of 2012 at Brown University, an Ivy League school in Providence, Rhode Island. It was the only college application he mailed and he did it largely at his mother's insistence. Like many kids with their diplomas in hand, Alex was directionless and had no idea what he wanted to do now that he'd graduated high school. And, true to his age, he never wanted to talk about it either.

"I'm not sure I want to go to Brown," Alex mumbled almost imperceptibly.

"What do you mean you don't want to go to Brown?" Tom shot back, unsettled by the barely audible announcement.

"I'm just not sure," Alex said as a feeble, teenage attempt at elaboration.

Beneath the table, I kicked Tom in the shin because I knew he didn't want to argue with Alex on his first full day at the farm. In his eyes, I saw a flash of pain, as well as subtle recognition about the message in my assault. He changed the subject.

"If you're done eating," Tom told Alex, whose plate looked like it had already been through the diner's dishwasher, "why don't you go check out the shops on Main Street? Nick and I will meet you at the truck in fifteen minutes."

"He's going to college," Tom asserted as soon as Alex exited the diner's front door. "That's not negotiable."

"I am not a parent, but I was a college student, and I can tell you that forcing him to go to college will only prove to be a waste of a lot of time and money. He'll party too much and not get what he should from the experience, mainly a direction for his life."

"So, I should just let him squander the time?"

"We are both old enough to know that life is a marathon, not a sprint. He'll go to college when he is ready. He's a smart kid. He's your son. Worse case is he waits a year, but he gets a lot more out of his time at the university."

"So, I should say nothing?"

"He knows you want him to go to college. There is really not much more for you to say. If you give him some time, I bet he comes around on his own."

"I don't know."

"I know you want him to stay at the farm for the summer—why don't you just focus on that objective for now?"

* * *

The old guesthouse was built in the 1950s, consisted of two rooms and a bathroom, once served as Marie's art studio, and currently functioned as a tool and potting shed. During Alex's second week working with us, we collectively decided to divert our efforts for a week, so we could refurbish it, and Alex could move into it. To do so, we had to relocate tools, haul off junk, tear out the old wood paneling, install new wallboard, and put a fresh coat of paint on the walls. After doing similar work in the main house last summer, Tom and I were confident we could accomplish this work in five days. This schedule change was largely a ploy on Tom's part to keep Alex in Shelbyville for the summer, but it was a project we were going to do anyway.

On Monday morning, Tom tasked Alex with cleaning the old guesthouse and tearing out the wood paneling. We planned to join him Wednesday afternoon for the installation of the new wallboard. When we broke for lunch on Tuesday, Alex showed us an interesting discovery he'd made when he ripped out some of the wood paneling.

"Look what I found in the wall," Alex declared, holding a large metal flashlight in his hand that looked like it was manufactured in mid-century.

"Where exactly did you find that?" Tom asked, glancing my way to gauge my interest in the steel flashlight.

I nodded my head slightly. I'd made the connection.

"Right here behind the paneling," Alex said, pointing to an open wall section. "The paneling didn't go all the way to the ceiling, and someone must've accidentally dropped it in there."

"Can I take a closer look?" Tom asked, taking the fifteen-inch-long cylinder from his son.

"They sure made things solid back then," Alex observed. "It must weigh five pounds."

Unlike modern flashlights, this one resembled a copper pipe that turned at a right angle near the top so that the light shined forward while its handle was perpendicular to the ground. Clearly in CSI mode, Tom examined the rusty flashlight by waving his hand at chest level to determine its weight, and it was solid and capable of delivering a substantial blow. Next, he studied the glass in front of the light bulb and noticed a deep crack running the entire diameter of the light. Finally, he ran his index finger up and down the steel outer casing of the flashlight and paused at the top where he noticed a flattened portion, a smooth area that wasn't rounded anymore. Tom pointed out that it was flat for about two inches, perhaps altered by something hard that it once struck. With his finger paused on the spot, his brow furrowed like he was deep in thought.

"Feel that," Tom said as he handed me the flashlight.

Manufactured by the Allbright Company in the 1940s, this model of flashlight was largely used by the U.S. military. During

World War II, Sam's uncle, Clive Corbett, served in the Navy on an aircraft carrier in the Pacific, and Tom speculated that his service must be the reason this military flashlight found its way to a farm in the middle of Pennsylvania. It wasn't something his grandfather or father or uncle bought because it would've cost considerably more than a standard flashlight.

"What are your thoughts about the flashlight?" Tom asked me later when Alex wasn't around.

"Well," I said, "the cracked glass and dented casing are suspicious, but the flashlight is seventy years old."

"Yeah, I know exactly what you mean—that damage could've happened in so many other ways."

"To me, the most significant aspect of the flashlight is where it was found—in Marie's art studio. She spent a lot of time in there and would've noticed that the wood paneling didn't go all the way to the ceiling in places. On the night your father died, if she wanted to hide the murder weapon, it makes perfect sense to me that she dropped it behind the wall. Heck, it took forty years for it to be discovered."

"If you first consider where the flashlight was found and then you consider the damage, it's incriminating."

"You're right about that," I told him, agreeing with his logic. "We can't be sure it's the murder weapon, but it's possible."

Chapter Fifty-Eight

I n Shelbyville, the summer holidays—Memorial Day, Fourth of July, and Labor Day—were celebratory occasions that drew visitors from across the state and across state lines. They flocked to Shelbyville for its pastoral beauty, idyllic downtown, and renowned street fairs. A town ordinance that dated back to 1977 required all businesses on Main Street be painted at least ninety percent Roman white, permitting other colors on the window trim and front doors only. These clean white facades were the perfect backdrop for holiday celebrations and gave the town a purity, simplicity, and innocence that truly befitted its small-town character. On each summer holiday, with all its storefronts draped in American flags, the town hosted a street fair, and the resulting scene was something that only existed in memory and Norman Rockwell paintings. Families with strollers wandered from booth to booth, the scent of fresh pastries and deep-fried delicacies drifted on the air, and cheesy renditions of bouncy songs by the high school glee club could be heard in the distance. When the mayor rolled down Main Street in a vintage T-Bird convertible with Beach Boys' tunes blasting from its speakers, visitors surely thought they'd actually gone back in time.

True to form, Memorial Day of 2012 was a glorious and festive occasion, but the "good vibrations" came to a crashing halt on the following Tuesday.

A little before noon, Police Chief Walt Garrison arrived at the colonial-style home of Robbie Reynolds to perform a wellness check after Robbie's assistant reported that he'd missed all his morning appointments and she was unable to reach him by phone. Chief Garrison, a retired Philadelphia police officer with a noticeable limp from an injury in the line of duty, called Robbie's cell phone from the front porch of the residence. He could hear it ring inside the home, but he didn't see any sign of Robbie's presence. After nine rings and no response, the chief checked the front door and the windows above the porch, but they were all securely locked. In the front of the home, he found no way to enter.

"Hey Robbie," the chief called out, "it's Walt. Are you in there? I need to make sure you're okay."

Despite his shout, the house remained still and silent; no doors or windows opened, and no curtains fluttered. The chief saw no sign of Robbie within the house so he proceeded from the front porch to the back door, hoping to find it unlocked so he could enter. On arrival, he turned the back door's antique knob and was quite surprised to find it locked also.

I wonder if Robbie left town for the long weekend, the chief thought. *It's not like him to lock the house so tightly.*

Standing beside the back door, the chief recalled one Saturday afternoon a couple of years earlier when Robbie called from an insurance seminar in Pittsburgh and asked him to retrieve a phone number from the desk in his home. At the time, he told the chief that he was pretty sure the back door was unlocked. When the chief arrived at Robbie's house half an hour later, all the doors were unlocked and most windows were wide open. Suddenly concerned, the chief removed his handgun from its holster and walked toward the garage.

Peering through the dirty side windowpane of the garage, the chief viewed a heartbreaking scene—Robbie's feet were dangling three feet above the concrete floor, and a thick rope encircled his neck. He was clearly dead and had been for some time. And, if the chief had any misgivings about the scene, the six-foot stepladder beside the stiffened body provided the additional details. The town's beloved hard court hero had hung himself. Though hardened by tragic scenes during his time on the tough Philadelphia streets, tears began streaming down the chief's face as he slowly re-holstered his gun. Devastated by the sight, a full twenty minutes elapsed before he regained his composure and called in his report. It took less time for the tragic news to be communicated amongst the townsfolk.

Chapter Fifty-Nine

A t sunset on a cold February evening, I interviewed Robbie for my *Sentinel* article about the twenty-fifth anniversary of his fabled jump shot that secured the state championship game for Shelbyville High School. As I entered the reception area, his last appointment of the day passed me on her way out, and I found Robbie in his office with the lights dimmed and a glass of scotch in front of him, a second glass on the corner of his desk in front of a leather chair, intended for me. In the corner of his office was an oak and glass trophy cabinet that showcased his many high school accomplishments: three large plaques for All-American teams, gold medallions for All-State honors, trophies for MVP honors, three conference championship trophies, and the Pennsylvania State Championship trophy, game ball, and clipped nylon net from the game.

"That case is obligatory," Robbie said as I viewed its contents, with neither pride nor satisfaction in his voice. "Everyone who comes into this office wants to talk about "The Shot." I spend the first fifteen minutes of every appointment reliving my high school days."

"That state championship means a lot to everyone in this town," I remarked, stating the obvious as Robbie overlooked it.

"I know," he returned solemnly.

Considering the celebrated nature of the event, the interview was subdued, like it concerned a defeat rather than a glorious triumph. Robbie seemed more resigned to our interview than engaged in it. As we conversed, his prior use of the word "obligatory" echoed in the back of my mind and I wondered if our anniversary interview was an extended version of his daily encounters where he simply fulfilled an unpleasant obligation. There was no gleam in his eye or enthusiasm in his voice as he recalled "The Shot." It was like he was fulfilling a duty. After an hour revisiting his glory days, one thing was clear to me: Robbie wasn't excited about the upcoming anniversary.

"Do you remember that night in high school when we went to that field on the edge of town to stargaze?" I asked him as we neared the end of the interview.

"Yeah," Robbie replied, smiling for a brief moment, the first time since I arrived, "that was a lot of fun."

"We saw a shooting star, and I remarked about its short-lived brilliance and sudden fade to black."

"I remember the shooting star."

"Do you remember what you said to me?"

"No, I don't."

"You said we were fortunate to have witnessed its brilliant moment."

"Hmmm."

"Robbie, this whole town feels that way about you."

* * *

After "The Shot," the life of the superstar known as "The Train" completely derailed. He suffered a severe knee injury during his first year at Notre Dame and was told by doctors that he would never compete again. He left college after one year, never graduated, and returned instead to Shelbyville to settle down and marry his high school sweetheart. Largely due to his anger and disillusionment over his canceled career, their marriage lasted only eighteen months and ended in divorce. At the age of twenty-three, while working in his father's insurance agency, his parents were killed in an automobile accident while traveling between Shelbyville and Philadelphia. On the spectrum of life where one end was fortunate and the other end was cursed, Robbie's life had clearly swung from shining and blessed to the other extreme.

As the basketball slipped through the net on that fateful March evening twenty-five years ago, Robbie Reynolds had every reason to believe his life would be exceptional. He was the best high school basketball player in the nation, a highly recruited college prospect, and destined for a professional career, with all the money, perks, and privileges that came with it. He was the holder of every significant record pertaining to the sport in the state of Pennsylvania, and similar college and professional records seemed inevitable. His career and personal life would be noteworthy, his lifestyle envied, his name renowned, and his contribution significant. It was all a certainty. An ordinary life was not a possibility because Robbie had potential and promise that almost exceeded the imagination.

Then, with one iniquitous turn of his knee, it was all gone. All his promise and potential was ripped from his being like the cartilage ripped in his knee. In that moment, his life went from exceptional to ordinary, and Robbie faced the difficult task of living with so much failed promise, so much lost potential. At a young age, he had experienced exceptional moments, heard the cheers of thousands, and accomplished so much—how could he possibly live an ordinary life? In the ordinary days that followed, every moment felt like failure. Robbie spent long days behind a desk in a dark office talking about life insurance, explaining the difference between term and whole-life policies over and over again. He spent long nights alone in the dark at home, drinking Kentucky spirits and mentally inventorying everything he'd lost. And, making matters even worse, every day, almost hourly, Robbie was reminded of his lost promise and potential as his neighbors and clients wanted to reminisce about "The Shot." In truth, that moment tormented him all his adult life.

In Robbie's mind, failing to fulfill a spoken promise was a lie, but failing to fulfill God-given promise was something much worse.

On a cluttered workbench in the small, one-car garage, just ten feet from Robbie's body, was a blank sheet of white paper and a black felt-tipped pen. Clearly, Robbie brought those items into the garage so he could leave a note. I was sure he stood over that sheet of paper with the pen in his hand but could not find the words. As a writer, I knew that struggle well; I knew that no words were always better than the wrong words. In the end, I guess Robbie came to that same conclusion. As editor of the town's newspaper, I also interpreted that blank sheet of paper as a message for me, a last request from Robbie concerning how I should handle his story. In his silence, he reminded me that no words were always better than the wrong words.

I believed I understood Robbie Reynolds as well or better than anyone, but I left his story untold, publishing only a fluff piece for the twenty-fifth anniversary article and a simple obituary after his death. I couldn't bring myself to publish the real story as I knew it in *The Sentinel*—I just couldn't do it. His was not the storied life everyone believed. It was actually quite tragic.

* * *

Some say our culture changed the day Marilyn Monroe was found dead on her bed in Los Angeles; some say our society changed the day Martin Luther King was shot on a hotel balcony in Memphis; some say our nation changed the day John Kennedy was assassinated in Dallas; some say the world changed the day terrorists attacked the World Trade Center on September 11th. Closer to home, I know that one small town in Pennsylvania changed the day that Robbie Reynolds killed himself. After his death, the moment that all the townsfolk cherished, the moment that always brought a nostalgic smile to the corners of their mouths, was now and forever tainted by tragedy. From that day forward, when they thought of Robbie Reynolds, they'd no longer think only of that beautifully arched final shot and the state championship it secured; they'd think of his suicide also. Smiles would be replaced by sadness; joy replaced by remorse. Much more was lost in that garage at the end of that rope than the quiet life of a heartbroken insurance salesman—the town lost its cherished moment and its innocence.

At The Bashful Rooster on the Wednesday following his suicide, and for many days thereafter, few words were spoken amongst the diners. In their usual chairs at their usual tables, the townsfolk nodded to one another and then dined without the usual conversation. In truth, nothing was "usual" about those days; their minds were heavy and their hearts were broken. They gathered at the diner to share their shock and grief in silence; the consolation came from the simple act of gathering together. For the townsfolk of Shelbyville, only one shooting star had ever flashed so brilliantly across the night sky and shined its light on their beloved town. And, its rarity made it all the more beautiful, and more special. For days following his suicide, in silence at the diner, the townsfolk were slowly coming to terms with the inevitable blackness that awaits those who gaze at shooting stars.

Chapter Sixty

Whenever AJ visited the farm, he always remarked that the front porch could easily adorn a home in Charleston, South Carolina, where porches were status symbols, open-air extensions of grand living spaces, and never an afterthought. Since we painted it last summer, the forty-foot porch has been inviting, comfortable, and as perfect a place to sip sweet tea on a warm summer evening as any porch in the Palmetto State. Once the sun began its descent toward the silo each evening and the air temperature became accommodating, we tended to drift toward the porch with its white Adirondack chairs and beautiful western view. In many homes, the most significant conversations and moments happened at the dinner table, but at the Corbett farm in the summer, those conversations and moments happened on the front porch.

"Why do you always stay one night and not the weekend when you come to the farm for a visit?" Tom asked AJ one evening as they sipped AJ's specialty, a spicy Bloody Mary that he claimed had the added benefit of cleansing sins.

"I don't like camping," AJ answered.

"You're not camping. You're sleeping in a bed in my house."

"I know," AJ replied, "but it's a farmhouse in the country, and that's as close to camping as I'm ever going to get."

"Are you saying that I need to earn a few more stars from the travel guides before you'll stay a full weekend?"

"I love you like a brother, Tom, but you'll never make a country boy out of me. It's just too damn quiet here. But, you have done a great job with the place."

"You'll stay the whole weekend when you get older."

"I will never get that old."

"How is our art gallery doing?" Tom asked.

"Fabulous," AJ said, smiling because he loved the topic. "The Miami gallery is three times as profitable as my other galleries. I should've opened it twenty years ago."

"I don't have to ask whether you're spending much time there. Your tan says it all. You look great; you look healthy."

"I feel great, but we both know it will only last so long."

"Don't talk like that, AJ. I have high hopes that you won't fall back on any of your old, bad habits. After all, you're both older and wiser now."

"We'll see. I may just move to Miami at some point. I'm so happy when I'm there. I must have Latin blood in me because that culture speaks to me. It's so rich and vibrant. I've even noticed that I walk differently when I'm strolling down the boulevard in Miami—my steps are lighter and more rhythmic."

"It wouldn't surprise me to learn that your ancestors came from either Spain or South America. You've always been the most passionate person I've ever known."

"What has your lawyer told you about Shannon's arrest?" AJ asked as he removed the celery stalk from his Bloody Mary and bit the stem off.

"She basically said it was both good news and bad news for me. On the one hand, I clearly have the high ground in the divorce, but, on the other hand, our assets will be closely scrutinized by the feds to determine whether they're ill-gotten gains."

"I hope the feds don't come sniffing around the Miami gallery. We don't need that kind of distraction."

"Yeah, I agree."

Tom hesitated because he knew his next topic was a sensitive one. While all conversations with AJ about Marie were emotional, this one had the potential to be even more difficult for him.

"I'm glad you came for a visit because there is something I want to talk about with you. I need your opinion."

"Well, you are in luck, Tom. I always keep plenty of those in my back pocket."

For the next twenty minutes, Tom enlightened AJ about his late Uncle Carl's suspicions about his brother's death as well as Tom's more recent conversations, memories, and discoveries that also had him questioning the circumstances of his father's death. He told him about his conversation with his mother's best friend while she lived in Shelbyville, Maddie Stover, and her disturbing revelations about his parent's marriage. He told him that his father verbally abused and battered his mother more and more with each passing year. He told him about his recollection of the violence that occurred on his father's last night and his mother's adamant declaration that "it will never happen again." Lastly, he told AJ about our theory concerning what happened on the night of his father's death and the discovery of the flashlight in the wall that seemed to corroborate it. Through it all, AJ was silent and dumbfounded, two adjectives seldom applied to him.

"Should I exhume my father's body?" Tom asked.

"You'd be accusing Marie of murder."

"Well, let's just say I'm acknowledging the possibility."

"Are you out of your mind?" AJ blurted. "There is absolutely no way Marie ever murdered anyone. She was the kindest and gentlest person I've ever known."

"I know you loved her, but the evidence is convincing."

"Not for me," AJ returned, ruffled. "I knew Marie very well, and it's simply not possible. I'm beginning to question how well you knew your own mother. She didn't kill your father."

"So, you're opposed to me exhuming my father's body."

"I don't give a damn about your father. I didn't know him, but you've told me he was a cruel man. I only know that exhuming the body to find out whether Marie killed him is ridiculous. What would be the point anyway?"

"We would know the truth."

"And what if the findings are inconclusive? What then? You will have besmirched her memory and good name for nothing. You will have labeled her a murderer. You can't just un-ring that bell."

Chapter Sixty-One

Tom and I sat on the front porch with a couple of cold beers and a bowl of tortilla chips in front of us after a long day of hard work.

"I think I found a bone today," Tom said.

"That's fantastic," I returned. "Is it one of his front legs?"

"It's too early to tell whether it's part of a front leg or a long finger. We'll know what we have when we get more bone exposed."

"You know, I was never one to get my hands dirty until I met you. Previously, I only worked with words and ideas. Now, I find myself refurbishing homes, building guesthouses, and digging up dinosaurs. It's quite a departure for me."

"And I only worked with antiques and appraisals, but we're better off now that we're doing some real work. Frankly, we were a couple of wimps in the past. There is a lot to be said for getting your hands dirty."

"We're going to have to dig a new hole for the septic system on the other side of the guesthouse."

"Yeah, I know," Tom said in a less-than-enthusiastic tone. "I've been putting it off. We'll need the excavator again, and God only knows what we'll find this time."

"Maybe we'll find Digby's wife—Gladys."

"Don't even joke about that."

"Do you realize that it has almost been a year since we first met in The Bashful Rooster?"

"We were two pretty pathetic guys back then," Tom said, shaking his head, "both of us running from mistakes and bad choices."

"I think we're both doing much better now."

"Mostly," Tom replied as an open-ended answer.

"What do you mean?" I followed up.

"When we first met, Nick, you were tormented by your past, by the tragic death of that police officer, so much so that you weren't living in the present. You lived your days in a drug and alcohol haze."

"That was true, alright."

"Now, you're doing so much better, and you have reclaimed the present, but you're still not looking to the future. In life, we all have pasts, presents, and futures. And frankly, our presents and our futures are the most important because we can impact them."

"I get that," I said, put off by his unsolicited psychoanalysis.

"I think you need to start looking ahead again. You need to start living with the kind of plans and aspirations that make life richer again. You're way too talented to spend your life publishing *The Sentinel* for this small-town audience."

"But, I'm happy publishing the newspaper."

"Who are you kidding? You're a Fenwick Prize winner. You have serious talent and a serious contribution to make to the world. A God-given gift like yours comes with an obligation to use it in the best way possible."

His words reminded me of Robbie Reynolds, his struggle with his unfulfilled promise, the guilt and regret that haunted him, and his recent death. I hesitated for a long moment before I finally responded.

"I'm afraid that's all in the past."

"Have you ever had a conversation with his widow?" Tom asked, following up on my reference to the past.

Whenever I thought about having a conversation with Sandra Maxwell, my words felt like confederate currency to me—worthless, ineffectual, meaningless, and of no use to anyone in the present day. No matter how many portraits of Jefferson Davis I placed on the table before her, she would never feel like my debt was paid, my obligation met. Sandra and I could never be even. No matter how fast I talked or how eloquently I crafted the English language, my words couldn't turn back the clock, reverse the bullets, and reunite her with her husband, the only actions that would truly right my mistake. I was a writer, and I'd always believed in the power of words, but my words were as useless now as the defunct currency of the Old South. Even in the broadest definition of currency—something given to settle a debt—there was simply no currency known to man that could ever satisfy this debt, no words that could ever make things better. Whenever a man finds himself doubting the one thing he wholeheartedly believes in, he is in a pitiful predicament, a miserable state. For me, that one thing had always been words. In all the time that has passed, I had not been able to bring myself to have a conversation with the widow. I'd lost my faith.

"I tried to talk to her, but I just couldn't do it," I said. "On many days, I sat in my car and watched her with her kids in a park near her home, but I just couldn't bring myself to approach her. I was a coward."

"You're not a coward. You just weren't ready yet."

"But it has been four years now. I've waited too long."

"I don't think so. You're going to have to talk with her if you ever want to put this mistake behind you."

"What would I say?"

"Just tell her what's in your heart, that you are sorry this tragic accident happened and you never intended it. I think it would mean a lot to both of you to have that conversation."

"What if she's angry at me? What if she hates me?"

"She may be angry, and she may hate you, but you'll just have to deal with that."

"That's much easier said than done."

"Where is Chelsea these days?"

"She is still in Los Angeles working on her cooking show. Why do you ask about her?"

"No reason."

Chapter Sixty-Two

In the three weeks that Alex had lived at the farm, we had developed a good rapport. I liked him. He was a smart kid with a lot of potential but clearly in that adolescent phase when he had no idea who he was or what he wanted to do with his life. In whatever ways I could, I wanted to be a positive influence and help him find his way.

Watching Tom, I could see this was a difficult time for him as a parent because it was a critical time in Alex's life, a real fork-in-the-road moment. Over the next few years, Alex would make decisions about dating, college, career, and marriage that would greatly impact his future. As Alex's father, Tom wanted him to make thoughtful, measured decisions, but young adults didn't tend to do that. Unfortunately for Tom, bad decisions and regrettable mistakes were a part of adolescence and a part of growing up. And parents like him were simply fated to suffer through it with their child.

"So, you grew up in Shelbyville?" Alex asked me one evening on the front porch.

"I did," I answered, "and I can't imagine a better place to grow up. It is the biggest, most beautiful backyard ever."

"Weren't you bored?"

"Oh, I'm sure there were times when I was a little bored, but growing up in the country in a small town like Shelbyville provides a young boy with a strong sense of community. Growing up, I felt very rooted here and that's important."

"Then why did you leave?"

"Because it is a small town. The time came for me to go off to college and experience more of the world than I could in Shelbyville. As much as I loved Shelbyville, I believed my life would be enriched by a wider range of people, places, and experiences."

"You must think my dad is right that I should go to Brown University in the fall?"

"No, actually I don't."

"Say what?"

"College can be the best time of your life and the time that you figure out what you want to do with your life, but only if you want to be there and embrace the experience. If you don't go to Brown in the right frame of mind it will be a waste of time and money."

"Did you know what you wanted to do with your life when you went to college?"

"I did. I knew I wanted to be a writer from a very young age, but I was clearly an exception. Most kids don't have any idea what they want to do with their lives before college; many still don't after college. When the time is right for you to go to college, just go with the expectation that it'll expose you to so much great stuff that you'll figure out where your interests and passions lie. Once you know that, you'll know what you want to do with your life."

"I wish I knew what I should be."

"You're eighteen, and you have a long journey in front of you. You don't need to know what you want to be right now—only that you want to be something. Don't think there is a timetable you should measure yourself against because there isn't. I will tell you this—don't hurry and don't waste time. Both are signs that you should probably adjust."

"You know something, Nick, I'm starting to like it here on the farm. This little town is growing on me."

"That's good. I really like it here, too. I've got a suggestion for you."

"What's that?"

"We're going to need a new hole for the septic system on the other side of the guesthouse and that means your dad will have to rent the excavator again."

"So?"

"So, you should tell him that you'll dig the hole if he'll give you the amount of the excavator rental to do it."

"It's a pretty big hole."

"It is. It'll be hard work. It'll probably take you a full day, but you'd be increasing your hourly rate by about four or five times because the day rate for the excavator is about five hundred dollars. It would be worth it."

"Do you think he'd do it?"

"I think he would. It's easier for him to pay you to do it than rent the excavator again. It's a win-win."

"I will talk to him about it. Thanks for the idea."

Chapter Sixty-Three

"How is the refurbished guesthouse working out for you?" Tom asked Alex in early evening while the sun lingered above the silo. It was mid-summer, and the two were aligned.

"It's good, Dad."

"I'm glad we fixed it up for you. You're much better off in the old guesthouse than the old folks home next door."

"That's for sure."

Twenty-three days into Alex's stay at the farm, there was still detachment between father and son, but Tom felt like he was making progress. It seemed like much of the anger and resentment had faded away, and he was now dealing with an eighteen-year-old's normal aloofness and reserve. Tom was determined to allow Alex the space a young man needed to find his way in life while also being there when he needed him. It was a delicate balancing act, but one Tom wanted to master.

"Do you think Mom is guilty of insider trading?"

"I don't know. The legal system and the courts will answer that question. Your mom is a very competitive and determined person, so it's very possible she broke the rules."

"Do you still love her?"

"Of course I do. I always will. Your mom and I shared a large portion of our lives together and created two beautiful children. Nothing will ever change that. We are divorcing because we are both better off separate going forward than together, but that doesn't change the past. I wouldn't change the past even if I could."

Those last nine words echoed in the back of Tom's mind like a call for help in a canyon, causing him to rethink what he'd said. After all, incidents from his past were haunting him like unpaid bills. His family dynamic during his childhood had caused him many sleepless nights, and he'd eagerly revisit that past and make significant, broad-brush changes. For starters, he'd amend his stint in Shelbyville and wipe away the violence and abuse from his family history. So, the truth was that if he could change the past, he most certainly would. And he would change a lot of it.

"I talked with Nicole today."

"What did she say?" Tom asked.

"She hasn't seen or heard from Scratch in almost a month. He is supposedly on tour with his band, but she doubts it."

"Well, that's not good but also not surprising. Scratch needs another decade of growing up before he'll be ready to be a father, if ever."

"He's a guy who isn't in touch with reality."

"I can't argue with that. I talk to her weekly, but she won't tell me about problems with Scratch. I'm glad you told me."

"Sure."

"I think Nicole enjoys being a mom."

"I think so too. I feel like I have to find something I enjoy."

"You know, Alex, about five years ago, I was on a business trip to Maryland and I spent an afternoon relaxing beside the Chesapeake Bay. For the better part of an hour, I watched a young man throw a red rubber ball about fifty yards into the bay, and his Labrador retriever swim out and get it. Over and over again, that dog swam with such joy and enthusiasm and purpose that I realized I was watching him do exactly what he was born to do, the thing that came most naturally to him. As I watched, I could see the beauty in that, the sheer joy of it, the fulfilled heart. I saw that in my mother when she was at an easel, I see it in Nick when he talks about writing, and I see it in Nicole when she is with Bart."

"Do you get that feeling from antiques?"

"I do. I get a sense of purpose and a feeling of fulfillment from my work. I truly love the artistic and historical aspects of my profession."

"How do I find what I was born to do?"

"I really don't know how that works—do we find it, or does it find us? I don't know. But I think the important thing is to keep your heart and mind open and have faith. It'll happen."

"We should ask Nicole to come to Shelbyville for a visit during the Fourth of July street fair."

"That's a good idea."

"I come bearing gifts," I said as I stepped through the screen door with three bottles of cold beer in my hands.

"Perfect timing," Tom replied, taking a last swig from his bottle.

"You know, Dad," Alex said as I handed him his bottle, "Nick told me we need a new hole for the septic tank."

"We do," Tom replied. "It'll be on the other side of the house, so we don't disturb Digby."

"How about I dig the hole and you pay me what it costs to rent the excavator?" Alex suggested to his father.

"It'll be very hard work and take at least a day. Are you sure you're up to it?"

"I am. I can do it."

"I paid five hundred fifteen dollars to rent the excavator last time, so I'll pay you that same amount, but the hole has to be the same size and shape as the first one."

"It's a deal."

"Well then, you've got the job."

We sat quietly for fifteen minutes until Tom broke the silence.

"Look at that," he remarked. "The sunset is almost perfectly lined up with the silo. In another ten days or so, it will be perfect. My mother always said that the days when the sunsets line up perfectly with the silo are magical days."

"Those days include your birthday, Tom," I added, reminding him of the remainder of his mother's sweet sentiment.

"They do indeed," Tom said as his eyes welled up.

"Your grandmother referred to this annual phenomenon as Shelbyville's miniature version of Stonehenge," I advised Alex.

"That sounds like Grandma alright," he returned.

Chapter Sixty-Four

"Hey Tom, it's AJ. I'm in Miami."

"Hey AJ."

"Are you sitting on the front porch? I thought I might catch you there."

"As a matter of fact, I am," Tom said into his cell phone. "I am sitting on the porch with Alex, wishing I had one of those great Bloody Mary concoctions you make."

"I'll return to the farm soon and make you one."

"I look forward to it."

"I want to talk to you about the conversation we had about Marie and your father a couple of weeks ago," AJ informed him with a wisp of remorse in his tone. "I basically want to retract everything that I said that day."

"How so?"

"As you well know, I am a homosexual addict who grew up poor in the south and was abandoned by my father at a young age. As such, I have faced a lot of hard truths in my life—you could say I am the queen of hard truths. And the one thing I know for certain about hard truths is that things get better once you face them. There is no peace until you do. Tom, I understand your need to know the truth about your family, so you have my full support if you decide to exhume your father."

"Thank you, AJ, that means a lot to me. I couldn't do it without your blessing. You are family."

"As I thought about it, the other thing I realized is that no matter what the outcome, it won't change my memory of Marie. I'll love her just as much. I don't think Marie killed your father, but if she did, she did it to protect you. Maybe even murder can be a beautiful act."

"I also recognize that no outcome will change the way I think about my mother, and so I'm gradually coming to the conclusion that I have to exhume my father. I need to know the truth."

"Let me know if you do. I'll come to Shelbyville to support you through the process."

"We'll talk soon."

Chapter Sixty-Five

W hat role does the past play in our daily lives? Is the past basically like hardened concrete within our brains, beyond shaping or correction? How should we manage our past?

I pondered these questions as I drove east on Interstate 76 toward Philadelphia—concrete I hadn't traveled over in almost four years. More so than the city, I felt like I was heading into the gray matter of my mind as the wheels of my pickup truck glided across the gray matter of the highway. In many ways, I was driving into my past, as the city was the backdrop of my time at *The Post* and my life with Chelsea, the site of the most significant moments in my life—both good and bad. For the last four years, I had done all I could to escape my past, to dodge the memories that haunted me like ghosts in the cluttered attic of my being. But not anymore. Early on a Saturday morning, I motored toward my old stomping grounds with a newly minted resolve to confront these painful memories and face up to my past mistakes. In my heart, I knew it was long overdue.

When I saw the city's skyline in the distance, I felt like I was looking into the forlorn face of a broken-hearted lover, one that I'd clearly disappointed who had every reason to simply turn and walk away. Hell, she had every right to spit in my face and then turn and walk away. But, instead of one face, three faces appeared in my mind: the faces of Officer Louis Maxwell, his widow, Sandra, and Chelsea. In a few short years, I caused these three good people more pain than I ever would've thought possible; my impact on their lives was troubling and tragic. Undeniably, I'd left a triple measure of heartbreak and unresolved emotions behind.

Overcome by my guilt as I drove, I tried to find consolation in the fact that, while some things in life can't be fixed, they can often be made better. For all concerned, I needed to try to accomplish that.

My itinerary for the day consisted of four locations that were the epicenters of my collapse so that I could acknowledge my past mistakes, offer remorse, find atonement, and move on. While I didn't have any training in grief therapy or healing, I instinctively believed that this was the way to move forward, the means to finally get on with my life. I would follow my heart for the first time in a long time.

Around 11 a.m., I guided my pickup truck into a still alleyway in the warehouse section of downtown where most activities ceased on the weekends. The alley was stained and littered with the byproducts of commercial enterprises, but no one was around. All was quiet. Across the alley from a plumbing supply company, I stopped beside a large mural of mountain scenery on the side of a one-hundred-year-old, red brick building that housed the Rockland Brewing Company. Beside the majestic Rockies, I climbed out of my truck, walked to a row of three dumpsters, placed a bouquet of flowers on the ground beside the last one, and stood in quiet reflection. I'd never been in this alley before, but I knew this location from the photographs of the crime scene. Years later, I was standing at the exact spot where the body of Officer Louis Maxwell was found.

An hour later, I repeated this same routine. As soon as I parked, I climbed out of my truck, walked a short distance, placed a second bouquet of flowers on the ground, and stood in quiet reflection. Only this time, I was in the cemetery at the grave of Officer Louis Maxwell. On the shiny black granite marker was carved: Louis James Maxwell 1974 – 2007. Once again, I'd never been here before, but I knew his gravesite because I watched his funeral from across the street. From my truck, I watched as his casket was lowered into his grave with his widow, two young daughters, and a large contingent of his fellow police officers in attendance. I watched as his devastated widow grasped dirt in her bare hand, crumpled it between her fingers, and allowed it to rain like tears into his grave. I'd never met him while he was alive, but I had a lot to say to this man.

"Officer Maxwell," I began as I stared at his marker, "I am Nick Sterling, the journalist who made the terrible mistake of publishing a photograph on the front page of *The Post* that cost you your life at the hands of gang members. My story about the death of those two little boys in the park a decade earlier resulted in a second tragedy, the death of a fine police officer and a family man. I cannot begin to tell you how much I wish I could undo that story. I wish I could go back in time, stop the printing presses, and pull that article. It was the biggest mistake of my life, and you paid the price."

I paused as I needed a moment to gather my thoughts and composure. It was early afternoon, but I was exhausted and drained already. Though I was speaking to a black slab of granite, it did not make the encounter any less personal, any less human. Officer Louis Maxwell was very real to me.

"I want you to know that I know the extent of the loss you suffered. I've seen your wife and two beautiful little girls, and I know I robbed you of a lifetime with them. The price that you paid for my mistake is both great and immeasurable. I would trade places with you in a heartbeat if it allowed you just one more hug from your wife and daughters, one more chance to tell them you love them. I know they miss you every day, and the pain of that loss will never end."

I paused again. I felt so weakened by this experience that I was on the verge of passing out. To conserve my strength, I sat on the ground at the foot of his grave. Fortunately, his stone was twenty feet from a massive maple tree with leaves the size of catcher's mitts that shaded the gravesite; otherwise, I probably would've fainted by now. But this reckoning had been a long time coming, and I was not about to cut it short. I needed to be forgiven—by both of us.

For the next hour or so, I just rambled. I told him that I knew a lot about him; I told him about myself; I told him about my days at *The Post*; I told him about Shelbyville; I even told him about Chelsea. I talked for so long and at such length that I finally passed out in the shade of the maple tree. I think I slept for a solid hour. When I awoke, the sun had moved thirty degrees to the west in the afternoon sky, and there was a beam of light passing between the branches and leaves of the maple tree that was shining directly on me, only on me. As I looked upward at the tree and the beam of light, it seemed to originate in heaven, pass through the branches and leaves of the large tree, and shine on me. The light felt like warm comfort, like a blessing. While I wasn't a religious man, I wanted to believe that the light was a sign, that the light was the manifestation of God's presence in this cemetery, that God had witnessed my contrition and shined his light of forgiveness on me. I so wanted to believe it. For as long as the warm light lingered, about another fifteen minutes or so, I bathed in its glow.

When the sun inched further west, and the beam of light ceased, I kneeled, leaned forward, and kissed the headstone, for no other reason than it seemed like the most personal gesture I could make to this good man. With tears streaming down my face, I softly whispered, "I am so sorry, Louis," and then I rose and walked away. Two hours earlier, I arrived at this cemetery seeking forgiveness from Louis, God, and myself. The exact tally was unclear as I walked back to my truck, but I felt a little better.

Chapter Sixty-Six

Coincidentally, and unbeknownst to me at the time, a second gravesite conversation occurred in Shelbyville in the middle of the afternoon. In the Corbett section of the cemetery, Tom stood before two side-by-side headstones that read Samuel Gerard Corbett and Carl David Corbett, his father and his uncle, one stone weathered by years on the hillside and one freshly carved. Seeing both names on the markers made him angry because he clearly had unresolved issues with both of them. He barely knew either man but this last year spent learning about his lineage had not been a pleasant one. He was silent for a long period, and then he finally spoke.

"Look at the two of you," he declared in a disgruntled tone, "lying there like a set of bookends on a shelf of books about mean and hateful human beings. Between you, each volume contains the vile-filled story of a wretched soul who inflicts pain and misery on the people in his life. The amount of suffering on the pages equals the amount that you doled out during your lives. Needless to say, the toll is significant, and the damage is not repairable. In all my life, I've never met two meaner men, and I'm ashamed to say that your blood courses through my veins."

His rant completed, Tom breathed a sigh of relief. He knew he had more anger in him these days than at any other time in his life, and he also knew it wasn't healthy. Having said his piece, he felt better.

"I obviously didn't come today to pay my respects," Tom continued in a more conversational tone. "Instead, I came with a message for both of you. Sam, I've decided to exhume your remains so a medical examiner can determine your cause of death. But I'm not doing this for either of you. With the two of you, I want to be clear about one thing—this exhumation has nothing to do with justice. Whether an act of karma or a blow to your head by my mother, justice was served forty years ago in that field. You were a miserable man, and you got what you deserved. In terms you will better under-stand, you reaped what you sowed. In my mind, either cause of death is understandable and acceptable. I just want to know the truth."

His message delivered, Tom stepped forward and ran his finger over the chipped top of his uncle's headstone, a lasting reminder of the metal box he hurled at it ten months ago. A satisfied smile appeared on his face as he turned away from the limestone markers and walked out of the cemetery in the direction of his truck.

Chapter Sixty-Seven

I n all the time that Chelsea and I lived in the row house, we never parked directly in front of it. Parking in our neighborhood was difficult. We kept our car in a parking garage four blocks away, but when we tried to park on the street near our home, we were never able to secure the prime spot directly in front. We always carried packages from at least a block away. As I turned onto our old street, I saw a car pulling out of the spot, and, for the first time, I parked directly in front of our old home, ten feet from the front door that Chelsea painted black the first weekend we owned it. Back then, I was amazed by how a little black paint so changed the home's overall curb appeal. She always had a way of making things better.

Chelsea would laugh so hard, I thought once I'd finished the always-tricky task of parallel parking, *if she knew I was finally parked in the spot directly in front of the home that we don't own anymore. She'd really appreciate the irony.*

This was the third stop on what I was starting to think of as my last chance at redemption tour, which was already running way behind schedule because it was almost 5 p.m. and I still had one more stop to make after this one, maybe the most important stop of the day.

From the four years that we lived in the house, I had both wonderful and sad memories, with the clear demarcation line being the day Officer Maxwell died. Until his death, it was a light and airy place filled with love and laughter. After his death, it was a dark and stifling place filled with tears and silence. Sitting at the curb, I tried to focus on the good memories, but our final night together refused to stay in the back of my mind. It kept fighting its way to the forefront of my thoughts, like childhood taunts or perceived inadequacies. Staring at the black door, I could hear the heartache and disappointment in Chelsea's voice when she found me stumbling down the hallway at 2 a.m. for the umpteenth time.

"I know the pain of losing a child," she said in a desperate and pleading tone. "I can help you with your pain if you'll let me in."

"I can't take it anymore. He is all I think about, every minute of every day."

Drained, I collapsed backward. When my head and back met the plasterboard, I slid down the wall until my butt found the floor. Engulfed by anguish, I sat on the floor with my back against the wall and my head in my hands. Anymore, I tried not to look into her eyes.

"Don't shut me out," she demanded, looking down at me. "We can get through this together."

"You don't understand," I responded, without looking up at her. "I don't think I'll ever get over this tragedy. The image of Officer Maxwell in that alley with his tongue cut out won't go away. It haunts me every time I close my eyes."

"I know your feelings of guilt are overwhelming, but drugs and alcohol are not the answer. You need to start your healing by stopping this destructive behavior. You're killing yourself."

"I need to numb my mind. I need to escape my thoughts. It's the only way I can make it through a day."

"I won't stand by and watch. I won't enable your behavior."

"No one is making you stay, sweetheart," I shot back at her. "Don't let the black door hit you on the ass as you leave."

I was high on cocaine and drunk from more than numerous shots of alcohol, but I don't think I'd ever said anything so stupid in all my life. In my altered state, I thought my black door reference was clever and humorous, but those words have weighed heavily on my conscience ever since that night, echoing often in my thoughts while I tried to focus on other things. How could I say such horrible words to Chelsea? How could I tell her to go away?

Saddened by that recollection, I looked for comfort in the memory of a more typical evening in our home, before grief and despair moved into our guest bedroom. From my favorite leather chair in the living room, I watched Chelsea as she prepared our dinner in the kitchen, and it was as entertaining for me as any Broadway show. Throughout the entire process, her movements were beautiful, joyous, and even sensual, and I was in awe of her. Chelsea was always radiant whenever she was in a kitchen cooking a meal; she lit up from within because she was doing what she loved most.

For almost twenty minutes, I was lost in that sweet memory until the loud honk of a car horn jolted me back into the present. Sitting in front of our old home, remembering my deep love for Chelsea, my feelings were now clear: I wanted my life back, I wanted Chelsea back, I wanted our life back. Tom was entirely right—it was time for me to look forward again. My last chance at redemption tour was having the desired effect, but I was running out of time, and I still had one more stop to make, the most difficult stop on the tour. Though unscheduled and long overdue, I needed to have a conversation with Sandra Maxwell.

Chapter Sixty-Eight

On a quiet street in South Philadelphia, the Maxwell home was a shoebox of a house, with three bedrooms and just a smidge more than nine hundred square feet of living space, washed-out, pale yellow paint and light blue shutters, and a large picture window in the living room, the perfect place for the Christmas tree during the holidays. It sat in a humble neighborhood of working class people, who wore overalls at work, punched time cards as they came and went, and owned little more than their homes, cars, and weekends. They were good people with strong work ethics and faith in God. On this street, people knew their neighbors by their first names, helped each other without being asked, and took pride in their community. Louis Maxwell grew up in this neighborhood, and the thought of ever leaving it never crossed his mind, not even for a moment. In his time, he wanted nothing more than to make it better.

I was parked at the final stop for the day, across the street from the Maxwell home with a clear view of the living room's large picture window. I could see into the living room, but in my short time on their quiet street, I hadn't seen anyone inside the house. I reached for the door handle to exit my truck, but as I did, my cell phone rang, and the name Tom Corbett appeared on the screen. Happy for the delay and distraction, I touched the screen to answer the call.

"Hello, Tom," I said. "What's up?"

"Hey, Nick. I'm calling to let you know that I've decided to go forward with the exhumation of my father's grave. You've been right all along—I need to know the truth about my family."

"I'm glad to hear that. I think it's the right decision for you."

"I'm will talk with a lawyer on Monday and get the process moving forward. I'm sure it will involve paperwork, court dates, and a lot of red tape."

"And an excavator," I said.

"Very funny," Tom returned.

"You know, Tom, I know a retired medical examiner in Pittsburgh who is now a private consultant involved in court cases that could do the examination for you. You'd have better control of the findings that way."

"That's a good idea," Tom said. "Give me his name when you come back to the farm. Where are you?"

"I'm sitting in my truck across the street from Sandra Maxwell's home."

"Are you going to talk to her?"

"That's why I'm here."

"I am proud of you. It's not going to be an easy conversation, but it's necessary."

"I know."

When I hung up from our call, my mind drifted to a video I once watched of Louis Maxwell at an awards ceremony for a little league baseball team that he coached in the spring of 2004. His daughters were too young to play on the team of eleven and twelve-year-olds, but he coached the squad anyway because he always looked for ways to impact young people. True to his nature, he was the only coach in the league who didn't have a child on his team. The video was recorded three years before his death, but someone posted it to the internet shortly after his death. I'm sure it was meant as a tribute to him. I recognized my stall tactic, but I touched my phone's screen to select the internet anyway and quickly located the video again. Along with his players, about thirty-five family members had gathered in a community center for the trophy presentation and cake and ice cream afterward. As the team's coach, Louis was the master of ceremonies for the event.

"I am so very proud of each of you," Louis began, directed at fifteen boys and girls seated in the front row of folding chairs, wearing baseball jerseys with "Firebirds" across the front.

"We had such a great season," he continued. "Fifteen wins, two losses, and the league championship—that's fantastic. And we had a whole lot of fun."

The family members clapped vigorously while Louis paused and smiled at the little leaguers. Unusual for children of their young age, the players were all quiet and well-behaved with no rambunctiousness or clowning in their seats. Looking at their shining faces, their admiration and respect for their coach were quite evident.

"It's great to be champions, but I want to talk to you about losing before I hand out trophies. It might seem like an unusual topic for this gathering, but it's relevant. As you grow up, you're not going to win every championship along the way, and that's okay. Many times, you will finish second or third or even tenth. There may be times when you don't finish at all. On the baseball diamond and in life, the most important competition is the one that takes place within your own self, within your own being. It doesn't matter whether you win or lose so long as you have put forward your best effort."

Originating in the back of the room, Louis was interrupted by applause again; apparently, the parents approved of his message.

He continued. "When you take these trophies home tonight, I want each of you to remember these words that I include with them— true accomplishment comes from bettering yourself, not defeating another. You see, team, self-improvement is the real victory. The ultimate competition in life is with yourself, to be better tomorrow than today, to be the best that you can be. That is the championship I want you to win."

Once again, the family members applauded enthusiastically and even whistled. For some reason, during this round of applause, the video lost sound, and the final seven minutes was silent as Louis handed out the trophies and shook the hands of his players. Everyone was smiling and happy and celebratory, but a ghostly silence existed during the awards portion of the ceremony. Once the trophies were distributed, parents came forward and seemingly thanked Louis for his efforts with their children, but those exchanges were shrouded in silence also. The lack of sound gave the video an eerie, haunting quality, at least for me. For the final minute, Louis was front and center, close-up, smiling and laughing with his friends and neighbors, who seemed really fond of him. In silence, I watched him, stared into his eyes, and knew he was a good man.

When I looked up from my phone, the light of day had faded away into the dusk, and several table lamps illuminated the living room of the Maxwell home. Through the window, I saw Sandra Maxwell walk across the living room and disappear from my view as quickly as she entered it. During her brief appearance, she called out to someone as she walked, signaling to me that at least one of her daughters was in the residence. I placed my hand on the door handle and began opening the truck door, but I stopped midway. With my hand wrapped firmly around the door handle, I hesitated.

I can't do this right now, I told myself. *I'm exhausted. I'm worn out. I shouldn't have made this stop the final stop of the day. I need to make this conversation the only stop on another day, so I can give it the focus it deserves. I won't insult Sandra by showing up in this worn-out condition.*

How much of my decision to delay my conversation with Sandra Maxwell was avoidance and how much was real concern about my tired condition, I didn't honestly know. It had, indeed, been a long, hard, emotional, and draining day. I watched the front window for another five minutes and then I started the engine of my truck and drove away. It looked like my last chance for redemption tour would roll into town again on another day. Now more than ever, I knew I needed to have a conversation with Sandra Maxwell.

I will come back, I promised myself.

Chapter Sixty-Nine

B y mid-July, we'd installed the blue metal roof and the guesthouse was fully enclosed, so we were eight weeks ahead of our original timeline, though we obviously had yet to learn how long any of the work took when we drew up the schedule. Enclosing the structure before harsh weather arrived was the most important milestone, and we'd breezed past it in mid-summer. As such, Tom and I felt good about our rate of progress on the project.

Our paleontological effort was progressing well also, as half of Digby's small front arms were now visible beneath his massive skull, and several of the vertebrae of his neck were visible behind his skull. In the wall of the hole, his enormous size was becoming evident, and he was starting to look formidable, a creature you wouldn't want to happen upon in a dark alley during its heyday. Beneath the spotlights at night, Tom had worked until well after midnight on several occasions as he was still fascinated with our fossil find. For reasons I didn't fully understand, he'd forged a relationship with Digby that went beyond our original intent of seeing a portion of the dinosaur unearthed. There seemed to be an ongoing connection between Digby, Tom, and his family tragedy. In some archaic way, I think Digby had become one more piece of the troubled past that Tom inherited on the farm. If I were to take a stab at psychoanalysis, I might even speculate that Tom and Digby were one and the same, as both suffered traumatic events while inhabiting this farm. While Tom was unearthing the dinosaur in the field, he was simultaneously unearthing his own history.

"Digby gets more real for me every day," Tom told me one evening after dinner though I wasn't sure what he meant. "He is here for a reason," he added. "He has a greater purpose than we know."

"He is one hell of an obvious metaphor," I said, grinning as I did. "Digby is an enormous secret from the past buried on the family farm in the same field where the murder of your father took place."

"You can't turn off that writer thing, can you?"

"It's an occupational hazard."

"Well, at least you're good at it."

"Is there any progress on the exhumation?"

"My lawyer filed the petition with the court, and she expects we'll hear something in a week or so."

"Then the body will be exhumed and transported to Pittsburgh for the examination?" I followed up.

"That's the plan."

"I've never been to an exhumation."

"Well, keep your work boots handy."

About 7:30 p.m., Alex returned from town in his Jeep Cherokee and drove across the open field toward the guesthouse with seven recent graduates of Shelbyville High School crammed within it, two boys and five girls. Twenty feet from the structure, the vehicle came to an abrupt halt, and everyone leapt out. Very quickly, Alex and his friends gathered around the perimeter of the hole and stared down at Digby.

"No way!" one of the boys called out, "that's one fierce-looking beast. I wouldn't mess with it."

"Digby was the badass of his day," Alex informed his friends. "He feared no other creature—they all feared him."

"His teeth look like they could rip you apart," the same boy commented. "I don't think he was a vegetarian."

"While he was alive," Alex replied, "those teeth were as sharp as samurai knives. He ripped his prey into little pieces."

"How old are those fossils?" one of the girls asked Alex.

"One hundred fifty million years old."

"Amazing," she replied, her eyes wide.

Even from a distance, the group dynamics were interesting and obvious. Alex was the only one of the eight who had ever lived in a big city, and the other kids admired him for that, thinking him sophisticated and worldly because he grew up in Philadelphia. When he told them about his home—a condo in a hi-rise building with a concierge in the lobby—he was suddenly the coolest kid they'd ever met, a real city slicker. In their minds, Alex had experienced things they could only imagine or view on the internet. Two of his new friends were going to colleges in large cities in the fall, and they asked him questions like he was an explorer for the crown who'd returned from distant and exotic locations. They wanted to know what to expect in those far-away worlds. The fact was that Alex was much cooler in Shelbyville than he ever was in Philadelphia.

"Some things never change," I remarked to Tom.

"Why do you say that?"

"It's obvious Alex is using Digby for his benefit."

"You think he's using him to be popular with the other kids?"

"I think he's using him to get laid!" I replied.

Tom's eyes widened. It was suddenly obvious to him.

"I'm glad we moved him into the old guesthouse," he remarked. "It'll save me from uncomfortable moments."

"It probably will."

Sitting on the porch that evening, neither Tom nor I made the logical connection and realized what would inevitably follow this visit—word of our dinosaur would spread amongst townsfolk as quickly as rumors of an affair or news of a death. Our Digby would suddenly be more famous than the original Digby, and he founded the town. Two days later, when we went to The Rooster for lunch, Tom and I first learned about this newly generated interest in our prehistoric houseguest. As we walked along Main Street toward the diner, townsfolk approached and asked if they could come to the farm to view our dinosaur; most said they wanted to bring their children or grandchildren. Some even jaywalked and crossed the street between traffic when they noticed us on the other side, determined to hear about the dinosaur firsthand. All told us they simply had to see it.

At our table in the diner, Tom and I barely had time to place our orders or nibble on our meals because we had non-stop visitors. Everyone wanted a moment with us. In between inquiries, I wondered whether there was a connection between the recent death of Robbie Reynolds and the frenzied interest in Digby. Either way, the town had clearly christened its newest hero in the form of a dinosaur. While he was indeed a longtime resident, it was still rather unusual when you considered the fact that Digby never played for Shelbyville High School, performed at a street fair, or competed at the county fair.

Back in the cab of my pickup truck, we were both dazed and confused by all the attention and excitement. Our quiet, small-town lives had suddenly been injected with a dose of craziness, a condition that didn't fit either of our personalities or manners of conduct. We were in demand, and neither of us wanted to be in demand. Sitting there, staring forward toward City Hall, we were startled when Donna Brinkley, a woman who worked at the drug store, tapped on the passenger side window and called out, "See you soon."

Tom shook his head. He fastened his seat belt.

"Can you believe what just happened?" he asked.

"I know what it felt like to be one of the Beatles in 1964. We are suddenly the 'Fab Two.' That was one crazy lunch."

"One mother asked me if she could have her daughter's tenth birthday party at the farm with Digby?"

"What did you tell her?" I asked.

"I said sure. What the hell else could I say?"

"Principal Harding told me they will want to schedule some field trips to the farm as soon as the children are back in school. He said we should sit down with a September calendar and plan the best dates for each grade."

"Oh, my God!" Tom exclaimed.

"I guess we'll have to purchase a couple of megaphones and prepare to give group tours at the farm. When I have some time, I'll write up a script for each of us to follow."

"Sometimes, your sense of humor really bugs me."

"If you can't find humor in this situation," I returned drolly, "something is wrong with you. Frankly, if you can't find humor in this situation, you have no sense of humor at all."

"You know, Nick," Tom said, smiling as he did, "you prepare for as much as you can in life, but you never think to plan for the impact that the discovery of a one hundred fifty million-year-old dinosaur on your property might have on your life."

"Now you're getting it."

I started the truck up and moved the lever into drive. As we pulled away from the curb, there was a fleeing sensation in our acceleration, and I checked my rearview mirror to see if there were any screaming townsfolk running after us like the Beatles all those years ago.

"We've got to get out in front of this craziness," Tom said.

"What do you have in mind?" I asked.

"You should write an article about Digby for *The Sentinel* and include a photograph of Digby as well as a picture and some history about the allosaurus."

"Isn't that just going to add fuel to the fire?"

"Maybe. But, in the article, you can specify that anyone that wants to see Digby can come to the farm on Sundays between 1 p.m.

and 5 p.m. That way, we won't have people showing up uninvited at all times of the day and night. We'll control it."

"That makes sense. After all, people really want to see Digby. I'll include an article about him in the next issue."

"Can you put it on the front page?"

"You got it," I replied. "I can't imagine I'll have any bigger, competing stories than the discovery of dinosaur bones on the outskirts of town."

"How about my father's planned exhumation because my mother is suspected of murdering him in our field forty years ago?"

"Well, I'll be darned, Tom—you do have a sense of humor after all," I said as I found amusement in his joke.

Chapter Seventy

On July 26th, the front page of *The Shelbyville Sentinel* heralded "Meet Digby" in bold text above a photograph of Digby's skull and small legs protruding from the wall of the hole beside the guesthouse. "One Hundred Fifty Million-Year-Old Allosaurus Found on Corbett Farm" supported the headline in smaller text. Immediately, this issue became my favorite issue of *The Sentinel* because I felt a real sense of pride about it.

As publisher of a small-town newspaper, I recognized that the subject matter of my articles seldom had significance beyond the limits of our little town. Most of my articles were human-interest pieces about the lives and times of the good people of Shelbyville—people whose daily activities consisted of hard work and community interaction but little of importance or noteworthiness. As I sat in my dark office and tapped away at the keyboard, I strove to make the stories interesting, but I knew they were not truly newsworthy. Unlike my early days at *The Philadelphia Post,* there was little chance that any of the major news services would pick up my little stories and distribute them to the major newspapers. The truth was that the sound of my voice contained on the pages faded into silence at the town's limits.

Working late into the night for several nights in a row, putting this issue together was different for me because the discovery of Digby was truly newsworthy. For the first time in a long time, I was writing about something that had relevance and significance beyond the town limits of Shelbyville, Pennsylvania. On the world stage, in the fields of archeology and paleontology, the discovery of Digby was a major event, a once in a generation occurrence that would have a significant impact on the ongoing study of dinosaurs, as well as our knowledge of the planet that existed long before we arrived. Beyond its scientific implications, this discovery would also encourage people everywhere to appreciate the magnificence of these creatures and wonder about our place in the world, our place in this universe. The resulting article was about Digby, the allosaurus, the study of dinosaurs, and how people in small towns still honored and preserved the past.

Without a doubt, I loved the people of Shelbyville and this town itself, but I'd forgotten how important my work as journalist was, how a well-written article about the right subject matter could affect lives. While working at *The Post,* I wrote many meaningful articles that impacted the city of Philadelphia and its citizens. In those days, I felt my words were important, and I thought I made a difference. Working on this issue restored my old enthusiasm for my chosen profession. I felt passion filling my body to the level I had at twenty years old. I felt renewed. Sitting at my desk, I felt like a world-class journalist again.

As a humorous sidebar, I included a box in the issue that I titled, "Why We Love Dinosaurs." It was a last-minute addition, a space-filler to complete the subject matter, but I got more reaction and emails about that little box than I ever expected. Much to my surprise, it truly touched people.

Michael Bowe

Why We Love Dinosaurs

For many of us, dinosaurs represent the past, a simpler time before man arrived with his inventions, the time before time when there weren't any clocks or schedules or deadlines. Whether a million years or twenty years ago, we know the world was simpler then because it gets more complex and confusing with each passing day. As we move forward in life, we yearn for simplicity because simple is comforting. For many of us, dinosaurs represent the world in its simplest age, a nostalgic period during its infancy while new and young and innocent. But, even dinosaurs couldn't hold back time, and they vanished from the world, leaving all of us in the modern world to ponder...

innocence and dinosaurs...two simple things that you can't find no more...this world is changing, and we can't ignore...the lack of innocence and dinosaurs.

Chapter Seventy-One

When the July 26th issue hit the newsstand on Thursday, there was sufficient excitement and buzz around town to cause Tom and I to realize that we better prepare the site for an onslaught of visitors. On Saturday, we spent the morning putting a chain link fence in place around the hole, with an additional fifteen feet of fencing beyond the hole so we could expand and expose more vertebrae and possibly part of his ribcage in the coming weeks. We hoped the new fence would keep visitors from falling into the hole or messing with Digby. As we worked on the fence, Tom received calls from several local vendors—Angelo's Brick Oven Pizza, Tito's Taco Truck, and The Cookie Mill—and, in turn, each requested permission to sell their wares at the farm on Sunday. These calls were more confirmation that visitors would overrun the farm, and Tom told the vendors that they were welcome.

More than one hundred fifty people arrived at the farm in the first half-hour on Sunday. Cars and pickup trucks were parked along the dirt road for nearly a quarter of a mile in both directions. Almost immediately, the line to walk past the chain link fence and view Digby wound and twisted from the guesthouse through the open field to the front porch of the farmhouse and was nearly seventy people in length. The decision to allow food vendors to work the event turned out to be wise as it alleviated some of the congestion that would've inevitably formed around Digby. The mayor and the police chief, along with three police officers, arrived around 2 p.m. after they noticed the event's popularity.

For most of the afternoon, Tom and I sat on the front porch and enjoyed the pleasant scene occurring before us, one very similar to one of Shelbyville's street fairs, as parents with children milled about in the field, viewed Digby in his hole, purchased lunch and snacks from the vendors, and generally enjoyed a beautiful summer afternoon. Most interesting to watch was the children's reactions as they saw a real dinosaur for the first time; their faces lit up with sheer joy and absolute wonder while their parents told them about Digby and his prehistoric sidekicks. When the dinner hour approached and the crowd began to dwindle, the final tally of visitors for the day was in excess of five hundred. Digby's popularity was confirmed.

In the ten days that followed the publication of the Digby issue, *The Philadelphia Post* picked up the article first, and then more than eleven hundred other newspapers across the nation followed suit. Two television networks included segments about the discovery of Digby in Shelbyville on their national news programs. It was all reinvigorating and a confidence builder for me.

"What a great article, Nick," Austin said when he called to congratulate me. "It's no wonder you have a Fenwick on your shelf."

"It's so nice to hear from you. I miss our daily chats."

"I do, too. Are you ready to come back to *The Post*? We'd love to have you on staff again."

"No, not just yet," I replied, "but I'm doing better these days. I'm starting to make plans again. Maybe soon. You know I think of *The Post* as my home in journalism."

"That's good to hear. I'm glad you're doing better."

"I'm finally making progress on putting the death of Officer Maxwell behind me. I'm doing my best to move on."

"It was a tragic accident, Nick, but it wasn't your fault."

"I'm starting to understand that."

"As part of your looking forward, I have something I want to mention to you. I'm only going to remain in the position of editor of *The Post* for another couple of years, and then I plan to recommend you as my successor."

"Well, I'd be honored to have your endorsement, but I don't know if it's the right job for me."

"That's why I want to mention it so far in advance. You'll have to decide if you want to keep writing or take on an entirely new challenge as an editor at a major newspaper. It will be a difficult decision for you."

"Thank you, Austin. I will give it a lot of thought."

"Where is Chelsea these days?"

"She is still in Los Angeles working on her cooking show. Why do you ask?'

"Just curious, that's all."

Five days ago, Tom told me he believed Digby was here for a reason, that his discovery on the farm had a much greater purpose than we realized. At the time, I didn't understand what Tom meant—I allowed his words to pass without question or comment. Five days later, I fully understood and agreed with him. I, too, believed Digby was here for a reason, and maybe as many as a handful of reasons.

Chapter Seventy-Two

During the three months Alex lived at the farm, there was a large dinosaur in the field and an even larger elephant in the living room. In many families, topics that are either too sensitive or too combustible become the elephant in the living room that no one acknowledges. Everyone acts like it isn't there; no matter how wildly the elephant swings its giant trunk. Alex knew the concept well because he grew up with an elephant in the living room in the form of his mother's drinking. No one ever mentioned her fourth or fifth glass of wine at dinner or the unpleasantness that often followed. And that elephant could really swing its trunk and raise a ruckus. All summer at the farm, the elephant in the living room had been whether or not Alex would attend Brown University in the fall. When Tom, AJ, and I discussed the issue earlier in the summer, we all agreed that it was better to let Alex initiate the conversation, let him approach us. So far, Alex had come to both AJ and I but not his father, which was understandable because he knew his father's opinion. On a Sunday morning in early August over waffles at breakfast, Alex finally engaged his father in a conversation about his college plans.

Heeding the advice AJ and I gave him, Tom remembered to listen more than talk.

"I'd like to talk to you about college if that's okay?"

"Okay," Tom said, trying to hide his eagerness.

"I keep thinking about something Nick said to me a while back," Alex observed in a contemplative tone unusual for his age.

"What was that?"

"He said that at my age, it's not important to know what I want to be, only that I want to be something."

"Nick is a smart guy."

"I want you to know I'm going to do something worthwhile with my life—I just don't know what that is yet."

"That's okay. Nick is right. Few kids your age know what they want to do with their lives. When I was your age, I didn't know what I wanted to do either."

"Brown University is a great school, and I want to go there, but I want to start in the fall of 2013 instead of this fall. I have applied for deferred enrollment."

"Well then, what will you do for the next year?"

"AJ told me he could hook me up with a job in Miami. He has all sorts of connections there. I want to work in Miami this winter, return to Shelbyville for the summer, and then go to Brown."

Considering his son's proposal, Tom hesitated for a moment and took on a thoughtful demeanor. While he originally wanted Alex to go to Brown in the fall and start his studies, he was pleasantly surprised to learn that Alex had a plan, and one that included real consideration. This represented a level of maturity Alex hadn't exhibited in the past. Further, AJ ran his offer by Tom before making it to Alex, so Tom wasn't surprised by that possibility. Always a realist, Tom recognized that a year in the real world before college might do his son a lot of good. After a few uneasy moments of silence for Alex, Tom surprised him with his next comments.

"That sounds like a really good plan, but you have to promise me something if you want my blessing and support."

"What's that?" Alex asked.

"You have to promise me that you will use your good mind in Miami, no DUIs or other trouble that could impact your future."

"That was a year ago, Dad," Alex said. "I've grown up a lot since then."

"You have indeed."

"I won't let you down."

"Then, I'm on board with your plan."

"Can I stay in the new guesthouse next summer?"

"I'm really happy that you're coming back to the farm for the summer. Let's wait until then to figure out the room assignments. You'll either be where you are now or in the new guesthouse."

"That sounds good."

"You've started to like Shelbyville, haven't you?"

"I have."

Chapter Seventy-Three

After the first Sunday afternoon, I expected interest in our dinosaur to wane. On each successive Sunday, I thought turnout would gradually lessen until no one showed up. Soon enough, we'd sleep in on Sunday mornings, and the field would return to its normally still state on Sunday afternoons. After all, how long could Digby continue to generate interest in this distracted, internet-obsessed world that we lived in? When all was said and done, Digby was really just a skull and a few bones in a hole. In my mind, I believed he'd be forgotten as quickly as an old issue of *The Sentinel*. Boy, was I wrong!

Each Sunday, turnout kept increasing until the third Sunday when the visitor count broke the one-thousand mark. On that day, we had five vendors participating in the event, three police officers assisting with parking and crowd control, and a line of ten portable toilets beside the barn. Cars and trucks were parked along the road for a mile in each direction, and, interestingly enough, ten or twelve states were represented by license plates, a few from as far away as Florida and Maine. Had everyone forgotten that Disney World,

Hershey Park, and Six Flags had even more to offer than the Corbett farm?

"I talked with a woman from Athens, Georgia," Tom said as he joined me on the porch, shaking his head in a confused manner as he lowered himself into an Adirondack chair. "She and her husband made the seven-hundred-mile trip to see Digby. She told me that they were absolutely thrilled to be here. I swear to you, Nick, this woman sounded like someone on a pilgrimage to the Holy Land."

"Well, that's nothing," I returned. "A guy from Tallahassee just asked me if he could be Digby's official agent in the Sunshine State. He wants to start a fan club."

"What did you tell him?"

"I said sure. You don't say no to someone like that! You just hope he forgets about the conversation when he returns to the asylum."

"What is happening here?"

"Digby is a phenomenon. That's what's happening."

"Why?" Tom asked with a befuddled look on his face.

"These kinds of things are always hard to understand, Tom, but I've seen it many times before; the public latches onto something innocuous, and suddenly it's relevant. A circular logic develops: It's relevant because many people are interested in it, and many people are interested in it because it's relevant. Some group dynamic takes over and creates interest that didn't previously exist, relevance with no basis in reality. There isn't a logical explanation—it just happens.

"Some guy told me Digby has a Facebook page with almost five thousand followers."

"Well," I said, "we're going to have a talk with Digby and suspend his internet privileges."

"Very funny."

"Hey, mister," a ten-year-old boy called up to me from the driveway, "do you work here?"

I smiled. "I guess I do."

"Where is the video games pavilion?"

"Sorry, kid, we don't have one."

"Aw man," he mumbled as he walked away, "this is the lamest amusement park I've ever visited."

Though we made light of the situation and thought it was all a bit absurd, Tom and I were concerned about the scene we witnessed in the field. Unlike restaurants and other public places, the field didn't have an occupancy limit set by the fire department, but, during the day, it sure felt like we approached it, whatever the hell it was. People were not shoulder-to-shoulder, but they were cramped and crowded and bumping into one another frequently. It felt like Black Friday at a shopping mall. Fortunately for us, the thirteen hundred visitors for the day were spread over five hours, which made it manageable for now. At its peak, three hundred wandered the field, and that crowd size made it clear that the field wouldn't accommodate five hundred at once. And the reality was that we could be just a few weeks away from that many. So far, there was no indication that the crowds would slow or lessen and no reason to believe that the tally wouldn't continue to climb. For Tom and me, we were anxious about the coming weeks.

"In all my fifty-five years on this planet," Mayor Pete Nash said when he joined us around 4 p.m., "this is the darnedest thing I've ever witnessed. I'm blown away by what I'm seeing on your farm."

"Digby is a phenomenon," I said. "The crowds get bigger each week."

"We need to find a way to incorporate Digby into the street fair that is coming up on Labor Day weekend," the mayor suggested in a calculating manner. "Somehow, we have to add your dinosaur to our promotion for the event."

"Oh, I don't know about that," Tom said. "I'm not looking for ways to make this any bigger. I already feel like I have a dinosaur by the tail here."

"But Tom," the mayor insisted, "this is much bigger than your little farm and the turnout here. Both hotels are booked solid, all tables at The Rooster are occupied, and retail sales are up at least thirty percent for the weekend. Digby is having a wonderful effect on our tourist trade."

"Well," Tom replied, "I'm certainly glad to hear that, Mayor. The fact is that plenty of positive things have happened since we found Digby, and Nick and I both feel obligated to look after him and protect him. We don't want this thing to get out of hand."

"I fully understand," the mayor said. "Why don't you come by my office this week and we can discuss it further? Maybe we can figure out a way to make this work for everyone."

"I'll give it some thought," Tom replied half-heartedly, "but I can't promise you anything."

Two hours later, the field had emptied of visitors, and Tom and I remained on the front porch with cold beers in front of us, watching as the vendors packed their wares. One by one, each seemed quite jovial as they shouted, "See you next week," at the porch and drove their trucks away from the trampled field, leaving little doubt that they had done brisk business and had a lucrative day. As the daylight was fading into twilight, Tom seemed quiet and reflective until he surprised me with his next comments.

"You should write another article about Digby," he said, and his words seemed to come out of nowhere. "I think you should dedicate another issue of *The Sentinel* to this crazy phenomenon we're witnessing around our dinosaur."

"It's certainly newsworthy, but it'll only draw more attention to Digby and more people to the farm. I've often thought about a follow-up article, but I didn't think you'd want me to do it."

"I definitely want you to do it."

"Why?"

"This afternoon, when I told the mayor that plenty of positive things have happened because of Digby, one of the main things I was referring to, was your first article about Digby. To me, it felt like that article was part of the reason we found Digby in the first place, like it was all destined to happen the way it did. Now, I would love to see a second article by you about the Digby phenomenon get picked up by all the big newspapers again. It would feel like Digby is fulfilling his purpose and adding additional meaning to his time with us."

"Well okay then," I told him, elated. "The next issue of *The Sentinel* will be headlined "The Digby Phenomenon," and it will include some of the photographs I took today."

"Great. Will you do me another favor also?"

"Sure, what is it?"

"Call your friend Augie and tell him it's time for his team to return to the farm with their ground-penetrating radar equipment and determine how much of Digby is in the ground."

"Are you considering donating Digby to the museum?"

"I don't know, but it's time to learn what we have here."

Chapter Seventy-Four

The finishing touches made the guesthouse a beautiful space and one that greatly exceeded my expectations. In the last three weeks, Tom and I installed gray, wide-plank flooring that coordinated well with the blue shaker cabinets and white quartz countertops in the kitchen; we installed white subway tiles in the bathroom and shower and even poured our own concrete sink for the bathroom; we hung a barn-style door made of reclaimed wood on rails as a room divider that could be open or closed depending on the need —closed created a living room and bedroom and open created one large space for a studio or office. When we sealed up the structure six weeks earlier, the guesthouse took shape, but with the interior almost complete, it had character and soul also.

Each evening before I turned out the lights, I paused to appreciate our work. I was proud of the end results. In my lifetime, I'd gotten a lot of satisfaction from my literary accomplishments, but this guesthouse taught me the special satisfaction that comes when accomplishing something outside your comfort zone, when you stretch to do something you never imagined you could. When we broke ground on this project last spring, I'd never used a jigsaw or router, and would've been hard-pressed to identify either on a workbench. Now, as a result of this project, I felt like a better, more rounded person and one with fewer limitations. We built a guesthouse and a lot more in the process.

"I think we can finish by Labor Day," I remarked as Tom and I walked toward the house on Monday evening.

"I think it will be early September," Tom replied, "because we have the exhumation coming up, and you have your next issue of *The Sentinel* to work on. We don't have a lot left to do, but we have some distractions in the next few weeks."

"Yeah, I guess you're right. I will have to dedicate a lot of time to the next issue. I want it to be as special as the first Digby issue."

Chapter Seventy-Five

"Before us lie two of the most miserable men to ever leave footprints on the face of this earth," Tom said hardheartedly as we arrived at the headstones of Samuel and Carl Corbett. He scowled at his relatives when he stopped at the foot of their graves.

"That's a little harsh, isn't it?" AJ asked.

"I don't think so," Tom returned. "I've spent the better part of a year learning about the lives of my father and his brother, and I've yet to hear anyone say a kind word about either of them. They were both mean, bitter men who never did anything for anyone."

"Well, you get to watch as they dig up your father's grave today," I said. "Maybe that will be cathartic for you."

"Maybe."

"Listening to your stories about your abusive father," AJ offered somewhat sadly, "makes me wonder if I was just plain better off without my father after he abandoned us. He couldn't have been much of a man either to walk away from his family. He was probably no better than your father."

"Which is worse," Tom asked, "staying and abusing your family or packing up and abandoning them?"

"They are different degrees of horrendous," I chimed in. "It doesn't really matter which one is worse. In both situations, the kids pay a steep price."

"How is your relationship with your father?" AJ asked me.

"He has always been good to me. He is a good man."

"That's good to hear," AJ said like my acknowledgment had restored his faith in humanity.

"One out of three," Tom observed. "I hope we're not an accurate sample group."

The exhumation of Samuel Corbett was scheduled for 6:30 a.m. because cemetery policy required all exhumations to happen at first light when there was little foot traffic on the grounds. Exhumations in the cemetery business were like cockroaches in the restaurant business —the public didn't want to see them or know they existed. Both were creepy and repulsive. As we waited beside the grave, a yellow excavator already parked alongside it, the air was cool and crisp, and the ground was glazed with morning dew. Tom's comments about his father and uncle made me wonder about his grandfather, and I made a mental note to see what I could find out about him; as a journalist, my curiosity was easily roused. I knew that human emotions traveled through stages, but Tom had been carrying his anger toward his father inside him for too long. Standing beside him before the source of his festering anger, I could only hope this exhumation helped him move forward.

"Good morning," a cemetery worker in tan overalls said as he approached us. "Which one of you is Tom Corbett?"

He was a lanky man with tattoos and a cigarette behind his ear.

"That's me," Tom answered.

"I'm going to start with the excavator," the cemetery worker, Seymour Hickok, stated as he began his explanation of the process, "and remove the top four feet of dirt and then I'll use a shovel to remove the last few feet of dirt. The tricky part will come when I put straps around the casket and try to lift it out of the grave with the excavator. This is a forty-year-old casket so you never know whether it'll hold together or break apart. Let's hope it stays together. Assuming it doesn't fall apart when we lift it out, the whole process will take about an hour at most."

"That's much quicker than I expected," Tom said.

"Once we exhume the remains," Seymour continued with his explanation, "we'll transport them to the address in Pittsburgh you provided. They should arrive by noon."

"Good."

"Our office will notify you when the casket returns and we are ready to put it back in the ground. You can arrange for a short ceremony if you like."

"That won't be necessary."

"Would you like to say a prayer before I start?"

"No, Seymour," Tom replied, "that won't be necessary either. Please start whenever you are ready."

The lanky man shrugged. He was confused. "What was your relationship to the deceased?"

"He was my father."

Now, he seemed to understand.

"I'll get to work, Mr. Corbett."

Tom and I appreciated good excavator work. We, too, had maneuvered the great beasts and challenged solid earth. With only ten or twelve jabs of the steel claw into the ground, Seymour removed the top four feet of dirt and left behind a perfectly rectangular hole just larger than a casket. His movements of the tractor, long arm, and digging claw were extremely efficient and accurate, and he climbed down off the big machine within fifteen minutes of climbing up on it. In the process, he hadn't consumed any unnecessary time or ounces of fuel to do the work. When he was done, I felt like we'd witnessed a master excavator at work.

"That was impressive," I said to Tom as Seymour grabbed his shovel from its spot against a tree.

"It sure was," Tom returned.

For the next twenty minutes, Seymour shoveled dirt from within the rectangular hole and built a pile along the side of the grave that, coincidentally, was about the size of a body. With each toss of dirt, a little more of the casket came into view and it looked like the wood on the bottom of an old boat, blackened by four decades in the moist ground. Tom, AJ, and I moved to the perimeter of the hole to assess the condition of the casket, as we all realized this exhumation would go much smoother if the casket didn't crumble when lifted from the earth. It appeared solid, but I knew that only the actual lift would reveal the true condition of the box.

"It looks solid," AJ remarked as we stared into the hole.

"It better hold together," Tom replied in a determined tone. "It's important that the remains not be dropped or jostled because that'll only complicate the medical examiner's work. I don't want him wondering whether the bones might have been damaged when the casket broke. That won't help me in my quest to learn the truth."

"It's going to come out of there in one piece," I said in my most optimistic tone.

With the digging complete, Seymour positioned the excavator arm over the grave and began wrapping straps around the casket that he attached to the claw. If all went well, the straps would cradle the casket while the excavator claw lifted it out of the grave. At one point, Seymour paused and told us that the casket looked intact and should come out of the hole without breaking apart. He said he'd seen caskets in much worse shape than this one.

"This is the moment of truth," Seymour observed as he climbed out of the hole and then up onto the excavator. "You might want to say that prayer now, Mr. Corbett," he added as he started the engine.

As Seymour moved the lever on the excavator forward, the straps tightened, and the claw began to lift the casket. Careful to avoid any jolts, he slowly lifted the casket into the air but only to a height of about a foot above sea level, not even knee level. For a long moment, the black box hovered over the hole. Watching it dangle, my breathing stopped. Anxiously, Tom, AJ, and I watched as the casket slowly moved from above the hole to the side of the grave opposite the pile of dirt, a journey of less than five feet, but it seemed to take forever. Seymour lowered the casket to the ground beside the grave with the delicacy of a heart surgeon.

"Well done, Seymour," Tom exclaimed as he made the thumbs-up sign.

We all breathed a collective sigh of relief.

When Seymour left to coordinate the pick-up of the casket by the cemetery van, the three of us were left standing beside the black casket, covered with a gooey, muddy substance where earthworms still writhed and squirmed. This moment was something right out of a horror movie. If it were night and dark outside, I would've gotten the hell out of there. Instead, with Tom on my right, I looked at the casket and wondered about the condition of the remains within.

"Will you be okay if Marie did it?" I asked AJ.

"She didn't do it, Nick!" AJ shot back angrily. "Marie is not a murderer. You never even met the woman."

"I'm just concerned about you, AJ."

He glared at me.

"One day when I was at Marie's home," AJ said, directed at me, "I noticed a baby raccoon in a small cage that Marie had taken in because its mother abandoned it. She found it in the alley behind her home and adopted it so it would survive. Who takes in a baby raccoon and nurses it back to health, Nick? That is certainly not the actions of a murderer."

"I remember that raccoon," Tom said, amused by the memory. "She kept it for almost a year until it bit her on the hand, and then she gave it to an animal rescue group to transport to another state and release it."

"She told me that the rescue group transported it to the Blue Ridge Mountains of West Virginia," AJ added.

"But in reality," Tom declared in an uncharacteristic moment, "raccoons are vicious, little creatures with sharp teeth, big claws, and rabies. Maybe Marie realized the true nature of her housemate and whacked it over the head with a flashlight. Maybe there was never an animal rescue group at all."

"Tom!" AJ shrieked, appalled.

"I'm sorry," Tom returned, retracting his thoughtless anecdote. "I shouldn't make jokes about this situation. I guess Nick's twisted sense of humor is finally rubbing off on me."

"That sounds like something I'd say," I observed.

"We'll know the truth tonight," Tom said, "when Dr. Aguilar calls with his preliminary observations. Until then, let's get some breakfast. We'll all feel better once we've eaten."

Chapter Seventy-Six

AJ Gaines was a Renaissance man, a man of many diverse talents and interests, and one who lived with deep-seated hunger and recklessness in his soul. Beyond his talent behind an easel, AJ was a licensed pilot, an expert in rare stamps, fluent in seven languages, and a world-class chef. In the kitchen, AJ made a potato-crusted halibut worthy of a five-star restaurant in Seattle, a chicken cordon bleu that rivaled the small cafe in Rouen where the recipe originated, and a shrimp gumbo that blared like the horns of Bourbon Street in New Orleans. Whenever AJ visited the farm, the star rating for the cuisine served in the farmhouse dining room improved by at least three stars.

While we waited for the preliminary results from the medical examiner, AJ prepared his legendary fried chicken, mashed potatoes, green beans with almonds, buttermilk biscuits, and gravy in the kitchen. Whether his intent or not, he was making comfort food. Alex, an infrequent presence at the dinner table on most evenings, never missed dinner when AJ cooked. Around 6 p.m., Alex, Tom, and I waited at the dining room table for tonight's southern fare. After AJ placed a plate of chicken breasts with crispy brown skin before us, he sat opposite Tom at the other end of the table. For the next hour, we ate, drank, and conversed with the comfort and familiarity of old friends with shared experiences.

"What is the word of the day?" Tom asked me.

His interest in my word of the day had waned, but he still asked occasionally.

"Reckoning," I responded, amused by the obvious irony.

"You're kidding me," Tom said. "You're just saying that to be clever."

"I'm serious. I couldn't believe it when I saw it this morning, either. Isn't life something?"

"What's the definition?" Tom asked, looking for proof that I wasn't simply making it up for my own amusement.

"The settlement of accounts or scores, as between entities or persons, sometimes in payment, other times by judgment."

"That's unbelievable," he said, dismayed. "That has got to be some kind of sign that higher powers are involved today."

"I'm not a religious man," I replied, "but I sure hope someone is watching over us today."

A half-hour and several servings later, AJ announced, "I have news that I've been asked to deliver."

"Good news?" Tom asked with a hopeful tilt in his voice.

"Not exactly," AJ informed him.

Easy does it, AJ, I thought, concerned, *the news we're waiting on already has the potential to be heartbreaking and devastating. We don't need to go out of our way to add more bad news.*

"Shannon asked me to update you on her legal situation," AJ continued. "She didn't want to tell you this news over the phone, so she asked me to tell you in person."

"What is happening?" Tom asked.

"Shannon and Martin Hastings have accepted a plea deal that includes three years in a federal penitentiary. They have decided that the case against them is too strong to contest. She'll report to prison near the end of October."

"Mom is going to jail," Alex blurted.

"It looks that way," AJ confirmed, placing his hand on Alex's shoulder. "With good behavior, she could be out in two years."

"Do you really think my mother is capable of good behavior?"

No one answered.

"I can't imagine Shannon in prison," Tom remarked, shaking his head in disbelief.

"It's not the time in prison that concerns me," AJ responded, "it's her adjustment once she gets out that truly concerns me. As part of the deal, she'll have to forfeit her license to trade securities, so I worry she'll be lost after her release. What will she do?"

"She won't be happy idle," Tom said. "She'll have to find a new pursuit, a second career."

At that moment, Tom's cell phone rang and vibrated, and "Medical Examiner" appeared on its screen. After an apprehensive pause, he touched the screen to accept the call.

"Hello, Dr. Aguilar," Tom spoke into his phone. "I'm here with several interested parties, so I have you on speaker."

"Good evening," the doctor announced. "I have finished my examination of the remains and formed an opinion regarding the cause of death. I will summarize my findings for you now, and I'll overnight the full report within a few days."

"That sounds good, Doctor," Tom responded with eagerness in his tone. "Please proceed with your findings."

"There are fractures to both the ribs and the pelvis which are consistent with the deceased having been run over by the wheel of a tractor. Those injuries are also consistent with the death certificate, where the coroner cited massive internal injuries as the cause of death. It is clear to me that those injuries were significant enough to have caused his death. On the back of the skull, I also observed a four-inch fracture that would most certainly have been the result of blunt-force trauma, meaning a hard blow to the head, and the cause of that fracture was a rounded weapon such as a baseball bat or a lead pipe."

"Could the weapon have been a metal flashlight?" Tom asked, interrupting the doctor.

"That's consistent with the injury I observed," the doctor said. "I can't say with certainty."

"Interesting," Tom mumbled.

"Now, the blow to the head that caused this fracture would have been sufficient to cause his death, but I cannot tell you how quickly death occurred. He could have died in seconds but probably no more than a few minutes. Therefore, I cannot conclude with certainty whether he died of massive internal injuries, as the coroner ruled, or blunt force trauma. Either would have killed him within a few minutes. Since the remains are forty years old, we will never know. Had the coroner been aware of the blunt-force trauma also during the original examination, he could have considered both injuries and determined which killed him, but it is too late now. In layman's terms, we know he was struck in the back of the head and run over by a trac-tor, but we don't know which actually caused his death, though both, independently, would have resulted in his death."

The phone was silent for almost a minute.

"That's a summary of my findings," the doctor added when no one said anything. "Do you have any questions?"

Still, no one said a word. It was like all the air and energy had been sucked out of the room, and we were sitting in a vacuum. It was the stillest, most silent moment I'd ever known.

"Are you still there, Tom?" the doctor called out from his end into the silence of our space.

"We are here, Dr. Aguilar," I responded as I reached across the table and picked up the cell phone. "Please forward the written report at your earliest convenience. Thank you for your efforts."

With that said, I touched the screen and ended the call.

Immediately, I looked at AJ, and he had tears streaming down his face. We didn't make eye contact because he was looking upward at the chandelier with a blank expression on his face. He was such a large man that his tears seemed incongruous on his cheeks, but he was also a sensitive man, and I knew his pain was real. He seemed to muster his strength and slowly rose from the table.

"I need to be alone for a while," he said in an anguished voice, and then he left the dining room. A moment later, I heard his footsteps on the staircase as he headed for his bedroom.

As AJ climbed the stairs, Tom rose from the table and walked out the front door without uttering a word. The screen door slammed behind him, and I heard him walk down the front steps. For five minutes, Alex and I sat at the table in silence with the leftovers from dinner before us. He looked dazed. Finally, he addressed me.

"My mother is going to prison, and my grandmother is a murderer," he said. "This has been quite a night."

"Quite a night," I repeated, at a complete loss for words.

Usually, words were my friend and always at my side but not at that moment. Even though I didn't know Marie, I, too, felt a sense of devastation, and I was unable to process my thoughts yet. After Alex departed for his room, I remained at the dining room table alone for over an hour.

If my sister is a nun, I thought to myself, *and I found out she is turning tricks at night, I'd probably experience feelings similar to what Tom, Alex, and AJ are feeling about Marie right now. I'd still love my sister just as much; I just wouldn't know how to process this new information about her. I'd wonder if she is the person I thought I knew.*

In the morning, little was said. Tom and AJ looked like two men who'd lost a piece of themselves and had no idea what to do to get it back. An unspoken pact was formed to save all conversation for a time when conversation could have value and meaning—now was clearly not that time. After cups of coffee at the dining room table, AJ grabbed his overnight bag and walked toward the front door. Tom and I followed. At the door, AJ hugged each of us like he wasn't going to see us again, but we all knew that wasn't the case.

"I'll see you soon," he told us as he walked out the door and climbed into his Porsche.

In silence, Tom and I watched the dust cloud move along the dirt road until the car finally slipped from view.

"Let's take a few days off the guesthouse project," Tom suggested as we walked back into the dining room. "You should focus on the next issue of *The Sentinel* anyway."

"Why don't we break until after Labor Day?" I proposed. "We'll take a week to focus on other things."

"That's a good idea."

Chapter Seventy-Seven

A t the southern edge of Shelbyville, in a bucolic meadow beside a small lake, was a quaint, one-room schoolhouse built in 1894 with a tall steeple and bronze bell. In 1959, when the new elementary school was built, the police department moved into the old school, painted it carmine red, and made it their headquarters. In 2012, the police force consisted of the police chief, Walt Garrison, and seven police officers that shared three police cruisers and two bicycles. It was small town, low budget, back-slapping law enforcement at its finest.

Old police reports and office supplies were stored in the attic of the police station, which could only be reached by climbing a twenty-foot wooden ladder to the access panel. While I spent time in town working on the next Digby issue of *The Sentinel,* I broke away period-ically to visit the police station and rummage through old police reports from the 1940s. It was difficult to work there because I couldn't stand up in the crawl space, the lighting was insufficient, and bugs and mouse poop were everywhere. Each day when I arrived at the station, the police chief and his team teased me as I put on my kneepads and headlamp before I climbed the ladder. While I moved around above them, one of the officers loudly remarked about raccoons in the attic and removed the ladder so I couldn't climb down on completion of my work. Absent any real crime to focus on, a fraternity-like quality had developed in our police department.

As I flipped through police reports from the 1940s searching for the name Wilbur Corbett, Tom's grandfather, I noticed that the name Corbett appeared on many of the reports. It seemed that Wilbur Corbett and his two brothers, Clive and John, were frequent recipients of police visits at their homes, and one theme was ever present in the details of the reports—the Corbett men liked to fight, with other townsfolk, their own family members, and even the police. In the dusty boxes, I found one police report, dated July 7, 1941, where a police officer responded to the farm after reports of fighting—the term domestic violence didn't seem to exist back then. The report stated that Darlene Corbett, Tom's grandmother, was bruised and bloodied, and Sam Corbett, about ten years old at the time, was transported to the hospital with a broken jaw. Neither Darlene nor Sam would implicate Wilbur Corbett in their injuries and gave ever-changing stories regarding the causes, but since Wilbur was the only other person on the property at the time and these occurrences were "frequent in the family," according to the officer, he wrote in his report that he suspected Wilbur had beaten both of them.

Almost immediately, I found a second report, dated December 5, 1941, where a different police officer responded to a violent argument at the farm and, once again, found Darlene battered and beaten and Carl Corbett with a dislocated shoulder. The opinion of the officer was the same as the first report, but since neither Darlene nor Carl would implicate Wilbur, the officer was left with no other option other than to transport Carl to the local hospital and simply write up a report. In all, I found nine police reports involving Wilbur Corbett between the years 1941 and 1943, and each one was similar in actions and tone. I was quite sure there would have been many more reports had I continued to advance forward through the years

311

for any length of time—it was a horrifying, habitual pattern of domestic violence and abuse.

"I think I hear a big rat in the attic again," one of the young officers remarked loudly beneath me. "We better take the ladder away, so it doesn't come down from the attic and attack anyone."

"Come on guys!" I shouted as I looked up from a police report dated August of 1943. "I can't wait here while you go to lunch again."

Chapter Seventy-Eight

On Saturday of Labor Day weekend, I had almost completed the next issue of *The Sentinel*, headlined "The Digby Phenomenon," so I broke from my task to wander around town on a beautiful end-of-summer afternoon and enjoy the sights and sounds of the street fair. American flags fluttered in faint breezes as fairgoers wandered from booth to booth and viewed hand-crafted items, purchased baked goods, ice cream, and other treats, or simply enjoyed the fine weather and festive atmosphere. Having grown up in this little town, I'd attended countless street fairs, but I still felt comforted by the Norman Rockwell-esque nature of the scene as I felt like I was strolling in an oil painting of another era rather than an actual town. From my experience as a reporter in Philadelphia, our city streets and suburban neighborhoods were tougher and grittier than ever before, so there was something comforting about small-town America. The feeling of community was stronger, the streets softer. Three times each summer, people drove long distances to Shelbyville to attend the street fairs, but the truth was that the booths weren't any different than the ones at the street fairs in their neighborhoods. They came to be comforted.

Unlike previous Sundays, visitors began arriving at the farm the following morning around 10 a.m., long before the vendors had arrived and set-up. These early arrivals added a chaotic and unstructured element to what was always a demanding day. On previous Sundays, visitors had been aware of and honored the 1 p.m. until 5 p.m. viewing hours we established, but the passage of time and influx of street fair visitors seemed to have swept that convention away. We didn't try to turn away the crowd but instead made our usual efforts earlier to form the necessary lines in the field. By the end of the day, we were grateful for the early start because it spread the almost two thousand visitors over three additional hours.

At 5 p.m., Tom and I sat in the Adirondack chairs and watched as the crowds dwindled and the vendors packed up. Since the exhumation, Tom had been quieter than usual and seemed a little down, even a little depressed. It seemed like his anger toward his father had been replaced by an overarching sadness. We hadn't talked about the exhumation results or how he felt about his mother having killed his father. Since almost a week had passed, I decided to inquire about his mental state.

"Have you had time to process the exhumation results?" I asked timidly.

"I've thought about it plenty, that's for sure. I don't know that I've come to any significant conclusions."

"You said previously that the results wouldn't affect your feelings toward your mother. Has that proven true?"

"Yes, it has," Tom said. "My thoughts don't have anything to do with my love for my mother. I'm thinking about the bigger picture—my father abused my mother, and she killed him. It's not the most ideal family history, not the most ideal start in life."

"But you came out of it okay, and I assume that was due to some wonderful mothering on the part of Marie."

"That's all true, but I still have to reconcile the big picture. To find peace in my life, I have to find a way to come to terms with the violence between the people who gave me life, as well as the homicide that resulted. I need to understand it. I need to make some sense of it."

"That could take some time."

"I know."

Chapter Seventy-Nine

Honk! Honk!

At almost 11 p.m., two blasts of a truck horn and two bright headlights pierced the tranquility of a quiet night with a bright full moon on Misty Hollow Road. Immediately, Tom recognized the beckoning horn as it was clearly from the early days of the automobile, and the headlights shining into his front room were familiar also. Alone in the dining room, he knew the past was summoning him; he knew his late night visitor was an unwelcome one with unsettled business from long ago. Always uninvited, this old pickup truck had parked in his driveway once before.

"You have to put that shotgun down, Calvin," Tom cried out from the open front door, "if you want to talk with me. I'm not coming out until you do."

Reluctantly, the old man placed the butt of the shotgun on the dirt beside him and leaned the barrel against a headlight. It had been nine months since their last encounter under similar circumstances. Once again, Calvin was standing between the brightly illuminated headlights of his depression-era Ford pickup truck. Tom took three steps forward to the front of the porch so that only twenty-five feet separated the men.

"I told you not to come back," Tom asserted.

"No one tells me what to do," Calvin returned.

"What do you want?"

"I see you dug Sam up," Calvin answered. "I want to know the outcome."

"What outcome?" Tom returned.

"Seymour told me you sent the bones to Pittsburgh. I want to know the outcome."

"That's a family matter," Tom replied flatly.

"I'm here for Carl, and he was family."

"You're not family."

"I want to know the outcome," Calvin repeated.

He picked up his shotgun. He didn't point it at Tom, but his threat was clear.

"The last time you were here, you insulted my mother. You need to get off my property."

"She did it, didn't she?" the old man said.

Tom took three steps forward and descended the porch steps onto the dirt driveway. He noticed Calvin's finger on the trigger of the shotgun, as well as the shaking motion of his unsteady hand. Whether shot intentionally or accidentally, Tom knew he'd bleed just as much. He was concerned about the old man's unsteady nature, both mentally and physically, but he wasn't going to give him what he wanted. He wouldn't give him the satisfaction of being right about his mother. Tom simply wouldn't allow this angry old man—this living, breathing proxy for Carl—to disparage his mother anymore.

"Get off my property!" Tom shouted.

"You better remember what I told you about old men and life sentences," Calvin snarled.

"Don't threaten me. If I report you to the police, you'll do six months in jail. For an old man in your health, that's a life sentence."

"She did it, didn't she?" Calvin blared once more. "Marie killed Sam. She drove the tractor right over him."

"Sam and Carl were nothing but cowards. They picked on someone smaller and weaker than them. Marie was kind and loving, and they reciprocated with meanness."

"Now there you go again. What did I tell you about badmouthing my friends? I won't hear it!"

In truth, Tom had heard enough. Surprising Calvin and himself, Tom marched straight toward Calvin within the beams of the headlights in a calm and unhurried manner. As he walked, he stared directly at Calvin, looked him right in the eyes.

The old man's eyes widened. Unsure of the threat, he raised his shotgun and aimed it forward. Though full of bluster and bravado, he'd never fired his gun at another human being and froze in place. With nowhere to go, he was trapped between Tom and his pickup.

Tom continued his march. After eleven paces, when Tom was directly in front of the pickup truck, he reached with his right hand, latched onto the steely barrel of the shotgun, and pointed it away.

BAM! The shotgun discharged in the direction of the open field. Both men were startled by the blast.

"Back off!" Calvin warned his assailant, more bluster.

Adding his left hand, Tom grasped the barrel again and violently jerked it from the old man's hands. He pulled it towards his own midsection.

Suddenly unarmed, Calvin appeared shocked and concerned.

Holding the shotgun in his hands, Tom glimpsed Calvin's face for the first time; Calvin looked like someone who had lived a hard life and seemed, to Tom at least, to be the embodiment of the difficult past that he had been contending with. His words were directed at Calvin, but they carried larger implications.

"Get the fuck off my property, Calvin," he growled at him. "If you ever come back, I'll shoot you with your own gun and be well within my rights."

Tom put the shotgun over his shoulder and walked back into the house, leaving the screen door flapping in the doorframe. Five minutes later, he heard the old pickup truck rattle and drive slowly away from the property. With the headlights gone, bright moonlight shone on the white curtains in the front window once again.

Back in the dining room, his mind cleared and adrenaline easing, Tom's hands began to shake uncontrollably.

Chapter Eighty

A wonderful coincidence, my follow-up article, "The Digby Phenomenon," appeared in *The Sentinel* and *The Philadelphia Post* on the same day that August Reese and his team from the Woodbury Museum traveled to the farm to analyze the completeness of Digby's remains with ground penetrating radar. Riding in his Range Rover at 9 a.m., with the same entourage as his previous visit, three students and a museum curator, Augie opened *The Post* to the third page and saw a nearly full-page article about the very reason he was traveling west on Interstate 76. He read its contents and learned that nearly five thousand people had made their way to the Corbett farm to view the dinosaur. He glimpsed the accompanying pictures depicting the large crowds and festival atmosphere in the field each Sunday and a calculating grin appeared on his face because he knew this backstory would make for a popular exhibit at the museum. A dinosaur with folk hero status would shatter previous attendance records.

"Our friend, Thomas Corbett," Augie said to his traveling companions at sixty miles per hour, "is causing quite a commotion in the Pennsylvania countryside with his dinosaur remains. People are coming from all over to view Digby the Dinosaur."

"When I was buying my coffee this morning," the curator added in an amused tone, "the kids in line ahead of me were talking about Digby like he is the latest reality television star. He definitely has celebrity status."

Augie winced at the observation and stated, "I sure hope that the dinosaur's newfound popularity won't make it more difficult for us to acquire the rights to the remains."

"On the other hand," the curator replied, "if we get the rights, Digby will be an extremely popular exhibit."

"On our visit today," Augie advised his team, "we are simply going to have to convince Thomas Corbett that Digby belongs at the Woodbury, that it's the right place for him. We all met Thomas, and he seems like a reasonable man."

When Augie and his team arrived at the farm, they unloaded a machine that looked like a push lawnmower, except instead of an engine and a blade for cutting grass, the machine had equipment that emitted radar waves into the ground as it rolled along. Essentially, the machine mapped the ground beneath the surface and highlighted areas that were denser than the normal soil. In other words, the skeletal bones would show as anomalies in the ground, different than the soil surrounding them. Once they rolled the machine over a mapped out grid, the radar mapping would tell us whether his skeletal remains consisted of his skull, front legs, and neck vertebrae (which we had already unearthed) or whether the entirety of his nearly forty-foot skeleton was beneath the topsoil. In a few hours, we would know how much of Digby's remains were in the field.

"I read your article on the way to Shelbyville," Augie said as he greeted us. "You're going to make that dinosaur into a folk hero."

"Well, Augie," I replied, "the world can use more folk heroes. Folk heroes remind us of all the good in the world."

"You've always had a brilliant perspective on the world, my friend," Augie said.

"You remember Tom," I said.

"Of course I do. I'm so happy you invited us back to the farm, Thomas. By the end of the day, my crew and I will enlighten you concerning exactly how much dinosaur you have in your field. Just so you know going in, any result over fifty percent is quite remarkable."

"Thank you for coming," Tom said as he shook his hand. "It's time we both know exactly what I've got in that field so we can make some decisions."

"Does that mean you're considering donating the remains to the Woodbury Museum?"

"I'm considering it, but let's not get ahead of ourselves."

While we caught up with Augie, Patricia Knox, the twenty-two-year-old with the black, onyx-rimmed glasses that told us about the allosaurus during their first visit, had connected a laptop to the radar equipment and was furiously typing away at its keyboard. As Augie enlightened us about a new exhibit at the museum, I was distracted by her typing speed, which was easily twice as fast as my normal pace, and I was a professional writer. I wondered why I hadn't gotten any faster over the years. Abruptly, Patricia halted her rapid typing, removed the white cable that tethered the equipment to the laptop, and walked over to where Augie, Tom, and I were standing.

"We're ready to begin, Professor," she announced. Her enthusiasm was evident on her face.

"Splendid," Augie replied, eager for the work to commence. "Set up a grid at least seventy feet by seventy feet, so we know we have it all."

"How many passes?" Patricia asked.

"Let's map it three times so we can be confident that we have good data. Take your team and start mapping and let me know if you encounter any issues."

"Will do," Patricia said.

"Should we follow so we can watch?" Tom asked.

"Oh God no, Thomas," Augie replied. "They will push that machine back and forth across the field for the next three hours.

Nothing is interesting but the end results. Perhaps we could continue our conversation over a cup of coffee in your home?"

"Of course," Tom responded, "follow me."

Just as Augie indicated, as we drank coffee in the living room, I saw his team through the front window rolling the ground-penetrating radar equipment across the open field at a snail's pace, slower than twenty feet per minute, an exercise in repetition and tedium. The team took turns methodically inching the machine along between the new guesthouse and the grove of birch trees at the edge of the property, only pausing periodically to check the control panel atop the sophisticated equipment. As I watched them at work, I realized the mapping process would take every bit of the three hours that Augie predicted and maybe more. It wasn't until well after 3 p.m. that I noticed the absence of the team from my western view.

"I think they might be finished, Augie," I notified him.

"Splendid," he returned, "they'll download the data to a laptop and do some analysis, and we should have our answers in the next hour or so."

Shortly thereafter, Patricia opened the screen door and hastily entered the living room, looking like she was in the middle of a once-in-a-career moment early in her young career. Her face was aglow, and she was about to burst.

"It's unbelievable, Professor," she exclaimed. "It is absolutely unbelievable!"

"What is it?" Augie asked. "What are the results?"

"The skeleton is more than ninety-five percent complete. It's basically all there!"

"Are you sure? That would be remarkable if true."

"Absolutely," she said, lit up and animated. "All three mappings validate one another, and the resulting approximation is more than ninety-five percent."

"He is all there," Tom repeated, looking in my direction, tears welling in his eyes, absolutely overcome with emotion.

I didn't respond because I was taken aback by Tom's overly

emotional response to the radar results. I was confused. While Augie continued to speak to the two of us, I was lost in my own thoughts and unaware of his words.

In the aftermath of traumatic events, people cling to whatever is available; whatever consolation and hope is within reach; whatever metaphorical life preserver is tossed their way. Strength during trauma is part of the survival mechanism in our brains that gets us through traumatic incidents. It's what gets parents through the loss of a child and the badly injured through to recovery. Many times, in my work, I'd witnessed it—I'd stared into glazed eyes and marveled at the resilience and persistence within.

For several months, I'd known Tom felt a kinship with our dinosaur, but I didn't connect the dots and realize how much was riding on this day, how important these ground-penetrating radar results were to him. He believed that if Digby could survive his traumatic event on the farm for over one hundred fifty million years, then Tom could too. If Digby was "all there" then that must mean that Tom could be whole again also. In his own way, Tom was clinging to Digby. Clearly, he was more traumatized by the upheaval in his life than I realized.

"Is anyone listening to me?" Augie asked when he noticed the far-away look in our eyes.

"I'm sorry," I responded in a repentant tone. "I think we're both overwhelmed by the results. We are fond of Digby."

"I understand," Augie returned, "but we must talk about the future of these remains. This significant scientific find should be unearthed and preserved by professionals."

For the next twenty minutes, Augie pleaded his case to Tom about why he should donate the remains to the Woodbury Museum, including the fact that the museum already had one of the largest and most significant dinosaur collections in the world. As he did, he talked about the founding of the museum, his early days as its curator, their previous acquisitions of dinosaur remains, and the impressive credentials of the current board. Augie even described his grand plans for Digby, including the room in the museum where Digby would reside and what the actual exhibit would involve. And all the while, Tom's facial expression still indicated that he was overwhelmed by the radar results and not listening to a single word Augie said. Once again, when Augie completed his passionate pitch, he needed to make a special effort to get Tom's attention.

"Are you listening?" Augie asked. "You seem distant."

"I am a little distracted," Tom replied.

After a brief pause, Tom continued. "I suggest you return to the museum and prepare the paperwork pertaining to the museum's acquisition of the rights to Digby and forward those documents to me. With the paperwork in hand, I'll decide whether to grant the rights to Digby to the Woodbury Museum. You should make sure that the package is detailed and complete, right down to clauses that specify that his name will remain Digby in all future exhibits and that his place of origin will always be noted as Shelbyville, PA. The more I have in writing concerning the intentions of the Woodbury, the more likely I will be to sign over the rights to Digby. Basically, I want to be sure the Woodbury is the right steward for Digby."

"I will email a complete package to you tomorrow."

In the days that followed the publication of "The Digby Phenomenon," more than one thousand newspapers picked up the article and four television networks included segments about Digby on their national news programs. As a result of my two articles, our dinosaur may or may not have been a bona fide folk hero, but he was definitely a household name, one like Madonna or Elvis who needed no last name. While I didn't have the results of an opinion poll to confirm it, I was confident that Digby and Dino (from the Flintstones) were the most recognized dinosaurs in America.

Chapter Eighty-One

O n September 20, after lengthy delays caused by Digby and the exhumation, Tom and I installed the wrought iron railing on the deck and hung three silver pendant lights near the kitchen. With the flip of the wall switch that illuminated the lighting, the construction of the guesthouse was officially complete. We were done. It was a project that produced much more than the actual guesthouse, as Tom and I both worked our way back from mistakes and humiliation while hammering, sawing, and sweating in the Pennsylvania sun. And as we built that guesthouse, we built a friendship as sturdy as the structures's foundation. Walking across the field with our project finally complete, I felt great satisfaction and pride in our efforts.

Chapter Eighty-Two

In the final days of September, the mood and pace on the farm changed significantly as the hours passed more quietly now that the guesthouse project was complete and Alex had relocated to Miami. Accentuating the change, the afternoon temperatures settled twenty degrees lower on the thermometer, and the sun shifted away to the south. The onset of fall, the season of winding down, had brought with it a quiet time for reflection when Tom was struggling with his parent's legacy and the single hardest question, we, as human beings, ever confront: why? When, where, and how are relatively easy questions compared to that always-perplexing question: why? In truth, why is seldom answered and generally leaves those who ask it feeling unsatisfied. Each evening, Tom sat in the living room in the darkness alone, with the memories of Marie and Sam Corbett who occupied his mind with the persistence of guilt or remorse, emotions that didn't wax and wane. In his heart, Tom knew he'd never rest easy until he found some sense of understanding regarding his parents.

Around 8 p.m. one evening, I turned on the lights, entered the living room, and sat down opposite Tom in a side chair. I'd been looking for the right moment to talk with Tom about Wilbur Corbett, and I could only hope that this was it. He had a concerned look on his face because he saw the concerned look on my face.

"I have something I want to talk to you about," I said.

I handed him nine photocopied pages of police reports from the 1940s. While he perused the pages, I sat quietly.

"It seems my grandfather was pretty much the same mean bastard as my father," he observed when he finished.

"That's what I want to talk with you about."

"Okay."

"Do you remember when I came to you six months ago with my theory about what happened in your field on the night your father died?"

"I do. It turned out we both had the same theory."

"Well, I've done some research and learned a few things in the interim, and I would like to amend that theory."

"How so?"

"Your mother, Marie, grew up in a loving house with great parents where she was encouraged to play the piano and paint and flourish as a child."

"That's true," Tom confirmed. "We visited my grandparents often, and they were great people."

"Marie knew the importance of a positive, loving home for children."

"She certainly did."

"But then she married into the Corbett family, a family where the men were violent and abusive to their family members. In her own home, her husband, Sam, beat and abused her regularly."

"He did," Tom replied, wincing.

"Tom, I went to the police department to learn more about your grandfather, Wilbur Corbett, because I know that these things do not happen in a vacuum. I showed you nine police reports from two years in the 1940s when your father was about ten years old. In those reports, the police were called to the Corbett home because Wilbur was battering his wife and children, and, very often, the result was that someone went to the hospital. Your dad and his brother Carl were frequent visitors to the emergency room because their father beat them."

"Evil begets evil," Tom said.

"Well, that is only partially true," I responded. "Evil does not necessarily beget evil, but it certainly cultivates it."

"I see your distinction."

"As the years passed and your father grew more violent and cruel towards her, I think Marie realized that this violence and cruelty was passed down from generation to generation in the Corbett men like some kind of horrible inheritance or genetic flaw. She saw the anger and meanness in her husband, and she saw it in his father, and she came to understand that there was a circle of violence in their family that went back many generations. When your father struck you that night, Marie realized that this was the first effort to pass that violence on to you, the first effort to extend that circle of violence for one more generation."

Tom was silent, but tears were streaming down his face. He was reliving painful memories with even more detail this time. He was a smart man, and he sensed where this conversation was going. I reached across, placed my hand on his knee, and continued.

"On your father's final night, I think Marie took a stand against the violence. She told herself that the circle of violence ended "right here and now." She knew that unless she did something drastic, Sam would batter you, you would batter your children, your children would batter their children, and so on and so on. Having grown up in a loving home, she wouldn't allow her home to be a link in this chain, she wouldn't allow her child to be initiated into the family tradition. I think Marie killed Sam because she couldn't allow him to hurt you, but also because she wasn't going to let this violent tradition continue to pass down through the generations, down through the lineage. Marie was determined to put an end to it that night."

"Oh my God," Tom exclaimed.

Tom lowered his head. His tears were now accompanied by periodic sobbing because he understood that his mother's abuse had started generations ago. Her pain was real enough to him without the added realization that many members of his family tree participated in the abuse. In a troubling way, it was almost as if the Corbett men ganged up on her and beat her down. Tom was clearly distraught.

"She was so out of her element," Tom muttered, "so isolated."

For a few minutes, I paused because I knew this was a lot to absorb. Whys can be elusive but also hard to accept if you actually find an answer. But there was still more about his family history I wanted to help him to understand, one final realization that might help him find peace amongst all this heartache.

"The one thing that is easy to overlook amongst all this pain and tragedy," I said to Tom as he sobbed, head in hands, "is the fact that your father was a victim also. The violence and meanness that you saw in Sam was beaten into him during his childhood when his father battered and verbally abused him. Children need to feel safe and loved to flourish like Marie, but Sam had a horribly violent and cruel childhood. He never felt safe, and he never felt loved. His home wasn't a place for flourishing; his home was a place for cowering. The simple truth is that Sam never really had a chance in life."

"I never thought about it that way," Tom mumbled, as he was barely able to speak the words.

"While I was with *The Post,* I wrote many articles on domestic abuse, and I learned about the circle of violence, where violence is passed down through families. One day in 2003, I interviewed an abuser named Darrel Spencer, a horrible man with more than twenty arrests for domestic violence, and a long history of substance abuse as well. He was a man who treated his family like punching bags and one who was hauled off to jail in the middle of night on a regular basis. Sitting in their cluttered and filthy living room, I couldn't help but notice that everyone present, his wife and three small children, was badly bruised. Point blank, I asked him why he beat his family?"

"If someone in the family gets out of line or acts the fool," Darrel replied, "it's the man's job to beat some sense into them."

"Those words stuck with me for a long time, rattling around in my mind as I tried to make some sense of them. My initial reaction was that the guy was simply subhuman; he was something even less than a horrible human being. But the more I thought about it, the more I realized that he was beaten so much while he was young that he was just plain damaged. Without condoning his actions, I believed I finally understood the impact of being beaten regularly by his own father, and watching his mother being beaten regularly. At a very young age, his empathy for other human beings was beaten out of him."

Tom was an emotional wreck. He said nothing more that night, and I could only hope I had done him a service and not harm. My intent was to help him to better understand his parents and the tragic incident they left him to figure out, but I really didn't know what his thoughts were at that moment. In silence, I sat with him for almost an hour before I left for my room. In the darkness of my bedroom, as I tried to fall asleep, I worried about my friend.

The next morning over coffee, Tom was in a quiet and reflective mood, much as I expected. We said very little to one another. I tried to give him space.

"Thank you for all you did on my behalf," he said at one point. "You're a good friend."

As he spoke the words, Tom forced a smile, and I took that as a positive sign. It might sound strange, but I saw his forced smile as a sign that he was forcing himself to deal with his difficult issues. In that forced smile, I sensed that my efforts had landed, that Tom had some thinking to do, but that he was closer to understanding than ever before. I had good instincts about people, and I believed Tom would be just fine.

One thing I knew for certain—we'd both come a long way since that day we met in the diner almost fifteen months ago.

Chapter Eighty-Three

The following Wednesday, Tom and I arrived at The Rooster for lunch at 11:45 a.m. As we made our way to our usual table, several diners greeted us with good-natured ribbing.

"Hey everyone," Davy Preston called out from his booth, "it's Tom Corbett and Nick Sterling, the world-famous dinosaur hunters of Shelbyville, PA. Have you guys found any more prehistoric animals on your farm that we should know about?"

"No, Davy," I responded as we passed, "it's been a slow week on the farm. We haven't found any new dinosaurs, but I swear I saw some Bigfoot tracks near the barn the other day."

"You know, guys," Walt Garrison, the police chief, called out to us, "if you'd been charging admission to view that dinosaur, you'd be rich by now."

"Well, I'll be darned, Walt," Tom replied, "all this time I've had a nagging feeling that I was overlooking something, and now I know what it is. Admission—we should've been charging admission."

Over the last few days, I noticed that Tom seemed to be in high spirits, like a man who had lightened himself of a heavy burden he had been carrying every day. He definitely seemed happier than he'd been in all the time I'd known him. Looking at him across the table, I wondered if he'd made peace with his past.

At 11:56 a.m., Chet Riley entered the diner and proceeded to his table. Waiting with Walt for the mayor to arrive, Chet heard a familiar voice call out to him from across the restaurant.

"Hey Chet," Martha Gladstone addressed him from a nearby table, "I wanted to buy a handsaw at your store the other day, but your price was twenty-nine dollars. How can a simple handsaw possibly cost twenty-nine dollars? I'll gnaw at the wood with my teeth before I'll pay that much for a damn saw."

"How many times do I have to tell you?" Chet said. "Things cost what they cost. I don't have any control over what it costs to manufacture a handsaw. We buy stuff, attach a reasonable markup, and then sell the stuff to the good people of Shelbyville."

"That's the same damn answer you give me every time."

"I have committed it to memory."

At 12:17 p.m., Hal Donaldson entered the diner and walked to the table where the police chief and Chet were already seated.

"Do you have any idea how long it takes to drive through the center of town on a Sunday afternoon?" Hal asked.

"From your tone," the police chief replied, "I am betting it's a lot longer than you think appropriate."

"It takes almost a half-hour!"

"Well, the town is getting a lot of visitors on Sundays these days. We have a famous dinosaur, you know."

"I know about the darn dinosaur. I just don't understand why we can't replace the four-way stop with a traffic light. The line was about twenty cars long when I arrived last Sunday at about 2 p.m."

"Well, that's horrible," the police chief said. "Where were you going on a Sunday afternoon that required such urgency?"

"I was on my way to my mother's house."

"Does she still spank you if you are late?"

Nearby patrons snickered at the remark.

"Damn it, Walt, that's not funny!" Hal responded. "It's time we acknowledge that a traffic light would be far more efficient and make the change."

"I don't know what to tell you, Hal, the mayor and city council considered your request and voted it down. Take it up with them again the next time they meet in November."

"There is no talking to anyone in this city government," Hal mumbled as he headed for his seat.

At 12:25 p.m., Milt Wallace entered the diner wearing a yellow rubber raincoat and yellow rubber hat, the kind that crossing guards wore at elementary schools on rainy days. On the coat, white splats were present where bird poop landed as he walked from his liquor store to the diner. At his table, Milt took the heavy raincoat off and placed it on the back of an extra chair at his table. Next, he placed the hat on top of the chair.

"What a beautiful day, Milt," Chet said.

"Unseasonably nice," Milt said as he took his seat at his table and picked up the menu.

"How is business?" Chet asked.

"Not good," he answered. "I have the only store in town not benefitting from the dinosaur. These families coming to town to see the dinosaur don't stop at my liquor store. They stop everywhere else but not my store. That's how business is!"

"I am sorry to hear that."

No one commented about the yellow raincoat or hat. Milt had been wearing the rain gear every day since before the start of summer, and it had become one of those quaint idiosyncrasies that you happen upon in a small town. Around Shelbyville all summer long, the single most asked question on the streets by visitors was: Why does that old guy walk around town in a yellow rubber raincoat when it is sunny and ninety degrees? In a hurried world where thirty-second sound bites and one hundred forty-character tweets were the norm, the answer given by townsfolk was also something unique to small towns anymore: the long story.

Chapter Eighty-Four

The most heralded locations for autumn foliage were in New England, mostly small towns in the mountains of Vermont and New Hampshire, but Pennsylvania was as spectacular in autumn as it was underrated. After all, the state's Latin name meant Penn's woods. In Shelbyville, the leaves turned resplendent shades of red, orange, gold, and yellow and fluttered to the ground every time the wind unsettled branches. With oak and maple trees abundant in the region, the leaves were as large as pie tins and painted the ground with bold strokes of color, like a modern artist with a four-inch brush. On a beautiful October afternoon, Tom tramped through fallen leaves in a peacoat as he made his way across the cemetery grounds to a familiar location, which he had visited several times. When he stopped in front of the grave markers of Samuel and Carl Corbett, his demeanor was markedly different from previous visits. Tom bowed his head in quiet reflection until he finally addressed his father's headstone.

"Since my return to Shelbyville sixteen months ago," Tom began, "I've learned a lot about you, your marriage to my mother, and your family. I learned that I was a child of rape, that you battered my mother regularly, and that you were not a kind or good man. I learned my mother killed you by striking your head with a flashlight and driving our tractor over your body."

On such a beautiful, blue-sky day, his subject matter seemed incongruous, even in a cemetery standing before headstones. Tom was composed, but the words were still difficult to speak out loud, difficult to push from his mouth. He was acknowledging a family history that had been hard to accept and even harder to understand. It was the type of family history seldom talked about. But Tom knew he wanted to talk about it.

"I learned that your childhood was horrible and that you never really had a chance in life. I learned that you were mean and abusive because your father was mean and abusive when you were a child. Since my return, my education about my parents and our family has been disheartening at best and painful at worst."

Tom paused for a moment to collect his thoughts. He knew it was important that he got it all out today. He wanted to speak his mind and say his piece, even though his audience was dead. The day of reckoning had long since passed—this was the day for atonement.

"I came here today to tell you that I understand why you were so mean and abusive and forgive you. For a long time, I was very angry with you, but now that I understand the violence and abuse you endured, I understand why you did what you did. While your actions were hurtful and despicable, they are also understandable. I forgive you, Dad."

He paused once again.

Staring at the ground, Tom found irony in the fact that his father's grave still looked like a fresh wound in the earth weeks after the exhumation when the truth was quite the opposite; after more than forty years, the wounds inflicted within his family were finally closed and healed.

Beneath a blue sky and warm sun, Tom glanced around the

cemetery at the fall scenery and the beautiful colors that painted the trees and the earth. As he did, his mind drifted back to the time when he was a small boy on the family farm. He suddenly remembered a day that he had long ago forgotten, a day similar to this one, warmed by the sun and painted by the season. On a beautiful autumn afternoon, Tom and his father were working side-by-side on the old barn together, replacing wood slats that were weathered and rotten. For more than an hour, his father held the replacement boards in place against the barn wall while young Tom placed a nail against the wood and hammered it into place. One board after another, they repaired the south wall.

"Good job, Tom," his father told him, halfway through their task, "that is the way to drive a nail in, nice and straight and with only three whacks. We'll be done in no time at all."

"The barn looks a lot better with the new wood in place," Tom said, proud of his handiwork.

"It sure does. I'll paint it tomorrow."

"Can I help paint also?"

"We'll see, I don't want a big mess."

"I can do it."

"We'll see, Tom.

"Okay."

"When we finish up here today, son, how about we go into town for ice cream? How does that sound?"

"That sounds great, Dad."

Tom remembered driving to town in his father's rickety pickup truck and enjoying a scoop of vanilla ice cream with chocolate syrup on it at the soda fountain at the pharmacy. His dad sat beside him and drank a cup of coffee. Tom was surprised by this sudden recollection, as it was his first positive memory of his father since his return to Shelbyville.

Returning from the sixties, Tom turned his attention back to the gray headstone at his feet, Samuel Gerard Corbett carved into it.

"This world was never kind to you, and I hope you are in a better place now," he offered as his parting thought.

During our conversation about Wilbur Corbett, Tom was emotional, shedding many tears then, as well as in the following days while he worked through the pain of his family's violent legacy. While granting forgiveness to his father, Tom felt true relief and a sense of peace. He shed no more tears. As he walked away from the headstone, he acknowledged his composed manner and thought it might be a sign that he'd finally come to terms with it all. He finally had closure. His traumatic, tumultuous, and difficult family history in Shelbyville was finally relegated to the past where it belonged. It was no longer in the front of his mind.

Tom tramped through the colorful, fallen leaves once again on the way back to his pickup truck. As he opened its door, he felt a vibration in his coat, and he retrieved his phone from his pocket. In his hand, Nicole was illuminated on its screen, and that brought a smile to his face. Settling in behind the steering wheel, he touched the screen to accept the call.

"Hi Nicole," he said as he turned the key to start the engine. As he did, an enormous yellow leaf fluttered down from a maple tree beside his truck and landed on his windshield.

"Hi, Dad," she returned.

"What is it? I can tell by your voice that something is wrong."

"It's Scratch, Dad. Scratch is what's wrong."

"What did he do now?"

"He finally showed up after more than a month on the road with his band, and he stayed with Bart and me for three days and then took off with our November rent money."

"Oh, for goodness sake," Tom replied. "He is never going to be a good husband or father. He is just too immature and stupid for both of those roles."

"I know."

"Do you want me to send you the money for your rent?"

"Well, that's why I'm calling. I'm really not happy here and I was wondering if Bart and I could come live with you for a while until I figure some things out? I need a little time to think about stuff."

"Of course, you can. I'd really like that."

"We'll come near the end of the month."

"Alex is doing well in Miami," Tom informed her so they could find lighter, more upbeat subject matter. "AJ set him up with a job waiting on tables just four doors down from his gallery, and Alex is enjoying it. I think it'll be good for him to deal with people daily. It'll help him get over his teenage shyness."

"Is he making good money?"

"You know AJ—leave it to him to get Alex into a chic Miami eatery where the line is long, and the tips are fantastic. AJ tells me Alex will make good money there."

"I'm glad to hear that," Nicole replied. "I haven't heard from Alex in a few weeks. I think he has been busy since he arrived in Miami."

"That's true."

"I think I might want to try my hand at painting while I am in Shelbyville this winter," Nicole remarked. "Maybe I inherited some talent from Grandma Marie. Her paintings are amazing."

"They certainly are. Your grandmother was amazing also. I think that's a good idea. You know, you could set up a studio in her old art studio."

"I'd like that."

"Well, let me know when you and Bart will be arriving. I am very happy you are coming."

"I love you, Dad."

"I love you, too."

For a few minutes, Tom relaxed in the seat of his truck with the engine idling and a satisfied smile on his face, marveling at how well things were suddenly turning out for him. Having his daughter and grandson coming to live with him was a welcome turn of events, and watching his daughter at work behind an easel in his mother's old art studio would surely bring pleasure and comfort to him. On the

Corbett farm, the forecast for the coming winter just got a whole lot warmer.

I sure hope Nicole inherited some artistic talent from my mother, Tom thought. *Otherwise, we're going to have paintings hanging all over the farmhouse that look like my grandson painted them.*

Chapter Eighty-Five

On Sunday evening in *The Sentinel* office, as I was working on the next issue, I saw the front door swing open and Tom enter as he stopped by for a visit around 8 p.m. True to my reformed work ethic, I was close to finishing the issue two days before the Tuesday deadline. My writing buddy, Glen (fiddich), was conspicuously absent and a tall bottle of Gatorade occupied his usual spot on my desk beside my laptop. As he arrived, I was happy to see Tom because I had really been enjoying his light and easy manner lately.

Ever since we met, Tom has had a lot on his mind. First, there was the whole Dream Squasher incident and the upheaval it caused in his life; then, there was the disintegration of his marriage and resulting divorce; finally, and most importantly, there was the discovery of abuse and murder within his immediate family that rocked his foundation. Without a doubt, it had been a trying period in his life, and a time that produced a lot of reflection and change. As he entered my office, it lifted my spirits to see this light and easy Tom Corbett.

Five days ago, Tom shaved his beard. Lighter in many ways, he was clean-shaven also. Since he left his job at Desjardins, he had been hiding behind facial hair; he was embarrassed to be recognized. For the first time in a long time, Tom was comfortable in his own skin.

"How is the writing going?" Tom asked as he sat opposite me in a wooden chair from the old schoolhouse.

"I'm close to completing the issue," I told him.

"I stopped in because I have something to give you."

With that said, Tom reached into the inner pocket of his topcoat, retrieved a cashier's check payable to Nicholas Sterling for five hundred thirteen thousand dollars drawn on the bank account of the Woodbury Museum Acquisition Fund, and placed it on the desk in front of me. I was so taken aback by all the digits on the check that I couldn't even bring myself to pick it up. Instead, I looked down at the check like it was a rare and delicate document that shouldn't be touched or handled. Several times, I looked at my name and the amount just to confirm what I thought I was seeing. I was stunned.

"What is this all about?" I asked.

"It's your half of the finder's fee for Digby. On Friday, I assigned the rights to his remains to the Woodbury Museum."

"Well, I'm glad you did that because it's the right place for him. But, he was on your property, in your field—why am I getting half of the money?"

"We found him together. Digby was always our find, not mine. I've always thought of him as our dinosaur."

"Okay."

"It is how it should be, Nick."

I stared at the check for another moment.

"It's all so absurd, isn't it?" I observed, shaking my head due to the wonder of it all. "We found a dinosaur together?"

"We not only found a dinosaur together," Tom said, "but that dinosaur changed our lives. How absurd is that?"

"It's been a great ride," I replied. "I think we are both better for it. I think that dinosaur healed us."

"A week ago," Tom began as a prelude to a story, "with the spotlights in the field on, I sat on the edge of the hole beside Digby while reviewing the museum documents and I swear I had the most profound and most ridiculous moment of my life at the same time. Sitting with Digby, contemplating his future, I couldn't ignore the absolute absurdity of the moment, but I also had this intense feeling come over me that I'm the most comfortable with myself that I've ever been in my entire lifetime. It's been quite a ride alright, and I feel like I've landed perfectly."

"I feel the very same way," I told him.

"I added a clause to the agreement," Tom said, "that specifies that the exhibit will always include both our names as finders of the remains."

"That's appropriate."

"It's not that I wanted billing for us, it's just that I wanted us to be there with Digby in some form."

"I get it."

"Do you have any plans for the money?"

"I hate to sound like this money is already spent, but I know exactly what I'm going to do with it."

"What are you going to do with it?"

"I'm going to take a large chunk of it and work with the Police Officer's Union to establish an anonymous college fund for Officer Maxwell's daughters. Like most fathers, I'm sure he dreamed of them going to college one day. I'd like to help make that happen."

"I think that's an excellent idea," Tom said. "What about the rest of it?"

"I'm going to use the rest of it to buy a home for Chelsea and me if she'll have me back. More than anything, I want to restart our life together."

"I think she'll have you back alright."

"Why do you say that?"

"Because the moment she sees you, she'll know you have recovered from your tragic mistake and are, once again, the fantastic guy that she first met. I see it, and she will too."

"I can only hope but thank you for saying that."

"Are you going to Los Angeles?"

"I have a plane ticket for a flight on Saturday, but I have something to do in Philadelphia first."

Chapter Eighty-Six

I stood in a small living room in a simple, working-class home—far too small to host a decent cocktail party, but that had never mattered to its humble residents. The large front window allowed a lot of sunlight into the bright and welcoming room, but I knew this room was the site of much grief and heartache. The small sofa, side chairs, and area rug were well worn and faded, each several years beyond any reasonable useful life. On the mantle of the white brick fireplace sat three framed photographs of proud parents and young girls, images that would never advance, never progress, remaining instead as reminders of a family changed by violence and tragedy. In one photo, the father wore the formal dress uniform of the Philadelphia Police Department and that image caused my eyes to well with tears. I knew he looked like a superhero to his daughters, but, unfortunately, on the streets of Philadelphia, even superheroes died. In the small living room, the woman in the photos stood directly in front of me, and, at the age of forty-one, she'd already endured enough heartache for twenty lifetimes. For four years, she'd struggled every day to be strong for her daughters, to restore a sense of normalcy to a home once filled with grief. There was no reason or

345

necessity for the arcs of our lives to ever intersect, but I knew this man, this woman, these girls, and this house better than I should. I knew their story; I was part of their story.

My path to this living room had been a long and difficult one. I had much to say to this woman and much to ask of her. In my mind, I had rehearsed this moment many times, and I knew all the necessary words, but as soon as my ass touched the threadbare fabric of the floral sofa, I broke down into tears and couldn't speak. I swallowed hard and tried to form the words that rolled across my mind, but I couldn't produce a sound. In truth, I was absolutely overwhelmed by her presence because this woman was the physical embodiment of a debt I knew I could never make good on. There were no words, no repentant acts, and no amount of money that would ever even this score. On the edge of the sofa, I sat silent and ashamed, with my head resting in the palms of my open hands. I waited for her wrath.

And then, extending incomprehensible kindness to a man she had every right to hate, Sandra Maxwell addressed me.

"It's okay, Nick," she whispered in an angelic voice while reaching out and placing her hand on my right shoulder. "I know you never meant for it to happen."

I nodded my head. I was shaking.

"On many days," she continued, "I saw you sitting in your car across the street from Middleton Park, watching my daughters as they played with the other children on the playground. I knew it was you."

I nodded again. I couldn't speak.

"I wanted to talk to you," Sandra told me. "I knew you were hurting just like me. But I just couldn't do it. I knew it would be too emotional for both of us."

From all the words I wanted to say to this woman, I finally managed to stammer just four of them.

"I am so sorry."

"I know you are," she said. "There is evil in this world. There are a lot of bad people. My husband became a police officer because he wanted to make the world a safer place for our children, a safer place for everyone. He died trying to make that happen. He died a hero."

"I am so sorry," I repeated.

Thus far, they were the only words I could manage. Because of her sweet voice and kindness, I was more overwhelmed than ever.

"Louis died because criminals who sell drugs to children wanted to protect their business. Money is more important to them than children, more important than human lives. It wasn't your fault. It was their fault—no one else."

"You don't blame me?" I asked.

"I never blamed you, Nick. Oh, I wished that picture had never been published, but I never blamed you. I never thought you intended for my husband to be murdered. I always knew you didn't. Inside of me, I had plenty of anger, but it was always directed at the drug dealers who murdered my Louis, never you."

"I blamed myself."

"I know you did. Looking at you in your car, I knew you were another victim of the drug dealers. I knew you were in pain, too."

"I wanted that article back. I wanted to undo what I'd done, but I couldn't. It just wasn't possible."

"After Louis was murdered, I was devastated. I couldn't get out of bed. I could barely function. But, as the first anniversary of his death approached, I realized those lowlife murderers were continuing to harm my family. They'd murdered my husband—I wasn't going to let them do more harm. I simply wouldn't allow it. And I wouldn't let Louis' life be defined by that last horrible day. He was so much more than that. Determined to overcome their impact, I reclaimed my life, and you need to do that, too. You need to move on. The good people of this world cannot surrender to the bad ones. Making myself move on with life was the best way I could honor my husband. In my heart, I know it's what Louis would've wanted for my children and me. It's what I want for you, Nick."

I believed that most lifetimes could be summed up by ten to twenty moments, meaningful little snippets that contained both the best and worst of one's character and experiences. Like a home movie on Super 8 film, twenty impactful moments that told the story of a life. In the small living room of her modest home, Sandra showed me that if we are graceful people and extend kindness and compassion to one another during those moments, we have the ability to impact one another's moments, to impact one another's lives. With measures of grace, kindness, and compassion that I had never witnessed before, Sandra Maxwell did that for me.

About the Author

A graduate of Georgetown University and a recipient of a Master in Business Administration (MBA), Michael Bowe is an accomplished businessman, entrepreneur, investor, and novelist, and a resident of Vashon Island, WA, a short ferry ride from Seattle. In 2020, his second novel, The Weight of a Moment, won the American Fiction Award for Literary Fiction.

Readers' Favorite Review

The Weight of a Moment is a beautifully written and inspiring story that is filled with realism and pathos. Told in the first person narrative voice, it captures the viewpoints of the characters with brilliance. There are insightful passages that compel readers to reflect on the human condition and the idea of meaning. The prose is excellent, and it is interesting how the author captures the life of the journalist. The themes of pain, the quest for meaning, friendship, and purpose are deftly handled. The reader quickly understands that life is shaped by moments, sometimes very brief, and these moments could be "first glances, tearful goodbyes, fortunate turns, unfortunate accidents, promises kept, promises broken, triumphs, failures, and regrets." The story is emotionally rich, psychologically exciting, and inspiring. Michael Bowe makes readers care about his characters and feel like a part of their world.

American Fiction Award
Winner
Michael Bowe

The
Enduring
Echo
of Words
Unsaid

Coming to Amazon
January 31, 2023

Made in the USA
Columbia, SC
01 February 2023